May Agnes Fleming

A mad Marriage

May Agnes Fleming

A mad Marriage

ISBN/EAN: 9783743308947

Manufactured in Europe, USA, Canada, Australia, Japa

Cover: Foto ©Andreas Hilbeck / pixelio.de

Manufactured and distributed by brebook publishing software
(www.brebook.com)

May Agnes Fleming

A mad Marriage

A
MAD MARRIAGE.

𝔄 𝔑𝔬𝔟𝔢𝔩.

BY

MAY AGNES FLEMING,

AUTHOR OF

"GUY EARLSCOURT'S WIFE," "A WONDERFUL WOMAN,"
"A TERRIBLE SECRET," "NORINE'S
"REVENGE," ETC.

"Such a mad marriage never was before."
Taming of the Shrew.

NEW YORK:

G. W. Carleton & Co., Publishers.

LONDON: S. LOW, SON & CO.,

MDCCCLXXVI.

PART III.

—:o:—

A MAD MARRIAGE.

CHAPTER I.

T lay down in a sort of hollow, the hillside sloping up behind, crowned with dark pine woods, shut in by four grim wooden walls, two dark windows, like scowling eyes, to be seen from the path, and was known to all as "THE HOUSE THAT WOULDN'T LET."

It stood neither on street nor high road. You left the town behind you—the queer, fortified, Frenchified town of Quebec; you passed through St. John's Gate, through St. John's street-outside-the-gate, to the open country, and, a mile on, you came upon a narrow, winding path, that seemed straggling out of sight, and trying to hide itself among the dwarf cedars and spruces. Following this for a quarter of a mile, passing one or two small stone cabins, you came full upon Saltmarsh—this house that wouldn't let.

It was an ugly place—a ramshackle place, the lonesomest place you could see, but still *why* it wouldn't let was not so clear.

The rent was merely nominal. Mr. Barteaux, its owner, kept it in very good repair. There was a large vegetable garden attached, where, if you were of an agricultural turn, you might have made your rent twice over. There was game in the woods; trout in the ice-cold brooks; but no

venturous sportsman took up his abode at Saltmarsh. It
wasn't even haunted ; it looked rather like that sort of thing,
but nobody ever went exactly so far as to affirm that it *was.*
No ghastly corpse-lights ever glimmered from those dull
upper windows, no piercing shrieks ever rent the midnight
silence, no spectre lady, white and tall, ever flitted through
the desolate rooms of Saltmarsh. No murder had ever
been done there ; no legend of any kind was connected with
the place, its history was prosy and commonplace to a degree. Yet still, year in, year out, the inscription remained
up over the dingy wooden gateway, THIS HOUSE TO BE LET ;
and no tenant ever came.

"Tom Grimshaw must have been mad when he built the
beastly old barn," the present proprietor would growl ;
"what with taxes, and repairs, and insurance, there it stands,
eating its own head off, and there it may stand, for what I
see, to the crack of doom. One would think the very trees
that surround it say, in their warning dreariness, as the sen-
tinels of Helheim used in Northern mythology :

"'Who passes here is damned.'"

If this strong language rouses your curiosity, and you
asked the proprietor the history of the house, you got it
terse and lucid, thus :

"Old Tom Grimshaw built it, sir. Old Tom Grimshaw
was. my maternal uncle, rest his soul ; it is to be hoped he
has more sense in the other world than he ever had in this.
He was a misogynist, sir, of the rabidest sort, hating a petti-
coat as you and I hate the devil. Don't know what infernal
mischief the women had ever done him—plenty, no doubt ; it
is what they were created for. The fact remains—the sight
of one had much the same effect upon him as a red scarf on
a mad bull. He bought this marshy spot for a song, built
that disgustingly ugly house, barricaded himself with that
timber wall, and lived and died there, like Diogenes, or
Robinson Crusoe, or any other old bloke you like. As heir-
at-law, the old rattle-trap fell to me, and a precious legacy
it has been, I can tell you. It *won't* rent, and it *has* to be
kept in repair, and I wish to Heaven old Tom Grimshaw
had taken it with him, wherever he is !"

That was the history of Saltmarsh. For eight years it was to be let, and hadn't let, and that is where the matter began and ended.

Gray, lonely, weather-beaten, so I had seen the forlorn house any time these twenty years ; so this evening of which I am to write I saw it again, with the mysterious shadow of desolation brooding over it, those two upper windows frowning down—sullen eyes set in its sullen, silent face. From childhood it had had its fascination for me—it had been my Bluebeard's castle, my dread, my delight. As I grew older, this fascinating horror grew with my growth, and at seven-and-twenty it held me with as powerful a spell as it had done at seven.

It was a cold and overcast February afternoon. An icy blast swept up from the great frozen gulf, over the heights of Quebec, over the bleak, treeless road, along which I hurried in the teeth of the wind. In the west a stormy and lurid sunset was fading out—fierce reds and brazen yellows paling into sullen gray. One long fiery lance of that wrathful sunset, slanting down the pines, struck those upper windows of Saltmarsh, and lit them into sheets of copper gold.

I was in a hurry—I was the bearer of ill news—and ill news travels apace. It was bitterly cold, as I have said, and snow was falling. I had still half a mile of lonesome high road to travel, and night was at hand ; but the spell of Saltmarsh, that had never failed to hold me yet, held me again. I stood still and looked at it ; at those two red cyclopean eyes, those black stacks of chimneys, its whole forbidding, scowling front.

"It is like a house under a curse," I thought ; "a dozen murders might be done inside those wooden walls, and no one be the wiser. Will any human being ever call Saltmarsh home again, I wonder ? "

" This house is to let ? "

I am not nervous as a rule, but as a soft voice spoke these words at my elbow, I jumped. I had heard no sound, yet now a woman stood at my side, on the snow-beaten path.

" I beg your pardon ; I have startled you, I am afraid.

I have been here for some time looking at this house.   I see
it is to let."

I stepped back and looked at her, too much surprised for
a moment to speak.   To meet a stranger at Saltmarsh, in
the twilight of a bitter February day, was a marvel indeed.

I stood and looked at her ; and I thought then, as I think
now, as I will think to the last day of my life, that I saw one
of the most beautiful faces on which the sun ever shone.

I have said she was a woman—a girl would have been the
fitter word ; whatever her age might have been, she did not
look a day over seventeen.   She was not tall, and she was
very slender ; that may have given her that peculiarly childish
look—I am a tall young woman, and she would not have
reached my shoulder.   A dress of black silk trailed the
ground, a short jacket of finest seal wrapped her, a muff of
seal held her hands.   A hood of black velvet was on her
head, and out of this rich hood her richer beauty shone upon
me, a new revelation of how lovely it is possible for a woman
to be.   Years have come and gone since that evening, but
the wonderful face that looked at me that February twilight,
for the first time, is before me at this moment, as vividly as
then.   Two great, tawny eyes, with a certain wildness in
their light, a skin of pearl, a red mouth like a child's, a low
forehead, a straight nose, a cleft chin, the gleam of small,
white teeth, rise before me like a vision, and I understand
how men, from the days of Samson the Strong, have lain
down life and honor, and their soul's salvation, for just such
women as this.   Surely a strange visitant to the house that
wouldn't let, and in the last hour of the day.

All this in a moment of time, while we stand and face
each other.   Then the soft voice speaks again, with a touch
of impatient annoyance in its tone :

"I *beg* your pardon.   You heard me ?   This house is to
let ? "

I point to the sign, to the legend and inscription affixed
to the gate, and read it stoically aloud : "This house to
be let."

" Evidently my lady is not used to being kept waiting," I
think, " whoever she is."

"Yes, yes, I see that," she says, still impatiently ; "there is no one living in it at present, is there ?"

"Madame," I say, briefly, "no one has lived there for eight years."

The wonderful tawny black eyes, almost orange in some lights, and whose like I have never seen but in one other face, dilate a little as they turn from me to the dead, silent house.

"Why ?" she asks.

I shrugged my shoulders.

"Need one ask that question, madame, after looking at the house ? Who would care to live in so lonely, so lost a place as that ?"

"*I* would. No one would ever think of coming here."

She made the answer almost under her breath, more to herself than to me, her pale face turned toward the house.

Its pallor struck me now, not the pallor of ill health, or of natural complexion, but such fixed whiteness, as some extraordinary terror may once in a lifetime blanch a human face.

"No one would ever think of coming here," I repeated, inwardly. "I should think not indeed. Are you in hiding then, my beautiful young lady, and afraid of being found out ? You are lovelier than anything out of a frame. You are one of the rich and elect of the earth, or you would not be dressed like that, but *who* are you, and what are you doing here alone and at this hour ?"

The last red light of the sunset had entirely faded away. Cold, gray, and overcast the wintry sky spread above us like a pall, and over Cape Diamond, with its citadel crown, swept the icy wind from the frozen St. Lawrence. One or two white flakes came sifting down from the fast drifting sky —night and storm were falling together, and it was still half a mile to my home.

"If you desire any information about this place, madame," I said, "you had better apply to Mr. Barteaux, No.— St. Louis Street, Quebec; he is the present owner. It is to let, and he will be very glad of a tenant. Good-evening."

She made no reply, she did not even seem to have heard. She stood, her hands in her muff, her eyes fixed with a strangely sombre intensity on the blank wooden wall, her profile gleaming cold and white in the steely twilight. I know little of passion or despair, but surely it was most passionate despair I read in those fixed, sightless eyes.

I turned and left her. I was interested of course, but it would not do, to stand mooning here and let night overtake me. Once, as I hurried along the deserted road, I looked back. The small lonely figure still stood as I had left it, motionless, a black speck against the chill darkness of the wintry sky.

"Something wrong there," I thought; "I wonder who she is and what has brought her here. None of the officers' wives or daughters—I have seen all of them at the major's. One thing is certain, Mr. Barteaux will never rent Saltmarsh to a slip of a girl like that."

And then the mysterious young lady and all connected with her slipped from my mind, for the red light from my mother's cottage streamed far afield, and the ill tidings I was bringing home filled my whole thoughts.

In this strange record which it becomes my duty to write, a few words of myself must be said, and may as well be said here and done with. I was Joan Kennedy then, and am Joan Kennedy still. I was seven-and-twenty years of age, and the sole support of a feeble old mother and a sister of twelve. My mother who had been a governess in her youth, and in her native city of Glasgow, had educated me considerably above the station I filled, giving me a very thorough English education, and teaching me to speak French with a fine Scottish accent. At my father's death, ten years before, I went out to service, and in service I had remained ever since. This night, as I hastened homeward through the snowy darkness, my errand was to tell my mother and sister that I had lost my place, and had no present prospect of being able to get another. That is Joan Kennedy's whole past and present history, so far as *you* need know it.

The darkness was all white with whirling snow as I opened the cottage door and entered. All was bright and cosy here. A large red fire burned on the hearth, the tea table was spread, a little snub-nosed teapot wafted its incense alow and aloft, my mother sat knitting in the ingle nook, and my pretty sister Jessie sang, as she stitched away, at the table. At sight of their snow-powdered visitor both dropped their work in amaze.

"Joan!" Then Jessie's arms were around my neck, and my mother's poor old face lit up with delight; "Joan! in this storm, and at this time of night and alone! *Are* you alone, Joan?"

"Who is likely to be with me, little Jess? Yes, I am alone; and you are likely to have more of my delectable society than perhaps may prove pleasant or profitable. Mother dear, I have lost my place."

"Joan!"

"I am not to blame, mother, believe that. Only (it is not a pleasant thing to tell) Mrs. Englehart has taken it into that supremely foolish head of hers to be jealous of me—of poor, plain Joan Kennedy! The major, a kind old soul, has spoken a friendly word or two in passing and—behold the result! Don't let us talk about it. I'll start out to-morrow morning and search all Quebec, and get a situation or perish in the attempt. And now, Mistress Jessie, I'll take a cup of tea."

I threw off my shawl and bonnet, laughing for fear I should break down and cry, and took my seat. As I did so, there came a loud knock at the door. *So* loud, that Jessie nearly dropped the snub-nosed teapot.

"Good gracious, Joan! who is this?"

I walked to the door and opened it—then fell back aghast. For firelight and candlelight streamed full across the face of the lady I had seen at the House to Let.

"May I come in?"

She did not wait for permission. She walked in past me, straight to the fire, and stood before it. Furs and silks were coated with the fast-falling snow. She drew her hands out of her muff, tossed it aside, drew off her gloves, and held to the blaze two small white hands, all twinkling with rings. Mother sat speechlessly gazing at this dazzling apparition. Jessie stood with eyes and mouth agape, and my own heart, I must confess, fluttered nervously as I looked. Who was she, and what did she want? For fully a minute she stood staring at the fire, then feeling that some one must say something, I took heart of grace, and said it.

"You have been caught in the snow-storm," I ventured, drawing near. "I was afraid you would. Will you please to sit down?"

She took no notice of the proffered politeness. The tawny eyes turned from the fire to my face.

"Will you tell me your name?" was the strange young lady's abrupt question.

"Joan Kennedy."

"You are a single woman?"

"I am, madame."

"You live here—in this house, with——" a pause and a stare at mother and Jessie.

"With my mother and sister—yes, at present. As a rule I live at service in Quebec."

"In service?" Another pause and a stare at me. "Joan Kennedy, would you live with *me?*"

This was a leading question with a vengeance. "With you, madame?" I gasped.

"With me. I want a maid, a companion, what you will. Wages are no object—to a trustworthy person. I will give anything she asks. I am all alone—all alone—" her lips trembled, her voice died away; "all alone in the world. I have had great trouble and I want some quiet place to live —some quiet person to live with me, for awhile. I am going to take that house to let. I was overtaken by the storm, just now, and followed you here, instead of going back to the hotel. I like your face—you look as though you may have had trouble yourself, and so could feel for others. I wish you would come and live with me. I have told you I am in dreadful trouble—" she paused, a sort of anguish coming over her face : "I have lost my husband," she said with a great gasp, and covering her face with both hands broke out into such a dreadful crying as I never heard or saw before.

"Oh, poor dear!" said my mother. For me, I stood still and looked at her. What could I say—what could I do? Great sobs shook her from head to foot. A widow! I glanced at her left hand.   Yes, there among the diamonds gleamed that plain band of gold that has brought infinite bliss or misery to millions of women—a wedding ring.   It lasted not two minutes.   Almost fiercely she dashed away her tears and looked up.

"My name is Mrs. Gordon," she said; "as I tell you, I am all alone.   I came to Quebec yesterday, I saw that house advertised, and so came to see it.   It suits me, and I will take it for the next six months at least.   Some one must live with me there.   I like your looks.   Will you come?"

Would I come? would I live in the House to Let?   I stood gasping—the proposal was like a cold douche—it took my breath away.

"I will pay any wages to a suitable person—*any wages,*" emphatically this; "and in advance.   It is a lonely place, it suits me the better for that, and you don't look like a young woman afraid of bogies.   If you won't come," haughtily, "of course I shall find some one else."

"I—I have not refused," I gasped; " —it's all so sudden.   You must let me think it over.   I will tell you to-morrow."

Her mood changed—she lifted a face to mine that was like the helpless, appealing face of a child—she held up two clasped hands.

"*Do* come," she said piteously; "I will pay you anything —anything!   I only want to be quiet for awhile, and away from everybody.   I am all alone in the world.   I have lost my husband—lost him—lost him—"

"The lady is going to faint!" screamed Jessie.

Sure enough! whether the heat of the fire had overcome her, or the "dreadful trouble" of which she spoke had broken her down, she swayed unsteadily to and fro, the words dying on her lips, and I caught her as she fell.

So it was that the first tenant of the House to Let came into my home, and into my life, to change it utterly from that hour.

CHAPTER II.

A WOMAN WITH A SECRET.

RS. GORDON did not leave our cottage that night —did not leave it for two whole weeks, and then the house that wouldn't let was let at last, and Saltmarsh had a tenant.

It would be of little use at this late day to detail all the arguments she used to win me for her attendant and companion—the most irresistible argument of all was wages, treble, fourfold what I had ever earned before, and paid in advance. Of her and her story I had very serious doubts, but beggars must not be choosers. I took her money and became her paid companion.

For hours that night, after mother and Jessie were in bed, I sat beside Mrs. Gordon, listening to the story she told of herself. Brief, vague, and unsatisfactory to a degree, that story was. She had been an orphan from childhood. She was not wealthy, but she had sufficient ; great trouble had suddenly come upon her, and she had lost her husband after four months of wedded life. That was all.

" Lost your husband ! " I repeated, curiously, looking at her. " Do you mean that your husband is dead ? "

A simple and natural question, surely ; but her face, pale before, turned of a dead whiteness from brow to chin.

" Dead of course," she answered, huskily ; " for pity's sake, don't ask me questions. It is only a week ago, and I cannot bear it. Only a week, and it seems like a century. And to think—to think of all the long, lonely, empty years that are to come ! Never to hear his voice, never to see his face more ! "

And then she broke down again and wept—oh, how she wept ! My heart was full of compassion, and yet—only dead one week, and running away like this, not in mourning, not a friend in the world, rich, young and beautiful. A queer story on the face of it—a very queer story indeed.

Who is to gauge the power of woman's beauty? If she had been a plain young person, I believe ten pounds a week would not have tempted me to take up with her and bury myself alive at Saltmarsh. But her wonderful beauty fairly fascinated me, her lovely face won me, even against my better judgment.

"And if that face can make a fool of you, Joan, my dear," I said to myself, as I went to bed, "what awful havoc it must make among mankind! How very unpleasant for poor Mr. Gordon to die and leave it, and how desperately fond she must have been of him, to be sure!"

"You will let me stay here until the house yonder is ready," she said next morning, with the air of one not used to being refused. "I dislike hotels—people stare so. I will make you no trouble, and I want to be perfectly quiet, and quite alone."

It was curious to see her with her lovely face, her elegant dress, her diamond rings, and her dark flowing hair, so strangely out of place in our small, bare, homely house. I hardly know whether she should have stayed or not, but our poverty pleaded for her, and I consented to all she proposed. To take the house for her, to see it furnished, to attend to everything, while she herself kept absolutely out of sight.

My new duties began at once. I went to Mr. Barteaux, and abruptly informed him I had a tenant for the House to Let.

"A widow lady, sir," I said; "a Mrs. Gordon. Any reasonable rent she is willing to pay, and I am engaged to live with her."

"Bless my soul!" said Mr. Barteaux. "You don't say so! A tenant at last. A widow lady, eh? How many in family, Joan?"

I knew the vision before Mr. Barteaux's mind's eye. A florid matron of fifty, with half-a-dozen strapping boys and girls.

"No family, sir. Quite a young widow. You must close the bargain with me, Mr. Barteaux; her loss is recent, she is in trouble, and doesn't feel like transacting business herself. There are no references; instead, she will pay in advance if you choose."

We closed the bargain there and then; and that very day Saltmarsh was thrown open to the sunshine and free winds of Heaven. What an odd, awesome feeling it gave me to go with my mysterious new mistress through the gruesome apartments, silent and forsaken so long. Four, out of the ten rooms the house contained, were chosen to be furnished and fitted up, papered, painted, whitewashed, carpeted, curtained. All fell to me, and all was done in two brief weeks, and well done, though I say it, and Mrs. Gordon and Joan Kennedy, it was known to all Quebec, were domesticated at Saltmarsh.

I wonder now, as I sit here and look back at that strange time, that even poverty could have tempted me to endure the life I led all those dreary months. The listless, lonely days spent in reading or rambling through the empty, echoing rooms, the long awesome nights when the winds held high carnival without and the rats high jinks within. No one ever came to the house, except a stout Frenchwoman, who did our washing and general drudgery, coming every morning and going every night. For me, my position was a sinecure, nothing to do, and treble wages for doing it, but the hardest work for all, that I ever did in my life.

And my mistress! Well, the days, and the weeks, and the months went by, and she was as great a mystery as ever. Where she had come from, how long she meant to remain, whither she intended going, were all sealed secrets to me. She never wrote letters, she never received any. She could not have been much more dead to all the world outside our wooden walls if she had been in her shroud and coffin.

She spent the heavy, aimless days sitting mostly at her chamber window—a dark-draped, slender figure, a dreary, lovely face, two great, hopeless eyes, a total wreck of life. The story of her life, whatever it had been, no common one be sure, was ended for the time; the play was over, the lights

out, and nothing left but to sit and look at the curtain.
A woman young as she was, of the wrong sort, of the silent,
secret sort, a woman with something on her mind, a woman
with a secret.

Two things I discovered—only two. One, that her husband was not dead, but deserted ; that she had run away
from him and was hiding here, in horrible dread of his ever
finding her out. Secondly, that in spite of this running away
and this constant terror, she still loved him, with a passionate and most despairing love.

I had gone into her room one night, and found her sitting
holding a picture before her, and gazing on it as if entranced.
It was her principal occupation. I had often found her so
before, but the picture itself I had never seen. To-night,
however, she called me to her in her abrupt way.

"Joan," she said, "come here."

She had been crying, I could see—silently and miserably.
I went and looked over her shoulder at the picture.

Photography was in its infancy in those days—every family
had not its picture gallery. This was a daguerreotype—the
portrait of a young, dashing-looking and rather handsome
man. A beardless and boyish face, yet a very manly one,
looking up at you with frankly smiling eyes.

"It is all I have left," she said, with tremulous lips. "I
will never see him again. I loved him and I have spoiled
his whole life. It would have been better for him he had
died than ever looked in my face."

"Indeed," was my rather stupid answer. But I was used
to her extravagant talk and not much affected by it. "He
is a friend of yours, madame ?"

She looked at her picture, and over her face there dawned
a light that made her beauty radiant.

"He is my husband !" she answered.

I drew back and looked at her—aghast, I must confess.

"Your husband !" I repeated. "Oh—*was* your husband,
you mean ? You told me he was dead."

"Dead to me. Oh, Joan ! dead to me, but alive and
well. Alive and well ; and though I should live to be a
hundred, I may never see his face again. Never again ; and

there are times when I would lay down my very life only to look upon him once more."

"You love him and—he has left you?" I ventured.

"I love him—and I left *him.* I love him with all my heart, and I have fled from him, and buried myself here for fear of him. I wonder I don't go mad, or die. Once I thought I would without him ; but somehow life drags on and on, and one is a coward, and afraid to end it one's self. He loved me once, Joan—ah, dear Heaven, yes! he loved me and made me his wife ; and now, and now, Joan, if ever he finds me, I believe he will take my life."

I looked back at the frank, fair, boyish face.

"He take your life!" I said ; "that bright-faced boy! No, Mrs. Gordon, murderers don't look like that."

"He is the truest, the noblest, the bravest of men, a loyal friend and a gallant gentleman."

"And yet his wife runs away from him, and says if ever they meet he will take her life."

She scarcely seemed to heed me. She laid her head on her folded arms as though she never cared to lift it again.

"Ah! let me alone," she said. "*You* know nothing about it. If I could but die and make an end of it all! Only this, Joan," she looked up suddenly, swift, dark terror in her eyes ; "I dreamed last night he was searching for me —that he was here. He came and stood before me, stern and terrible, holding my death-warrant in his hand! Don't let him come! don't let any one come! If ever we meet, I believe in my soul he will kill me."

Was Mrs. Gordon going mad? that was the very serious question uppermost in my thoughts when I went to bed that night, and for many nights after. It was a very queer and uncomfortable affair altogether, and the sooner I got out of it the better ; and just as I was beginning to think of tendering my resignation, behold the climax all at once came of itself.

March, April and May had passed—it was the close of June. I had gone into the city one afternoon for our weekly store of groceries, finished my purchases, and, basket on arm, was going home. My way led up St. Louis Street ; and passing the office of Mr. Barteaux, I saw him in his own doorway, deep in conversation with a stranger. A look at that stranger, and with one great jump my heart was in my mouth. For it was the original of the picture—it was Mrs. Gordon's husband. "The hour and the man were come!"

Neither saw me. I paused a second and looked again. The same, beyond doubt; the same, with a difference—worn and haggard, set and stern—the same, yet *that* was the face of a frank, happy boy, this of a reckless, desperate man. A straw hat was pulled over his eyes, a gray summer overcoat was buttoned up—a soldier and a gentleman, that was evident at a glance.

I turned up a side street and hastened breathlessly on. My first duty was to my mistress. I must tell her that what she dreaded had come—that the husband from whom she had fled, was here. I walked at my utmost speed, and in half an hour was at Saltmarsh.

"She said he would kill her!" I thought, turning hot and cold; "and who knows that he will not? He would not be the first husband that has killed a runaway wife."

I ran through the rooms, all flurried and breathless, calling out her name.

She was not in any of them. Of late, since June had come, the fine weather at times had tempted her out. This, most unfortunately, was one of the times. I knew pretty well where to find her—on the river bank below there was a strip of yellow sand, where she was fond of walking up and down in the sunshine. She was sure to be there now.

I rushed out, looking wildly around. Yes, there was the tall, soldierly figure in the straw hat and summery overcoat, coming rapidly toward me at a swinging pace.

I declare I almost screamed, so nervous and overwrought had I become.

If he was before me—if he came upon her suddenly, the shock alone might kill her, for she was far from strong of late. I turned and fled headlong down the steep hillside path, still calling her name. Yes, there, quite alone, pacing slowly up and down the sandy riverside path, looking at the fast-flowing water, Mrs. Gordon walked.

She paused in her slow walk, and turned to me in wonder at my break-neck descent.

How beautiful she was ! even in that supreme moment, I remember that was my first thought.

" For pity's sake, fly !" I cried out ; "fly at once. He is here !"

She laid both her hands suddenly over her heart. Across her face there flashed the electric light of a great and sudden joy.

" Who ?" she said, almost in a whisper.

" Your husband, the man whose picture you showed me. Fly at once if you are afraid of him. I saw him, I tell you he is coming. Oh, Heaven !—he is *here !*"

I fell back in consternation. Yes, he had followed me ; he was coming down the path, he was here.

I turned to my mistress. Would she faint ? would she fly ? Neither.

Who is to understand men's wives ! Terror was there, in that wild, white face, it is true, but over and above it all, such rapture as I never before saw in the face of man or woman. She loved him and she saw him again—all was said in that.

He walked down the path. She came a step forward, with that transfigured face, and held out to him both arms with an eloquent cry :

" Gordon ! Gordon !"

CHAPTER III.

THE DECREE OF DIVORCE.

T had come. I could do no more. Nothing remained for me but to retreat into the background, and wait with bated breath and beating heart for this play of "powerful domestic interest" to play itself out.

He had descended the steep, hillside path and stood on the strip of yellow sand, face to face with the wife who had deserted him. The full light of the June afternoon fell upon his face as he stood there before her, a face more hollow-eyed and haggard, more worn, than it had even looked to me first. A face set and stern, with little of mercy or pity in it.

He waved her back. Only the slightest motion of his hand, but she shrank and shivered like a child who has got a blow.

"No nearer," he said in a voice as cold and steady as the chill gray eyes that looked upon her. "Unless your sense of hearing has become dulled since the night of Lovell's death, when you played eavesdropper so well, you will be able to hear all I have to say, where you stand. I will not detain you long, and you need not wear that frightened face. I am not going to kill you—the time for all that is passed. But let me tell you this : If you had *not* played eavesdropper that memorable night five months ago, if you had not fled as you did, if I had found you before me when I returned, you would never have lived to see the morning. The greatest fool that ever walked the earth I had been—if you and I had met that night I would have been a murderer as well."

All this he said in a slow, self-repressed sort of tone, but the deep gray eyes that watched her were full of such hatred as no words of mine can tell.

2

"Spare me, Gordon," she answered, with a sobbing cry.

"Spare you?" he repeated, with cold scorn; "have I not said so? I would not lift a finger to harm a hair of your head, or to save your life if I saw you drowning in the river yonder. You are as dead to me as though I had gone home and strangled you that eventful night. The madness of love and rage, alike, are past forever. I have cut you off utterly and absolutely from my life. You have been in hiding here, they tell me, in daily dread of your life no doubt. Let us end all that. You are free to come and go where and how you will. After to-day I will never look upon your face again of my own free will, alive or dead."

She gave a shrill cry, like a culprit under the lash, her hands still held out to him in dumb agony.

"I have not even come to Quebec now in search of you," the cold, pitiless voice went on; "don't think it. I came to visit General Forrester, stationed yonder at the Citadel, before leaving this accursed Canada forever—accursed since in it I met *you.*"

Her outstretched hands went up, with a dull moaning sound, and covered her face.

"Would you care to know how I found you out, and why I came?" he slowly went on. "Listen: Last night at mess the fellows were speaking of a widow lady, a most mysterious widow lady, young and beautiful, so rumor said, who had taken a desolate old house in a marsh, and there shut herself up, hidden from mortal man and light of day. Her name was *Mrs. Gordon.* Where she came from, who she was, why she had come, no man could tell. Before the name was uttered I knew it was you. Knew that when you fled from Toronto you fled here; knew that the lost woman who had been my wife was found."

Her hands dropped. For the first time she stood upright before him and looked him full in the face, stung, it would seem, into turning at bay by these last words.

"Who had been your wife!" she cried, passionately; "who *is* your wife, Gordon Caryll! Nothing," a sort of exultation lit her face as she said it, "nothing but death can ever alter that!"

For fully a minute he stood silently looking at her, a smile on his lips, a pitiless triumph in his eyes.

"Nothing can change that?" he repeated; "nothing but death? Well, I will answer that before we part. Let me go on. I knew it was you, this woman they talked of, and I said to myself: 'I will find her to-morrow; I will look upon her face once more, for the last time, and I will see *what* there was, if I can, in its wax-doll beauty, its yellow-black eyes, its straight nose and silken hair, to turn men into blind, besotted fools.' Take down your hands, Rosamond, and let me look at you."

She had shrank from him, from his smile, in some nameless, dreadful fear, that made her cover her white face once more. She dropped her hands now, at his bidding, looking up with dilated eyes.

"Gordon, have mercy on me. I love you!"

Again she stretched forth her hands to him with that piteous cry. Again he motioned her imperiously back, his lips set, his eyes pitiless, his face like stone.

"Stand still!" he ordered.

She obeyed.

For fully two minutes this strange tableau was before me, and all unseen, in my obscure nook, I stood gazing with an interest that held me rapt and spell-bound. He, drawn up to his full height, his face like white stone, so hard, so cold, that chill, half smile still on his lips. She, half cowering before him, her lovely, colorless face uplifted, her eyes full of dreadful terror, her loose, feathery hair blowing in the wind, —young, fair, innocent to *see*, at least. So they stood— stern young judge, quivering little criminal, until it grew almost too much even for my nerves to endure.

"You are a beautiful little woman, Rosamond," he said, at length; "one of those exceptional women, who, like Ninon de L'Enclos, will be beautiful at eighty. And that fair face of yours will do its devil's work, I don't doubt, to the end of the chapter. To possess that face for four short months I have lost all that man holds dear—name, honor, home, friends, fortune—all. For the name that *you* have borne and disgraced, I will bear no longer. I have sold out

—do you know it? my father has disinherited me—I am the laughingstock of all who ever knew me. I look back and wonder at my own infatuation. I loved you—I trusted you. Oh, God!" he cried out, a spasm of anguish distorting his face; "I *married* you—you! You played your game well, you and Lovell. It was your trade ; and with such a fool as I, it was an easy game enough. But you had cause to fear, and you knew it—I say again you did well to fly. I went out from Lovell's death-bed a madman—if I had found you on my return, by the light above us, I would have murdered you!"

She shrank back from him, trembling with pure physical terror now, from head to foot.

"No need to tremble—no need to fear *now*," he went on, his voice losing its sudden fury, and sinking to its former cold monotone ; "I have told you all that is past and done with. But before we part, I should like to hear once from your own lips, just once (not that I doubt) that Major Lovell's story was true."

Her only answer was to cower still farther away, and with a great, heart-wrung sob, to bury her face once again in her hands.

"Ah, hide it," he said bitterly ; "hide it forever from the sight of man—the fairest, falsest face ever made. But speak —if such lips as yours can speak truth, and tell me that Lovell's story was true."

"Gordon! have mercy."

"Was it true?"

"I loved you, Gordon! As there is a heaven above us, I loved you with all my heart."

He half laughed—even in that moment.

"Your heart—*yours* ! What witty things are said by accident! Never mind your heart or your love. I know what both are worth. Answer my question. Was Lovell's story true. One word—yes or no."

"Gordon, I was faithful. Oh! *what* shall I say to him to—"

"Was it true? Yes or no?"

"Gordon, I swear—"

"Was it true?" he cried, his eyes flashing fire; "no more words! Yes or no."

"Yes, but—"

"That will do. We won't waste words about it. You would swear black was white, I daresay, but keep your histrionic talents for the New York stage again—you may need them before long. Let us get back to what you said a moment ago. 'You are my wife—nothing but death can change that.' Do me the favor to look at this."

He drew a newspaper from his pocket and handed it to her. Something in his face as he did so frightened her as nothing had frightened yet. Her hands shook—she strove to open the paper and failed. She looked at him with piteous eyes and trembling lips.

"I can't," she faltered; "Gordon, what is it?"

"It is a decree of divorce," he answered, in his cold, sombre voice. "One week after Lovell's death and your flight, I instituted a suit for divorce, and obtained it. You can read the details in that paper, at your leisure—it may help while away an hour. This is what has kept me in Canada so long. In two days I leave it forever. Chance has brought us together this once, for the last time."

He paused, half turned away, then suddenly stopped. She had made some kind of gesture, but it was not for that; she had said "*wait!*" in a hoarse whisper; but it was not that. It was the ghastly change that had come over her face as he struck his last merciless blow. For a moment, I think, it startled even him.

"This is true—this that you tell me—this—divorce?"

She spoke the words in a husky, breathless sort of voice, her face all distorted, clutching the paper hard.

"It is perfectly true," his chill voice answered. "Read and see."

"I am no longer your wife?"

"You are no longer my wife—thank Heaven and the merciful law of the land."

"After this day, you never mean to see or know me again?"

"I never mean to see you again if it be in my power, alive or dead."

" Then hear *me* /" She drew herself upright, her small figure seeming to dilate and grow tall. " Lovell's story was true—true I tell you in every particular except this: that I married you for your rank, and your name, and your wealth. I married you for these, it is true; but beyond these, because I loved you with all my heart. Oh, yes, Gordon Caryll ! even such women as I am can love ; and in deed, and thought, from the hour you placed this ring on my finger, I was your true and loyal wife. I would have gone with you to beggary—I would have died, if need were, for your sake. Now I am divorced and cast off forever, you say. Well, then we *shall* meet again one day, so surely as we both live. This cold-blooded divorce I will never forgive. Go, Gordon Caryll ! but remember this, one day or other, so surely as we both stand here, I will make you suffer for this !"

He laughed as he listened—a low, contemptuous laugh, that would have goaded any infuriated woman to madness.

" You do it very well, Rosamond," he said; " but so many years' hard practice on the stage of the Bowery Theatre could hardly fail to tell. For the rest, it is rather wasted on an unappreciative audience at present. If I should be so unfortunate as ever to meet you again, I trust, even then, to be able to take care of myself."

He turned without another word and left her, striding up the steep path, and never once looking back.

She stood where he left her, watching him out of sight, the color fading from her face, the life from her eyes. So, standing motionless there, she saw him pass from view, heard the last echo of his footsteps die away. Then I came forward, for the look on her face frightened me. She turned to me slowly, the fatal paper held in her hand.

" I dreamed he came with my death-warrant," she said; " here it is."

And then without word or cry to warn me, she went down in a dead faint on the sands.

How I brought her to, how I got her home, I can never tell. I did it somehow, and laid her on her bed as the June moon rose and the stars came out. Old

Bettine, the French charwoman, was still pottering about the kitchen. In her charge I left my mistress, and fled into town for a doctor. For she was very ill—so ill that it seemed doubtful whether she would ever live to see day dawn.

The clocks of Quebec, high up in steeples, silvered by the quiet summer moonlight, were chiming eleven as our first visitor entered Saltmarsh—the doctor.

And when the lovely June morning dawned, and the swallows twittered in the eaves, Gordon Caryll's child lay in my arms, and Gordon Caryll's divorced wife lay white and still, with Life and Death fighting their sharp battle above her pillow.

CHAPTER IV.

A STRANGE ENDING.

IFE won. Days passed, two weeks went by, and the struggle was at an end. Pale and shadowy that marvellously fair face lay among the pillows, but all doubt was at an end. Mrs. Gordon would live.

Saltmarsh was a deserted house no longer. A ponderous nurse had come from Quebec, the doctor was a daily visitor, and old Bettine spent her nights as well as her days with us. There was nothing to fear any more ; the man she had longed for and feared had come and gone, to come no more forever. The baby fell almost entirely to me—a charge as pleasant as novel, for I must own, spinster that I am, to a tender weakness for babies. It lay in my arms all day ; it slept in its crib by my bedside at night.

" The smallest mite of a baby *I* ever see," observed Mrs. Watters, the fat nurse ; "and I've seen a regiment of 'em, little and big, in my day. I should say now it wouldn't weigh five pounds."

It *was* small. A tiny, black-haired, black-eyed speck, its pink dot of a face looking weird, lit by those black, blinking eyes.

One thing was strange—was unnatural. From its birth its mother had never seen it, never asked to see it. One evening, when Bettine had called nurse down to supper, and I sat watching in her room, she spoke of it for the first time.

It was a lovely July night, under the brilliant summer moon, the St. Lawrence ran between its green slopes like a belt of silver light. The white, misty moonlight filled the chamber, the lamp had not yet been lit, and the pale glory illumined the face, whiter than the lace and linen against which it lay. She sat partly up in bed, propped by pillows, gazing with dark, sombre eyes out at that radiance in Heaven and on earth—that glory from the skies upon river and shore. For more than an hour she had been sitting motionless, her dark, brooding eyes never leaving the fairy scene, as though she saw her own future life over there beyond that shining river. In the dim distance, baby lay in its crib fast asleep ; deepest silence reigned within and without. That silence was suddenly and sharply broken by the shrilly, feeble wail of the child as it awoke. As I rose and crossed the room to take it, she spoke : "Joan, bring it here."

" H'm ! high time for you to say it," I thought, but in silence I obeyed. There had been something revolting to me in her utter want of mother-love ; in her unnatural indifference ; I carried it to the bedside and stooped to place it beside her.

" No, no," she said with a quick, petulant gesture of repulsion ; "not there ; I don't want it. I always hated babies. I only want to look at it."

" Shall I bring in the lamp ? " I asked.

"No ; the moonlight will do. What a dot of a baby ! Joan, who is it like ? "

" It has your eyes," I answered ; " beyond that it is impossible to tell. Mrs. Watters says, though, it is your very 'moral.' It is certainly the tiniest baby that ever was born."

" My very moral," she repeated, with a feeble laugh. " I hope so ! I hope it may be like me. I hope it may never resemble *him,* in any way. I hope it may live to help avenge its mother yet ! "

I was silent—shocked and scandalized beyond power of replying. Here was a Christian woman and mother, just saved from death, talking like some heathen, of revenge !

" Is it a girl or a boy ? " she inquired next, after a pause.

" Girl," I answered, shortly. " It is time you asked."

She glanced at me in surprise, but in no displeasure.

"Why should I ask ? It didn't matter much. A girl ! If it had only been a boy ; and yet, who can tell, if she is like me, and is pretty, she may do great things yet. She may help, *me.* That will do, Joan. Take it away."

She turned her face from the light, and lay for a long

2*

time still, brooding over her own thoughts—dark and wicked thoughts I well knew. Whoever or whatever this Mrs. Gordon might be, she was not a proper or virtuous woman, that seemed pretty clear—a wife whose husband had been forced to put her away—a mother who only looked forward to the future of her child as an instrument of vengeance on its father. There are some services that no wages can repay—to my mind this was one. The moment Mrs. Gordon was well enough to be left, that moment I would leave her.

"And what will become of you with such a mother, Providence only knows," I apostrophized the little one on my lap. "You poor, little, spectral, black-eyed mite! I wish you belonged to me altogether."

From that evening Mrs. Gordon rallied, and asserted her power once more as mistress of the house. Her first act of sovereignty was to dismiss the nurse.

"All danger is over, the doctor tells me," she said to Mrs. Watters a few days after. "Joan Kennedy can take care of me now. I shall not require you any more. Joan, pay Mrs. Watters her due. She leaves to-night."

Mrs. Watters left. Next morning Mrs. Gordon asserted herself still further—she insisted upon being dressed and allowed to sit up. She had her way, of course, and I wish I could tell you how fair and youthful and lovely she looked. Youthful! I declare, whatever her age really was, she did not look a day over sixteen. But there was that in her quick, black eyes, in her colorless face, in those latter days, not pleasant to see—something I could not define, and that confirmed me in my resolution to leave her very soon. Of her child, from the evening of which I have spoken, she took not the slightest notice. I truly believe she never once looked at it again; when it cried she had it impatiently removed out of hearing. She sat thinking—thinking steadfastly, with bent brows and compressed lips, of what—who could tell ?

"I'll give her warning to-morrow," I said resolutely to myself; "my month is up in a week. I'll never live another with you, my pretty, mysterious little mistress."

Her eyes lifted suddenly, and fixed themselves on my face as I thought it. Did she divine my very thoughts? The faint smile that was on her lips almost made me think so.

"Joan," she said, in her pretty, imperious way, "come here, child; I want to talk to you. You have been a good and faithful companion in all these dreary, miserable months, to a most miserable and lonely woman. Let me thank you now while I think of it, and before we say good-by."

"Good-by!" I repeated, completely taken aback. "Then you are going away?"

"Going away, Joan; high time, is it. not? All is over now—there is nothing to fear or hope any more. One chapter of my life is read and done with forever. The day after to-morrow I go out into the world once more, to begin all over again. Up to the present my life has been a most miserable failure—all but four short months." She paused suddenly; the dreary, lovely face lit up with a sort of rapture. "All but four short months—oh, let me always except that— when he made me his wife, and I was happy, happy, happy! Joan, if I had died three weeks ago when *that* was born, you might have had engraven on my tombstone the epitaph that was once inscribed over another lost woman ; ' I have been most happy—and most miserable.' "

I listened silently, touched, in spite of myself, by the unspeakable pathos of her look and tone.

"All that is over and done with," she said, after a little. "I am not to die, it seems. I am going to begin my life, as I say, all over again. Nothing that befalls me in the future can be any worse than what lies behind. It does not fall to the lot of all women to be divorced wives at the age of eighteen."

She laughed drearily. She sat by the window in her favorite easy-chair, looking out while she talked, with the rosy after-glow of the sunset fading away beyond the feathery tamarac trees and the low Canadian hills.

"I feel something as a felon must," she dreamily went on, half to herself, half to me, "who has served out his sentence and whose order of release has come, almost afraid to face the world I have left so long. I did not come to this

house a very good woman, Joan—that, I suppose, you know ;
but I quit it a thousand times worse. I came here with a
human heart, at least, a heart that could love and feel remorse ; but love and remorse are at an end. I told him I
loved him and had been faithful to him, and he laughed in
my face. Women can forgive a great deal, but they do
not forgive that. If he had only left me—if he had not
got that divorce, I would never have troubled him—
never, I swear. I would have gone away and loved him,
and been faithful to him to the end. Now—now—" she
paused, her hands clenched, her yellow eyes gleaming cat-
like in the dusk. " Now, I will pay him back, sooner or
later, if I lose my life for it. I will be revenged—that I
swear."

I shrank away from her, from the sight of her wicked
face, from the hearing of her wicked words,—the horror I
felt, showing, I suppose, in my face.

" It all sounds very horrible, very shocking, does it
not?" she asked, bitterly. "You are one of the pious
and proper sort, my good Joan, who walk stiffly along
the smooth-beaten path of propriety, from your cradle to
your grave. Well, I won't shock you much longer, let that
be your comfort. The day after to-morrow I go, and as a
souvenir I mean to leave *that* behind me."

She pointed coolly to the crib in the corner.

" You—you mean to leave the baby?" I gasped.

" I—I mean to leave the baby," she answered, with a
half laugh, parodying my tone of consternation; "you
didn't suppose I meant to take it with me, did you? I
start in two days to begin a new life, as a perfectly proper
young lady—young lady, you understand, Joan? and you
may be very sure I shall carry no such land-mark with me
as that of the old one. Yes, Joan, I shall leave the baby
with you, if you will keep it, with Mrs. Waters if you will
not."

" Oh, I will keep the baby and welcome," I said ; " poor
little soul !" and as it lay in its sleep, so small and helpless,
so worse than orphaned at its very birth, I stooped and
kissed it, with tears in my eyes.

You are a good woman, Joan," she said, more softly; "I wish—yes, with all my soul, I wish I were like you. But it is late in the day for wishing—what is done is done. You will keep the child?"

" I will keep the child."

" I am glad of that. It will be well with you. One day or other I will come and claim it. Don't let it die, Joan ; it has its work to do in the world, and must do it. I will pay you, of course, and well. The money I had with me when I came here is almost gone, but out yonder, beyond your Canadian woods and river, there is always more for busy brains and hands. The furniture of these rooms I leave with you to sell or keep, as you see fit. Wherever I may be, I will give you an address, whence letters will reach me."

" And you will never return—never come to see your child?" I asked.

" Never, Joan,—until I come to claim it for good. Why should I? I don't care for it—not a straw—in the way you mean. One day, if we both live, I will claim it ; one day its father shall learn, to his cost and his sorrow, that he has a child."

That evil light flashed up into her great eyes for an instant, then slowly died out : but she spoke no more— her folded hands lay idly on her lap, her moody gaze turned upon the rapidly darkening river and hills. The rose light had all faded away—the gray, creeping, July twilight was shrouding all things in a sombre haze. The baby awoke and cried ; I had its bottle ready—I lit the lamp and lifted it. As it lay in my lap, placidly pulling at its feeding-bottle, its big black eyes fixed vacantly upon the ceiling, its mother turned from the window and stared at it silently.

With its little white face, and large black eyes, and profusion of long black hair, it looked more like some elfish changeling in a fairy tale than a healthy human child.

" It's a hideous little object," was Mrs. Gordon's motherly remark, after that prolonged stare ; "but ugly babies they say sometimes grow up pretty. I want it to be pretty—

It must be pretty. Will it, do you think, Joan? Will it really look like me?"

"I think so, madame—very like you. More's the pity," I added, under my breath.

"Ah!" still thoughtfully staring at it, "is there any birthmark? The proverbial strawberry on the arm, or mole on the neck, you know? that sort of thing?"

"It has no mark of any kind, from head to foot."

"What a pity; we must give it one, then. Art must supply the deficiencies of nature. It shall be done to-morrow."

"*What* must be done? Mrs. Gordon, you don't surely mean—"

"I mean to mark that child so that I shall know it again, fifty years from now, if need be. Don't look so horrified, Joan,—I won't do anything very dreadful. One marks one's pocket-handkerchiefs—why not one's babies? You may die; she may grow up and run away—oh, yes, she may! If she takes after her mother, you won't find it a bed of roses bringing her up. We may cross paths and never know each other. I want to guard against that possibility. I want to know my daughter when we meet."

"For pity's sake, madame, what is it you intend to do?"

"You have seen tattooing, Joan, done in India ink? Yes. Well, that is what I mean. I shall mark her initials on her arm to-morrow, exactly as I mark them on my handkerchief, and you shall help me."

"No, madame," I cried out in horror, "I will not. Oh, you poor little helpless babe! Madame! I beg of you—don't do this cruel thing."

"Cruel? Silly girl! I shall give it a sleeping cordial, and it will feel nothing. So you will not help me?"

"Most assuredly I will not."

"Very well—Bettine will. And lest your tender feelings should be lacerated by being in the house, you may go and pay your mother and sister a visit. By the by, you don't ask me what its name is to be, Joan."

"As I am to keep it, though, supposing you don't kill it to-morrow, I shall be glad to know, Mrs. Gordon."

"I don't mean to kill it—never fear; I don't want it to die. If it had been a boy, I always meant—in the days that are gone, mind you—to have called it for its father."

She paused a moment, and turned her face far away. On *this* point, even she could feel yet.

"It is a girl, unluckily," she went on again, steadily, "but I will still call it for him. Gordon Caryll—a pretty name, is it not, Joan? an odd one too, for a girl. Until I claim it, however, and the proper time comes, we will sink the Caryll, and call it Kennedy. Kennedy's a good old Scotch, respectable name—Gordon Kennedy will do. As I said, to-morrow I will mark the initials 'G. C.' upon its arm; and whatever happens, years and years from now, if my daughter and I ever meet, I shall know her always, and in all places, by the mark on her arm."

I could do nothing. My heart sickened and revolted against this cruelty, but she was mother and mistress, and could do as she pleased. I would not stay to see the torture; Bettine might help her or not, as she pleased; I would go.

Next morning, immediately after breakfast, I quitted the house, and spent the day at mother's. In the gray of the summer evening I returned, to find the deed done, the babe drugged and still asleep, lying in its crib, the arm bound up, Bettine excited, Mrs. Gordon composed and cool.

"Did it cry?" I asked, kissing the pale little face.

"Ah, but yes, mademoiselle!" Bettine cried, in her shrill, high French voice; "cried fit to break the heart, until madame double drugged it, and it lay still. The arm —the poor infant—will be sore and inflamed for many a day to come. It is a heart of stone. Mam'selle Jeanne— the pretty little madame."

That was our last evening in Saltmarsh—a long, quiet, lonesome evening enough. I distrusted her—in some way I feared and disliked her; and yet I felt a strange sort of compassion for the quiet little creature, sitting there so utterly desolated in her youth and beauty—wrecked and adrift on the world at eighteen.

She sat in her old place by the window so still—so still —the fair face gleaming like marble in the dusk, the dark, mournful eyes fixed on the creeping darkness shrouding the fair Canadian river and landscape.   It all ended to-night— the peace, the safety, dreary though it may have been—and to-morrow she must go forth out into the great, pitiless world, with only her beautiful face and her wicked heart to make her way.   What dark story lay behind her ? I wondered ; and was this fair, forsaken wife most to be pitied or blamed ?

The hours of the evening crept on—ten, eleven ; she never stirred. · And when, sometime before midnight, I crept away with my baby to my room, the motionless little figure was there at the window still.

Next morning dawned cloudless and fair.   Bettine was up betimes to prepare breakfast—for the last time I served my little mistress.   She was dead silent through it all, and ate it in her travelling suit of dark gray, all ready to depart. There was a train at nine ; it was half-past eight now, and the cabriolet ordered from Quebec was at the door.   She stooped for a moment over her babe ; but even in this part- ing hour she never kissed it, and my heart hardened against her once more.

"It is as Bettine says," I thought ; "she has the face of an angel and the heart of a stone."

Even as I thought it, she arose and looked at me—that charming smile upon her charming face, that had bewitched me against my will the very first time we met, that bewitched me out of my hot anger once again.   She held out her hand.

" Good-by, my solemn Joan.   Don't think too badly of me when I am gone—a poor little woman with whom life has gone hard.   You are a good girl, and I shall always keep a grateful remembrance of you in my none too tender heart. Take good care of my baby—you shall be amply rewarded. I *may* come back years from now to look at it—who knows ? At all events you will hear from me monthly.   And, if we never meet again, let me thank you once more for your faithful and patient companionship all these months."

They were the last words she ever spoke in Saltmarsh

In the yellow sunshine of the soft summer day Mrs. Gordon passed out of the House to Let, and out of my life forever. I watched her enter the cab, caught one last glimpse of a pale, lovely face, of a little gloved hand waving from the window, then the driver cracked his whip, and they were whirling away in a cloud of dust to where quaint, gray, silent old Quebec slept in morning quiet, the golden sunshine flooding its steep streets, its tin roofs, its lofty spires, its high stone walls. Mrs. Gordon was gone.

Before nightfall I had taken the baby home and dismissed Bettine. Part of the furniture I kept, part I sent into Quebec and sold. Late in the evening I carried the key to Mr. Barteaux, with his rent, and on my return my own hands replaced the placard over the gate. Saltmarsh was once more a " House to Let."

She had come among us a mystery—she left us a greater mystery still. I write this record for the child's sake—one day it may need it. I feel that the story I have told does not end here, that it is but the prelude to what is to come. So surely as that woman and this child live and meet, trouble —sad and deep trouble to that man Gordon Caryll—will come of it. I say again I write this for the child's sake. One day, even what I have set down here may be of use to her. If I die I will place it in safe hands, to be given to her, and so I sign myself

JOAN KENNEDY.

CHAPTER V.

AT CARYLLYNNE.

ANY miles away, many miles of land, many leagues of sea, far beyond that "city set on the hill," Quebec, far away in fair England, lay the broad domain of Caryllynne, Gordon Caryll's ancestral home.

It lay in one of the brightest, sunniest of the sunny seaside shires, a fair and stately inheritance, stretching away for miles of woodland and meadowland, to the wide sea, sparkling in the late August sunshine, as if sown with stars.

Under a massive Norman arch, between lofty iron gates, you went up a sweep of broad drive, with a waving sea of many-colored foliage on either hand, slim, silver-stemmed birches, copper beeches with leaves like blood-red rubies, sombre pines, hoary oaks, graceful elms, and whole rows of prim poplars, those "old maids of the wood." Far away this brilliant forest of Caryllynne stretched to the emerald cliffs above the bright summer sea, to the little village nestling between those green cliffs, a village which for two centuries had called the Squire of Caryllynne, lord.

You went up this noble avenue for a mile or more past the picturesque Swiss cottage that did duty as a gate lodge, past green and golden slopes of sward, past parterres bright with gorgeous autumnal flowers, to the Manor house itself, an irregular structure of gray stone, turreted and many-gabled and much ivy-grown. There was a stately portico entrance, a flight of shallow-stone steps, and two couchant stone dogs, with the ancient motto, "*Cave canim.*" It was a very old house, one portion as old as the reign of the greatly-married-man, Henry the Eighth. A gift, indeed, from his Most Christian Majesty to Sir Jasper Caryll, Knight, and cousin of Katherine Parr, on the happy occasion of his last marriage.

Sir Jasper Caryll, Kt., had been sleeping beneath the chancel of Roxhaven Church for three hundred odd years, with a brass tablet above him recording his virtues ; and many Carylls had been born and married, and had died, within those gray stone walls since. The old, old business of life, " Hatching, Matching, and Dispatching," had gone on and on within those antique chambers ; and Mistress Marian Caryll, widow of the late Godfrey Caryll, reigned now in the Manor alone.

The old house had been modernized. Plate-glass windows, a tessellated hall, velvet-carpeted stairways, conservatories gay with flowers, these made the ancient dwelling bright. Flowers, indeed, were everywhere, in gilded vases in half a hundred nooks, in swinging baskets from the ceilings, and over all the amber August sunshine slanting like golden rain.

The last light of the brilliant autumn day was falling softly over sea and woodland, meadow and copse ; the western windows of the Manor, facing seaward, glinted through the trees like sparks of fire. The sweet, tremulous hush of eventide lay over the land, as through the park gates a pony phaeton dashed up the long, tree-shaded drive. Two black high-steppers, a dainty little basket carriage, and a lady sitting very erect and upright, driving with a strong, firm hand—a lady in sweeping crapes and sables—in widow's weeds—the mistress of this fair domain.

A groom came forward to hold the horses. As she flung him the reins and stepped out you saw that Mrs. Caryll was a very tall and stately lady, bearing her forty years of life well. A tall, pale, rather cold, rather stern, rather haughty lady, handsomer perhaps in her stately middle age than she could ever have been in youth.

"I have driven the ponies very fast from Dynely Abbey, Morgan," she said to the groom ; "see that they are slowly exercised and well rubbed down. Has the post arrived ?"

The man made a sort of half military salute, as to his commanding officer.

"Post came 'alf an hour ago, ma'am. I'll attend to the ponies, ma'am, all right."

Mrs. Carvll passed on with a slow and measured sort of tread up the stone steps, past the great couchant dogs, along the vast domed hall, hung with suits of mail and antlered heads, up the wide stairway and into her own rooms. The rose light of the sunset filled those elegantly appointed apartments, and lying upon an inlaid table the mistress of the Manor saw what she looked for—a sealed letter. Her heart gave a bound, cold and well disciplined as it was, but (it was characteristic of the woman) before taking it up, she slowly laid aside her bonnet and veil, drew off her gloves, and then deliberately lifted it. A moment she paused to glance at the free flowing writing she knew so well, then she opened and read :

LONDON, *August 25th,* 18—.

MY DEAREST MOTHER :—I have arrived but this moment. By the first train I leave for home. I write this simply to announce my coming. I will be with you almost as soon as my note. I know that in spite of all you will grant me this last interview at least.

Your affectionate son,
GORDON CARYLL.

She crushed the brief letter in her strong white hand. Her fixedly pale face, even in the glow of the sunset, seemed to grow paler, her firm lips set themselves in one tight unpleasant line.

"'My dearest mother!' 'Your affectionate son,'" she said, bitterly, looking at the letter. "Yes, I will see him— he is right—for the last time. After to-night I shall be as though I never had a child."

She folded the letter, laid it aside methodically in a drawer with many others. Slow, methodical habits had become second nature to Mrs. Caryll. "Yes," she thought, "I will see him once more—once more. Whatever he may have to say in his own defence I will hear. To him and to all mankind I trust I shall always do my duty. But come what may, after to-night I will never see him again."

She looked at her watch—the train that would possibly bring him was due even now. In a little time he would be with her. For two years she had not seen him—he had been her darling, the treasure of her heart, the apple of her eye, the "only son of his mother, and she was a widow." Her whole soul cried out for him, and she stood here, and crushed down every voice of nature, and calmly resolved after this once to see him no more forever.

She walked across the room, and paused before the chimney-piece. Two pictures hung above it—the only two this room contained—two portraits. One, the one at which she looked, was the portrait of her husband, painted twenty years ago, in the gallant and golden days of his youth, a present to his bride. A handsome face; the Carylls had ever been handsome men; and this proud, self-contained woman had loved her husband with a great and deathless love. Now, he too lay in Roxhaven church; only a month ago they had laid him there, glad to escape by death the shame brought upon him by an only son.

"There are some things that Heaven itself will not ask us to forgive," was her thought—"this is one of them."

Beneath this portrait hung the other, a smaller one, of her son. Two years ago that had been painted, on the eve of his departure for Canada with his regiment. The frank fair face of the lad of twenty, gray-eyed and yellow-haired, smiled at her from the canvas. With a resolute hand she took it down, and turned it with the face to the wall. A little thing again, but it told how small the mercy Gordon Caryll might expect when he stood before his mother.

It had grown dark—the pale August moon rose up the misty sky. The trees, waving faintly in the salt sea wind, cast long, slanting shadows across the dusty whiteness of the high road, as from the town beyond, from the brightly lit station, a fly from the railway drove through the gates and up the moonlit avenue to the house. A young man sprang out, paid and dismissed the man, and paused a moment in the pallid light to look about him. Only two years since he had stood here last—two years. Nothing had changed—nothing but his life, and the hot fever of his own youthful fancy—

the fair, treacherous face of a woman had spoiled that forever.

He lifted the heavy bronze knocker and sent the echoes
ringing dully down the great hall. The man who opened
the door, an old family servant, started back with a cry of
surprise and delight.

"Sure to goodness, if it isn't Mr. Gordon come back !"

"Mr. Gordon come back—bad shillings always come
back, don't they? How are you, Norton? Is my mother
in ? "

"Yes, Mr. Gordon. In her own rooms. You know the
way—"

"Go and tell her I am here, Norton, and be quick about
it, will you? I'll wait."

The man stared, but obeyed. Gordon Caryll stood in the
long, echoing, deserted hall, staring moodily out at the
moonlight, and not at all sure, in spite of his letter, whether
his mother would deign to see him or not. But his doubts
were speedily set at rest. Norton reappeared.

"My mistress will see you, Mr. Gordon, sir. She bids
you come to her at once in her morning room."

He waited for no more; she would see him; he had
hardly dared hope it; she *might* forgive him—who knew?
He ran lightly up the stairs and tapped at the familiar door.

"Come in," his mother's calm voice said, and, hat in
hand, he entered.

Mother and son stood face to face. A cluster of wax-
lights lit the room brilliantly. In their full glow Mrs,
Caryll stood, her tall figure upheld at its tallest, her widow's
weeds trailing the carpet, her widow's cap on her dark, un-
silvered hair, her face like a face cut in white stone. In
that moment, if he could have but seen it, she bore a curious, passing likeness to himself as he had stood, pale and
relentless, before the girl who had been his wife.

"Mother ! "

She made a sudden, hasty motion for him to stand still and
back, a motion again like his own as he had repelled his
most miserable wife. He obeyed, closing the door, and
knowing his whole fate in that second of time.

She stood for fully a minute, silently looking at him, never softening one whit. She saw the cruel changes those two years had made plainly enough, the youthful face grown grave and worn, the hollow eyes, the colorless cheeks. He had sinned, but he had also suffered. Well, it was right ; here and hereafter is not suffering the inevitable penalty of sin ?

"Mother," he said, "forgive me."

She made a motion of her hand toward the picture above the mantel.

"You know that he is dead?" were her first words.

"I know it. Oh, mother, I acknowledge all my wrong-doing, my shame, my sin, if you will call it so. I was mad. All I could do to atone, I have done. Mother, forgive me, if you can ! "

" Forgive you !" Her eyes blazed out upon him for one moment with a lurid fire. " I will never forgive you so long as we both live !"

He walked over to the low mantel, laid his arm upon it, and his bowed face on his arm. She stood and looked at him, her breast heaving with strong, repressed emotion, her eyes glowing like fire in her pale face.

" For three hundred years," she said, in that tense tone of suppressed passion, "the Carylls have been born, have lived and died beneath this roof, brave men, noble gentlemen always. It was left for my son to bring shame and dishonor at last. The name was never approached by disgrace until you bore it. Your grandfather married a duke's daughter ; you, the last of your name, take a wife from the sweepings of New York city—an actress—a street-walker—a creature whose vile, painted face was displayed nightly in the lowest theatre of the worst of American cities. *My* son, did I call you? I take it back. After to-night I have no son ! "

He never moved ; he never spoke. His hidden face she could not see. That very silence was as oil to fire.

"One month ago your father died—died of your shame. You stand there as much his murderer as though you had stabbed him to the heart. He died unforgiving you—every rood of land, every shilling of fortune left away from you.

Not an inch of Caryllynne is entailed—that you know—not one farthing of the noble inheritance that was your birthright shall you ever possess. The name you dishonor is yours beyond power to recall ; but that alone—not one thing more. And after to-night you never cross this threshold again."

Still no reply—still he stood like a figure of stone.

" You say you have atoned," his mother went on, in that low, passionate voice. " Atoned ! That means you have dragged the name of Caryll through the mire and filth of a divorce court—that your story and hers, that lost wretch, is in the mouths of all men in Canada and England. Your atonement is worse than your crime. Your atonement shall last your life long. Now go ! All I wish to say, I have said—I will never forgive you—I will never look upon your face again ! "

The very words he had spoken to his divorced wife ! What fatality was at work here ? She ceased speaking, and Gordon Caryll lifted his haggard face and looked at her—to the day of her death a look to haunt her with a pain sharper than death itself.

" It shall be as you say," he answered, very quietly. " I don't think I expected anything else—I suppose I deserve nothing better. I will not trouble you again. For the name I have dishonored, have no fear—it shall be dishonored by my bearing it no more. I leave it behind with all the rest. Good-night, mother, and good-by."

And then he was gone. The door closed gently behind him, and she was alone. Alone ! she would be alone her life-long now.

She was ghastly white—ashen white to the lips. But— she had done her duty ! That thought must console her in all the long, lonely years to come. She stood for nearly half an hour in the spot where he had left her, stock-still. Then she slowly turned, walked across the room, lifted a velvet curtain, and entered what seemed an oratory. Over a sort of altar, a painting of the Madonna di San Sisto hung—an exquisite copy ; and the heavenly mother, with the serene, uplifted face, holding the child-Christ in her arms, was there before the earthly mother, who for one rash act, had cast her only son off forever.

On a prayer-desk, before this altar, a Bible lay. At random she opened it—in a blind sort of way seeking for comfort. And this is what she read:

"Behold the king weepeth and mourneth for Absalom. And the victory that day was turned into mourning unto all the people, for the people heard say that day how the king was grieved for his son. But the king covered his face, and the king cried with a loud voice, 'Oh, my son Absalom! Oh, Absalom, my son, my son!'"

8

CHAPTER VI.

GORDON CARYLL'S STORY.

IS trial was over, his sentence was passed, and Gordon Caryll went out from his mother's presence an outcast and banished man.

"All for love, and the world well lost," he said to himself, with something that was almost a smile. "Ah, well! Come what will, I have been blessed. For four months I had my fool's paradise—let that thought console me, in all the years of outlawry that are to come."

He did not leave the house directly. On the landing he paused a moment irresolute, then turned, ran up another stairway, opened one of the many doors that flanked the long corridor, and entered the rooms that had been his own. Only the moonlight lit them, but that was brilliant almost as day. With that slight, sad smile on his lips he walked through them. Everywhere traces of his dead father's pride in him, his mother's love for him, were scattered with lavish hand. More luxurious almost were those rooms than his mother's own.

"They will serve for my mother's heir," the young soldier thought—" whoever that may be. Lucia Dynely's little son Eric, very likely. She was always fond of Lucia; so, for that matter, was I. My pretty cousin! It is but seven miles distant, and there is time and to spare. Suppose I look her up for the last time before I go forth into the outer darkness, and be heard of no more?"

He selected a few trifles, a picture of this mother, another of this "Cousin Lucia" of his thoughts, a gold-mounted meerschaum pipe—then with a last backward glance of farewell at the pretty moonlit rooms, he ran down the stairs, out of the silent house, the great door closed with a clang behind him, and all was over.

He made his way to the stables, startling grooms and stable boys as though he had been a ghost.

"Saddle Dark Diamond, Morris," he ordered; "I'm going to Dynely Abbey, and will leave him there behind me. You can go over for him to-morrow."

He vaulted lightly into the saddle, cantered down the avenue, out of the great gates, and beyond the far-stretching park that was never to call him master.

As he stopped for one last look, never, it seemed to him, had the old ancestral home looked so noble and desirable as on this August night, under the yellow light of the summer moon.

"A fair and stately heritage to yield for a girl's face," he thought, bitterly. "May my successor be wiser than I, and be kept from that maddest of all man's madness—loving a woman!"

His horse was a fleet one—he spurred him on to a gallop. For miles, as he rode, the woods of Caryllynne stretched, on the other hand the cottage lights twinkled, the village forge flamed forth lurid red, old familiar landmarks met him everywhere, and far beyond the broad sweep of the silver-lighted sea.

Less than half an hour brought him to his destination, Dynely Abbey, the seat of Viscount Dynely—a huge historic pile, that long centuries ago had been a Cistercian monastery, in the days when the "Keys and Cross and Triple Crown" held mighty sway through all broad England. As he rode at a gallop up the entrance avenue, in view of the great gray Abbey, pearly white in the moonlight, his horse shied at some white object, so suddenly and violently as almost to unseat his rider. Gordon Caryll laughed as he leaped off and patted him soothingly on the head.

"So ho, Diamond! Easy, old fellow. Does the sight of my pretty Cousin Lucia, in her white dress and shawl, upset your nervous system like this?"

He threw the bridle over a tree, and advanced to where a lady, in a silk dinner dress, and wrapped in a white fleecy shawl, stood.

"Lady Dynely," he said, lifting his hat, "good-evening."

She had been slowly pacing, as though for an evening constitutional, round and round a great ornamental fish-pond. As horse and rider appeared she had paused in some alarm—then, as the unexpected visitor approached, and the bright light of the moon fell on his face, she had uttered a low cry of great surprise and delight, and held out to him both hands.

"Gordon!" she cried. "Oh, Gordon! Can it be you?"

She was a pretty woman—three-and-twenty, perhaps, with a fair blonde face, a profusion of pale blonde hair, a tall, willowy, fragile figure. The fair face, the pale blue eyes, lit up now with genuine delight.

"I, Lady Dynely. You hardly looked for me to-night, did you? And yet, you must have known I would come."

Her color rose. She withdrew the hand he held still.

"I did not know it. How could I tell? Your mother was here to-day—she said nothing about it. When did you come?"

"Two hours ago. And as to-morrow morning, by the first train, I leave again for good, I ran the risk of not finding you at home, and rode over to say good-by. By the way, it's rather a coincidence, but one August night two years ago, you and I shook hands and parted on this very spot. You were dressed in white that night, too, I remember, and looked as you always do look, *belle cousine*, fair and sweet, and pale as a lily."

Again her color rose, but the blue, startled eyes fixed themselves on his face.

"Say good-by—leave for good!" she repeated. "What is it you mean? Gordon, have you seen your mother?"

"Yes, Lucia, I have seen my mother. I have just come from Caryllynne. I have bidden farewell to it and to my mother forever."

She stood looking at him in painful silence—that sensitive rose-pink color coming and going in her cheeks. In the crystal moonlight she could see the great and saddening change in him. She clasped both hands around his arm, and looked up at him with soft, pitiful eyes.

"Gordon—cousin," she said, gently, "is it true, this story they tell, that is in the papers, that all London rang with before we left? It must be true, and yet—oh, Gordon! unless you tell me with your own lips I *cannot* believe."

"Then I tell you," he moodily answered, "it is true."

"That you married an actress—an—oh, Gordon!" she said passionately, "I would rather see you dead!"

"You are not alone in that, I fancy," he said, with a drearily reckless laugh. "All the same, I have done it. All the same, too, I have had enough of reproach and bitterness for one night—it is my last, remember—don't you take up the cry against me. Those gentle lips of yours, *ma belle*, were never made to say cruel things. We have been good friends always—let us so part."

She sighed wearily, her hands still loosely clasped his arm, her blue, pitying eyes still fixed on his face. His gloomy gaze was bent on the water-lilies in the pond, whose pale heads he was mercilessly switching off with his riding whip.

"I am sorry—I am sorry. But your mother, Gordon, surely she pities you and forgives you. I know how stern and resolute she can be where she thinks her duty is concerned; but you, her only son, whom she loves so dearly—"

"She has disinherited and cast me off forever. It is all right, Lucia. I don't deny the justice of my sentence, only you see one looks rather for mercy than for justice from one's mother."

"But she does not mean it—she speaks in anger. She will repent and call you back."

He smiled—a slow, hard, inexorable smile.

"It is a little late for all that. What is done is done. I will never go back. She says truly, I have disgraced the name—the only atonement I can make is to renounce it. She has ordered me from her sight and her home forever— one does not wait to be told that twice."

"How could she—how could she!" his cousin murmured, the soft blue eyes filling and brimming over; "you, her only son—all she has left—whom she loved so dearly.

Oh! how could she do it! Gordon, I, too, have a son,
my little Eric, and I love him so devotedly, so entirely, that
I feel, I know, no crime he could commit, though it were
murder itself, could ever for one second change that love.
Do what he might—yes, the very worst man can do, I
would still love him and take him to my heart."

Her pale face glowed, her pale eyes lit, her voice arose.
Her cousin looked at her tenderly.

"I can believe that," he said; "but you see, Lucia,
there are mothers and mothers—and Viscountess Dynely
and Mrs. Caryll are of two very different orders. I never
did prefer the Spartan sort myself, ready to run the knife
through their nearest and dearest at a moment's notice.
Still, I repeat, my sentence has been deserved, and is just."

"Gordon, tell me all about it, will you? I know so little, I read the papers, of course, but still—"

"Is it worth while, Lucia? It is not a pleasant or profitable story. Do you really care to know?"

"Gordon!"

"Oh, I know all your affectionate interest in me and my
concerns, fairest cousin, and I don't mind boring you with
the details of a young fool's folly. Folly! good heaven
above! What a fool I was! What a gullible, wooden-
headed, imbecile idiot I must have been!"

"You—you loved her, Gordon?"

"Well, yes, I suppose it was love, that blind and besotted fever her beauty and her witcheries threw me into.
She was a sorceress whose accursed spells sent every man
she met under sixty straightway out of his senses. Why
she threw the rest over for me (she had half the battalion at
her feet) was clear enough. I was the youngest, the richest,
and the greatest ass in Toronto. She turned scores of
other heads, but not to that pitch of idiocy which proffers
wedding rings. I had only seen her six times when I asked
her to marry me—you may faintly guess the depth and
breadth of my imbecility when I tell you that."

"She was handsome, Gordon?"

"She was more than handsome, Lucia. She had a
beauté du diable whose like I have never seen—that no man

could resist—a dark, richly-colored, Southern sort of beauty, of the earth earthy. She was small and slender, with a waist you could snap like a pipe-stem, two large black eyes, like a panther's, precisely, and a smile that sent you straight out of your senses. All the fellows in Toronto raved of her—she was the toast of the mess, the talk of the town. Only the women fought shy of her—they took her gauge by intuition, I suppose. Before she had been a week in 'Toronto, Major Lovell and his daughter were *the* topic, in ball-room, and boudoir, and barracks."

"She was a Miss Lovell?" Lady Dynely asked, in a constrained sort of tone. One hand still rested on his arm, and as they talked they walked slowly round and round the fish-pond. In the days that were gone she had been very fond of her dashing boy cousin and playmate—very fond—with sisterly fondness she told herself—nothing more.

"You will hear. I had been a year in Toronto before she came, a dull and dreary year enough, with nothing but the daily drill, the parade, the routine of military life, the provincial balls and dinner parties, the provincial flirtations with dark Canadian belles to break the monotony. All at once she came, and everything changed. Major Lovell brought his daughter among us—and it seemed to me my life began. He was a disreputable old duffer enough, this Lovell, a drunkard, a sharper at cards, a rooker at billiards, living on his half-pay and his whole wits. He was a widower, with a daughter out in Bermuda with her mother's friends, who declined to live with her rascally old father. He was in the habit of disappearing and reappearing in Toronto at odd times—this time, after a longer absence than usual, he reappeared with his daughter.

" He met me one bleak autumn night lounging aimlessly down one of the principal streets, dressed for a heavy sacrificial dinner party, yawning at the boredom in prospective, wishing all civilian dinner-givers at the deuce, and, willy-nilly, he linked his seedy old arm in mine.

" 'En route for Rogers', dear boy?' he said, with a grin, ' and looking ennuied to death even at the thought of what is in store for you. Why make a martyr of yourself, Gor-

don, my lad—why sacrifice yourself on the altar of acquaint-
anceship? Throw over the bloated timber merchant, come
to my lowly wigwam, and let's have a friendly game at ecarte,
I'll give you a deviled kidney, and a glass of sherry—you
can drop in at Rogers' when the heavy feeding's over.
Besides,'—after a pause, this, and with a sideling glance—
' I want to show you my little girl—bless her ! She's come
to keep house for her old dad at last.'

" I made some faint resistance—only faint, and yielded.
I had a weakness for ecarte ; the major was past-master of
the game, although he made his lessons rather expensive to
youngsters like myself.

" ' Neville and Dalton and two or three more of Yours
are coming,' he said, as he inserted his latch key. ' Rosie
will give you a bit of supper by and by, and sing you a
song, if you like that sort of thing. Come in, Gordon—
come in, my boy, and thrice welcome to the old man's
modest mansion.'

" And then I was in, out of the cold, dark Canadian night,
in a fire-lit, lamp-lit parlor, looking with dazzled eyes down
upon the loveliest face, I thought, that firelight or sunlight
ever shone on.

"She had sprung up at our entrance—she had been
crouched in kittenish fashion on the hearth rug, and two big,
wonderful eyes, of tawny blackness, were looking up at me.
I thought of Balzac's ' Girl with the Golden Eyes '—these
were black or yellow, just as the shifting firelight rose or fell.
As I stood staring in a stupefied trance of wonder and admiration, the major's fat, unctuous old voice droned in my
ear.

" ' Rosamond, my child—my young friend, Mr. Caryll,
of Caryllynne, Devon, England, and Her Majesty's—the
Royal Rifles, Toronto, Canada. Gordon, my boy—my little
daughter Rosie.'

"Then a little brown hand slipped out to me, the dark
luminous eyes and the red dimpling lips smiled together.

" ' I am very pleased to meet Mr. Gordon Caryll of ——
what's all the rest, papa? Very pleased to meet anybody,
I'm sure, in this cold, nasty, dreary Canada.'

"'You don't like Canada then, Miss Lovell?' I managed to stammer. 'I am sorry for that. We must try and change your opinion of it before long. What with skating and sleighing, it isn't half a bad place.'

"She pouted and laughed like a child. She was singularly childish in form and face, hardly looking sixteen.

"'Not half a bad place! Where you grill alive three summer months and shiver to death nine winter ones. Oh, my dear Bermuda! Where the hearts were as warm as the climate, and the faces as sunny as the skies. No fear of being lonely, or miserable, or neglected there. If papa would let me, I would go back to-morrow.'

"'But papa won't,' the major put in with a chuckle; 'papa can't spare his one ewe lamb yet. Mr. Caryll here, I am sure, will do his best to make time pass, little one. Hark! I hear a knocking in the south entry—the other fellows at last.'

"Then with much laughter, and stamping and noise, three or four military men came clattering in out of the cold and damp darkness, and were presented to 'My daughter, Rosamond.'

"I don't know how it was with them; I can answer for myself—from the first moment I looked on Rosamond Lovell's face I lost my head. You know me well enough, Lucia," the speaker broke off with a half laugh, "to know I never do that sort of thing by halves. But this was different from anything that had gone before. I looked on those wonderful dusky eyes only once, and said to myself, 'I will win Rosamond Lovell for my wife, if it be in the power of mortal man to win her.'

"I lost no time in setting about my wooing. No wonder the other fellows laughed. They admired old Lovell's daughter, too, no doubt—that was a matter of course—but not to the depth of lunacy. They left that for me. I declined ecarte, I declined deviled kidney, declined the doubtful sherry—I was sufficiently intoxicated already. The peerless Rosamond smiled upon me but shyly; she was not accustomed to such sudden and overpowering devotion —timid angel! Still, she did smile, and let me accompany

3*

her to the distant corner where the piano stood, while the other men played for ponies in the distance, and the major with great impartiality fleeced all alike. She played for me on the jingly piano ; she sang for me in a rich contralto.

" I can see her now as she sat there that first fatal night, in a pink dress, white roses in her belt and in her bosom, the lamplight streaming across her rich, dusk loveliness. Paugh ! the smell of white roses will turn me sick all my life.

" It was late when we broke up, and Miss Lovell, shrinking pettishly from the other men, held out her hand with a soft good-night to me. I went out from the warm, bright room, into the black, rain-beaten midnight, with head and heart in a whirl. The others, not too pensive over their losses at first, chaffed me clumsily, but the hospitable major had bled them all so freely at ecarte, that their deadly, lively jokes soon lapsed into moody silence. To-morrow evening, they were to go back for their revenge, and the friendly major had asked me too.

" ' Though you *did* throw us over, Caryll, my boy.' he said in his big debonnaire voice, ' you'll keep little Rosie from moping herself to death. Yes, yes, come to-morrow and fetch her the new songs. She has a passion for music, my little one, and a voice that would make Lind look to her laurels if the poor old dad could afford to cultivate it.'

" I tossed feverishly through the dark morning hours. ' Rosamond ! Rosamond ! ' I kept repeating ; ' there is music in the very name, music in her voice when she speaks, music celestial in her tones when she sings. And to think that my little white " Rose of the World " should be daughter to such a confounded old cad as that. But I will marry her and take her home to Caryllynne and my mother,' I thought ; and I could picture to myself my mother's whole heart going out in love and welcome, to her son's fair young bride. I didn't much fear a rejection—I was constitutionally sanguine, and she had been as kind as heart could desire. Unless—and I grew cold and hot at the mere fancy—unless she had left a lover behind in Bermuda.

' At the very earliest possible hour next morning, I made

an elaborate toilet and sallied forth for conquest. I purchased an armful of music, and presented myself at Major
Lovell's dingy little cottage. The major was out—Miss
Rosamond was in—that was what the grimy maid-of-all-work
told me. I entered the parlor, and Rosamond was there to
meet and welcome me, more fresh, and youthful, and lovely
in the broad, bright sunshine, than even under the lamplight last night.

"'Oh, what quantities of music! Oh, how kind of me!
All the songs she liked best. Oh, how could she ever
thank me enough!'

"'By letting me come to—to see you every day. By—
caring for me a little. By letting me say how happy it will
make me to be welcomed here by you.'

"Stammering over this speech, blushing and floundering
like any other hobbledehoy in the agonies of calf-love, I
lifted her hand to my lips, *à la* Sir Charles Grandison, and
kissed it.

"I can imagine now how she must have been laughing inwardly at the green young fool she had hooked. But
private theatricals were in her line, her maidenly confusion
and embarrassment were done to the life.

"I lingered for hours, while she tried over the songs, and
dimly realized two facts : that her knowledge of piano-forte
music was but meagre after all, and that she had really very
little to say for herself. Only dimly ; I was much too far
gone to realize anything very clearly, except that she was
the loveliest little creature the Canadian sun shone on.

"That evening I was back. Again Rosamond and I had
our corner, our singing and our *tête-à-tête ;* again that old
wolf, Lovell, fleeced those big innocent military lambs—as
a shearer his sheep. That was the story over and over for
a week—at 'the end of that time, I walked up to Major
Lovell one forenoon, and demanded the priceless boon of
his daughter's hand. The old rascal's start of amazement
and consternation was capital.

"'His daughter! his Rosie! his little girl! And only a
week since we had met! The difference in our positions,
too! *What* did I mean!' Here the major inflated himself

like an enraged turkey-cock, and glared fiercely out of his
fiery little eyes. ' Not to insult him, surely ! A poor man
he might be—alas ! was, but always an officer and a gentleman.'

" Here he stopped sonorously to blow his nose. ' Very
little of a gentleman,' I remember thinking, even then.

" ' Have I taken a viper into the bosom of my family ? '
pursued the old humbug, melodramatically. ' You, Mr.
Gordon Caryll, sir, are heir to a large estate and fortune—the last of an ancient and distinguished line ; it is
also true that I am but one remove from a pauper, still—'

" ' Good Heaven, Lovell ! ' I cried out, impetuously cutting short this rhodomontade. ' What bosh are you talking ?
I mean what I say, I mean it more than I ever meant anything in my life. Insult—nonsense ! I love your daughter,
and I ask you to give her to me for my wife. We have
known each other but a week, it is true. What of that ?
Love is not a plant of slow growth—it can spring up like
the gourd of Jonas, fully grown in a night.'

" I think I must have read that somewhere. It struck
me even at the time as sounding rather absurd, and I looked
to see if the major was laughing. No doubt the old villain
was, for he had turned away to the window, and was elabor-
ately wiping his eyes.

" ' And she—my Rosamond,' he said, at length, in a
voice husky with emotion and much whiskey-punch—' my
little one, who, only a year ago, it seems to me, played with
her dolls, and—and marbles, and—er—that sort of thing,
can it be that she is indeed a woman, and returns your—er
—'pon my life, very flattering passion ? '

" I smiled exultantly as I recalled a little scene of last
night, in that musical nook of ours, the lamp turned low,
the music at a stand-still, and ' I mark the king, and play,'
' Your deal, Deverell,' ' Five to one on Innes,' coming from
the unromantic ecarte players at the other end—a scene
where I, holding Miss Rosamond Lovell's two hands in
mine, had poured forth a rhapsodical story of consuming
passion. And the hands had not been drawn away, and,
as the exquisite face drooped in the dim light, she had

whispered that which had made me the happiest man on
earth.

" 'Yes,' I told the major, ' that was all right; she had
consented to be my wife—nothing was needed but his
sanction. And I hoped he would agree to the marriage
being at once. What need was there of delay? I was of
age, and two months over—what need of waiting? I
wanted to make sure of my prize.'

" It was the most out-and-out case of insanity on record.
I was mad—sheer mad. I cannot account for my besotted
folly in any other way. The old fox made a feint of not
consenting at first. She was too young—our acquaintance
was so scandalously short—what would Toronto say?
What would my father and mother say? The thing was not
to be thought of.

" But I would listen to nothing. What did it matter *what*
Toronto said? Toronto might go hang! My father and
mother had no thought but for my happiness; their ultimate
consent was all right. For the rest, if he dreaded the
world's tongue, let the marriage be private, just as private as
he pleased, and in a month, or two months, or whenever I
could get leave of absence, I and my wife would sail for
England. When the thing was inevitable, talk would die
out. Marry my darling I must; life without her was insupportable, etc., etc., etc.

" I grow sick at heart, Lucia, when I recall that time.
And yet I was blindly, insanely happy—with that utter bliss
that in the days of our first youth and grossest folly we can
only know. We were married. Rosamond had but one
female acquaintance, a young lady music-teacher—she, of
course, was bridesmaid, and Singleton, of Ours, was best
man. We were married in the cottage parlor, one dark
autumnal morning, all on the quiet. Clergyman, groomsman,
bridesmaid, all promised secrecy. Rosamond remained at
the cottage with her father as before. I kept my rooms in
the town. I did not write to announce my marriage—time
enough for all that, I thought. I would get leave of absence
and take Rosamond home—they would have to look in

her face but once, to forget my rash haste, her poverty and obscurity, and take her to their hearts forever.

"But days and weeks and months slipped away—four passed ; and leave had not yet been obtained. As might be expected, our secret had leaked out, and was our secret no longer. The story of my mad marriage was whispered throughout the town, and only my blindness was upon me still, I must have seen the looks of pity that met me at every turn—pity blended with amusement and contempt. But I saw nothing, suspected nothing, and when the blow came, it fell like a thunderbolt, indeed.

" I have said this girl I had married was a perfect actress —I say it again. Love itself she could counterfeit to the life ; she fooled me to the top of my bent ; she made me believe her whole heart was mine. Her face lighted when I came, saddened when I went, ay, after four months of matrimony she held her dupe as thoroughly duped as on the first day. Something preyed on her mind, *that*, at least, I saw. She looked at me at times as though she feared me ; she looked at the major as though she feared him. The old fellow had taken to drinking harder than ever, had been at death's door with delirium tremens more than once since my marriage, and in his cups (I learned after) babbled of what he had done.

" 'We hooked him, sir,' the tipsy major would hiccough, winking his bleary old eyes, and tottering on his rickety old legs, ' hooked him like the gonest coon ! Oh, Lord ! what fools young men are ! a pretty girl can twist the biggest of you gallant plungers around her little finger. I've known regiments of fools in my lifetime, but that young ass, Caryll —oh, by Jupiter ! *he* puts the topper on the lot.'

" It was the major himself who threw up his hand, and showed me the game he had played at last.

" He had caught cold after a horrible fit of D. T., and I suppose his devil's race was run—typhoid fever supervened, and the gallant major was going to die. Rosamond, with him still, nursed him faithfully and devotedly, and tried with all her power to keep me from seeing him at all.

" 'You can do no good, Gordon,' she would plead ;

'keep away—don't go in. You may catch the fever. He wants no one but me.'

" The bare thought of my entering the sick room seemed a perpetual terror to her. She would have no nurse, she would wait upon him herself, she almost tried by force to keep me from seeing him. Off and on he was delirious; as a rule he had his wits about him though, and would grin like a satyr to the last.

" ' She's afraid I'll peach, Caryll,' he whispered to me one day, with a wink. 'Blessed if I won't, though. *I* never cared about her, and it would be a shame, a cursed shame, to go off hooks, you know, and not tell.'

" ' Not tell what ? ' I asked, sternly.

" ' Never you mind, Gordon, my boy, you'll hear it all fast enough. You ain't half a bad sort, hanged if you are, and I'm sorry—yes, I'm sorry I did it. It was a devilish unhandsome trick for one gentleman to play on another; but it was good fun at the time, that, you'll be forced to admit yourself. Hush-h! here she comes, not a word to *her*. I'll tell you all by and by.'

" I was bewildered—half startled also ; but I set it down to delirium. She came in, looking with quick, apprehensive eyes from his face to mine.

" ' Has he been talking? ' she asked.

" ' Nothing *you* would care to hear, Rosie, my girl,' he cut in, with a feeble chuckle ; 'not a word about you—ask him if you like.'

" I set it all down to delirium. ' Whom the gods wish to destroy they first make mad.' My madness had lasted over four months—I was destined to become sane again.

" The major sank lower and lower. His last hour was near. Rosamond never left him when she could ; she still strove with all her might to keep us apart. I sometimes wonder now she did not hasten his end. She was quite capable of it, I believe.

" One night I was to dine in the town. I had left the cottage and nearly reached my destination. It was a stormy February night, the streets white with drifting snow, a sleety wind blowing piercingly cold. Some unaccountable depression had weighed upon me all day ; my wife was strangely changed of late; I could not. understand her. The major was very low, almost at his last. What if he died while I was absent, Rosamond and the servant-maid all ~alone. I turned hastily back ; I would share my dear girl's vigil, I thought—nay, I would compel her to go to bed and to sleep ; she was utterly worn out, and I would watch alone.

" I returned to the house, and entered softly. The maid-servant was alone in the sick room. Miss Rosamond had fallen asleep at her post from sheer weariness, and had been persuaded to go to her own room and lie down.

" ' You did quite right,' I said ; ' I will share your watch. I don't think he will last out the night.'

" The sick man's eyes opened—a cunning leer in them to the last.

" ' Don't you, Gordon, my boy—don't you think I'll last out the night? Then, by Jove ! it's time to make a clean breast of it. Where's she ? Your wife ? '

" ' Up-stairs in her own room, asleep.'

" 'That's right. When the cat's away the mice can play. Send that woman back to the kitchen—I've a word or two for your private ear.'

" I obeyed. The woman went.

" ' Now lock the door, like a good fellow, and come here. Sit close, for my wind's almost gone, and I can't jaw as I used. And I say ! look here, Caryll ! no violence, you know. I'm an old man, and I'm dying, and I'm sorry— yes, blessed if I ain't—that I ever fooled you as I did. All the reparation I can make, I will make—that's fair, surely. Now, listen, here, Caryll ; this has been a put-up job from first to last. Rosamond's not my daughter ¡'

" ' Not your—'

" I sat staring at him aghast.

" ' Not my daughter—no, by George ! My daughter, the one in Bermuda, you know, is in Bermuda still, and a deuced hard-featured young woman—takes after her mother, and wouldn't touch her disreputable old dad with a pair of tongs. No, Gordon, lad, the girl you've married isn't my daughter. I don't know who's daughter she is. She doesn't know herself. She's your wife—worse luck; but she's nothing to me.'

" I sat stunned, dumb, listening. If my life had depended on it, I could not have spoken a word.

" ' I'll tell you how it was, Caryll,' the dying old reprobate went on. 'Give us a drop of that catlap in the tumbler first. Thanks. It was in New York I met her first— in New York, just a month before I brought her here. Strolling down the Bowery one night I went into a concert-room, or music-hall, of the lowest sort. Bowery roughs, with their hats on and cigars in their mouths, were lying about the benches yelling for " Rosamond " to come out and give them a song. Presently the wretched orchestra began, the green baize drew up, and, in a gaudy, spangled dress, a banjo in her hand, tawdry flowers in her hair, " Rosamond " came bounding forward, smiling and kissing hands to her vociferous audience. So I saw her for the first time—I swear it, Caryll--the girl you have made your wife !'

" ' She sang song after song—you can imagine the highly-spiced sort of songs likely to suit such an audience. They applauded her to the echo, stamping, clapping, whistling, yelling with wild laughter and delight, and all the while I sat, and stared, and wondered at her beauty. For tawdry, and painted, and brazen as she was that night, her beauty, in all places and at all times, is a thing beyond dispute. It was then, sitting there and looking at her, that the plot came into my head, put there by *her* guardian angel, the devil, no doubt. This is what it was :

" ' Take that girl off the stage, clothe her decently, drill her in her part for a week or two—she's a clever little baggage—take her back to Toronto, and pass her off as your daughter. She's got the beauty and grace of a duchess, and there's more than one soft-headed, soft-hearted fool among the fellows there, who will go mad over her black eyes, and be ready to marry her out of hand before she's a month among them. There's that young chap, Caryll, for instance—oh, yes. Gordon, my boy, I pitched upon you even then—he's the heir to one of the finest fortunes in the kingdom, and the last man on earth likely to doubt or inves-tigate. The thing's worth trying. Of course, when the fish is hooked *I* come in for the lion's share. Ecarte's not an unprofitable amusement, but there may be better things in this wicked world even than ecarte.

" 'It was a brilliant idea—even you must own that. I lost no time in carrying it out. I hunted up Rosamond behind the scenes. Good Ged! such scenes! and there and then had a long and fatherly talk with her. She gave me her history frankly enough ; she had no parents, no friends to speak of, no relations. She never *had* had a father so far as she knew, and her drunken drab of a mother had died two years before. She was sixteen, and had made her debut a year before, under the friendly auspices of a negro minstrel gentleman, who had taught her to strum the banjo and play upon the piano.

" ' I said nothing of my plan that night. I slept upon it, and found it rather strengthened than otherwise by that process. I hunted up Mlle. Rosamond (in private life they called her Sally) next morning, in her Bowery attic, and laid my plan before her. Gad, Caryll, how she jumped at it! Her eyes glittered at the mention of the fine dresses and gay jewelry—she had ambition beyond her sphere, had devoured a great deal of unwholesome light literature, and was equal to anything. I found her cleverer even than I had dared to hope—the girl had been more or less educated at a public school, and could actually talk well. The negro minstrel gentleman thrashed her when he got drunk ; she was tired of her life and Bohemian associates, to call them by no fouler name, of this dirty Quartier Latin of New York, and eager and ready to go.

" 'What need to waste words, Caryll—the thing was an accomplished fact in three weeks. The rest you know— "we came, we saw, we conquered," more's the pity—for *you*. The little Bowery actress played her part *con amore*— the pretty little yellow-eyed spider wove her web, and the big, foolish fly walked headlong in at first sight. You married her !'

" He paused a moment, and motioned me to give him his cordial. The clammy dew of death was upon his face already, his voice was husky and gasping, but he was game to the end and would finish. I held the drink to his lips in a stupid, dazed sort of way, far too stunned to realize what I heard as yet.

" ' You married her, Gordon,' he went on, ' and—give the devil his due—I believe she's fond of you. That wasn't in the bond, but she is, and her efforts of late days to have me die and "make no sign" were worthy a better cause. But I ain't such an out-and-out bad 'un as that, Caryll—'pon my word I ain't ; and then, money can't do a man any good when he's going to die. So I've made a clean breast of it, my boy, and you can do as you please. You're awfully spoony on her, I know, and if you like, why, say nothing about it ; stick to her through thick and thin. Other men have married girls like Rosie—and she's fond of you, as I say, poor little beggar, and you can take her to England and no one will be the wiser. The fellows here won't peach ; they know it, Caryll ; the thing's leaked out somehow, and—'

" He stopped. I had risen to my feet. I don't know what he saw in my face, but he held up both hands with a shrill cry of horror, not to kill him. The next I remember, I was out in the black, storm-beaten street. It was close upon midnight. At that hour and in that storm there was no one abroad in Toronto. A wheel of fire seemed crashing through my brain, some nameless, awful horror hadfallen upon me. In a stupefied way I was conscious of that—of no more. And then—all in an instant it seemed to me the night had passed and the morning had broken. I had spent hours in the freezing streets. With the morning light the mists of my brain seemed to clear, and the full horror of this most horrible thing came upon me—this unheard-of, shameless deed.

" The girl I had loved, had trusted, had married, was the vile thing he made her out—the offcast of the New York streets. And the man who had blindly loved her she had fooled and laughed at from first to last ! A very

demon of fury seemed to enter me then.   I turned, and
went home—with but one resolve—to have her life, and
then end my own.

"She was not there.   She had seen my first entrance;
she had stolen down, listened, and heard all ; she had gone
back to her room, dressed herself for the street, taken all
her money and jewels, and fled.   They told me all this—
three or four of our fellows were there, and a strange, gloomy
hush lay over the house.   Major Lovell was dead.

"After that, for a week or two, all is chaotic.   I did not
end my life—I hardly know how I was kept from that last
coward's act—the fact remained.   They buried Lovell ; and
in a quiet way, the story of old Lovell's plot, and old
Lovell's daughter, was over the town.

"I made no attempt to follow her.   The first paroxysm
of fury passed, a sullen, dull reaction set in.   I filed a
suit for divorce.   A mere separation would not do—every
tie must be cut that bound me to her.   I wrote home, telling my father and mother all—all—hiding nothing.   Then
my leave came, and I quitted Toronto forever.   Months
passed.   I lived in hiding in Montreal ; then the decree of
divorce was granted—I was free !

"I was going home.   Before quitting Canada to return
no more, I went to Quebec to visit my mother's old friend
and my godfather, General Forrester.   My story had rung
through Quebec, of course—was it not ringing over the
length and breadth of the land?   But the kind old general
made no mention of it, and insisted upon my joining them
the day of my arrival at mess.

"I agreed.   I had lived a hermit life for five months—I
longed to see familiar faces once more.   At the mess dinner, while jokes and stories were being bandied round, some
one jovially proposed the health of the 'Sleeping Beauty of
the Enchanted Palace,' and it was drunk with laughing enthusiasm.   I naturally made inquiry concerning this celebrated lady, and learned, that in the present instance, her
mortal name was Mrs. Gordon, a youthful widow of fabulous beauty and wealth, who had come to Quebec five
months before, and had shut herself up in a deserted old

rookery, to weep in silence, no doubt, over the dear departed. Like a flash the truth came upon me.

"'Most thrilling indeed, Ercildoun,' I said; 'here's towards her! Which are we to drink—*belle* blonde, or *jolie* brunette?'

"'Brunette, brunette! a picture by Titian. Eyes like sloes, and hair like that what's-his-name's wing!' shouted Ercildoun.

"The toast was rapturously taken up. I was as hilarious as any of them. There are times when thought *must* be drowned, no matter how.

"Next day I deliberately hunted her down. Her servant was pointed out to me on the street; I followed her. And walking up and down by the river side, in the summer sunset, I came full upon the girl who had been my wife.

"I believe at first she imagined I had come to kill her. I speedily reassured her. What need, Lucia, to speak of that interview? It was brief, indeed. I have looked my last, I hope, on the woman who was for four months my wife. I hope—and yet, so surely as I stand here, I believe she will cross my path again. She vowed it, as we parted that night, and for good or for evil she is one to keep her word."

The story was told rapidly, at times almost incoherently, but told. He stood beside her in the moonlight, with color-less face and eyes full of passionate despair.

"The remainder you know," he said, after a pause; "the shame that broke my father's heart and sent him to his grave—that has parted my mother and me forever. For the rest, whatever fate befalls me in the time to come, it is a fate richly earned. I blame my mother in no way. Your son Eric, or General Forrester's baby daughter, will inherit Caryllynne in my stead. So let it be. I go from here to-night, in all likelihood forever. Before the week is out I shall have left England."

She had turned her face away from him, but he knew that her tears were falling.

"Where do you go?" she asked.

"To India. I have exchanged into a regiment ordered

out at once. When one's life comes to an end at home, it is well to be of some service abroad. And so, Lucia, my best cousin, you at least will bid me good-by and good speed before I go."

He took both her hands, looking down into the fair, drooping face.

"And you," he went on, "are *you* happy, Lucia? You are pale and frail as a shadow. Tell me, does Dynely—," he paused. She drew her hands from his clasp, her face still turned away.

"I made a mercenary marriage," she answered, sudden coldness and hardness in her tone; "that you know. All the happiness such marriages bring, I have. While I possess my boy, my Eric, I can never be utterly miserable, Gordon!" She looked up suddenly, her fair face crimsoning. "You knew Lord Dynely before his marriage—you were with him one autumn in Ireland, were you not? Tell me—" she stopped.

"Well, Lucia? What?"

"It may be only fancy, but I *have* fancied there is some —some secret connected with that Irish summer. It is seven years ago—you were only a boy at the time. Still—" again she paused confusedly.

"Well?"

"There was no one, no girl, no peasant girl to whom Lord Dynely paid attention that summer in Galway? I have heard a rumor—" for the third time she broke off, afraid, it seemed, to go on.

Her cousin looked at her in some surprise.

"You know what Lord Dynely is—was, I mean, in his bachelor days," he said, quietly, "an admirer of every pretty girl he met, whether peeress or peasant. There were many handsome Spanish-looking women to be seen that long ago summer we spent fishing at the Claddagh, on the Galway coast. His lordship admired them all, I am bound to say ; I am also bound to say, impartially, so far as I could see. Don't take fancies into your head, Lucia—facts are enough. And now I must go. By Jove! how the time has flown! I have kept you here an unconscionable time in the falling dew.

Good-by, Lucia, keep a green place in your memory for the black sheep of the flock. Kiss little Eric for me. Once more, good-by."

Holding her hands in his, he bent down and touched her cheek. She broke suddenly into a passionate sob.

" Oh, Gordon, cousin, it breaks my heart to see you go ! "

He smiled.

" It is best so," he said.

He dropped her hands, turned with the words, walked rapidly away, and disappeared.

CHAPTER VII.

HOW LORD VISCOUNT DYNELY DIED.

HALF an hour had passed away, and still Lady Dynely paced slowly where her cousin had left her, heedless of falling dew, her thin dinner-dress damp and heavy already in the night. In the days that were gone she had been very fond of her boy cousin, three years her junior in actual years, twenty in worldly wisdom and judgment. There had never been any thought of love or love-making, marrying or giving in marriage, between these two; she had given Viscount Dynely her hand of her own free will, and yet, the sharpest, keenest pang of actual jealousy she had ever felt, she had felt when she first heard of Gordon Caryll's marriage. Not a very fierce pang, though, after all—it might have been said of her as of Lady Jane, in the poem:

> "Her pulse is calm, milk-white her skin;
> She has not blood enough to sin."

It had been considered a very brilliant match, *the* match of the season indeed, when Lucia Paget won Alexis, Viscount Dynely and twentieth Baron Camperdown. She had been taken up to London at eighteen, and presented by her kinswoman, the Countess of Haldane. She was tall, slim and white, fair and fragile as a lily, "a penniless lass wi' a lang pedigree"—a trifle insipid to some tastes, but she suited Lord Dynely. He came home from a yachting cruise around Norway and the Hebrides, presented himself suddenly in Vanity Fair, the most desirable prize of the mall, with mansions and estates in four counties, a villa at Ryde, a shooting-box in the Highlands, and an income that flowed in

like a perennial golden river. He was a prize that had
long been angled for (his noble lordship was in his five-and-
fortieth year), maids and matrons had put on their war paint,
and set their wigwams in order, long and many a day ago,
for him. But in vain ; his scalp-lock hung at no belt. He
admired all, ballerinas, as a rule, more than baronesses,
actresses more than duchesses. But his day came at last ;
he saw Lucia Paget, by no means the beauty of the season,
and after his own impetuous fashion, where his own gratification was concerned, threw up the sponge to Fate at once,
and surrendered at discretion. He proposed, was accepted,
and the wedding-day named, before Vanity Fair could re-
cover its breath. It was the wonder of the day—that pale,
insipid nonentity—that blasé, fastidious, worn-out roué—
What did he see in her ?

> " There were maidens in Scotland more lovely by far,
> Who would gladly be bride to the young Lochinvar."

But he had passed them all by, and thrown the handkerchief
at the indifferent feet of this pale-haired lass. Before the
end of the season they were married.

He was very much enamored of his bride, there no was
denying that. Fickle, in his fancies, to a proverb, he was
yet loyal here. He took her over the Continent for a year,
then returned to England, with them " little Eric ; " and
Lord Viscount Dynely was the fondest of fathers as well as
the most devoted of husbands. But from the birth of his
son a change came over him. He took a habit of falling
into moody, darksome reveries, he dropped mysterious and
unpleasant hints of some wrong-doing in the past, he spoke
gloomily of his infant heir and some sin, sinned against *him*.
Lady Dynely grew pale as she listened—it was no common
wrong-doing of a man of the world of which he hinted—it
was something that might influence the future of his son, of
herself — some crime against them both. He spoke a
woman's name in his disturbed, remorse-haunted slumbers—
" Maureen "—his wife could catch. What did it mean ?
She had never loved her husband, she had always been a
little afraid of him—she grew more and more afraid of him

4

as the years went on. Years did go on. Eric was five ; the
secret, whatever it might be, was Lord Dynely's secret still.
Only once he had said to her :

"Lucia, if I die before you, I have something to tell
you that you won't like to hear. People always make death-
bed confessions, don't they ? On the principle, I suppose,
that come what may, they are past hurting. I wonder if
they sleep any easier in their six feet of clay, for owning up ?
I'll write it down, and leave it sealed with my will, and then
if I'm cut off in a hurry (and it is an interesting trait in the
Dynely succession that we always *are* cut off in a hurry), it
will come to light all the same. There's one consolation,"
he said with a short, reckless laugh, " you never cared over
and above for me—it was the title you married and the set-
tlements, and you'll have them, you know, to the end of
the chapter, so you won't break your heart."

He had whistled to his dogs and walked moodily off, saying no more ; and his wife, listening with pale cheeks and
dilated eyes, asked no questions. She was not strong,
either mentally, morally, or physically ; she shrank from
pain of all sorts, with almost cowardly fear. If Lord Dynely
had wicked secrets, she wanted to hear none of them—she
desired no confessions—it was cruel of him to talk of making them. As he had kept his dreadful masculine secrets in
life, let him keep them in death.

She stood vaguely thinking this where Gordon Caryll had
left her, looking like some spirit of the moonlight in her
white robes, her light, floating hair, and colorless face. And
even while she thought it, the messenger was drawing near
to summon her to hear that secret told.

The stable clock chiming loudly eleven awoke her from
her thoughtful trance. She started. How late it was, how
chilly it had grown ! She shrank with the first sensation she
had felt of cold and damp, and turned to go. But she
stopped, for the sylvan silence of the summer night was
loudly broken by the ringing clatter of horses' hoofs dashing up the avenue. Was it Gordon coming back ? Little
things disturbed her—her heart fluttered as she listened.
Horse and rider came in view ; the man espied her and

vaulted off. No, this small, middle-aged man, was not her tall cousin, but Mr. Squills, the village apothecary.

" My lady ! "

He took off his hat and stood bowing before her. In the moonlight my lady could see the frightened look the man's face wore.

" What is it ? " she asked.

" Oh, my lady—I don't want to alarm you, I'm sure— they told me to break it to you, but it's so hard to break things. There's been an accident, my lady. The 9.50 express from Plymouth, and don't let me frighten you, my lady—his lordship was in it, and——"

She laid her hand over her heart, turning for a moment sick and faint. Then she rallied.

" Lord Dynely was on that train ? There was an accident, you say. Was he——"

" Oh, my lady, prepare yourself. It—it's a dreadful thing to break things to——"

" Was Lord Dynely hurt ? " she asked.

" Yes, my lady, very badly hurt, I'm sorry to say."

" Dangerously ? "

" We're afraid so, my lady. Mr. Glauber is with him, and they've telegraphed to London for Doctor—"

" He is alive ? " she interrupted, her voice sharp with horror and pain.

" Alive, my lady, but—it is best you should know the truth—he won't be alive by morning. The clergyman is with him, but he calls, my lady, continually for you."

" Where is he ? "

" At the inn, in the village—the ' Kiddle-a-wink.' And, my lady, there is not a moment to lose."

She turned from him and ran to the house. On the way she met one of the grooms, and ordered the carriage at once. She fled up to her room, threw a dark mantle over her white evening-dress, put on her bonnet with trembling fingers, and turned to depart. A sudden thought came to her—she turned into an adjoining room—the nursery, where her boy lay asleep.

The night-light burns low; he lies in his downy, lace

draped bed, a lovely baby-vision of health and beauty. Flushed, dimpled, his golden curls falling over the pillow, a smile on the rosy lips—he is a sight to make any mother's heart leap. · She stoops and kisses him with passionate love. "Oh, my baby, my angel!" she whispers, "you are all I have on earth. While I live, no harm, that I can avert, will ever come to you."

Then she flits out of the room—out of the house. The carriage is waiting, and in a moment more she is rapidly whirling through the still, white midnight to the village inn where her husband lies dying.

They lead her to the room. Physician and priest fall back, and give way to the wife. The wounded man lies propped by pillows, his head bandaged, his face awfully bloodless and ghastly in the wan light. She has heard no details of the accident, she has asked none. He is dying—all is said in that.

His eyes light as they turn on her, but his brow is frowning.

"Send them all away," are his first words.

She motions them out of the room. She sinks on her knees by the bedside. Her dark drapery slips off; her white dress, her soft laces, her fair, floating hair, seem strangely to contradict the idea of death. She is trembling from head to foot—her teeth chatter with nervous horror, her eyes fix themselves, all wild and dilated, upon his face. She never speaks a word.

He lies and looks at her—a long, steadfast, frowning gaze.

"I am dying," he says; "you know it. You never cared for me—no, never—not even in your wedding hour. You never cared for me—why should I care for *you?* Why should I hesitate to tell you the truth?"

It has been the thorn in his rose-crowned life—this fact, that the portionless girl he married, never gave him her heart.

"Tell me now," he says, still with that dull, frowning gaze, "I was too great a coward ever to ask you before—tell me now—you married the rank and the rent-roll, not the man?"

" I did wrong," she says, huskily, " but I have tried to do my duty as your wife. Forgive me, Alexis."

" Ah !" he answers bitterly, "we have both something to forgive—it makes us quits. I have been a coward, a coward to you, a coward to *her*. It is hard to say which has been wronged most. But you shall hear the truth now, and you shall do as you see fit after. Draw near."

She bends closer above him. He takes her hand in his cold fingers, and whispers, hoarsely and brokenly, his death-bed confession.

Half an hour passes, an hour, another, and still from that closed room there is no sound. It is very strange. Mr. Glauber, the doctor, and Mr. Texton, the rector, think un-easily, looking at their watches, outside. It is quite impos-sible Lord Dynely, in his fast-sinking state, can be talking all this time—impossible, also, that he can have fallen asleep. Presently Mr. Texton takes heart of grace, and taps at the door. There is no reply. He taps again. Still silence. He opens the door and goes in. Lord Dynely has fallen back among his pillows, dead, that frown forever frozen on his face ; my lady still kneels by the bedside—as rigid, as upright, as white, as cold, as though turned to stone.

"My lady !" She does not speak or stir. " My dear Lady Dynely," the rector says, in an unutterably shocked tone.

She moves for the first time, and lifts two sightless eyes to his face. He holds out his arms, for she sways unsteadily, and catches her, as without word or sound she slips heavily back, and faints away.

PART SECOND.

CHAPTER I.

IN THE ROYAL ACADEMY.

HE brilliant noontide of a brilliant May day was passed—all London looked bustling and bright under a sky as cloudless as that of Italy. In Trafalgar Square there was a mighty gathering of carriages, an army of coachmen and footmen in liveries, of all sorts and colors, for it was the opening day of the Royal Academy.

The rooms were full—full to repletion, filled with a jostling crowd of well-dressed ladies and gentlemen, but then "a mob is a mob though composed of bishops." Languid, dilettante-looking swells, with eye-glasses; painters with long hair, and picturesque faces; art critics, book and pencil in hand; academicians, receiving congratulations; picture dealers, marking the quarry on which they meant presently to swoop; stately dowagers, sweeping their silken trains over the crimson drugget; slim, young English girls, with milk-and-rose complexions and gilded hair.

The clock of St. Martin's-in-the-fields was striking four as there entered two ladies and a gentleman, who moved slowly through the swaying throng, and who, even there, attracted considerable attention. One of the ladies was approaching middle age, a fair, pale, pensive, *passée* looking woman, with a stamp of high rank on every faded feature, in every careless gesture. *She* was not the attraction. The escort was a very tall, very broad-shouldered, very powerful·

looking young man, muscular Christianity personified, with a certain military air, that bespoke his calling, a thick, reddish beard and mustache, reddish, close-cropped hair, and two light, good-humored eyes. *He* was not the attraction. Terry Dennison's face was as well known about town as Landseer's couchant lions around Nelson's pillar, in the square beyond. It was the third of the trio, a girl, tall and slender, and very graceful, with a figure that was rarely perfect, and a way of carrying herself that was altogether imperial. A dark beauty, with a warm, creamy, colorless skin, two vivid, hazel eyes, a profusion of hazel hair, arranged *à la mode*, a handsome, decided, square-cut mouth, and a general air of imperious command that said to all

"Incedo Regina !
I move a queen."

She was dressed *en passant*, as it were, with a careless simplicity that was the perfection of high art. An Indian muslin robe, a scarf of black lace, caught up on one shoulder with a knot of yellow roses—on her head a touch of point-lace, with just one yellow rose over the ear, and in her pearl-kidded hand a bunch of the same scented yellow roses.

A covey of idle, elegant dandies of the Foreign Office, and guardsmen, lounging in one of the door-ways, put up their glasses and turned to look again, roused for the moment almost to interest.

"Something new in Vanity Fair," one said, "and the best thing I've seen this season. Know who she is, any one ? "

No one knew.

"Altogether new, as you say, Danby. Jove ! what a regal air ! There is nothing on the walls—not a nymph or goddess of them all, with a lovelier face. *Who* is she ? "

"Her companion is Lady Dynely," remarked a third.

"And her escort is Terry Dennison. He has placed them before *the* picture of the year, that thing by Locksley, and has left them. Here he comes. I say, Dennison ! who is she ? "

"Who is who ? asked Mr. Dennison, the sandy-haired and whiskered young man, approaching. " ' Who is she ? ' isn't

that the question the cynical old French party always asked,
when any fellow he knew came to grief?"

"Don't be analytical, Terry, it isn't your *mètier*. Who is
that lady you accompany? Handsomest thing out."

"That," answered Terry, thoughtfully stroking his beard,
"is my Lady Dynely; and where have you kept your eyes
all these years not to know it—"

"That will do. We don't want chaff. Who is that
girl?"

"All yellow roses and black lace, like a picture by Tit
ian," another murmured.

"Who is she, Terry?" chorus all.

"Oh!" said Terry, opening his light blue eyes with an innocent air, "that's what you mean, is it? That girl is
France Forrester."

"France? Named after the dominion of his Imperial
Majesty, Nap the Third?"

"Her name is France—Frances, if you like it better," answered calmly Mr. Dennison.

"But who is she? *Who* is she, Terry? She's new to all
of us, and the handsomest debutante of the season. Open
the mysteries a little, old man; and end our agonizing suspense."

"There's nothing mysterious about it," responded Terry
Dennison with a suppressed yawn; "she is France Forrester, as I say, only child and heiress of the late General
Forrester, distant connection of Lady Dynely, and adopted
daughter and heiress of Mrs. Caryll, of Caryllynne. 'To
her that hath shall be given.' I have spoken!"

"Like an oracle. Go on—tell us more."

"There's no more. Her mother a French Canadian,
from whom mademoiselle inherits her gypsy skin and *beaux
yeux*, died when she was six. Her father placed her in
a Montreal convent, and there she lived until she was fifteen.
Then *he* died, left her a fortune, and made Mrs. Caryll her
guardian. That was three years ago; and if your limited
knowledge of arithmetic will permit you to add three to fifteen you will come at Miss Forrester's age. Mrs. Caryll,
then and at present in Rome, had her ward conveyed to the

Eternal City. Until two months ago she moved and had her being there—now she has come over, to come out under the auspices of Lady Dynely. I wish you fellows wouldn't make me talk so much," says Terry, with a sudden sense of injury, "the thermometer is high, and I ain't used to it."

Then Mr. Dennison strolls away, and the four men from the F. O. stand and gaze with languid interest at the Canadian-Roman beauty and heiress.

"Safe to make a hit," one said ; "haven't seen anything so thoroughbred for three seasons. What with mademoiselle's beauty and grace, and *that* poise of the head, and two fortunes tacked to her train, and her twenty quarterings (they're an awfully old family, the Forresters), she ought to make a brilliant match before the season ends."

"Ah! I don't know," another responded, "it doesn't always follow. The favorite doesn't always win the Derby. Mrs. Caryll's heiress—him-m! I say, Castlemain! You ought to know—wasn't there a son in that family once ? "

"Gordon Caryll—very fine fellow—knew him at Oxford," Castlemain answered, "commission in the Rifles—old story that—sixteen years ago—all over and forgotten for centuries."

"Dead?"

"Don't know—all the same—extinct. Made a horrible mesalliance out there in Canada—scandal—divorce—exchanged—went to India—never heard of more. *Sic transit* —fate of all of us by and by. Deuced slow this," struggling with a yawn ; "I say—let's hook it."

The quartette move on, others take their place, and the men, one and all, turn for a second look at the fair, proudlooking beauty. With Lady Dynely, she still stands where Mr. Dennison has left them, gazing at the picture that has made the hit of the year. It is by an artist unknown to fame and Trafalgar Square—it is marked in the catalogue "No. 556—*How The Night Fell.*"

It is not an English scene. Tall, dark hills in the background lift pine-crowned heads to the sky, clumps of cedar, and tamarac, and spruce, painted with pre-Raphaelite fidelity, dot these dark hill-sides. A broad river, with the last red

4*

light of dying day glinting along the water, and over hill-side and tree-top and flowing river, the gray darkness of coming night shutting down.   On the river-side two figures stand, a man and a woman.   One red gleam from the western sky falls full upon the woman's face, a face darkly beautiful, but all white and drawn with woman's utmost woe.   Passionate despair looks out of her wild eyes at the man who stands before her.   Her hands are outstretched in agonized appeal.   For the man, he stands and looks at her, one hand slightly upraised as if waving her off.   His face is partly averted, but you can guess the hatred that face shows.   You see that her doom is sealed beyond redemption.   Over all, the creeping night is darkening land, and river, and sky.

The two ladies gaze in silence for a time—Lady Dynely looking weary and rather bored—Miss Forrester's fine eyes bright with admiration.   She is new to general society as yet, and when eye, or ear, or heart are delighted, the expressive face shows it.

" It is beautiful," she says in a low voice ; "there is nothing like it in the rooms.   Look at that wonderful effect of light on the woman's face, and slanting along the river, and the gray darkness that you can almost *feel* there beyond. Those trees are tamarac—can it be a Canadian scene. ' How The Night Fell,' " she reads from her catalogue. " Lady Dynely, I must know the painter of that picture."

" My dear France !"

" ' G. Locksley.'   H–m–m—a new candidate, probably. Certainly I must know him.   In Rome, we—Mrs. Caryll and I—made a point of taking up every young artist who appeared.   She was known as the patroness of art.   Our rooms on our art-reception nights used to be crowded.   The man who painted that is a genius."

" Mrs. Caryll was the patroness of struggling artists for this reason, I fancy—her son was a devotee of art once himself, and studied for a year in Rome before entering the army."

" Her son," Miss Forrester repeated dreamily, " Gordon Caryll.   Perhaps so, she very seldom spoke of him, poor fellow.   What a very striking scene it is ! " looking again at the picture through her closed hand ; "there is a fascination for me in the anguish and despair of that woman's face. A beautiful face, too. I wonder if the artist painted his picture from life ? "

" My dear France, no. They are all imaginary, are they not—suggested by books, or something of that kind ? "

" Ah, I don't know. Artists, and poets, and novelists, all turn their sorrows to account in these latter days," says Miss Forrester cynically ; "they paint their woes in oil and water colors, write them in hexameters, and make money of them. Like Lord Byron, if they weep in private, they certainly wipe their eyes on the public."

" My dear child," says Lady Dynely, looking shocked, "where have you learned your cynicisms so young ? "

Miss Forrester laughed.

" I am but a debutante," she answered gayly, "not come out yet before the foot-lights ; but I have seen a deal of life, I assure you, behind the scenes. Here comes Terry." She glances over her shoulder. " If the artist of ' How the Night Fell,' be present, Terry shall fetch him up and introduce him."

" But, France—"

Miss Forrester laughs again—a very sweet, low laugh. She is unlike most English girls—in fact, she is *not* an English girl. She has her French mother's blood and vivacity, as well as her dark complexion, and dark eyes, with something of the frank-spirited independence of an American girl. With these and her late Roman experiences, she is a bundle of contradictions, and a bewilderingly charming whole.

" But, Lady Dynely," she repeats, "I warned you fairly in Rome what you might expect when you consented to become a martyr, and bring me out. I have had my own way ever since I was born, and always mean to—if I can. I have lived in a perpetual atmosphere of artists for the past three years—the long-haired Brotherhood of the Brush have been 'the playmates of my youth—the friends of my bosom.' " Here, catching sight of Lady Dynely's horrified face, Miss Forrester breaks off and laughs again, the sweetest, frankest, merriest laugh, that ever came from rosy lips.

" What's the joke ? " asks Mr. Dennison, sauntering up ;

"I don't see anything in that black, glowering man, and that woman of the woful countenance to excite your ill-timed merriment, Miss Forrester."

"Terry," says Miss Forrester, "do you know the artist?"

"Miss Forrester, it is the proud boast of my life that I know every one. Locksley? Yes, I know him—he's in the rooms now, by the same token. Look yonder—talking to Sir Hugh Lankraik, the great academician—very tall, very fair man. Crops his hair, and doesn't look like an artist—more of the heavy-dragoon cut than anything else. See him?"

"Yes," the young lady answered. She saw, as Terry Dennison said, a very tall, very fair man, with blonde hair and beard, a complexion fair once, tanned to golden brown, two grave, gray eyes, and a thoughtful, rather worn, face—a man looking every day of his seven-and-thirty years. Not a particularly handsome face, perhaps, but a face most women liked. Whether Miss Forrester liked it or not, who was to tell?

"Not bad looking?" commented Terry interrogatively. Mr. Dennison belonged to that large *nil admirari* class to whom the acme of all praise of mortal beauty is "not bad looking."

"Women admire him, I believe," pursues Dennison, "but he rather cuts the sex. I give you my word, he might be the pet of the petticoats all this season after that picture, but he won't. Lives for his art—capital fellow, you know, but doesn't care for women."

"Interesting misogynist! Bring him up here, Terry, and introduce him."

"France!"

"Is your hearing deficient, Mr. Dennison? I said, bring him up here and introduce him."

"Now, France, what has that poor fellow ever done to you? He cuts the fair sex, and is a happy and successful man! Do let him be. I know the havoc you made among those painting fellows in Rome, but you can't expect to do in London as the Romans do. She made it a point—I give you my word, Lady Dynely—of breaking the heart of every young artist in the Eternal City, and now she wants to add poor Locksley, as harmless a fellow as ever breathed, to her ' noble army of martyrs ! ' "

" Little Terry Dennison ! will you hold your tongue and fetch Mr. Locksley here ? "

Miss Forrester lifts her gold-mounted eye-glass and looks at him. Miss Forrester's brilliant, hazel eyes are not, in the slightest degree, short-sighted ; she merely wears this eye-glass as a warrior his sword. When she particularly wishes to annihilate any one, she lifts it, stares speechlessly for five seconds, and the deed is done. Mr. Dennison knows the gesture of old, and shows the white-feather at once.

" Mr. Locksley's picture pleases me. I wish to know Mr. Locksley."

"Yes'm, please'm," says Terry, meekly ; " hanything else ? "

"Mr. Locksley has ceased talking to Sir Hugh. Lady Dynely admires ' How The Night Fell,' and does him the honor of permitting him to be presented. You understand, little Terry ? "

Terry Dennison, from the altitude of his six feet, looks down upon his dashing little superior officer, with a comical light in his blue eyes, laughs under his orange beard, and turns to obey.

" As the queen wills," he says ; " but, alas ! poor Yorick ! He never did me any harm—Locksley, I mean, not Yorick. It is rather hard *I* should be chosen, as the enemy to lead him to his doom." He makes his way to where the painter of the popular picture stands, and taps him on the shoulder. " If you are not done to death with congratulations already, Mr. Locksley, permit me to add mine. There is nothing else on the walls half-a-quarter so good. Lady Dynely is positively entranced, has been standing there for the last half hour. Will you do her the pleasure of coming and being presented ? "

" Lady Dynely ! " The artist paused for a moment with an irresolute look, and glanced doubtfully to where her lady ship stood.

" My dear fellow," Terry cut in in some alarm, " don't refuse. I know you give 'em all the cold shoulder, but you
will really be conferring a favor in this instance. She—
Lady Dynely I mean of course—is quite wild on the subject
of art and artists. Never heard her so exercised as on the
subject of that picture of yours."

" Lady Dynely does me too much honor," said the artist
smiling gravely, and Dennison linked his arm in his own,
and bore him off in triumph.

" Lady Dynely, permit me—the artist whose picture you
so greatly admire, Mr. Locksley. Mr. Locksley—Miss
Forrester."

Both ladies bowed graciously. Lady Dynely addressed
him.

" It is the gem of the collection—but Mr. Locksley must
be weary of hearing that," she said.

" An artist never wearies of such pleasant flattery," Mr.
Locksley smilingly answered ; " and whether false or true,
the flattery is equally sweet."

" And like all sweets unwholesome," said Miss Forrester
with her frank laugh, " so we will spare you. But it is wonderful—wonderful—that woman's face. Where did you find
your model, Mr. Locksley ? "

" The face—the whole picture—is painted from memory,"
was his answer, very gravely made.

The moment he had spoken first, Lady Dynely had
turned, and looked him full in the face. What was there in
his voice and face so oddly familiar ? That face, bronzed
and bearded, was not like any face she knew, yet still—.
He stood talking to France Forrester, while she thoughtfully
gazed, striving in vain to place him.

" How goes the enemy ? " Terry cried, pulling out his
watch ; " ten minutes of five. Lady Dynely, there was talk
of a Keswick flower show—"

" And we are overdue—we must go instantly, France.
Mr. Locksley, let me congratulate you once more on your
success—I am sure it is but the forerunner of even greater
things. I have some examples of the old Italian school,
which I shall be very happy to show you, if you care to see

them. I am at home every Thursday evening to receive
my friends." She gave him her card, and took Mr. Dennison's arm. Miss Forrester murmured some last, gracious
words, bowed with easy grace, and moved away with her
friends.

"How your ladyship stared," was her remark, as they
entered the barouche and were whirled away ; " have you
ever met this Mr. Locksley before ? "

" I have never met Mr. Locksley before, I am quite sure,"
her ladyship answered; "it is not a face to be easily forgotten. It is a striking face."

"A very striking face," Miss Forrester agrees decidedly.
" He reminds you of some one, possibly ? "

She hesitates a moment—then answers :

"Of one who must have died, in exile, years ago. When
he spoke first, it was the very voice of Gordon Caryll."

CHAPTER II.

AT the window of one of her private rooms, Lucia, Lady Dynely, sits in deep and painful thought. The fair, smooth brow is knit, the delicate lips are compressed, an anxious worried light is in her pale-blue eyes. It is Thursday evening; she is dressed early for her reception, and in her flowing silks and soft, rich laces, looks a very fair patrician picture. But the slender, ringed hands are closely locked, as in physical pain; mentally or bodily, you can see, she suffers as she sits here.

The twilight of the May day is closing—a soft primrose light fills the western sky—a faint young moon lifts its slender sickle and pearly light over the Belgravian chimney-pots—a few stars cluster in the blue. A silvery haze hangs over the streets—the "pea-soup" atmosphere of dingy London is softly clear for once, and the gloomy grandeur of these West End stuccoed palaces is tenderly toned down. The room in which Lady Dynely sits is her sleeping room, an apartment as beautiful and elegant as wealth and taste can make a room. About it, however, there is this notice-able—there is but one picture. That picture is a portrait, painted *en buste*—it is as though that portrait were held so dear no other picture must be its companion. It is a por-trait of Eric Alexis Albert, Lord Viscount Dynely, and twenty-first Baron Camperdown.

You pause involuntarily and look at his pictured face; it is one that at any time or in any place must strike the most casual observer, if only for its beauty. Either the artist has most grossly flattered his subject, or Eric, Vis-count Dynely, is an uncommonly handsome man. The face is beautiful—with the beauty of a woman—its great drawback that very womanliness. The curling hair is golden, the eyes sapphire blue to their deepest depths, the features faultless, the smiling mouth sweet and *weak* as a girl's. There in its nook of honor this portrait hangs by night and day in Lady Dynely's room, the last object her eyes look on at night, the first that greets them when they open to the new day. He is her idol—it is not too much to say that—her hope—the very life of her life. At present he is abroad, has been for over a year, and is expected home now daily. His majority comes in August, and it is to be celebrated down at Dynely with feasting and rejoicing, with the slaying of huge bullocks, and the broaching of mighty vats of ale.

But to-night in the misty May gloaming it is not altogether of her darling and her idol my lady sits thinking. Surely all thoughts of him should be bright and pleasant—is not his majority at hand—is he not to marry her pet, France Forrester, and live happy ever after? But the thoughts she thinks as she muses here are neither pleasant nor bright.

All her life long, Lady Dynely has been a weak woman, timid and vacillating, good, gentle, charitable, but wanting "back bone." Her son inherits that want. You may see it in his smiling, painted face. Her mind drifts about irresolutely now. She thinks, first of all, of the grave, bearded artist, met yesterday in the Royal Academy.

How like these deep grave eyes to other eyes, passed forever out of her world—how like and yet how unlike. How like the voice—deeper, graver in its timbre, and still the same. Even a slight trick of manner, characteristic of Gordon Caryll, in shaking impatiently back his fair hair, this artist had. It was odd, it was almost painful, this passing likeness, and yet it made her well disposed toward this Mr. Locksley, made her absolutely anxious lest he should fail to put in an appearance at her reception to-night.

Gordon Caryll! all at once as she sits here, that long ago moonlight night is before her again. She sees the huge fish-pond, a sheet of silver light at their feet ; she sees his tall figure casting its long shadow on the velvet sward, sees herself, pale and shivering, clinging to his arm, as she listens to that sombre story of man's reckless passion and woman's shameful deceit. Again his hands clasp her own, again his farewell sounds in her ears.

"I will take nothing—not even my name. I leave it behind with all the rest when I sail for India next week."

He had gone; and far away under the burning Indian sky, six feet of ground held perhaps what had once been the cousin she loved.

"Ah, poor Gordon!" she sighs, and then for a while her train of thought breaks, and there is a blank.

It is taken up again; that same night and her husband's death-bed is before her. The dimly-lighted chamber of the inn, the man wounded unto death, and she kneeling beside him, listening to his dying words. Dying words so dreadful to hear, that, in the soft warmth of her room now, she shivers from head to foot as she recalls them. That terrible night has stamped its impress upon all her after life.

Slowly and wearily her mind goes over all that came after. The solemn and stately funeral, the sad droning service, the bare bowed heads of the mourners, and she herself in her widow's weeds, white and shuddering, but weeping not at all, her little azure-eyed golden-haired boy by her side. He is dressed in black velvet, but not a shred of crape, and people wonder a little at this strange neglect. His mother would have it so—almost passionately she had torn off the band and shoulder-knot of crape they had placed upon the baby viscount, and had caught him to her breast, crying wildly:

"Oh, my Eric! my baby! my baby!"

They buried the dead lord of Dynely Abbey—laid him beneath the chancel of Roxhaven Church, where scores of dead-and-gone Dynelys lay. There was a tablet of wonderful beauty and cost erected above him, with a long inscription, setting forth his virtues as a man, a magistrate, a husband, a father. "And his works do follow him," said the glowing record. Was it in bitter satire they had added *that*, she wondered, or was it ominously prophetic?

All was over, and then into Lady Dynely's life came a

weary gap—a blank of months. Months when she sat
alone in the grand, luxurious, lonely rooms, white and still,
never crying, never complaining, borne down by the weight
of some great and hidden trouble. Her health failed under
it. By spring she was the veriest shadow, and the family
physician shook his professional head, and ordered imme-
diate change; Italy, the south of France, a milder climate,
cheerful society, change, etc., etc. She refused at first
peremptorily, then all in a moment changed her mind, left
little Eric in charge of his governess and the housekeeper,
and started upon her travels. Not to Italy or France,
though; but, to the intense disgust of her maid, to Ireland.
Ireland, of all places in the world, and to the wildest of all
wild Ireland—Galway.

She had some object in view—Hortense, the maid, could
see that; some object that lent a glow to her pallid cheeks, a
light to her dim eyes, an energy to her listless movements,
that marvellously astonished that handmaiden. In the *claddagh* on the Galway coast her Irish journey came to an end.

She left her maid behind her the day of her arrival in the
town, and went on alone to this wild village of Galway
fishermen. She made her way to the cabin of one Mickey
Gannon, and came among them, in their squalor and their
poverty, almost as a visitant from another world. Her apology for entering came to hand readily enough.

"It had begun to rain"—her seal jacket was drenched;
"might she seek shelter here for a few minutes, until the
storm abated? She was a tourist exploring the west." That
was her faltered excuse.

They gave her the best seat and the cordial welcome for
which the Irish heart is famous, and which bursts out even
in their national motto, *Cead mille failthe*. They gave her the
place by the fire, and drew back in respectful silence to
gaze at the pale, fair English lady.

There seemed to be a dozen children, more or less,
swarming about the cabin. With keen anxiety in her eyes,
Lady Dynely looked from face to face, and finally her gaze
lighted and lingered on one. It was a little lad of seven,
rather more of a tatterdemalion, if possible, than even the

rest, with a shaggy crop of red, unkempt hair, and two big blue eyes, round with wonder as midnight moons.

"Are all these children yours?" she asked the matron of the house; but that lady shook her head; she could not speak a word of the Sassanach tongue.

"But, sure Biddy can spake the English illegant," suggested the father of the family; and Biddy was summoned—a strapping lass with rose-red cheeks, gray eyes, jet-black hair, and a musical brogue—a very siren of western Ireland. Biddy came, made a bashful courtesy to the quality, and stood waiting to be questioned. My lady repeated her query.

"Are all these your brothers and sisters, my good girl?" with a smile; "so many of them there are."

"All but one, yer ladyship—the red-headed gossoon beyant in the corner. He's me sisther's chile," responded bashful Biddy.

"Oh—you have a married sister then?" Lady Dynely said.

"Not now, yer ladyship—sure she's dead, God be good to her, an' it's poor Terry's an orphan this many a day."

"An orphan?" her ladyship repeated, still gazing very earnestly at Terry, who, quite overcome with bashfulness, put one grimy finger in his mouth and turned a very dirty little face to the wall. "It is rather hard upon your father, having to provide for his grandchildren, isn't it? Is—" Lady Dynely paused, and over her pale face there flushed a crimson light,—"is the lad's father dead?"

Biddy shook her head, and her blue, handsome eyes flashed angrily.

"I don't know, yer ladyship, an', savin' yer presence, I don't care. Oh! but it was the misfortinit day for this house whin that black-hearted villain iver set fut in it!"

"Did he—" again she faltered—"surely he did not deceive your sister?"

Biddy looked at her, and drew her fine figure—a figure that had been left, like Nora Crena's, to "shrink or swell as Heaven pleases"—to its full height.

" Desave her, is it ? He was her husband, if that's what
yer ladyship manes, married by Father O'Gorman, himself,
in the parish chapel beyant. Oh, faith ! he knew betther
than to come palaverin' here widout the ring. He was an
Englishman—bad cess to him wheriver he is—kem here for
the fishin' one summer, an' met Maureen on a summer even-
in', comin' home from a fair. Oh, wirra ! that he iver laid
eyes on her ! sure from that day he was at her heels like
her very shadda."

" Was she handsome, this sister of yours ? " Lady Dynely
asked, with curious interest in this lowly romance.

" The purtiest girl in Galway, an' that's a big word.
Och ! but wasn't he afther her hot fut, mornin's, noon, an'
night, an' niver a day's pace wud he give her, till she said
the word, an' they wint up to Father O'Gorman, an' were
married."

" And then ? "

" An' thin he tuk her away wid him, an' for a year or
more we seen nor heerd nothin' av aither av thim. Sure
poor Maureen cud naither read nor write. An' thin all at
wance she kem back one fine mornin' wid Terry there, a
weeny baby in her arrums, an' from that day to this we niver
seen hilt nor hair av her fine English husband. The curse
o' the crows an him this day ! "

" He deserted her ? "

" Sure he did. What else cud ye expect, a fine illegant
gentleman like that, as bould as brass an' as rich as a lord,
an' herself wid nothin' at all but two blue eyes an' a purty
face."

" A lord, did you say ? " Lady Dynely repeated. " Surely
he was not—"

" I don't know what he was," said Biddy, shortly ; " no
more did Maureen. He called himself Dennison, an' was
married by that name. But, maybe it wasn't—sure the
divil himself cudn't be up to the desate av him. Och !
Father O'Gorman warned her, but she wudn't be warned.
An' that day six months, afther she kem back, she died here
wid Terry in her arrums, an' a prayer for *him*, the villain av
the world, on her lips."

"And the child remains here since? A fine boy, too. Come here, Terry—here's a shilling for you."

But Terry, altogether aghast at such a proposal, shrank away into his corner and glued his grimy countenance to the wall.

"Arrah! Come here, Terry, come here, avic, an' spake to the lady," said Biddy, in persuasive accents. Then, as the dulcet tones produced no effect, she whipped him up bodily with one strong, round arm, and bore him over to be inspected.

"Sure, thin, he's dirtier than a little baste," said Biddy, with considerable truth. "It's himself does be rowlin' undher the bed wid the pig from mornin' till night."

Lady Dynley smiled in spite of herself. Terry's face was really picturesque, frescoed so to speak, with dirt. She held out a handful of loose silver, which Terry grabbed with ravenous eagerness.

"Would you part with the child?" she asked, after a pause, and Biddy regarded her with silent wonder. "I may as well acknowledge it," her ladyship went on, her delicate face crimsoning painfully. "I once knew this—this child's father. He has spoken of him to me, recommended him to my care. Hush!" she said authoritatively as she saw Biddy about to flame forth; "not a word. He is dead. In the grave let his sins rest with him. Suffice it to say, I will take this boy and do better by him than you can ever do. In fact—so far as I may,"—she paused, and grew very white—"so far as I may," she repeated, steadfastly, "I will atone for his father's wrong. If you decline to let him go—well and good—I shall trouble you no more. If you consent, you shall be amply repaid for all the trouble and expense of the past. I will take him, educate him, and treat him in all respects as my own—yes, as my own son. Now, tell your parents, and bring me word this evening. Go to the inn in the village and ask for Lady Dynely."

She arose and left the cabin. The rain had ceased, and with the look of one who had done a hard and humiliating duty, Lady Dynely went back.

That evening Biddy came. Her ladyship was very good,

and they would humbly accept her offer. It had been a hard season in the Claddagh—only for that they would never have let Terry go. There was but one stipulation—Terry must be brought up in the faith of his mother.

Next day Lady Dynely started on her return journey, with Terry washed and clothed, and looking a new little being, in her train. She went to Dublin, and there for good and all dismissed the maid who had accompanied her. All clew to Terry's antecedents must be lost. In the Irish capital she engaged another who would act as nurse to Master Terence, and maid to herself for the present, and pursued her journey to England.

She went to Lincolnshire, and there left her charge. It was her native place, and the Vicar of Starling was an old friend. With the vicar and his family the lad was placed. The vicarage lay down in the dreary fen country, with flat, dank marshes all about it—the flat sea, lying gray and gloomy beyond the sandy coast. He was a poor man, rich only in many daughters, and Lady Dynely's proposal that they should bring up Terry was gladly accepted. Her account of him was brief. He was Terence Dennison, the orphan son of a distant cousin of her late husband. An Irish cousin—a very distant cousin—still a cousin, and as such, with a claim upon Lord Dynely's widow. He was poor and utterly alone in the world. Would Mr. Higgins take him as one of his family, let him grow up among them, educate him and accept in return—

The offer was munificent in Mr. Higgins' eyes—the bargain was closed there and then, and little Terry Dennison's life began anew.

He could not tell these good people much about his early life—he was a slow child, but they could easily see he had been brought up among the very poor. Until he was fifteen he remained at the vicarage—then he went to Eton with little Eric, Lord Dynely, and the two lads got acquainted. That Christmas for the first time he spent the vacation at Dynely Abbey, and thenceforth alternately passed his holidays at the vicarage and the Abbey. It would be hard to say which the boy liked best. At the vicarage, Mr. and

Mrs. Higgins had been as father and mother to him, and there was little Crystal, his baby sweetheart, the prettiest fairy in all Lincolnshire. But at the old ancestral Abbey dwelt the angel of his life, Lady Dynely. It was wonderful—it was pathetic, the admiring love and veneration Terry Dennison had for this lady. Of all women she was the most beautiful, of all women the best. He could now realize all she had done for him, and it filled his slow soul with wonder, the greatness of her goodness. From the depths of poverty and misery she had descended like an angel of light to rescue him.

All that she did for her own son she did for him; he had even more pocket money than Eric. This Christmas she gave him a gold watch, the next a pony—she loaded him with costly presents and kindly words always. Costly presents and kindly words, but never once—no, not once, one caress. Instinctively she shrank from this boy she had adopted with a look absolutely of repulsion—absolutely of terror at times. This Terry did not notice. I have said he was slow, but his heart yearned vaguely sometimes for just one touch of her white, slim hand on his shaggy, tawny head—for just one of the kisses she lavished on her son. He envied Eric—thrice happy Eric—not his beauty, not his title, not his wealth; ah, no! but one of these motherly embraces showered on him like rain. Eric shook her off, impatient, boy-like, of kisses and fondling, and then Lady Dynely would see Terry's round, Celtic eyes lifted wistfully to her face with the longing, pathetic patience you see in the eyes of a dog. This love, little short of worship, grew with his growth—to him she was the perfection of all that was purest, fairest, sweetest, noblest, among women. He never put in words—most likely he could not—one half the veneration with which she inspired him. And partly for her sake and partly for his own, for the gallant and golden beauty that charmed all hearts, he loved Eric, as once upon a time Jonathan loved splendid young David—" With a love surpassing that of women."

Terry grew to manhood, went up to Oxford, reached his majority, and then his benefactress bestowed upon him the crown of his life, the desire of his heart, a commission in a crack regiment. He could have cast himself at her feet and kissed the hem of her garment, so grateful was he, but he only turned very red indeed, and looked foolish and awkward, after the fashion of your big-hearted men when they feel most, and stammered incoherently two or three stupid phrases of thanks.

"No, don't thank me, please," Lady Dynely said hurriedly. "I can't do too much for you, Terry. You—you are a relative of my late husband's, you know. In doing this I am only doing my duty."

"Only her duty." Ah, she made him feel that, feel it ever. Always duty, never love.

"Five hundred a year has been settled upon you, also," her ladyship went on; "this, in addition to your pay, will probably suffice for you. Your habits are not expensive, Terry," with a smile; "not like Eric's for instance, who spends more in a month for bouquets and kid gloves than you do in a year. But if it should *not* suffice, never hesitate to draw upon me freely, and at all times. My purse is open to you as to my own son."

"Madame, your goodness overpowers me," is all poor Terry can answer, and there is a choking sensation in his throat, and tears, actual tears, in the boy's foolish blue eyes.

She sits and looks at him as he stands before her, big, broad-shoulders, sunburned, healthy, not in the least handsome, not in the least graceful or refined, with the grace and refinement that is her darling Eric's birthright, but a gentleman from head to foot. She takes his hand and looks at him with wistful eyes.

"Terry," she says, "I have done my best for you, have I not? I have tried—yes, Heaven knows I have—to make you happy! And you are happy, are you not?"

Happy! he—Terry! A curiously sentimental question, surely, to ask this big dragoon, with his hearty face and muscular six feet of manhood. It strikes Terry in that light, and he laughs.

"Happy!" he repeats. "The happiest and luckiest fellow in England. Haven't a wish unsatisfied—give you my honor, wouldn't change places with a duke. Happy! by

5

Jove, you know I should think so, with a commission and five hundred a year, and the pot I made on Derby, and—er—*your* regard, you know, my lady. Because," says honest Terry, turning very red again and floundering after the fashion of his kind in the quagmire of his feelings, "your regard is worth more to me than the whole world beside. I ain't the sort of a fellow to speak out—er—um—what I feel, but by Jove! I *do* feel you know, and I'm awfully grateful and all that sort of thing, you know. And," says Terry, with a great burst, "I'd lay down my life for you willingly any day!"

And then he pulls himself up, and shifts uneasily from one foot to the other, and looks and feels thoroughly ashamed of himself for what he has said.

"I know that, Terry," her ladyship answers, more touched than she cares to show. "I believe it, indeed. You are of the sort who will go to death itself for their friends. The motto of our house suits you—'*Loyal au mort.*' One day I may call upon that loyalty, not for myself but for Eric. One day, Terry, I may remind you of your own words, and call upon you to redeem them."

"When that day comes, my lady," he answers, quietly, "you will find me ready."

"Yes," she went on, not heeding him, "one day I may call upon you to make a sacrifice, a great sacrifice, for Eric and for me. One day I shall tell you—" She paused abruptly, and looked at him, and clasped her hands. "Oh, Terry! be a friend, a brother to my boy! He is not like you—he is reckless, extravagant, easily led, self-willed, wild. He will go wrong—I fear it—I fear it—and you must be his protector whenever you can. Let nothing he ever does, nothing he ever says to you, tempt you to anger against him—tempt you to desert him. Promise me that!"

He knelt down before her, and with the grace a Chevalier Bayard might have envied, the grace that comes from a true heart, lifted her hand to his lips.

"Nothing that Eric can ever do, can ever say, will tempt me to anger—that I swear. For his sake, and for yours, I will do all man can do. You have been the good angel of my life. I would be less than man if I ever forgot your goodness."

She drew her hands suddenly from his clasp, and bowed her face upon them.

"The good angel of your life!" she repeated, brokenly. "Oh! you don't know—you don't know!" Then as suddenly, she lifted her face, took Terry's between her two hands, and, for the first time in her life, kissed him.

He bowed his head as to a benediction; and a compact was sealed that not death itself could break.

*   *   *   *   *   *   *   *   *

With a start Lady Dynely awakes from her dream. The soft darkness of the spring night has fallen over the great city; its million gas-lights gleam through the gray gloom; carriages are rolling up to the door, and Terry Dennison goes down the passage outside, whistling an Irish jig. She rises. As she does so, her eyes fall upon her son's picture. The light of a street lamp falls full upon it, and lights it up in its smiling beauty.

"My darling!" she whispers, passionately, "my treasure! what will you say to your mother on the day when you learn the truth? It is due to you, and ah! dear Heaven! it is due to *him*. Poor Terry! poor, foolish, generous Terry!—who holds me little lower than the angels—who loves me as you, my heart's dearest, never will—what will he think of me when he learns the truth?"

CHAPTER III.

WAY beyond the stately and stuccoed palaces of Belgravia, beyond the noise and bustle of the city, the fashion and gayety of the West End, Mr. Locksley, the artist, stands watching the afternoon sun drop out of sight beyond the green lanes, and quaint, pretty gardens of old Brompton. His lodgings are here in a quiet, gray cottage, all overgrown with sweetbrier, climbing roses, and honeysuckle. It is here he has painted the picture that is to be his stepping-stone to fame and fortune, " How the Night Fell."

He stands leaning with folded arms upon the low wicket-gate, among the lilac trees and rose-bushes in the old-fashioned, sweet-smelling, neglected garden, smoking a little black meerschaum, his friend and solace for the past sixteen years. Profound stillness reigns. In the west the sunset sky is all rose and gold light; above him, pale primrose, eastward, opal gray. A thrush sings, its sweet pathetic song in an elm-tree near, and artist eye and ear and soul drink in all the tender hush and loveliness of the May eventide—unconsciously, though, for his thoughts are far afield.

Two years have passed since this man's return to England from foreign lands, and during these two years he has looked forward to one thing, half in hope, half in dread, half in longing. That thing has come to pass. It is yesterday's rencounter with Lucia, Lady Dynely. She is of his kin, and he has yearned to look once more upon a kindred face, to hear once more a familiar voice—yearned yet dreaded it too; for recognition is the one thing he most wishes to avoid. The past is dead and buried, and he with it. The world that knew him once, knows him no more. It is a past of shame and pain, of sorrow and disgrace. It is all over and done with—buried in oblivion with the name he then bore. In that world few things are remembered long; a nine days' wonder; then the waters close over the drowning wretch's head, and all is at an end.

In the park, lying back listless and elegant in her silks and laces, he has seen Lady Dynely often during the past season; face to face never before. He stands thinking dreamily of yesterday's meeting, as he leans across the gate and smokes, and of his invitation of to-night.

"She did not know me," he thinks; "and yet I could see it, something familiar struck her, too. Sixteen years of exile—twelve of hard campaigning in India and America—would change most men out of all knowledge. They think me dead beside—so I have been told. Well, better so; and yet, dead in life—it is not a pleasant thought."

The blue, perfumy smoke curls up in the evening air; the thrush pipes its pensive lay. He pauses in his train of thought to listen and watch, with artist eye for coloring, the gorgeous masses of painted cloud in the western sky.

"This Terry Dennison," he muses again, "who can *he* be, and how came Lucia to adopt him? It was not her way to take odd philanthropic whims. A distant connection of the late viscount's—humph! That is easily enough believed, since he resembles sufficiently the late viscount, red hair and all, to be his own son. His own son!" Mr. Locksley pauses suddenly; "his own son! Well, why not?"

There is no answer to this. The serenade of the thrush grows fainter, the rosy after-glow is fading out in pale blue gray, the moon shows its crystal crescent over the elm-tree. His pipe goes out, and he puts it in his pocket.

"France Forrester, too," he says to himself; "the baby daughter of my old Canadian friend, the general, grown to womanhood—Mrs. Caryll's adopted daughter and heiress, *vice* Gordon Caryll, cashiered. They will marry her to Eric Dynely, I suppose, and unite Caryllynne and the Abbey. A handsome girl and a spirited—too good, by all odds, for that dandified young Apollo, as I saw him last at Naples. A girl with brains in that handsome, uplifted head, and a will of her own, or that square-cut mouth and resolute little chin belie her character. Still, I suppose, a young fellow as faultlessly good-looking as Lord Eric needs no additional virtues, and your women with brains are mostly the greatest fools in matters matrimonial."

With which cynical wind-up Mr. Locksley pulls out his watch and glances at the hour. Eight. If he means to attend my lady's "At Home" it is time to get into regulatior costume and start.

" I shall be an idiot for my pains," he growls, "running the chance of recognition, and only invited as the newest lion in the Bohemian menagerie. And yet it *is* pleasant to look in Lucia's familiar face once more—to make one again in that half-forgotten world. Besides"—he adds this rather irrelevantly as he starts up—"Miss Forrester interests me. What a face that would be to paint ! "

He turns to enter the house—then stops. A phaeton with two black, fiery-eyed steeds, whirls up to where he stands, the reins are flung to the groom, and a gentleman springs down, lifts his hat and accosts him.

" Mr. Locksley ! "

He is a small, elderly, yellow man, shrivelled and foreign-looking, with glittering, beady-black eyes. Beneath the light summer overcoat he wears the artist catches sight of a foreign order on the breast. He speaks the name, too, with a marked accent, as he stands, and bows and smiles.

" My name is Locksley," the artist replies.

The small, yellow man hands him his card. " Prince Cæsare Di Venturini," Mr. Locksley reads, and recognizes his interlocutor immediately. The prince is perfectly familiar to him by sight, though for the moment he had been unable to place him. He is a Neapolitan, the scion of an impoverished princely house, and a political exile.

" At your excellency's service," Mr. Locksley says, looking up inquiringly; " in what way can I have the pleasure of serving you ? "

" That picture, ' How the Night Fell,' is yours, monsieur ? "

Mr. Locksley bows.

"It is not sold?"

"It is not."

"It is for sale?"

Mr. Locksley bows again.

"It is not yet disposed of. Good! Then, monsieur, a lady friend of mine desires to do herself the pleasure of becoming its purchaser, and I am commissioned as her agent to treat with the artist. Its price?"

Mr. Locksley names the price, and inquires, rather surprised at the suddenness and rapidity of this business transaction, if the Prince Di Venturini will not come in.

"No, no—it is but the matter of a moment—he will not detain Mr. Locksley." He produces a blank check and pen there and then, scrawls for a second upon it, then with a low bow, a smile that shows a row of glittering teeth, passes it across the little gate. The next instant he has leaped lightly into the phaeton, and the fiery-eyed, coal-black horses, that look as though they had but lately left the Plutonian stables, dash away through the dewy darkness. Mr. Locksley stands with his breath nearly taken from him by the bewildering swiftness of this unexpected barter, and looks at the check in his hand. It is for the amount named—the signature is his excellency's own, but he had said the picture was for a lady.

"Who can she be, I wonder?" thinks the artist, pocketing the check and going into the house; "a personage of rank, or—stay! this popular danseuse from over the water, whose name rings the changes through London, and whose beauty and whose dancing are the talk of the town. The Prince is known to be the most devoted of her devotees— some men lay heavy odds he'll marry her. I must drop in, by the by, some night at the Bijou, and look at her. So, my picture is sold at my own price. Lady Dynely's fashionable doors are thrown open to me——surely a turn in fortune's wheel, this."

He laughs slightly. He is the possessor of more money this evening than he has owned any time the past sixteen years. In the days that are gone he has known poverty in its bitterest shape, the bitter poverty of a man born to the purple and fallen from his high estate.

He divested himself of his picturesque, paint-stained, velvet blouse, and got himself into a dress-coat and tie. All the while he kept wondering vaguely who had purchased his picture. " If by any chance the Prince is present at Lady Dynely's, I will inquire," he thought, as he pocketed his latch-key and left the house; " I really should like to know."

He really would, no doubt. Interested as he was in this unknown lady, he would have been more interested probably had he been present in the academy that afternoon.

The rooms, as usual, were filled ; as usual, too, the centre of attraction was "How the Night Fell." Very shortly after the doors were thrown open there had entered a lady and gentleman—whose entrance created a sensation, and who divided the interest with the pet picture of the year. The gentleman was the Neapolitan Prince, the lady the most popular danseuse in London, Madame Felicia.

She came moving slowly through the throng, seeing and enjoying the sensation she created, a plump, rather petite beauty, her dark face lit by two wonderful eyes, long, sleepy, yellow-black. She was of a beauty, in a dark way, simply perfect, and she was dressed in the perfection of taste. A silver-gray silk, with here and there vivid dashes of scarlet and touches of rare old lace, the masterpiece of a masculine mantua maker of the Rue de la Paix. Every eye turned to gaze after this lionne of Coulisses, the most perfect dancer they said that ever bounded before the footlights since the days of Taglioni. The Prince hung devotedly upon her lightest word, but she turned impatiently away from him, glancing with a scornful little air of disdain along the walls.

"Always the same," she said, pettishly; "simpering women, glowering women, wax-doll misses with yellow hair and china-blue eyes, insipid as their own nursery bread and butter. Bah ! why does one take the trouble to come at all ? "

" Will madame condescend to look at that ? "

He led her before *the* picture—the group surrounding it

fell back a little. She lifted her eyes, bored, disdainful, then—a sudden stillness came over her from head to foot. All languor, all ennui, fled from her face, its rich coloring faded—she grew ashen gray to the very lips. So for the space of fully five minutes she stood.

"How does madame find it?" the suave voice of the Italian asked.

She neither moved nor answered. She never took her eyes from the picture. Slowly life and color returned to her face, slowly into the great topaz eyes, sleepy and half-closed like a panther's, there came a vivid light. One small gloved hand crushed her catalogue unconsciously—as if fascinated she stood there and gazed.

"Thou art pleased with the picture then, madame?" Di Venturini said, softly, in French.

"Pleased with it?" she repeated, a slow, curious smile dawning on her lips. "Prince, I must have that picture!"

"But, if it is already sold? True, the star is not affixed, but——"

"I must have that picture!" madame repeated, with a flash of the black eyes; "sold or not, I still must have it. How do they call the artist?" She looked at the catalogue. "'G. Locksley.' The name is new—is it not, Prince?"

"Altogether new, madame. If you really wish it, I will discover this M. Locksley and purchase the picture if still in the market."

"I do wish it, Monsieur Prince. That picture I must have though it cost half a fortune. 'How the Night Fell!'"

She turned back to it, and looked and looked as though she could never look enough.

"It is an odd fancy," said Prince Di Venturini, after a pause; "an absurd one, you may think, madame, but the face of that woman in the picture is very like *yours*. Not one half so lovely, but very like, nevertheless. Does madame perceive it?"

"Does madame not?" madame responded, that slow, sleepy smile still on her lips. "Who could fail? And yet, mon Prince, you cannot fancy me with *that* expression, can

5*

you ?   He is leaving her—is it not ? and her heart is breaking.   Bah ! it is like the egotism of men, they desert us and we die—or so they think !   Prince, that picture must be mine before I sleep.   You hear ? "

"And live but to obey ! " with a most profound bow ; " the picture shall be yours ! "

He escorted her to her carriage.

At sunset across the gate of the Brompton cottage the bargain was struck, and " How the Night Fell " became the property of Madame Felicia, the actress.

CHAPTER IV.

LADY DYNELY'S THURSDAY.

BRILLIANTLY lit, brilliantly filled, Lady Dynely's elegant rooms were a study of color in themselves for a painter when Mr. Locksley arrived. He was rather late—dancing was going on, as he made his way to his hostess' side to pay his respects.

In his ceremonial costume, the artist looked something more than well, and that military air of his was more conspicuous than ever.

> "You may break, you may shatter the vase if you will,
> But the scent of the roses will hang round it still,"

quotes Miss France Forrester to Mr. Terence Dennison. "I would know the stalk of a trooper (and have seen it more than once) under the cowl of a monk. Your Mr. Locksley, Terry, is the most distinguished-looking man in the rooms."

"I never said he was my Mr. Locksley. So you find the painter as attractive as the painting, France, and you will be good to him, and smile upon him, and turn his head, for the space of a week. The last victim was the popular new poet, the Cheapside tailor's son. Ah! poor Locksley!"

"Terry," Miss Forrester says severely, "small boys should never attempt the sarcastic—you least of all—for some years to come. I am interested in aspiring geniuses—as a soldier's daughter, in all soldiers. Where did you say Mr. Locksley had served?"

"India and America. Indian mutiny, and American civil war, with great distinction in both. A professional free-lance, and, I have heard, brave as a lion."

"He looks it," France said, dreamily. "He has the true *air noble*. Surely that man is well born, or else the

old adage, that blood tells, is false.   And Lady Dynely says
he resembles Gordon Caryll."

" Never saw Gordon Caryll," Terry sleepily responds,
" Heard of him though.   Went to perdition for a woman,
didn't he?   A common case enough.   And you take him
to your heart of hearts for that resemblance, don't you, Miss
Forrester ?   I know you have set up this Gordon Caryll as
a sort of demi-god, my hero-worshipping young lady."

She smiled, then sighed.   She was looking brilliantly
handsome to-night in pink silk, pink roses in her brown
hair, caught back by gleaming diamonds.   She had a love
for bright colors and rich gems, and looked with contempt
on the white tulle and pale pearls of her young lady friends.

" What clergyman was it said once when he introduced
operatic airs into his choir, that it was a pity the devil
should have *all* the good tunes.   On the same principle, I
say it is a pity your married women should monopolize the
brightest colors and richest jewels.   The English Miss has
been trampled upon long enough—let me be the heroine to
inaugurate a new era."

This is what Miss Forrester had said to Lady Dynely,
this very evening, when slightly remonstrated with on the
subject of her magnificence.   The vivid colors, the vivid
gems, the roses and laces, suited her dusk, warm loveliness,
and she knew it.

Terry had been her companion for the past hour.   The
Canadian heiress had a very affectionate regard for Mr.
Dennison, and made no secret of it.

" I am awfully fond of 'Terry,'" she was wont to say ;
" the best fellow alive and the greatest simpleton ever created."

" She treats me like a small boy of ten, at home for the
holidays," Mr. Dennison would supplement with a groan.

They both pause for a moment while they discuss Mr.
Locksley, and look at him.   Many others look, too.   " How
the Night Fell " has made a sensation ; they feel a languid
interest in the painter.

" France," Mr. Dennison says, after that pause, " I have
an idea."

"Have you, Terry? Cherish it then, my dear boy, for you are never likely to have another."

"Madame," Terry responds, "your sex protects you! Here is my idea. What if that fellow should be the long-lost heir of Caryllynne, returned to the halls of his fathers, and all that sort of thing, once more, to cut you out of a fortune. It would be uncommonly like a thing on the stage, now wouldn't it?"

"Certainly like a thing on the stage," Miss Forrester disdainfully replies; "therefore very unlike anything in real life. Ah, no! that would be too good to be true. Gordon Caryll, poor fellow, is dead. The likeness Lady Dynely sees, if indeed she sees any, is but a coincidence. See, she is beckoning—let us go over."

They cross the room. Miss Forrester, with a frank smile of welcome, and looking very bright and lovely, gives the artist a most gracious greeting.

"I saw you were not dancing, France, and want you to do the honors of my picture gallery. You could not have a better cicerone, Mr. Locksley. France has lived as she says in an atmosphere of paintings all her life."

"And familiarity breeds contempt," murmurs Mr. Dennison.

"Only in the case of stupid dragoons," retorts Miss Forrester. "How often have I tried to impress upon you, Terry, that sarcasm isn't your forte. I shall have much pleasure in displaying our art treasures to your critical eyes, Mr. Locksley. I always feel *en rapport* immediately with artists—they were the staple of my acquaintance in Rome. It is the hot-bed of genius. You have studied there, I can see."

"For three years, Miss Forrester. And," he smiles as he says it, and Miss Forrester marvels to see how that smile lights up his dark, grave face—"I have seen *you* there many times."

"Indeed! But you must, of course; I spent half my life sketching in the galleries. The very happiest days of my life were spent in Rome."

He looks down upon the dusk lovely face with gravely admiring eyes.

"But so little of your life has come," that gaze says to her, "you have not yet begun to live."

"There is one thing about Rome which must strike the most casual observer," says Dennison, suddenly, seized with a second idea, "and that is, the lamentable dearth of Roman noses! They were snubs, give you my word, when I was there, one half. My own," says Terry, glancing complacently at an opposite mirror, "was the noblest Roman of 'em all!"

Miss Forrester giving the prominent feature Terry admired a rebuking tap with her fan, led the way into an anteroom, hung with crimson velvet, emblazoned with the arms and motto of the Dynelys :

"Loyal au mort."

He glances at these emblazoned splendors as he passes, and follows his fair leader into a long gallery, hung from floor to ceiling with pictures.

"Lady Dynely is a lover of art, and her collection is very fine. Here is a face by Titian, one of the gems of the room."

"Doesn't look unlike you, France—'pon my word it doesn't— the eyes, the hair, and the yellowish complexion— well, it isn't yellow, but you know what I mean. One of his wives, isn't it ? These old masters always had three or four, hadn't they—one buried, 'tother come on. You ought to marry a man of genius, France ; you would make a capital wife for one, wouldn't you ? a sort of moral spur in his side, urging him on to perpetual efforts. If he were in Parliament you would have him a premier, if he were an artist you would have him a Michael Angelo, if musical, a Beethoven, eh ? wouldn't you ?"

"I have seen geniuses," Miss Forrester makes answer, "I have also seen their wives. And, my dear Terry, the wife of a man of genius is a social martyr, who carries the cross while her husband wears the crown."

"And *vice versâ*," says Terry ; "or, stay—is it *vice versâ ?* The husband of a woman of genius is a—"

"There are no women of genius," answers France, with a little sarcastic shrug. "You monopolize all that. Women never write books, or paint pictures, or carve statues. George Eliot, Rosa Bonheur, Miss Hosmer, etc., all are myths. Genius is the prerogative of our lord and master—Man."

"You infringe on your master's prerogative then," says Mr. Locksley, smiling. "How very cynical you are pleased to be, Miss Forrester."

"I have always thought it a thousand pities France wasn't born in New York," cuts in Mr. Dennison. "She could mount the rostrum, as they all seem to do there, and spout until the welkin rang on the subject of down-trodden woman and her natural enemy and tyrant—Man. She is fearfully and wonderfully strong-minded, is Miss France Forrester. And now if you can possibly survive half an hour without me, France, I'll tear myself from your side. I am engaged for the next waltz, and I hear the opening bars afar off."

Then Mr. Dennison saunters leisurely away, and Miss Forrester and Mr. Locksley are alone among the pictures. They linger long, criticising, admiring, talking of Rome, of art and artists, and the picturesque, poetic life there. "I think I was born to be a Bohemian," she says, with her frank laugh, "and have somehow missed my destiny. It is such a free, bright, untrammelled sort of life, ever new and full of variety. Here it seems to be over and over the same tiresome, treadmill round. I haven't wearied of it yet in spite of my scepticism, the bloom is not yet brushed off my peach, but I know that day will come. Mr. Locksley," changing tone and subject, abruptly, "is your picture sold?"

"Sold two hours before I came here," he answers, and tells her of the hurried transaction over the garden gate.

"The Prince Di Venturini," she repeats; "and for a lady. Who can she be? The prince is here to-night—I shall ask him. I am sorry it is sold. Lady Dynely wishes very much to add it to her collection. The face of that woman has haunted me ever since."

His bronzed face pales a little, a troubled look comes into his eyes. She sees it, and her girlish curiosity deepens. She cannot understand her interest in this man, her interest in that picture, but both are there.

" Is she still alive ? " she asks, carelessly—"your model ? "

" Miss Forrester, I painted that picture from memory, as I think I have told you."

" Then, your model was in your mind. But you have not answered my question. Is the owner of that wonderful face still alive ? "

" I beg your pardon. I believe not—I hope not."

" Mr. Locksley ! "

" I hope not," he repeats, moodily. " A wicked wish, is it not, Miss Forrester ? But such women as that are better out of the world than in it."

" How very beautiful she must have been," France says, dreamily ; " even with that tortured look you give her, she is beautiful still."

" She was. The most beautiful woman I ever saw."

It is not a flattering answer, but France Forrester is not offended. A little out of the line of demure young ladyhood, she certainly might be frank and outspoken at times to a startling degree, but honest as a child and vain not at all.

" I wonder if you are her judge and accuser in that picture ? " she thinks, and looks up at him. " I wonder in what way that woman ever wronged *you* ? "

He catches her glance and understands it. A smile breaks up the dark gravity of his face as he looks down at her.

" You honor my poor painting too much, Miss Forrester, by your interest," he says ; " for the story it tells—that is over and done with many a long year ago. The woman I have painted is one not worthy a second thought from you— a woman who spoiled my whole life, whom I have reason to believe dead, and whom, were she alive, I would go to the other end of the earth sooner than meet. Why I painted that I hardly know—it was the whim of a moment—that it would have the success it has met with I did not dream."

She colors slightly, he seems to have rebuked her irrepressible curiosity. There is a romance then in this man's life—girl-like, that thought deepens her interest in him. A gentleman born she instinctively feels he is, this artist who paints for his daily bread, who has been a soldier of fortune for twelve years. Miss Forrester is by nature a hero-worshipper, as Terry has said. And Mr. G. Locksley, whoever he is, takes his place immediately on some vacant pedestal in her mind, to be numbered among the heroes of her dreams henceforth.

They say no more about "How the Night Fell." They linger, though, yet a little longer among the immortals in the long gallery. Mr. Locksley seems in no haste, and France feels an odd, altogether new pleasure, in lingering and listening to his grave, quiet remarks, an odd distaste for returning to the perfumed warmth, and glitter, and crush of the outer rooms. But they go there presently, for all that, and at her suggestion. She will be missed, and she has a vague recollection that she has promised the Prince Di Venturini a waltz.

"And I will find out who has purchased Mr. Locksley's picture," the little diplomat says to herself; "it is evident he is as curious about it as I am."

Prince Di Venturini is talking Italian politics eagerly to a knot of starred and decorated gentlemen, but he breaks away, and comes up to France as their waltz begins. As they float slowly away she plunges into her grievance at once.

"It is unpardonable of you, prince, to have purchased the gem of the Academy. I mean of course 'How the Night Fell.' I intended to have had it myself."

"*Mais, Mon Dieu !*" cried the prince, in his shrill Neapolitan French. "I did not purchase it. All the ladies fall in love with it at sight, I believe. How fortunate are these artists."

"You did not purchase it !" France repeats in surprise. "Mr. Locksley told me—"

"Ah, yes, Mr. Locksley told you, without doubt. Still, I did not buy the picture for myself—I am not the pet of the public. I have not thousands to throw away on a whim. It was Felicia."

" Felicia, the actress ! the—"

" Star of the Royal Bijou Theatre. Yes, mademoiselle, and at a most fabulous price. To wish and to have are synonyms with Felicia."

There is silence as they float around. Miss Forrester's dark, rose-crowned head is lifted over the top of his small, yellow excellency's two good inches. She feels it to be something more than annoying—a positive adding of insult to injury, that this popular danseuse should have won what she has lost.

It wears late ; the evening ends. One by one coroneted carriages roll away, and Mr. Locksley comes after some lofty personage, with ribbons and orders, and takes leave of Lady Dynely.

" We hope to see you every Thursday, Mr. Locksley," that lady says, very graciously, and Mr. Locksley murmurs his acknowledgment, and pledges himself to nothing.

" How do you like your genius, France ? " inquires Terry Dennison. " Does he bear the ordeal of close inspection, or does distance lend enchantment to the view, as in the case of the Cheapside tailor's son ? "

" Mr. Locksley isn't a genius," Miss Forrester replies, trailing her silk splendor up the stairs, " only a clever artist, who has painted one good picture, and may never paint another. There are many such in all walks of life, my dear child. Good-night, Terry—pleasant dreams."

" Good-night, France—morning rather ; and my dreams will not be of you."

" Ingrate ! Of whom then ? "

" Of a little girl down in Lincolnshire. You don't know her, Miss Forrester, and she would stand abashed in your regal presence. But, ah ! there's nothing like her under the London sun."

And Terry's blue eyes are absolutely luminous as he vanishes.

" Another heart gone ! " reflects Miss Forrester, as she closes her door ; " and so it goes on. ' Men may come and men may go, but *that* goes on forever ! ' Poor, good, honest

Terry ! I hope your course of true love will run smooth at least. You are one of the exceptional men who do make the women you marry happy."

Miss Forrester rings for her maid, and her mind goes off at another tangent.

"So Felicia has purchased Mr. Locksley's picture ! The dancer has taste. By the bye, we're due at the Royal Bijou to-morrow night. She is very handsome ; but these people owe all their beauty, I suppose, to paint, and powder, and wigs. She dances exceptionally well, too ; but she need not have been in such haste buying that picture."

She pauses in her wandering thoughts. Her eye falls upon a letter lying on her dressing-table, under the clustering wax-lights. It bears the Roman post-mark, and, with a little exclamation of joy, Miss Forrester snatches it up.

"From grandmamma !" she says.

Mrs. Caryll is in reality but her father's distant cousin, but so it pleases France to call her. She breaks the seal and reads eagerly through. After a few preliminary paragraphs, this is what the letter said:

" You say nothing, my dear France, of Eric's return. Has he *not* returned then ? It is really unpardonable of him to linger so long, knowing you are in London. Oh, my daughter ! I hope—I pray nothing may occur to break off this alliance. I am fond of Eric—I love you. To see you his happy wife is the desire of my heart. It is his mother's dearest wish also. In every respect it is most suitable—both dowered with youth and wealth and beauty. He loves you I am sure, France, and would have spoken before now had you let him. But you have laughed at him and made light of his wishes hitherto. And you are of so peculiar a nature, my dearest child, so unlike other girls of your age, so self-willed, and radical in your opinions, that I fear for you. Not that you would ever marry beneath you. I have no dread of that, you are far too proud ; but you may meet some one whom your fancy will idealize, whom you cannot marry, and who will wreck the happiness of your life. Something—I do not know what, tells me this will be so. Guard against it—let your engagement with Eric be announced to the world immediately it takes place. And write at once, my dear, dear daughter, to your most affectionate

"MARIAN CARYLL."

She threw the letter aside with a quick gesture of irritated impatience. As a rule, she was not petulant, and all Mrs. Caryll's wishes carried force, but just now she felt intolerant of this husband thrust upon her, whether she would or no.

"Eric Dynely," she said, "a masculine wax doll, a perfumed coxcomb, a dandy of the first water ! I hate dandies ! I detest pretty men ! I would sooner marry Terry Dennison any day !"

One of the windows stood open ; the soft, chill morning breeze stirred the curtains of silk and lace ; she put them aside and leaned out into the fresh coolness, the faint light of the dawn glimmering on her pink silk, her roses and diamonds.

"The day for this sort of marriage should have ended a century ago," she thinks, full of impatient pain ; "this kind of alliance should be left to royalty. But *noblesse oblige,* it seems to be my fate. He is very well, the best waltzer I know, the best second in a duet, he has the bow and grace of a Beau Brummel—the good looks of an Apollo —what more can one want ? And yet one does. Loves me, does he, grandmamma ? Ah, no ! Eric, Viscount Dynely, fell in love many years ago—with himself, and will be the victim of that passion all his life. And after all the dreams and the hero worship they laugh at, I am to marry Eric Dynely !"

Then through the mists of the morning there floats before her a face, brown, bearded, grave, with deep lines of care and thought seamed upon it, with threads of silver gleaming through the fairness of his hair, a man who had been a leader of men, a man who had lived and suffered.

"You may meet some one your fancy will idealize, whom you cannot marry, and who will wreck the happiness of your life."

Was Mrs. Caryll among the prophets ?

CHAPTER V.

HE leafy greenness of May, the soft and veiled warmth of June, had passed ; the feverish noontides of July had come, and Lady Dynely's only son had not returned from his idle wanderings to woo and win his bride.

To France Forrester this first season of hers had been bright and beautiful as a fairy tale. She had been presented by Lady Dynely, had created, as the critics of the Academy had predicted, a sensation. A certain royal personage, whose approval was a patent right and seal of popularity in itself, had condescended to place his gracious stamp of approbation upon her, and Miss Forrester awoke and found herself "the fashion." "The fashion !" these two magic words told the whole story. Women slandered her fiercely, hated her bitterly, and copied everything she wore, from her coquettish head-gear to her little boots. Men diplomatized for the favor of a waltz, as they might for princely preferment. In the ride, in the ball-room, and opera-box, Miss Forrester was still the best surrounded lady of the assembly, the *belle des belles.* "And *why* is it ? " her envious compeers asked. "It isn't her beauty ; there are scores more perfectly and classically beautiful than she, with her dark skin and irregular features." Was it the dashing independence of her manner, the careless audacity with which she looked into their eyes, and laughed at their flatteries, and threw them lightly over as whiffs of thistle-down ? She was so thoroughly heart-whole, so perfectly indifferent to their homage, that she piqued their vanity—always a man's strongest feeling—and rendered them, by that imperious grace of hers, her veriest slaves. Whether she talked Italian politics to Prince Di Venturini, with his wizen, murky face, and beady black eyes, or the newest opera with Signor Carlo Dolce, the new Venetian tenor, whether she discoursed art with long-haired, dreamy-eyed students, and stately academicians, or the latest Belgravian gossip with a dashing military duke, it was all the same. She was interested in the theme, not the man; her heart, if she possessed one, was triply clad in steel—no one, it seemed, had power to touch it. And then, presently it leaked out that she had been engaged for years to Lord Dynely, and that the engagement would be publicly anounced to all whom it might concern, immediately upon his return to England. " He must have great faith in his affianced," said the sneerers; he certainly seemed in no hot haste to join her. This was after Miss Forrester had said "no" to two of the most eligible gentlemen of the season, and who had followed her about the summer through, like her lap-dog or her shadow.

This season, which had been such a brilliant career of victory to Miss Forrester, had been a very busy one for Mr. Locksley the painter. Orders flowed in—his fame and fortune seemed made. Madame Felicia sent by the prince for a companion picture to "How the Night Fell." The Marquis of St. Albans had ordered a Canadian winter scene. Lady Dynely wished to have her own portrait painted for her son. The sittings for this portrait necessitated many visits to the Brompton Studio, and Miss Forrester was almost invariably my lady's companion. She wandered about among the paintings at will, whilst the elder lady sat or lay back, and listened with half-closed eyes to Mr. Locksley talking whilst he painted. He talked well, and as he seemed to have been pretty much everywhere, found subjects enough. Anecdotes of his Indian life, the fighting, the campaigning, the pig-sticking, stories of the American civil war, thrilling and vivid as truth could make them, of Canada, with its brief, hot summers, and long, cold winters, until the hours of each sitting were gone like a dream.

" Really, Mr. Locksley is a charming companion," Lady Dynely was wont to say; "talks better than any man I know. What a traveller he has been—been everywhere and seen everything."

It was a subject upon which Miss Forrester was suspiciously reticent—Mr. Locksley and the charm of his conversation. And yet, though she would not have owned it even to herself, those hours in the Brompton cottage, sitting by the open window watching the afternoon sun sink behind the tree-tops, leaving a trail of splendor behind, with the scent of the summer roses perfuming the air, while Mr. Locksley painted and talked, and Lady Dynely sat and listened, were the pleasantest hours of her life. All were pleasant; this summer took a glory and a bliss none other had known; but these were the foam of life's champagne.

She and Mr. Locksley met tolerably often elsewhere. He still attended at intervals Lady Dynely's Thursdays, and there were literary and artistic gatherings where Miss Forrester met him. It was curious on these occasions to note the restless light in the great hazel eyes, the quick, impatient glances at the door, the sudden stillness that came over her when a new name was announced, the swift shade of annoyed impatience, or the glad, quick light and warmth that spread over her face, as it was or was not the name she wished to hear. And somehow—certainly it was not Mr. Locksley's doing; he was the most modest, least presuming of men—presently he found himself by Miss Forrester's side, holding the little gloved hand she extended in frank, friendly greeting, and basking in the sunshine of her sunniest smiles. In the park, too, leaning over the rails, smoking his twilight cigar, Mr. Locksley was often favored with a gracious bow from a certain coroneted carriage, and a dark, lovely face, framed in a marvel of Parisian lace and rosebuds, shone upon him for an instant like a dusk star. That tall, soldierly figure, that bronzed, bearded face, that grave smile of recognition, Miss Forrester would have known among ten thousand.

And still Lord Dynely did not come.

"It is *very* strange—it is incomprehensible, it is most annoying," Lady Dynely said, over and over again, to herself, or to Terry, knitting her blonde brows; "I can't understand. So fond as he used to be of France, too, and see her now flirting with half the men in London."

"I don't call it flirting," Terry would respond. "France can't help smiling on men and turning their heads any more than the what's-its-name—sunflower—can help turning the sun. And if the sun scorches and shrivels them a little, I don't see that the sun is to be blamed either. Sounds poetical, that, don't it?" said Terry, rather surprised at his own performance.

"It is unpardonable of Eric," Lady Dynely would retort, vexed, and *almost* angry with her darling; "and so I shall tell him when I write. Here it is the end of July, and we go down to Devonshire next week. His birthday is in August, and who is to tell us whether he will even come then. Of course France must feel piqued, though she conceals her feelings so well."

"Uncommonly well," says Terry. "So well that I for one am disposed to think that she isn't in the least annoyed. Where is Eric loafing now?"

"Eric is still in Spain, and is evidently enjoying himself," says Eric's mother, irritably.

"'The girls of Cadiz,'" hums Terry, under his breath. "Well, don't worry. I'll go over and fetch him if you like."

"Nonsense, Terry! don't be a simpleton. What would France and I have done all this summer without you for an escort? You have been the best of boys, and I know you have been longing more than once to break away and go down to Lincolnshire."

"Your pleasure must ever be first with me," Terry answers, but he smothers a little sigh as he says it. Truth to tell, he *has* been longing many times to break away from flower show and opera, party and park, dining and dressing, and all the rest of it, and rush down into Lincolnshire, to the old vicarage of his boyhood, where his loadstar shines. But Lady Dynely wills it otherwise, and Lady Dynely's lightest word is law to Terry.

"If I could only have got off duty for a week—just a week," he had said pathetically once to France, "I wouldn't so much mind. You see, she's just the dearest, sweetest little darling in the world—"

"Of course," interrupts France, gravely.

"And I've been awfully fond of her ever since I wore roundabouts, and she short muslin frocks, tied up on the shoulder, and I'm dying to tell her the good news, my commission and the five hundred a year and—and something else." Terry suddenly turns very red. "A fellow could marry and keep a wife on his pay and five hundred a year, couldn't he, France? Just a little suburban villa, you know, a pretty parlor maid, and a boy in buttons, and a one-horse shay—eh? Couldn't they, France? My tastes ain't expensive, as Lady Dynely said the other day, and she—ah France! I see lots of girls, you know—jolly girls, and dashing girls, and pretty girls, but not one—no, I give you my word, not one-half as good, or sweet, or pretty, as my little Crystal!"

Miss Forrester is Terry's confidante; he gets on with her. For Lady Dynely, much as he loves and venerates her, or rather because of that great love and veneration, he stands in awe of her. But France sympathizes with him, more than ever in these later days, and listens dreamily, while Mr. Dennison pours forth the story of his love.

"What a good fellow you are, Terry," she says now regretfully. "It is a pity to throw you away upon any insipid little country girl. (I know by her photograph she is insipid.) I have half a mind to fall in love with you myself."

"Oh, but don't, please!" says Terry, piteously; "let it be half a mind, don't make it a whole one. If you insisted upon it, I should knock under at once—women can always do what they please with me, and then two clever people should never marry—it doesn't work; besides, you belong to Eric."

"Do I?" France responds, gravely. "I am not so sure of that. Eric seems in no hurry to come and claim his belongings."

"It's a shame," says Terry; "and so Lady Dynely has just been saying. She's awfully angry. Eric deserves to be shot."

"'The absent are always in the wrong,'" Miss Forrester

C

quotes. "I don't see why my lady should be angry with
Eric—I'm not. Let the poor boy enjoy himself. But, for
you, Terry, you shall go down to Lincolnshire to-morrow, if
you wish it. It is too bad, and too selfish of us, to keep
you tied to our apron-strings when the prettiest and sweetest
girl in England is pining for you among the Lincolnshire fens
and marshes. I shall speak to Lady Dynely, at once.
Yours is the most aggravated case of 'cruelty to animals' on
record."

"No, no! It may annoy Lady Dynely—I would not for
the world. My affairs can wait," Terry remonstrates in
alarm.

"So can ours. I am very fond of my lady, but I don't
worship the ground she walks on, as some people do. I
shall ask her."

Miss Forrester kept her word. She sought out Lady
Dynely, and broached the subject at once.

"Lady Dynely, can't you let Terry off duty for a couple
of weeks? The poor fellow is falling a prey 'to green and
yellow melancholy,' and the 'worm i' the bud is preying on his
damask cheek.' In plain English, he's in love ; and now
that your generosity has given him something to live on, he
naturally wants to go and tell her—wants to lay his hand
and fortune at her feet, and do the 'come, share my cottage,
gentle maid' sort of thing, you know."

France spoke lightly. Lady Dynely laid down her pen—
she was writing that indignant protest to Master Eric—and
looked up with a face that turned to the color of ashes.

"Wants to marry!—Terry!" was all she could say.

"Naturally. We have made him our 'fetch and carry'
spaniel, I know ; but he is a man for all that. We have
treated him as though he were a page or footman ; but he is
a lieutenant of dragoons, and nearly twenty-four years old.
Not a Methuselah, certainly, but old enough to take unto
himself a wife if he wishes to perpetrate that sort of imbecility."

"Terry! a wife!" Then Lady Dynely sits still, and
over the gray pallor of her face a look of anger flashes.
"It is absurd!--it is preposterous! Terry with a wife!

Why, he is only a grown-up baby himself. I will not hear of it."

" He is more than three years older than Eric," says Miss Forrester, her eyes kindling at this injustice. " When it is Eric's lordly will to take a wife, you won't put in that plea of youth, will you? "

" The cases are altogether different—there is no comparison," says Lady Dynely, coldly. " Who is the girl? "

" She is one of the Miss Higginses. There are nine Miss Higginses," says France, with a slight shudder. " She is the youngest but one, poor thing. Terry and she have been in love with each other ever since they ate pap out of the same bowl and wore pinafores. And I think it is a little too bad, Lady Dynely," concludes France, indignantly, " that poor Terry can't have a wife if he wants one."

" Send Terry here," is Lady Dynely's answer. " I will speak to him on this subject."

" And don't be too hard on the poor fellow," pleads France, imploringly. " Oh, Lady Dynely, he loves you as it is the fate of few mothers to be loved. So well that I believe if you order him to give up this girl, to go away and turn Trappist, he will obey you. As you are strong, be merciful—don't be hard on Terry."

Then she goes, and Terry comes. He looks uncommonly foolish and guilty, much as he used to do when caught apple-stealing down in Lincolnshire long ago, and was called up before the vicar to answer for his crime. Her ladyship is still pale, very pale, her lips are set, her eyes look anxious, the hands that are folded in her lap tremble nervously at his approach.

" What is this, Terry? " she asks, and her clear voice is not steady. " Is it a jest of France's, or do you really wish to—"

" Marry Crystal Higgins? Yes, Lady Dynely, with your permission," Terry answers, looking up firmly enough.

" You really wish it? "

" I really wish it, with all my heart."

" Silly boy," Lady Dynely says, " what folly is this? You are too young. Oh, yes, Terry, you are—you are ten years

younger than your years—in spite of all you have lived in
the world, you are as ignorant of it as a girl in her teens.   I
don't object to that ; I like you the better for it indeed.   But
you are not up to the rôle of Benedick, the married man.
And besides, the income that is sufficient for you, with your
simple habits, will not suffice for a wife and family.   I can't
conceive of you in love, Terry, you who treat all the young
ladies of your acquaintance with an indifference as unflatter-
ing as I am sure it is sincere."

"I love Crystal," is Terry's answer, and his blue eyes
light.   "I have loved her pretty much, I think, since I saw
her first."

"And she—"

"Oh, I don't know—she likes me, that I am sure of.
She is only seventeen, Lady Dynely, and knows nothing of
the world beyond the vicarage, the village, and her native
marshes.   And yet I think when I ask her to be my wife
she will not refuse."

"You mean to ask her then ? "

"With your permission, Lady Dynely."

She lays her hand on his head ; her lips tremble.

"You are a good boy, Terry ; it would be difficult to be
hard to you if one wished.   But I don't wish.   I only ask
this—postpone your visit for a little, don't ask her to be
your wife until—until Eric comes."

He lifts her hand and kisses it.

"It shall be as you please," he answers.

"Until Eric comes," she repeats, and that grayish pallor
is on her face, that troubled look in her eyes.   "I have
something to tell him—something to tell you.   When that is
told you shall do as you please—you will be absolutely your
own master thenceforth."

"You are not angry, Lady Dynely ? " Terry asks, in a
troubled tone.

"Angry ! with you ?   Ah, no, Terry ; you have never
given me cause for anger in your life."   She sighs heavily ;
she thinks of one, as dear to her as the very heart beating in
her bosom, who has given her cause for anger often enough.

"It is a compact between us. You will wait until I have told you what I have to tell before you speak?"

"I will wait," he answers. And then, with a troubled, mystified look on his face he goes out. "Something to tell; what can it be?" Mr. Dennison wonders. He is not good at guessing; mysteries have never come near his simple life, and they sorely perplex and upset him when they do. For Lady Dynely, she drops her face in her hands with a passionate cry.

"I have put it off so long," she sobs, "and now the day is here—is here."

"Well," says Miss Forrester, imperiously, "has your superior officer given you leave, Mr. Dennison?"

Terry explains—stammering a good deal. Not just yet— he is to wait until Eric comes home.

"Until Eric comes home! Grant me patience!" is Miss Forrester's prayer. "Now what under the sun has Eric to do with it? If Lady Dynely could, the whole world would revolve at Eric's pleasure, the sun only shine when it was his sovereign will. I need not ask, Mr. Dennison, if you mean to obey?"

"You need not, indeed, Miss Forrester," he answers, coolly; "I mean to obey."

She looks at him curiously—almost pathetically—and yet with admiration too.

"I think better of my fellow-men, Terry, since I have known you. You give me an exalted idea of human nature. I thought gratitude an extinct virtue—went out with the dark ages—you teach me my mistake. You love and venerate Lady Dynely in a way that is simply wonderful."

"She has done so much for me," Terry says, "no gratitude can ever repay her."

"Yours will, don't be afraid. You will have chance enough of showing it." Miss Forrester has thrice the worldly wisdom of poor Terry. "How was it all? Your relationship to the Dynely family seems somehow such a hazy affair. What was your life like before she came for you?"

But on this point Terry's recollections are misty. A troubled look crosses his face—it was all wretchedness and squalor that he vaguely remembers, also that those with whom his early years were spent were kind to him, in a rude sort of way. Out of this blurred picture, the rainy day upon which she entered their hovel, like a very angel of light, with her fair face and rich garments, stands out clear. She came, and all his life changed. No mother could do more for a son than she had done for him.

"Could they not?" Miss Forrester says, rather doubtfully, thinking how differently the lives of Eric and Terry are ordered. But she will not throw cold water on his enthusiasm. It is beautiful in its belief and simplicity, this worship of Lady Dynely in a world where gratitude is the exception, not the rule.

"But why did she do it? And what claim have you really upon her?" she asks.

Here Terry is "far wide" again. His father was some sort of relation of the late Lord Dynely, that much her ladyship told the Vicar of Starling, and that meagre scrap is all Mr. Dennison knows of himself or his history.

"Curious," France says, thoughtfully, looking at him. "Lady Dynely is the last to adopt a ragged child through a whim and do for him as she has done for Terry. There is something on the cards we don't see, and something I fancy not quite fair."

So all thought of going down into Lincolnshire and making the eighth Miss Higgins blessed for life, was given up by Mr. Dennison for the present, and he resumed his "fetch and carry" duties as France called them, and dutifully escorted his two lady friends everywhere. Even down to the Brompton studio, which bored him most of all, for he didn't care for pictures, and Mr. Locksley—a good fellow enough—was monopolized by the ladies and had no time to attend to him. The bright brief season—for Parliament closed early that year—was at its end, all the world of western London were turning their thoughts countryward, the last sitting for Lady Dynely's portrait was to be given. While she sat, Miss Forrester prowled about as usual among the pictures, and lo! brought one to light that was a revelation.

She had seen them all again and again. The Canadian

winter scene for the Marquis, a view from the heights of Quebec, with the river a glistening ribbon of frozen silver-white, and the ice cone of Montmorency Falls piercing the vivid blue sky—the glimpses of green Virginian forests, picturesque negro quarters, rich sketches of northern autumnal forests, all gorgeous splashes of ruby-red maple and orange hemlock, and anon a glimpse of Indian life, dusky white-veiled Arabs, and dreary sketches of sandy plain. The companion picture for Madame Felicia was not yet begun. And thus it was that suddenly France came upon her treasure-trove.

It was hidden from view in a dusky corner covered by half a dozen larger canvasses—a little thing, merely a sketch, but struck in with a bold hand, with wonderful gradation of light and shade. This is what she saw :

An old-fashioned garden ; a tangled mass of roses and heliotrope and honeysuckle ; a night sky, lit by a faint, new moon ; the dim outline of a stately mansion rising in the background over the black trees ; a girl in a white dress, her face uplifted to the night sky. In the dim distance, a darker shadow among the shadows, his face entirely obscured —the tall figure of a man stands unseen, watching. The face of the girl is France's own. The blood rushed to her forehead as she looked, with a shock, she could hardly have told—whether of anger or joy. She understood the picture in a moment, and in that moment understood herself. The figure in the background was *his*—and he was bidding her a last farewell. That look of passionate love, of passionate despair—how dared he ! With the crimson of conscious guilt still red in her cheeks, her eyes flashed. Did he suspect what until this moment she had never suspected herself? A suffocating feeling of shame, of terror, seized her. Did he suspect—did he dare suspect that she had stooped to care for him unsought ?

Yes, stooped ! Was he not a nameless, struggling artist, one of the toilers of the earth? And she—and then France stopped and knew in her inmost soul that though he were a beggar, he was the one man of all men born to be her master.

She sat like one in a trance looking at it—heedless how time flew, until suddenly a slip of paper attached to the back caught her eye.

It was a short printed poem that told the story of the picture. Mechanically she took it and read :

> " So close we are, and yet so far apart ;
>   So close I feel your breath upon my cheek ;
>   So far that all this love of mine is weak
> To touch in any way your distant heart ;
> So close, that when I hear your voice I start
>   To see my whole life standing bare and bleak :
>   So far, that though for years and years I seek,
> I shall not find thee other than thou art."

She laid it down. There was a step behind her, and then lifting her eyes they met his full. He turned quite white, and made a motion as though to take the picture from her hand.

"Miss Forrester !   I did not mean that you should see that."

"So I presume. You must pardon me for having seen it, all the same. May I ask for which of Mr. Locksley's patrons is this ? "

"Miss Forrester does me less than justice," he answered ; "I have not been so presumptuous as that. This picture is not to leave my studio. Have you seen the poem ? Yes—well, the fancy took me to put the story it told on canvas. Almost in spite of me the girl's face became yours. It is but an instant's work to dash it out if it displeases you."

"The picture is your own ; you will do as you please," she said, frigidly. "*Ma mère*, is the sitting over at last ? Shall we go ? "

"Your picture, France ? " Lady Dynely said, glancing at the apple of discord, and putting up her glass. "Really ; and very well done. 'The Last Parting.' But what a despairing expression you give her, Mr. Locksley. Who ever saw France with such a look as that ? "

"No one, mother mine," France said, gayly. There were

times when she called Lady Dynely by this title and thus gladdened her heart. "Nor ever will. But these artists have such vivid imaginations."

"I should like you to paint France's portrait, really," said her ladyship. "I have none. What do you say? Throw over your engagements and come down to Dynely and do me this favor."

"It is quite impossible, madame," the artist answered, moodily, standing by his handiwork and looking down at it with gloomy eyes.

And then all of a sudden a change came over Miss Forrester. The look of hauteur broke up, disappeared, and a smile like a gleam of sunshine after a storm lighted her face.

"No one ever says impossible to Lady Dynely," she said, in her old, imperiously charming tone; "least of all with that look. And I really should like to see myself as others see me, on canvas. *That* is not I, for I could by no possibility ever wear such a look as that. You shall paint my picture not once, but twice—once for Lady Dynely and once for a dear old lady in Rome, who will prize it above rubies—Grandmamma Caryll."

He looked up, a faint flush under the golden tan of his skin.

"You mean that?" he asked.

"Most certainly. Let Felicia wait, and you may follow us down to Dynely."

"I shall take it as a favor," chimed in Lady Dynely.

There is a moment's pause, of strong irresolution, France can see. Then he looks up and meets her eyes again.

"You are both very good," he says, quietly. "I will come."

R*

CHAPTER VI.

"THE LORD OF THE LAND."

ALKING up and down the pier of Saint-Jean-sur-Mer, on the Brittany coast, under the broiling sea-side sun, waiting for the English packet anchored out in the roads, is a young English gentleman. The July sky is blazing blindingly here by the sea; the heat quivers like a white mist over the water; not a breath of air stirs the chestnuts or laburnums, and the streets of Saint-Jean lie all baked and white in the pitiless, brassy glare of that fierce midsummer sun.

But in all this tropical dazzle and heat the young Englishman saunters up and down, and looks cool and languid still. His summer suit of palest gray is the perfection of taste; his boots, his gloves, perfection also; and the handkerchief which he flirts once or twice across his face is of finest cambric, embroidered with a coronet and monogram, and perfumed with attar of violets. He is tall and very blonde, as shapely as a woman, broad-shouldered, slender-waisted, long-limbed, and *very* handsome. His complexion is delicate as a girl's; for such blue eyes and blonde curls many a fair one might sigh with envy; very handsome, very effeminate. He has a little golden mustache, waxed into minute points; a straw hat is thrown carelessly on his fair hair. He is the most beautiful, the most noble, the most perfect of all men, in one woman's eyes at least. He is Eric, Lord Viscount Dynely. He walks up and down, and waits for the boat which is to convey him across the channel, to his home and the lady he is to marry. But he is in no hot haste about it; he has put off the evil day as long as possible.

France Forrester is a pretty girl, an elegant girl, a clever girl; a suspicion has entered Lord Dynely's handsome blonde head more than once that she may be even cleverer than himself. *That* is a drawback. In common with all men of good taste and sense, he dislikes clever women ; a suspicion of blue in the stockings would outweigh the charm of the daintiest foot and ankle on earth. Still it is a settled thing among the powers that be, and poor France expects it, no doubt ; and it is less of a bore, on the whole, to yield gracefully, and sacrifice himself in his youth and loveliness on the altar of filial duty, than make a fuss about it. And, besides, as a wife, he really doesn't know any lady he would prefer to Mrs. Caryll's heiress.

At half-past ten he came down to the pier ; it is a quarter of eleven now, as he sees by the small jewelled repeater he draws from his pocket, and Lord Dynely frowns a little.

"Confound it !" he mutters ; "she promised to be here at half-past, sharp, and now it is a quarter of eleven. The boat starts at eleven. Won't she come after all ? and have I been ruining my complexion and eyesight in this beastly glare for the last thirty minutes for nothing ? "

Then he pauses, stops, smiles. *She* is coming—a dark-eyed, coquettish little Frenchwoman, charmingly dressed, and who possesses the good looks that come from youth, good health, good taste, and fine spirits. She is Lord Dynely's last flirtee, met at a Saint-Jean ball, where in ten minutes she had waltzed herself completely into his fickle affections. He had come to Saint-Jean, from his Spanish loiterings, with the intention of crossing over at once, and lo ! a fortnight had passed and two merry black eyes and a vivacious French tongue had held him in rose chains ever since. The two weeks' passion had grown *triste* now, and he was going, and madame had promised to trip down and bid him adieu on the pier. Such was the gentleman decreed to become France Forrester's lord and master.

The fifteen minutes pass ; they talk very affectionately, he with his tall, fair head bent devotedly over her, his eloquent blue eyes speaking whole encyclopædias of undying devotion. He is one of those men who naturally delight to play at love-making, and throw themselves into the moment's

rôle with all the depth that is in them. One of those men
born to be worshipped by women, and to make them suffer
mercilessly at his hands. Not robustly bad in any way,
but simply without an ounce of ballast in him, body or
soul.

Eleven strikes from all the clocks of Saint-Jean-sur-Mer—
the fatal hour has come. There are tears in madame's black,
doll-like eyes as she whispers adieu ; beautifully pale, sad
and tender Lord Eric looks. He waves the perfumed
coroneted handkerchief from the upper deck as long as she
is in sight, still mournful and pale to look upon despite the
height of the thermometer. Then he laughs, puts the handkerchief in his pocket, lights a rose-scented cigarette, selects
a shady spot on deck, orders his valet to fetch him that last
novel of George Sand, and in five minutes has as completely
forgotten the woman he has left as—the girl he is going to.

He reaches London. It is a desert, of course. Everybody has gone. Some three million are left, but they don't
count. He looks in weary disgust at the empty, sun-scorched
West End streets, at the bleached parks, the forsaken
Ladies' Mile, and goes down at once to Devonshire. And
in the cool of a perfect summer evening he reaches the village station, and as he is not expected, is driven in a fly, like
an ordinary mortal, to the Abbey gates. There is a garden
party of some kind, he sees, as he strolls languidly up to the
house. This gentleman, who has not attained his majority,
has a certain weary and worn-out air, as though life were a
very old story indeed, and rather a tiresome mistake—the
"nothing new, and nothing true, and it don't signify " manner to perfection.

It is a most exquisite evening. Overhead there is a sky
like Italy, golden-gray in the shadow, primrose and pink in
the light, a full moon rising over the tree-tops, a few bright
stars winking facetiously down at grim old earth, a faint
breeze just stirring the roses, and clematis, and jessamine, and honeysuckle, and wafting abroad subtle incense,
and the nightingales piping their musical, plaintive vesper
song. It is unutterably beautiful, but to all its beauty Lord
Dynely is deaf and blind. It has been a hot, stifling day,

that he knows ; it is rather cooler now, that is all. What he does see is a group of fair English girls, in robes of white, and pink, and pale green, playing croquet under the beeches, and his tired eyes light a little at the sight. Wherever and whenever Lord Dynely may light upon a pretty girl, or group of them, all his earthly troubles vanish at once. It was a weakness, many cynical friends said, inherited honestly enough from his late noble father.

The group clicking the croquet balls did not see him, but as he drew near, a lady standing on the terrace, gazing thoughtfully at the twilight shadows, did, and there was a quick start, a quick uprising, and a rush to meet him, a glad, joyful cry:

"Oh, Eric ! my son ! my son !"

He permitted her embrace rather than returned it. It was too warm for powerful domestic emotions of any sort, Eric thought, and then women always went in for kissing and raptures upon the smallest provocation. He let himself be embraced, and then gently extricated himself, and glanced backward at the group.

"A croquet party, mother !" he said. "Do I know them? Ah, yes, I see the Deveres and the Dorman girls? Is France—? How is France? She is not among them ?"

"France is somewhere in the grounds. Oh, my boy ! how good it seems to have you at home again—how anxiously I have awaited your coming. We expected you in London at the beginning of the season."

"We?" his lordship says, interrogatively.

"France and I. Do you know, Eric, that France has been the sensation of the season, the most admired girl in London. Lord Evergoil proposed, and was rejected; but, Eric, you ran a great risk."

"Did I? Of losing Miss Forrester ? I could have survived it," he answers, coolly.

"Don't say that, Eric—you don't mean it, I know," Lady Dynely says, with a singularly nervous, frightened look. "You cannot do better—it is impossible. She is of one of the oldest families in the kingdom ; she is handsome, accomplished, and fascinating, and she comes into two fortunes,

her own and Mrs. Caryll's. Eric, I shall break my heart if
you do not marry her."

"Hearts don't break, dear mother—physicians have discovered that; it is an exploded delusion. And as to Miss
Forrester's accomplishments and fascinations, do you know
I rather find that sort of young person hang heavy on hand
—I prefer people of less superhuman acquirements. For
the fortune—well, I may not be a Marquis of Westminster,
but the rent roll is a noble one, and its lord need never sell
himself."

Lady Dynely has turned quite white—a dead, gray pallor
—as she listens. Is he going to throw over France and
her fortune after all? Must she tell him the *truth* in order
to make him speak? Before she can turn to him again, he
speaks, more cheerfully this time.

"'Time enough for all that," he says; "don't look so pale
and terrified, mother mine. One would think I were a pauper, reduced to heiress-hunting or starvation. Where is
France? I will go in search of her, and pay my respects."

"She went down the lime walk half an hour ago with Mr.
Locksley."

"Mr. Locksley? A new name. Who is Mr. Locksley?"

"Mr. Locksley is an artist; he is painting France's portrait. He made a hit at the Academy this year, and I prevailed upon him to come with us down here."

"Oh, you did! And he is received *en famille*, I suppose,
and France takes solitary strolls with him, does she?" responds Eric, lifting his eyebrows. "It seems to me, my good
mother, you don't look after your only son's interests so very
sharply after all. The lime walk, did you say? I will go
and flush this covey at once."

He turns away. His mother stands where he has left her
and watches the tall, slender figure, the slow, graceful walk.

"He grows handsomer every year," she thinks in her love
and admiration. "Go where I will I see nothing like him.
Oh, my boy! if you only knew that you may be a very
pauper indeed. That on the mercy of Terry Dennison
your whole fortune may hang. If I could only summon
courage and end all this deception, and secrecy, and sus-

pense at once.   Terry is so good, so generous, he loves me
so ; he is fonder of Eric than any brother ; he would rather
die than give me pain.   That is my only hope.   If the sins
of the father *must* be visited on the children, oh, let not my
darling be the one to suffer."

A selfish, a weak prayer, but passionately earnest at
least.   Her darling had faded from her view, and her tear-
filled eyes turned to another figure taller still, with all the
grace and elegant languor wanting, only manly strength and
vigor in their place.   His deep laugh comes to her at the
moment, clear and merry as any school-boy's.

"Terry will have mercy," she thinks ; "he is the soul of
generosity, and his wants are so simple, his ambitions so
few.   With his commission, his five hundred a year, and the
vicar's daughter for his wife, he will ask no more of fate.   I
will tell him when he returns from Lincolnshire, and I know,
I feel, all will be well.   And yet,"—her eyes went wistfully
over the fair expanse of park and woodland, and glade and
terrace, flower garden and fountains, all silvered in the radiance of the summer moon—"it is a great sacrifice—a sacrifice not one man in a hundred would make."

Meantime Lord Dynely had strolled down the lime walk,
and emerged upon a sylvan nook, commanding a view
of forest near, and the distant shining sea.   Its soft wash
reached the ear—the moon left a track of radiance as it
sailed up the serene sky.   And this is the picture his lordship saw :

In a dress of gauzy white, Miss Forrester sat in a
rustic chair, blue ribbons floating, trailing roses in the rich
brownness of her hair, a great bunch of lilies of the valley
in her lap, another cluster in the bosom of her dress.   Her
coquettish "Dolly Varden" hat lay on the grass beside her
—her eyes were fixed, full of dreamy light, on the shining
sky and sea, and the man who lay on the sward at her feet,
reading aloud.   Poetry, of course, Tennyson of course, and
"Maud" as it chanced.

> "I said to the rose, ‘The brief night goes
> In revel, and babble, and wine ;

Oh ! young lord lover ! what sighs are those,
  For one who will never be thine,
But mine, but mine !' So I swear to the rose,
  ' Forever and ever mine.' "

Pleasant first words to greet Lord Dynely's ears, pleasant tableau vivant to greet his eyes.

Confound the fellow ! A strolling artist, too. What presumption ! Good looking, no doubt ; those painting fellows, with their long hair, and picturesque faces, and velvet blouses, always play the mischief with women. Reading poetry, at her feet. France Forrester's—whom he used to think one of the proudest girls he knew. He had fancied her pining for him, piqued at his absence. Certainly, flirtation was a game for two to play at. She could amuse herself very well at home, it seemed, while he amused himself abroad.

"Taking people by surprise is a mistake, I find," he said, advancing. "If I don't disturb the exercises, Miss Forrester, perhaps you will turn round and say good-evening."

He stood before her, holding out his hand, a smile on his lips. She half arose, turning very pale.

" Eric ! "

" Eric, Miss Forrester—at last. I have been standing for the last five minutes enjoying the poetry and the very pretty picture you two make here in the twilight. Pray present me."

"There is no need, Miss Forrester. Unless Lord Dynely's memory be of the shortest, think I he will recall me."

Locksley arose to his feet as he spoke, and Lord Dynely saw him for the first time. His face lit up—a look of real pleasure came into his eyes—he grasped the hand of the artist with a genuine warmth, all unusual with him.

"Locksley? My dear fellow, what a surprise this is, you know. My mother mentioned your name, but it never occurred to me *you* were the man. Who would look for you in England?"

Locksley smiled.

" My headquarters is Italy, certainly; but I come to England, nevertheless. I have been here two years."

" You have met before," France broke in ; " you never told me, Mr. Locksley."

" Was it necessary ? I had the pleasure of doing Lord Dynely some slight service two years ago, and saw a good deal of him for some weeks after. But how could I tell he would remember ? Two years is a considerable time."

" Cynical, as usual—a Diogenes without the tub and cabbage leaves. A slight service ! Yes, I should think so. He saved my life, France—my boat upset in a squall in the Bay of Naples, and only he took a header gallantly to the rescue, the Dynely succession would then and there have been extinct. Odd I didn't remember your name the moment I heard it, but I am very pleased to meet you here all the same."

They had turned, and as by one impulse, walked back towards the house. It was quite night now, the trees making ebony shadows across the ivory light. The croquet players had adjourned to the house, and the balls and mallets had given place to piano music and waltzing. On the portico steps stood Terry, whistling and looking at the moon. He came eagerly forward with outstretched hand, his honest eyes shining with pleasure.

" Dear old man ! " he said, giving Eric's delicate digit a grip that made him wince ; " glad to have you back. Thought you were never coming—thought some old Spanish hidalgo out there had got jealous, and pinked you under the fifth rib in some dark corner. The *madre* is beside herself with delight."

" Softly, Terry—softly," says Lord Dynely, withdrawing his hand with a slight grimace. " A moderate amount of affection I don't object to, but don't let the grip of the muscular hand express the emotions of the overflowing heart. They are tripping the light fantastic in there — shall we join them ? "

They enter the drawing-room—there are more greetings and a few introductions. The lord of the land has returned —the seigneur of Dynely, the master, is in the house, and his presence makes itself felt directly. He is in excellent spirits—throws off his languor, forgets to be blasé, and waltzes like a student at Mabille.

France declines; it is too warm, she says; she will relieve Lady Dynely, and play. Mr. Locksley makes his adieux speedily and departs.

"How have you come to pick up Locksley, France?" Eric asks, later on.

"Pick him up? I don't quite understand. He painted the picture of the year, sold it for a fabulous sum, was overflowing with orders, and, as a special favor to Lady Dynely, consented to throw over everything else, follow us down here and paint my portrait."

She speaks with a certain air of constraint, which Lord Dynely does not fail to notice.

"Ah, very kind of him, of course. Very fine fellow, Locksley, and very clever artist, but a sort of reserve about him, a sort of mystery, something on his mind and all that. One of the sort of men who have an obnoxious wife hidden away in some quarter of the globe, like Warrington and Rochester in the novels. I must see the portrait—is it a good one?"

"Very good, I believe—I have given but two or three sittings as yet."

"How long has he been here?"

"A fortnight."

A pause. He looks at her as he leans over the back of her chair. She is slightly pale still, rather grave, but very handsome—*very* handsome. She has improved, Eric thinks, complacently, and dark beauties are his style, naturally. A very credible wife, he thinks; a fine, high-bred face to see at one's table; and if there be a trifle more brains than one could wish, one can excuse that in a wife.

"I must get Locksley to make me a duplicate," he says, bending over her, and putting on his tender look. "France, you have not said you are glad to see me yet."

"Is it necessary to repeat that formula?" she answers, carelessly. "That is taken for granted, is it not?"

"I was detained at Saint Jean," he goes on. "I have

been longing to see you once more ; how greatly, you can imagine."

" Yes, I can imagine," France answers, and suddenly all her reserve gives way, and she looks up and laughs in his face. " I can imagine the burning impetuosity, the fever of longing with which you rushed across the Pyrenees, across France, and home. Eric, that sort of thing may do very well in Spain, but don't try it with me."

" Merciless as ever. Your London season has agreed with you, France. I never saw you look so well. And the fame of your conquests have reached even the other side of the Pyrenees. How others slew their thousands and Miss Forrester her tens of thousands. How men went down before her dark-eyed glances like corn before the reaper."

" My dear Eric," Miss Forrester replies, politely shrugging with a yawn, " don't you find it fatiguing to talk so much ? It was never a failing of yours to make long speeches. But I suppose two years' hard practice of the language of compliments must tell."

" Come out on the terrace," is what he says, and in spite of her faint resistance he leads her there. He is growing more and more charmed every moment—not deeply in love, just epris of this new and pretty face. He is as much fascinated now as he was by madame last week, as he may be by any one else you please next, and thoroughly in earnest at the moment. Why should he delay ? Why not come to the point at once ? Really, France would do credit to any man in England.

The moonlight is flooding the terrace with glory, the trees are silver in its light, the stone urns gleam like pearls, the flowers waft their fragrance where they stand.

" Oh !" France sighs, " what a perfect night !"

" Yes," Eric assents, looking up with his poetic blue eyes to the sky ; " very neat thing in the way of moonshine. And moonlight hours were made for love and all that ; the poet says so, doesn't he, France ? "

" *The* poet, which poet ? Don't be so vague, Lord Dynely."

" Ah, France, you may laugh at me—"

"I am not laughing; I never felt less facetious in my life. My principal feeling, at present, is that it is half-past eleven, that I am tired after two hours' croquet, and that I should—and will say good-night, and go to bed."

"Not just yet." He takes her hand and holds it fast. "What a pretty hand you have," he says, tenderly; "a model for a sculptor. Will you let me put an engagement ring among all those rubies and diamonds, France? I wanted to once before—in Rome, you remember, and you wouldn't allow me."

France laughs, and looks at him, and draws away her hand.

> "There came a laddie here to woo,
>   And, dear, but he was jimp and gay;
>   He stole the lassie's heart away,
> And made it all his ain, Oh."

"You certainly lose no time, Lord Dynely. Really the haste and ardor of your love-making takes one's breath away. I have more rings now than I know what to do with—another would be the embarrassment of riches. Eric, let us end this farce. You don't care a straw for me. You don't want to marry me any more than I want to marry you. Why should we bore each other with love-making that means nothing. It will disappoint two good women a little—but that is inevitable. Go to your mother, like a good boy, and tell her she must make up her mind to another daughter-in-law."

His eyes light—opposition always determines him for right or wrong.

"I will never tell her that. I love you, France—have loved you always—you alone shall be my wife."

"Eric, do you expect me to believe that?"

"I expect you to believe the truth. And if after all these years—after what has passed between us, you mean to throw me over—"

"After what has passed between us!" she repeats, looking at him full, "I don't understand that, Eric. What has ever passed between us?"

"You know I have loved you—you did not quite cast

me off—you know it has always been an understood thing
we were to marry."

"And you mean to hold me to such a compact as that?"

"I mean I love you, and will be most miserable if you
do not become my wife."

"Ungenerous," she says, under her breath. "You will
hold me to this tacit understanding—to which I have never
been a party, mind—whether I will or no?"

He only repeats :

"I love you, France. I want you for my wife."

She stands looking at the softly luminous night, at the
dark trees and white shadows, her face pale, her lips set,
her eyes darkly troubled.

"It is unfair—it is ungenerous," she cries out, presently,
"to hold me to a compact to which I have never consented.
I will not do anything dishonorable, but, Eric, it is most
unkind. You do *not* love me—ah, hush—if you protested
forever I would not believe you. I know you, I think,
better than you know yourself. You mean it at this moment—next week you may forget my very existence. I am
not the sort of wife for you—you want an adoring creature
to sit at your feet and worship you as a god. There !" she
turns impatiently away; "let me alone. I can give you
no answer to-night. The dew is falling ; let us go in. I hate
to grieve Mrs. Caryll, I hate to disappoint your mother—for
your disappointment, if any there be, I don't care a whit."

"France, you are heartless," he says, angrily.

"No—I only speak the truth. Give me up. Let me go,
Eric—it will be better for us both."

"I will never let you go," he answers, sullenly. "If you
throw me over, well and good—I must submit—only it will not
be like France Forrester to play fast and loose with any man."

Her eyes flash upon him in the moonlight their angry fire.

"You do well to say that," she retorts. "You of all
men ! Give me a week ; I cannot answer to-night. If at
the end of that time you are still of the same mind, come
to me for your answer."

She passes him, returns to the drawing-room, and leaves
him on the terrace alone.

CHAPTER VII.

A WEEK'S REPRIEVE.

ISS FORRESTER goes to her room and sits at the window, after the fashion of girls, and looks out. She had never taken this affair of the proposed alliance seriously for a moment before. She had said, and with truth, that she understood Eric better than he understood himself. Somewhere in his wanderings he felt he would come upon some gypsy, girlish face, that would captivate his susceptible, romantic heart—no, not heart—*fancy;* and very probably there might be an impromptu marriage, and an end of all worry for her. He was just the sort of man to sneer at matrimony, because it was a cynical, worldly, correct sort of thing to do, and rush headlong into it upon the slightest provocation. To be "off with the old love and on with the new," at a moment's notice, was my Lord Eric's forte.

She had not disliked Eric, she had rather liked him, indeed —laughed at his love-making, parodied his pretty speeches, mimicked his languid drawl, and weary, used-up manner; treated him much as she treated Terry, with a sort of fun-loving, elder-sister manner; only she had a real respect for Dennison she never felt for Dynely.

"I never could marry such a man as you, Eric," she was wont to say. "You have a great deal fairer complexion than I have, and I don't like dolly men. You curl your hair; you wax that little callow mustache of yours; you perfume yourself like a valet; you think more about your toilet and spend longer over it than a young duchess; and you haven't an ounce of brains in you from top to toe. Now if I have a weakness, it is this—that the man I marry shall be a manly man and a clever man. You, my poor

Eric, are neither, and never will be. And besides you're too good-looking."

"First time a lady ever objected to that in the man who adored her," Eric drawled.

"You're too good-looking," Miss Forrester repeats with a regretful sigh; "and over-much good looks are what no man can bear. You're a coxcomb, my precious boy, of the first water—a dandy *par excellence.* Why, you know yourself," cries France, indignantly, "your sobriquet at Eton was 'Pretty Face?'"

"I know it—yes," Eric answers, with an irrepressible smile.

"Then you see it's quite impossible—utterly impossible and preposterous, Eric," Miss Forrester was wont to conclude; "so let us say no more about it. I don't object to your making love to me in a general way—it's your only earthly mission, poor fellow, and to veto that would be cruel. But let it be general—let us have no more foolish talk of present engagements and prospective weddings, and that nonsense. Because you know it can never be."

"Never, France—really?"

"Never, Eric—really; never, never, never. I wouldn't marry you if you were the last man on earth, and to refuse involved the awful doom of old-maidenhood. I like you too well ever to love you. And I mean to love the man I marry."

"Really!" Eric repeats, lifting his eyebrows, and pulling the waxed ends of the yellow mustache, intensely amused.

"Yes, Eric, with all my heart. Ah, you may smile in the superior god-like wisdom of manhood, but I mean it. He is to be a king among men—"

"*Sans peur et sans reproche?*" puts in young Lord Dynely.

"Without fear and without reproach. Yes, exactly. Not a man about town, mind you; an elegant tailor's block, too much in love with himself ever to love his wife; but a strong man, a brave man, a hero—"

"'I'm Captain Jinks, of the Horse Marines,'" hums Lord Dynely, that popular ditty having about that time burst upon an enraptured world.

"A man I can look up to, be proud of, who will do something in the world; anything but a handsome dandy who parts his hair in the middle, who wears purple and fine linen, and whose highest aim in life is to lie at young ladies' feet and drawl out the eternal passion that consumes him—a gentleman whose loves are as numerous as the stars, and not half so eternal."

In this spirited way Miss Forrester had been used to rebuff her would-be lover, and did sometimes succeed in piquing Eric into deserting her in disgust.

A young lady so strong-minded as this at sixteen, what was she likely to be at twenty? He pitied her for her lack of taste—other girls went down before those blue eyes of his, for which Miss Forrester expressed such profound contempt. It had never really meant much with either of them until this night on the terrace. And this night on the terrace Lord Dynely had been in earnest at last.

In some way her honor was bound—more or less, while she had laughed at the wished-for alliance, she had yet accepted it. Miss Forrester had a very high sense of honor, and was an exceedingly proud girl. To play fast or loose with any man, as Eric had said, was utterly impossible. In no way was she a coquette. Men had admired her, had fallen in love with her, had wanted to marry her; but the mistake had been of their own making; she had never led them on. If, indeed, then, her honor and truth stood compromised here, she must marry Eric. He did not love her—*that* she knew as well now as she had known it always; if she married him, she would be a most unhappy, unloved and neglected wife— that she also knew. And yet if he held her to it, if Lady Dynely held her to it, if Mrs. Caryll held her to it, what was she to do? To grieve those that loved her was a trial to her generous nature, and she was of the age and the kind to whom self-sacrifice, self-abnegation, look great and glorious things. Yes, it would resolve itself into this—if Lord Dynely held her to their compact, she must marry Lord Dynely.

And then out of the mist of the moonlight, the face of Locksley arose, the grave, reproachful eyes, the broad, thoughtful brow, the firm, resolute lips, hid behind that gold, bronze beard, France thought the most beautiful on earth. She covered her face with both hands as if to shut it out.

"I cannot! I cannot!" she said. "I cannot marry Eric. It is most selfish, most ungenerous, most cruel to hold me to a promise I never gave."

Then there came before her a vision—a vision of what her life might be as Locksley's wife. With her fortune and his genius, loving and beloved, what a beautiful and perfect life would lie before her.

Suddenly the carelessly spoken words of Eric came back to her:

"One of these mysterious men who have an obnoxious wife hidden away in some quarter of the globe." She turned cold at the thought. Was there anything in it— anything beyond a jealous man's malicious innuendo? There was that strange picture, "How The Night Fell" —his own strange remarks concerning it. Who was to tell what lay in the life behind him? Somehow, he looked like a man who had a secret, who had lived every day of his life, and that life no common one. She sighed ; her train of thought broke ; she got up abruptly, closed the window, and went to bed.

She was looking pale next morning when she descended to breakfast, in spite of the rose-pink cashmere she wore ; a shade too pale, fastidious, Eric thought, but very handsome, with the ease of high-bred grace in every word and act ; a wife, he repeated again, who would do honor to any man in England. How well she would look at St. George's in bridal veil and blossoms, white satin and Honiton lace, and how all the men he knew would envy him. In his love-making, as in every pursuit of life, self was ever uppermost with Lord Dynely.

"Is this one of the Locksley's painting days?" he asked after breakfast ; "because I want to see the picture. Does he come here or do you go there? Does Mahomet come to the mountain, or does the mountain, etc.? I must have that duplicate I spoke of, France. To possess the original

7

will not content me ; I must have the counterfeit present-
ment also."

This in a tender whisper and a look from under the long,
blonde eyelashes that had done killing execution in its time.
It missed fire, however, so far as France was concerned.

"I doubt if Mr. Locksley will take time to paint duplicates, Eric. Men who make their mark, as he has done,
do not generally devote themselves to portrait painting.
Here he comes now."

Her color rose as she said it—her pale cheeks took a tint
rivalling her dress. Lord Dynely saw it and frowned.
Mentally, that is ; so ugly a thing as a frown seldom marred
the smooth fairness of that low brow.

"Capital fellow, Locksley," he said, carelessly. "Saw a
great deal of him at one time in Naples. Can tell a good
story, and knock off a neat after-dinner speech better than
any man I know. The set he lived among—painting fellows
all—used to drop hints, though, about that discarded wife.
There is one somewhere, depend upon it, and Locksley
didn't act over and above well in the business, it was understood."

France turned upon him, herself again, a look of cool
contempt in her eyes.

"Eric, don't be ill-natured. I hate womanish men, and
there's nothing on earth so womanish as to slander absent
friends. *We* do that ; but let us retain the copyright."

And then she turns away and goes over to Mr. Locksley,
looking proud and lovely, and holds out her hand in cordial
welcome.

"One may have a look at the portrait, I suppose, Locksley ?" Eric suggests, unabashed.

Mr. Locksley assents ; and they adjourn to the painting-
room—Terry, who drops in, following in their wake. It is
in an unfinished state as yet, lacking in all details, but it is
a beautiful and striking picture.

From a cloud of misty drapery the face looks vividly out,
the lips gravely smiling, the serene eyes earnest and
luminous to their very depths, an etherealized expression
intensifying its beauty. He has idealized it unconsciously

—a handsome girl has sat to him—he has painted a divin‑
ity.

France stands and looks, and her face flushes. Ah ! she
has never worn that look. She knows she is of the
earth, earthy—very little of the angel about her, after all.
And he has painted more an angel than a woman.

" He'm," says Eric, with his hand over his eyes, critically,
" very good—very pretty, indeed. Paint a halo round her
and call it St. Teresa, or St. Cecelia at once—it looks like
that sort of thing, you know. It's a pretty picture, but it
isn't you, France ; that is not your natural expression."

" No," France says, under her breath. " I am sorry to
say it is not."

" And I prefer your natural expression," goes on Eric.
" It is very well done, as I said before, but it doesn't do you
justice."

" And I think it is grossly flattered," puts in Terry,
gruffly.

France bestows upon him a look of absolute gratitude.

" Flattered ! I should think so, Terry. *That* face Mr.
Locksley has painted out of his inner consciousness, and is
what France Forrester should be—what, I regret to add, she
is not."

Mr. Locksley takes no part in the discussion ; he goes
steadfastly on with his work. Terry yawns loudly, whistles
in an aimless way, thrusts his hands in his pockets, and
stares at the artist's rapid movements, until France, whose
nerves he sets on edge, orders him peremptorily to leave the
room. Eric lingers, lounging in a deep window, looking
unutterably patrician and handsome in his black velvet
morning coat, contrasting so perfectly with his pearl-like
complexion and fair hair. He remains all through the sitting, he follows France out into the Italian rose garden
when it is over, he hangs about her like her shadow all day,
and makes tender little speeches when he can. At dinner
it is the same—in the evening it is worse. He is really and
truly in earnest for the time. Whilst he was sure of her he
was indifferent—now that he stands a chance of losing her
he works himself into a fever of devotion. She is in love

with Locksley, Locksley with her—that he sees. That hit
about the hidden wife has stung. The green-eyed monster
blows the slight fire of his affection into a blaze. He will win
and wear Miss Forrester, or know the reason why. France en-
dures it as long as she can. That is not very long. At no
time are patience and meekness her most notable virtues;
as Eric bends persistently over the piano for an hour at a
stretch, the slight thread of that patience gives way at last.

"Eric, do give me a moment's peace," she cries out.
"Go and play chess with your mother; go and talk to
Terry or Mr. Steeves; go and make love to Miss Hanford;
go and smoke a cigar in the dew; anything, only leave me
alone."

He starts up, his pride fairly stung.

"As you please. As I am so disagreeable to you, suppose I take myself away from the Abbey altogether."

"I wish you would," she answers cordially, "for this week
at least. You irritate me beyond measure haunting me in
this way. Leave me alone, Eric, if you really care for my
decision."

"If I really care!" he reproachfully repeats.

"The more generous you are, the better your chances
will be. When the week is up, come back if you like, for—
for your answer."

"France! and if that answer be favorable. If! Good
Heaven, it must be," he cries.

"Then"—her voice trembles, she turns her face away
from him in the glow of the waxlights—"then you will
never more hear me complain of your attentions."

He lifts her hand and kisses it.

"I will go," he says, gently. "Forgive me, France, but
the thought of losing you is so—"

"Don't," she says, in a voice that is almost one of pain.
"Where will you go?"

"To Lincolnshire—to Sir Philip Carruthers' place. I
have had a standing invitation to Carruthers' Court for the
past two years."

"What's that about Lincolnshire?" Terry asks, appear-
ing. "I'm off there—are you on the wing again, Eric?"

"For a week, yes—to Carruthers'. You're a Lincoln-shire man, Terry—do you know it?"

"Do I not? It is three miles from Starling vicarage. Shall be glad to meet you there, dear old boy. Capital fishing, best trout streams anywhere, prime shooting a little later on. We will—

"'We will hunt the bear and bison, we will shoot the wild raccoon,
We will worship Mumbo Jumbo in the Mountains of the Moon!'"

spouts France. "There are nine pretty Misses Higgins—aren't there, Terry? Don't let Eric poach on your manor—it is in his line, you know."

France was herself again. The prospect of a week to quietly think the matter out was a great deal. And who knew what even a week might bring forth?

It was settled that they should go together; Lady Dynely's consent had been won at last.

"But, remember," she said at parting, looking anxiously into Terry's eyes, "you are to return in a week, and mean-time you are to say nothing to Miss Higgins. This I insist upon. When you have heard what I have to say—"

He looked at her in anxious wonder. What could it be, he thought, to make Lady Dynely wear that face of pale affright? What secret was here? He would obey her in all things; she hardly needed the assurance, and yet it was with a darkly troubled face she stood on the portico steps and watched the two young men disappear.

"Thank fortune," France breathed devoutly, "we shall have a quiet week. Men are a mistake in a household, I begin to find. Like yeast in small beer, they turn the peaceful stream of woman's life into seething ferment."

"France," the elder lady said, taking both the girl's hands, and looking earnestly down into her eyes, "you are to give Eric his answer when he returns—I know that. When does he return?"

"In a week."

"And the answer will be—"

"Lady Dynely, you have no right to ask that. When the

week ends, and Eric returns to claim it, the answer shall be given to *him*."

She dropped the hands and turned away with a heavy sigh.

"I will do my duty, I hope—I pray," France went on, quietly. "If Eric's happiness were involved—if, indeed, he loved me, after the tacit consent I have given all these years—I would not hesitate one moment, at any sacrifice to myself. But he does not love me—he is incapable of loving any one but himself. Oh, yes! Lady Dynely, even you must hear the truth sometimes about Eric. As a brother, I could like him well enough—be proud of his good looks, his graceful manner, as you are ; as a husband, if he is ever that, I shall detest him."

"France !"

"I shock, I anger you, do I not ? It is true, though, and he will tire of me before the honeymoon is over. If we marry, it will be a fatal mistake ; and yet, if you all hold me to this compact, what is left me but to yield ?"

"You are a romantic girl, France ; you want a hero—a Chevalier Bayard—a Sir Launcelot. Dear child, there are none left. Like the fairies, they sailed away from England years ago—went out of fashion with tilt and tournament. You will marry Eric, I foresee, and make a man of him. He will go into parliament, make speeches, and be a most devoted husband to the fairest and happiest wife in England. Oh, France, take my boy ! I love you so well that I will break my heart if this marriage does not take place."

"And I will break mine if it does," France answers, with a curious little laugh. "Let us not talk of it any more, *ma mère.* We are due at De Vere's, are we not ? We have a week's grace, and much may happen in a week. I have the strongest *internal* conviction that I will never be Lady Dynely."

CHAPTER VIII.

"WHO IS SHE?"

SCENE, an old-fashioned country garden of an old-fashioned country house; time, the mellow, amber hour before sunset; dramatis personæ, a young man and a young girl; names of dramatis personæ, Mr. Terence Dennison, of Her Majesty's ——th Dragoons, and Miss Christabel Higgins, eighth daughter of the Rev. William Higgins, Vicar of Starling, and beauty of the family.

A beauty? Well, as Tony Lumpkin says, "That's as may be." If you liked a complexion of milk-white and rose-pink, the eighth Miss Higgins had it; if you liked big, childish, surprised-looking, turquoise blue eyes, there they were for you; if you liked a dear little, dimpled, rosy mouth, there it was also; if you liked a low, characterless forehead, a round, characterless chin, and a feathery aureole of palest blonde hair, the eighth Miss Higgins rejoiced in all these pretty and pleasant gifts. If you fancied a waist you might span, a shape, small, slim, fragile as a lily-stalk, little Crystal would have been your ideal, certainly. Pretty? Yes, with a tender, dove-like, inane sort of prettiness, that does its work with a certain sort of men. Mind, she had none; depth, she had none; knowledge of this big, wicked world, she had none; in short, she was man's ideal of perfect womanhood, infringing on no claim whatever of the lordly sex. And Terry Dennison was her abject slave and adorer.

She was seventeen this sunny August afternoon. It seemed to Terry he had idolized her—idolized was the way Mr. Dennison thought it—ever since she had been seven. She knew she was pretty—dove-like innocence to the contrary—and rejoiced in that prettiness as thoroughly as any embryo coquette.   Had she not been caressed, and kissed, and praised for those blue eyes and golden tresses ever since the days of bibs and tuckers?   Had she not seen her seven elder sisters snubbed and passed over, and the cakes and the sugar-plums always presented to her?   It would be so forever, Crystal thought.   In the eternal fitness of things it had been ordered so—the seven elder Cinderellas worked in kitchen and chamber, sewed, baked, and mended; she, like the lilies of the field, toiled not nor spun.   The cakes and sugar-plums of life were to be hers always; they belonged by right divine to pretty people with pale yellow hair and turquoise eyes.   Let the snub-noses, and freckled complexions, and the dry-as-dust colored hair do the work.   She would marry Terry Dennison some day, and be, as Terry was, an offshoot of the aristocracy.   This great lady, who was Terry's patroness and friend, would take her up, would present her at court, would invite her to her parties, and the world of her dreams would become the world of realities.   She would see this handsome Lord Eric Dynely, of whom Terry never tired talking—this elegant Miss France Forrester, who was to marry him.   And, who knew—these beings of the upper world might condescend even to admire her in turn.

Miss Crystal Higgins, strolling with her Tennyson or her Owen Meredith in her hand through the old vicarage garden, had dreamed her dreams, you see.   That was the simple little life she had mapped out for herself.   She would marry Terry—that was settled.   Terry had never asked her, but, ah! the simplest little lassie of them all can read mankind like a book when they have that complaint: Terry was in love with her, had always been; she knew it just as well as Terry himself.   And she liked Terry very well; she wasn't in love with him at all, but still she was fonder of him than of any other young man she knew; and he was a dragoon, and *that* threw a sort of halo over him. It was a pity, she was wont to sigh, regretfully, that he was so homely; even being a dragoon could not entirely do away with the fact that he was homely, and had red hair.

None of the heroes of Miss Higgins' pet novels ever had
hair of that obnoxious hue.   Still one mustn't expect everything in this lower world—papa and mamma instilled that
into her sentimental little noddle—it is only for beings
of that upper world—like Miss Forrester, for instance,
to look for husbands handsome as Greek gods, titled,
wealthy.   Less-favored mortals must take the goods their
gods provide, and be thankful.   The wife of a dragoon, with
five hundred a year, looked a brilliant vista to the "beauty
daughter " of the Vicar of Starling.

   And now the question resolved itself.   Why didn't Terry
speak ?   He had written of his good fortune, of Lady
Dynely's boundless kindness, and the Reverend Mr. and Mrs.
Higgins congratulated themselves that "Crissy's" fortune
was insured.   Crissy herself simpered and cast down her
blonde eyelashes, and saw with secret satisfaction, the sour
and envious regards of the seven elder Misses Higgins, who
were verging helplessly toward the sere and yellow leaf.
Then Terry wrote of his speedy visit.   "And I really think,
Christabel, my love," said Mamma Higgins, "we might
begin making up the outfit.   It will take some time, and of
course he comes down with but one intention, that of proposing immediately."   And a few things were commenced.
The first week of August came, the big dragoon with it, his
frank face and good-humored eyes fairly luminous with delight at being with them again.   Those eager, loving eyes
actually devoured Crystal ; not for five minutes at a stretch
could they leave that pretty doll face.   He haunted her
everywhere, as a big, lumbering Newfoundland might follow
a little curled, silky King Charles.   He looked love, he
hinted love, he acted love, in ten thousand different ways,
but he never spoke it.   He blushed if she suddenly looked
at him, stammered if she suddenly addressed him, touched
the little lily-leaf hand she gave him with the timidity characteristic of big, warm-hearted men, very far gone indeed ; but
beyond that he never got.   "Miss Crystal Higgins, will
you marry me ?" was a conundrum he never propounded.
And Mamma Higgins' matronly eyes began to look at him
wrathfully over her spectacles, the seven elder Misses Higgins

7*   ·

to cast sisterly, satirical glances after the beauty, and Crystal herself to open those innocent turquoise orbs of hers to their widest, and wonder what made Terry so awfully bashful. The last day but one of the visit had come and Terry had not spoken.

It was Crystal's birthday, and there was to be a little fête; croquet in the back garden—the family bleaching-ground on ordinary occasions—a tea-drinking under the apple-trees afterward, and a dance by moonlight.

The company had begun to gather; but there were Mamma Higgins and the seven other Misses Higgins to receive and entertain them, so Terry drew his idol's hand inside his coat-sleeve, and led her away for a little last ramble "o'er the moor among the heather."

"I go back to-morrow, and I cannot tell exactly how long Lady Dynely may detain me, so let me gather my roses while they bloom," said Terry, growing poetical, as many young gentlemen do when in love.

"It seems to me, Terry," said the eighth Miss Higgins, rather pettishly, "you are a sort of companion for Lady Dynely's lap-dog, to fetch and carry, to come and go, as you are told. You are too big, I should think, to let yourself be treated like a little boy *all* your life."

It was not often Mlle. Crystal made so determined a stand as this, or uttered so spirited a speech. But mamma had told her this very day that something must be done; that if she couldn't bring Terry to the point herself, papa must ask his intentions. A little firing of blank cartridge is very well, but if you want to bring down your bird, you must use real powder and shot.

Terry's face flushed. He understood the reproof, and felt he deserved it. Love may be blind, but not quite stone blind; he saw well enough what was expected of him by the vicar's family, by the little beauty herself, and knew he was exciting anger and blame for not doing what he was dying to do. He deserved this reproof, and reddened guiltily. What if Crystal knew it was by Lady Dynely's command he did not dare speak, how she would despise him? And for the first time it occurred to him that perhaps it was rather unkind of that best of women to have bound him to this promise.

"I should never have come down here at all until I was free to say all that is in my heart," he thought. "Oh, my darling! before the sun sinks out of sight yonder, you would know life holds no thought half so sweet as the thought of making you my wife."

She was looking very lovely in this roseate evening light—but Terry thought when did she not look lovely? She wore flowing white muslin—she was that sort of ethereal creature who seemed born to wear white muslin. She had a bunch of roses in her breast, roses in her sash, roses in her hand, and a heart-breakingly coquettish "Dolly Varden" on her head. She had a cascade of white wax beads around her long, slim throat, and knots of blue ribbon streaming from her golden locks. The yellow sunshine fell full upon the perfect face without finding a flaw in it ; the little snowdrop of a hand rested on his arm ; the soft, affectionate, reproachful eyes looked up at him waiting in pathetic appeal.

"You know I like you ; I know you love me ; then why don't you say so, Terry, and please mamma and me? You have only to ask and receive ; I think it is a little too bad of you to go on like this." That was what that reproachful little look said, and Terry groaned in spirit as he saw and understood and chafed against the fetters that bound him.

"See here, Crystal," he said, "there's something I want to say to you"—Crystal's heart gave a little flutter beneath the roses, Crystal's lips parted in an irrepressible smile—"but I can't say it just now."

He paused, for the smile faded away, and the light blue eyes looked up in anger and alarm to his face.

"I can't say it just now," pursued Mr. Dennison, with a great gulp, "because—because I've promised. I don't know why, I'm sure, but there's something to be told, and I'm to go back and hear it before I return and speak to *you*."

Lucid this, certainly. With dilated eyes and parted lips, Miss Crystal Higgins was staring up at him, while Terry floundered hopelessly through this morass of explanation.

"I'm going to-morrow," went on the dragoon; "I told
her I would; but I'm coming back—back immediately,
mind. And then I shall have something to say to you,
Crissy, that I've been dying to say for the past year. To-
day I can explain no further. Only—you won't be angry
with me, Crystal, and you'll be patient, and trust me, and
wait until I come back!"

He looked at her imploringly—a woman blind, and deaf,
and dumb, might have understood all he meant. But Miss
Crystal was a kittenish little coquette, and her eyes were
cast down now, and the rose-pink color had deepened, and
she was pulling her roses to pieces and scattering them with
a ruthless hand.

"I don't understand a word you are saying, Mr. Dennison," was her answer. "What did we come here for, I
wonder? Let us go back. I'm dying for a game of croquet,
and all the people must have come."

"Won't you promise me, then, Crystal?"

"Promise you what, Terry?"

"To wait until I return. To—to not forget me," says
poor Terry, with a sort of groan.

Miss Higgins laughs. When a girl's lover stands before
her in an agony of masculine awkwardness and bashfulness,
that girl is immediately at her ease.

"Wait until you return? I have no intention of running
anywhere, you stupid Terry. Forget you? Now how
could I forget you if I tried, when your name is a household
word with the girls from morning until night? Do let us go
back and play croquet."

"Wait one moment, Crystal. I bought you this, this
morning. Wear it for my sake until I return, and then I
will replace it with a diamond."

He produces from an inner pocket a tiny case, from the
case a tiny ring of pearls and turquoise only made for
fairy fingers. But it slips easily over one of Miss Christabel's.

"Wear it, Crystal," he says, softly, "for my sake."

And Terry kisses the little hand, and Crystal looks up in
his face, and they understand one another, and there is no

more to be said. She is a good little thing after all, and not
disposed to play with her big, awkward lover. It is all
right; Terry is a dear, good fellow, and she will tell papa
not to demand his intentions.

They stand a moment still. Over the flat, distant marshes
the August sun is setting, turning the pools that lie between
the reeds into pools of blood. The distant sea lies sleeping
in the tranquil light. It is very pretty—quite Tennysonian,
Miss Higgins pensively thinks; but her soul is with the
croquet players. "Let us go back, Terry," she is on the
point of saying for the third time, when she stops, surprised
by the look Terry wears. He is staring hard straight before
him, a look of mingled doubt, recognition, and pleasure on
his face. Crystal looks too, and sees coming towards them
a man.

"It is!" says Terry, in delight. "By Jove! it is!"

"It is whom, Terry?"

"Eric. I wondered he hadn't looked me up before. He
has been stopping at Sir Philip Carruthers' place for the last
five days. Yes, it *is* Eric."

" Eric ? "

"Yes, Eric—Lord Dynely, you know. No, by the bye,
you don't know, but you have heard of him often enough
from me."

Yes, Miss Higgins certainly had, and looked with a little
flutter again, beneath the roses, at the young nobleman approaching, who had been described to her by enthusiastic
Terence Dennison "as the best-looking fellow in England."

Miss Higgins looked, and saw a young man of twenty-one,
with fair hair, handsome blue eyes, a little golden mustache,
and the worn-out air of a centenarian, who has used up all the
pleasures of this wicked world some sixty or seventy years
ago.

"Eric, old boy, glad you've looked me up at last," was all
Terry said, but his whole face lit as if the mere sight of the
other were pleasant to him. "Let me present you to Miss
Crystal Higgins. Crystal, the friend of my youth, the play-
mate of my happy childhood, as the novels have it—Lord
Dynely."

Lord Dynely lifted his hat and bowed with that courtly grace for which he was celebrated. His languid eyes kindled as the warrior's when he sees the battle afar off. Terry had said she was pretty. Pretty! Terry was a Vandal, a Goth; the girl was a goddess!

"Are you a good one at croquet, Eric?" inquired Mr. Dennison. "If so, you may come along. This is Crystal's birthday; there is a croquet party at the vicarage, and good players are in demand. Crystal's past mistress of the art; as the old song says:

> " ' She's a hard un to follow,
> A bad un to beat,'

and as a rule, croquets *me* off the face of the earth in two minutes and a half."

"If Miss Higgins will permit me, I shall only consider myself too happy," murmurs Dynely, with a look that has done its work before, and that sets Crystal's foolish, rustic heart fluttering, and tremulous blushes coming and going.

"Oh, yes, thank you!" is what she says, in her dire confusion of blushes, and she clings unconsciously to Terry's arm, and feels that the days of the demi-gods are not extinct, since this seraphic young nobleman exists.

"Don't be afraid, Crissy," says Terry's loud, jolly voice, as he pats the small clinging hand confidingly. "Eric's not half so ferocious, bless you, as he looks! Heard from France or the *madre* since you came?"

Eric gives him a look and a frown. Terry has no tact. Is this a place to talk of—h'm—France?

"I had a note from my mother by this morning's post," he answers. "She bade me tell you not to fail in returning. That is why I looked you up. Had I known you were dwelling in paradise," he adds, gayly, "I would have hunted you up long ago."

They reach the vicarage. Lord Dynely is presented to Mr. and Mrs. Higgins, the Misses Higgins and their guests, and strikes all the ladies mute at once by his good looks, his courtly grace of manner, his magnificent condescension.

Yes, he can play croquet, and play it well. He and the heroine of the fête come off triumphant in every game. They play croquet, and that other classical game yclept "Aunt Sally," and he lingers by Crystal's side, and for the one thousandth time his inflammable fancy fires, and a new fair face enchants him.

They go to tea under the gnarled old apple-trees. There is a snowy cloth, old-fashioned china cups of pearl and blue, fragrant tea, home-made pound cake and jelly; and Eric, whose luncheon has been a glass of sherry and a biscuit, and who has not dined, makes a martyr of himself, and drinks the tea, and partakes of the pound cake and jelly and helps the young ladies, and pays compliments, and tells pretty little stories.

The moon has arisen before they have done, and they dance by its light to the music of the jingly vicarage piano, upon which the nine Miss Higginses have practised for the last twenty years. Then they adjourn to the drawing-room, and there is more dancing, and presently it is eleven o'clock, and the party breaks up.

"You go back to-morrow then, Dennison?" Lord Dynely asks, carelessly, as they shake hands at parting.

"Yes; and you?"

"I remain two or three days longer. Carruthers wishes it, it's rather a pleasant house, and he's a good fellow. Capital quarters you have here, old man—a very seraglio of beauty."

"How do you like *her?*" Terry inquires.

"Which her? there are so many. Oh, the little queen of the revels, of course. As charming a little woodland nymph as ever I saw. My taste doesn't generally run to rustic beauties, but she's as sweet as one of her own roses. When am I to congratulate you, Terry, my boy?"

"Soon, I hope," Terry answers, with a laugh and a happy light in his eyes; and Lord Dynely looks at him with a curious smile as he rolls up a cigarette to light him on his homeward way.

She sees him to the gate—how he manages it no one can tell, but he is exceptionally clever at these things. She goes with him to the gate and gives him a shy little hand across it, the hand that wears Terry's ring.

" May I come again, Crystal ? "

Her name comes naturally and he speaks it. It fits her somehow, and Miss Higgins is a horrible cognomen for this pearl of price. What she answers, the stars and Lord Dynely alone know. It is satisfactory, doubtless, for that half-smile is still on his lips as he saunters, smoking, home.

"The most charming little fairy I've seen this many a day," he thinks. " And she is to marry Terry ; big, uncouth, lumbering Terry. It would be a sacrilege. How she blushes, and shrinks, and trembles—one sees so little of that sort of thing that its novelty charms, I suppose. One of those tender little souls whose heart a man could break as easily as I knock the ash off this cigarette."

It is midnight when he reaches the Court. He goes to his room, but not to bed. He sits staring abstractedly out, and smoking no end of cigarettes. Wonderful to relate, he is thinking. It is something which, on principle, Lord Dynely never does, but he does it to-night. The result is the writing of a letter. He flings away his last cigarette, sits down to his writing-desk, and dashes this off :

"CARRUTHERS COURT, *August 5th,* 1870.

" MY DEAR FRANCE :—Since we parted I have been think- ing over what you said, and I have come to the conclusion that you were right, that it *is* unjust and ungenerous to hold you to a compact made without your consent. I love you devotedly—that I must ever do ; but I shall never compel you to marry me if you do not love me in return. No, France, at any cost to myself, at any suffering—and that I shall suffer need I say ?—I will resign all claim to your hand. Unless you feel that the devoted affection I offer, you can return, then far be it from me to force you into a loveless union. *I* may be wretched, but you shall be free.

" I see plainly now how selfish I have been in urging my claims upon you in the past. Unless your own heart responds, believe me, they shall never be forced upon you in the future.

Write to me here—it will be less painful for both of us than a personal interview. If you can care for me, then call me back, and I will fly to you, with what joy you can imagine ; if you find you cannot, then I bow my head and submit to your decision.   "Ever devotedly,
                              "ERIC."

Here was a generous piece of composition ! Lord Dynely actually felt in a glow of admiration over his own nobility, generosity and self-sacrifice, as he sealed and addressed it. Not every man would give up the girl he loved in this heroic fashion and resign himself to life-long misery ! Not many, by Jove ! and so France must think. Only—this in some alarm—she was an odd girl ; he hoped she wouldn't feel called upon to be equally generous and insist upon accepting him whether or no.

By next morning's post this letter went off to Devonshire. The train that would take away Terry started about 12:50. A few hours later, irreproachable in the negligent elegance of his costume, Lord Dynely presented himself at the vicarage door.

They were all very jolly girls, except the three eldest, who were scraggy and old ; but Crystal was a pearl among pebbles. She improved upon acquaintance he found ; she sang for him in a sweet mezzo-soprano ; she wandered with him in the garden, and inserted one of her rose-buds in his button-hole. She was altogether delicious, and next day his lordship came again.

That evening's post brought him a letter. He turned cold as he looked at it—France's bold, firm hand, and the seal and crest of the Forresters. It looked big and square, and belligerent, and altogether formidable. Still it must be read—six crossed pages at the least, he thought with a groan. Girls never lose an opportunity of inflicting that sort of thing on their victims. He opened it. It consisted of three words—three of the shortest in the language :

          "DYNELY ABBEY, Thursday, *August 7th.*
"DEAR ERIC : *Who is she?* Affectionately.
                              "FRANCE."

N the evening of the day that was to bring Terrence Dennison to the Abbey, Lady Dynely sat
alone by her chamber window waiting. It had
been a sultry August day; the air, even now,
was oppressive, sky and atmosphere heavily charged with
that electricity which precedes a thunderstorm. In the
breathless gloaming, not a bough stirred, not a leaf trembled,
not the faintest puff of wind came to relieve the oppressed
lungs or cool the hot forehead. Lady Dynely leaned wearily against the glass. At all times pale, she was almost
ghastly in the livid twilight as she sat here. She was waiting
for Terry, and in all the years that were gone, in all the years
that were to come, she was in all probability the only
woman who had ever trembled or faltered at the approach
of Terry. It was not Terry she feared, but that which she
had to tell Terry, that which had lain on her conscience,
destroyed her peace of mind, embittered every day of her
life for the past sixteen years. A secret that, when given
into her keeping first, had been the secret of another's
wrongdoing and cruelty, but which had since become
the secret of her sin. She was a good woman, a con-
scientious woman, doing her duty to all men according
to her light; a kind mistress, charitable benefactress, a loving mother, a loyal friend. In all her life she had wilfully
wronged but one fellow-creature, and that one the man who
venerated and loved her above all women on earth—Terry.

But she was a weak woman, weak in her pride and the intensity of her love for her son. That pride and that love
had stood between her and duty, had sealed her lips, and led
her into sin. She had wronged Terry, deeply and deliberately wronged him, and she had paid the penalty in a re-

morse that never left her, that preyed on health of body and mind at once, that made her life miserable. The burden of her guilt was a burden to be borne no longer—this evening the truth should be told; then, come what might, her conscience would be free.

But it was hard—how bitterly, humiliatingly hard, only her proud heart knew. She dared not think of her dead husband, lest she should be tempted to hate his memory; she dared not think of her son, and of the passionate anger and reproach with which he would overwhelm her, should this ever reach his ears. She hardly dared think of Terry— the loyal, true-hearted lad, who trusted her so utterly, who believed in her so implicitly, whose affection and gratitude were so profound. On all sides the path was beset with thorns, but the path must be trodden.

"Help me, oh, Heaven!" was the bitter prayer of her heart; "my cross seems heavier than I can bear."

There came a step she well knew down the corridor—the step for which she waited and watched. There came a tap at the door. A moment she paused to gather strength. Then, "Come in," she said, faintly, and Dennison entered.

She shrank back into the shadow of the curtains. In the obscurity of the twilit room he could not see the fixed pallor of her face; yet something in her manner, as she sat there, startled him. He advanced and took her hand.

"There is nothing the matter?" he anxiously asked. "You are not ill?"

"I am not ill," she answered, in that faint voice. "Sit down, Terry. I am going to tell you a story to-night. I should have told you long ago, but I have been a coward— a weak and wicked coward—and I dared not—I dared not."

He seated himself on a hassock at her feet, and looked up at her in silent wonder and alarm.

"You have trusted me, Terry, been grateful to me, loved me. Ah! my poor boy! that trust and love of yours have been bitter to bear. I have deserved neither from you —nothing from you but contempt and scorn."

"Lady Dynely!"

"I have prayed for strength," she went on, "but strength did not come. I saw my duty to you and to Heaven, and to my own conscience, but I would not do it. I have concealed the truth, and gone on in secrecy and wronged you from first to last."

"Wronged me! my dear Lady Dynely!" he exclaims, in consternation. "Do you know what you are saying?"

"Ah! do I not?" she answers, bitterly. "It sounds strangely, Terry; but wait until you hvve heard all. Then you will despise me a thousand times more than you have ever loved me."

"*That* I will never do," he answered, steadily. "Tell me what you will, nothing will ever alter the affection and gratitude I feel for you. It has grown with my growth; it is part of my life; I could almost as soon lose faith in Heaven. When I cease to believe in *your* goodness I shall cease to believe in all goodness on earth."

"Don't! don't!" she says, in a voice of sharpest pain. "Wait until you hear. Terry, has it ever occurred to you to wonder why I took you from the Irish cabin and charged myself with your care and education through life?"

"Well," the young man answers, in a troubled voice, "at times—yes. But I took it for granted the meagre story I heard of myself was the true one. I am the orphan son of some distant connection of your late husband, and, in your goodness of heart, you sought me out and provided for me. That is the story, is it not?"

"Ah, no, no, no!—not the story at all. *My* goodness of heart! What bitter satire it sounds from your lips. A distant connection of my late husband! Terry—you are his son!"

"Lady Dynely!"

"His son, Terry—his elder son!"

He sat stricken mute, looking at her. Was Lady Dynely insane? What was this she was telling him? Lord Dynely's son! And then over Terry's face there came a sudden, deep, burning flush. Lord Dynely's son.—And his mother had been a peasant girl. What need to say more?—all the story was told in that.

He dropped his face in his hands like a man stunned by a blow. There are few men, even the worst, who do not venerate more or less, the memory of their mothers. To Terry's simple soul she had been a tender, idealized memory—to keep in his heart of hearts, to speak of never. And now his father had been Lord Dynely !

" Lady Dynely," he said, huskily, " why have you told me this ? "

She laid her hand upon his bowed head.

" It is not as you think, Terry," she said, sadly. " I know what you mean—it is not that. Your mother was Lord Dynely's wife, as truly as ever I was. You are Lord Dynely's son, as truly as Eric is. More—you are Lord Dynely's heir."

He scarcely heard the last words, so swift and great a rush of joy and thankfulness flooded his heart at the first.

" Thank Heaven ! " she heard him whisper ; " *that* would have been hard to bear. But—Lord Dynely's son ! Oh, Lady Dynely, pardon me, but I find this very hard to believe."

" It is a surprise, no doubt. But do you fully understand, Terry ?—You are not only Lord Dynely's son, but Lord Dynely's heir."

" His heir ? " he repeated, bewildered.

" You are three years older than Eric. Do you not see ? Your mother was Lord Dynely's wife ; you are not Terrence Dennison, but Viscount Dynely."

He lifted his head and looked at her, a sort of horror in his eyes. " And Eric is—what ? "

" Yes—what ? " Eric's mother cried, wildly. " He is Eric Hamilton—the younger son, with a portion about half of what he spends yearly for cigarettes and bouquets. You are the heir and the lord of the land ; he is the younger son and brother. That is the secret I learned to my cost sixteen years ago, by your father's death-bed—the secret of my so-called generosity to you, the secret that has poisoned and blighted my whole life. If I had been as strong in my wickedness as I am weak, I would have kept it to the end ; but that I could not do. It is told ; a load is off my soul at last; you know the truth, and my son and I are at your mercy."

Then there was long and deep silence in the room. She was sitting upright in her chair, her face gleaming out like marble in the gray gloom, her slender hands clenched together in her lap, her eyes dry and haggard, looking straight into vacancy. For Dennison, he sat stunned, absolutely stunned, trying with his whole might to realize this. His head was in a whirl. He Lord Dynely's eldest son and heir ! —not Terry Dennison, the dependant, the poor relation, but a peer of the realm ! Eric, lordly Eric, his younger brother, with no claim to the title he bore, to the thousands he squandered ! Not a powerful mind at any time, never a deep-thinking brain at best, mind and brain were in a helpless whirl now.

"Tell me all about it," was the first thing he said, in his dazed bewilderment.

She drew a long, heavy breath, and set herself to the task. The worst had been told—it was bitter almost as the bitterness of death, and yet it was easier telling Terry than telling most men. Her secret had weighed upon her so long, tortured her so unbearably, that she absolutely felt a sense of relief already.

"Tell you all ?" she repeated; "it seems very little to tell when all is told. I suppose most of life's tragedies can be told in few words—this certainly. On the night of Lord Dynely's death—sixteen years ago this very night; was it not fit to choose that anniversary ?—I learned it first myself. I recall that night so well—like no other in all my life. My cousin had come to me—you have heard of him, Gordon Caryll, poor fellow !—to tell me his story. It was a brilliant moonlight night. Arm-in-arm we walked round the fishpond, while he told me his life's tragedy, in brief, bitter words. I see it all," she said, looking before her with dewy eyes, her voice softening, "like a picture. The white light of the moon, the long, black shadows, the fish-pond like a sheet of circular glass, the scent of the flowers, and the coolness of the evening wind. There he said good-by—and he left me, my poor Gordon ! and I have never seen him since.

That man, Locksley, reminds me of him somehow; my heart warms to him whenever we meet for that chance resemblance."

She paused. She had drifted from the thread of her story, thinking of the soldier cousin from whom she had parted this night sixteen years ago.

"He left me," she continued, after that pause, "and I still lingered out there, thinking what a mistake life was for most of us, how we seem to miss the right path, where happiness lies, and love and ambition alike lead us astray. He had married for love—I for ambition; the end was the same to both—darkest, bitterest disappointment. I had never cared for Lord Dynely; he was many years my senior, and, though I never was a sentimental girl, all the liking I ever had to give had been given to Gordon Caryll. I had to do my duty as a wife in all things, but I was not a happy wife, had never been; and, when they brought me word my husband had met with an accident and lay dying, it was the horror we feel for the merest stranger who meets a tragic end that filled me, not the despairing sorrow of a loving wife.

"I hastened to him. He lay dying indeed—life was but just there when I reached him. But he was a man of most resolute will; he would *not* die until he had seen me. He had been very fond of me—ah, yes! I never doubted that, in his own selfish, passionate way, he was very fond of his wife. He had spared himself all his life, but now that he lay dying he would not spare me. Thorough and utter selfishness has ever been the chief characteristic of his race —I wonder sometimes, Terry, how you managed to escape."

She paused again and sighed. She was thinking of her son. Blindly, devotedly as she loved and admired him, she could not be utterly blind to his faults. Thoroughly and absolutely selfish all the Dynelys had been, thoroughly and utterly selfish was the last Lord Dynely.

"As I knelt by his bedside there, Terry, he told me in few and broken sentences the sad and shameful story. In his wanderings through Galway he had met Maureen Gannon, a dark, Spanish-looking beauty, as many of these Galway girls are, and, in his usual hot-headed fashion, he fell in love with her. He had been noted for running recklessly after any woman who struck his fancy his life long; another trait of his you seem to have escaped and my poor Eric to have inherited. You know what Irish girls are—the purest women under heaven—love-making that did not mean marriage was utter madness. He was mad where his own selfish gratification was concerned. He married Maureen Gannon."

Again she paused, catching her breath with a painful effort. It was quite dark now, and the rising wind, precursor of coming storm, soughed through the park. An elm just outside tapped with spectral fingers on the glass. She shuddered as she heard it, and drew closer to her silent and listening companion.

"He had called himself Dennison from the first, and under that name he married her. The ceremony was performed in the little rustic chapel by the parish priest. Of his class and friends there were naturally none present; her humble friends and family—that was all.

"He took her away at once, and they saw no more of her at home until she returned to die. She came back with you in her arms, and the story of her life was at an end. It was such an old story—hot fancy at first, cooling fancy after, coldness, indifference, utter neglect, and finally desertion. She died, and you were left, and Lord Dynely was free to woo and win another.

"I was that other. Of the girl whose heart he had broken, of his only child in poverty and neglect in Ireland, I believe he never once thought—until Eric was born, and then remorse and alarm awoke within him for the first time. She had been his lawful wife, you were his lawful son and heir. He loved me, as I say, in his selfish fashion; he also loved little Eric, and a great fear of the future of his youngest son began to come to him.

"But he told no one, he took no steps about you, he just drifted on to the end, putting all troublesome thoughts away from him, as was the habit of his life. Only when he lay dying this night, and thought that in some other world he might have to atone for the crimes of this, he turned coward —once more self became his first thought. What did it matter what became of Eric or me so that he atoned and escaped the consequences of his wrongdoing. He sent for me and told the truth.

"'You'll find it all down in writing in my desk,' he said. 'I've made a clean breast of it. The marriage certificate and the youngster's baptismal record are there too. The law might pick a flaw in an Irish marriage like that, but, Lucia, when a man comes to die he sees these things in another light from the law of the world. I couldn't meet that poor girl in the next world, as I *may*, and look her in the face, and know the wrong I've done her son. He's the heir, Lucia, mind that—not Eric, poor little beggar. And I want you to do, when I am gone, what I never had courage to do myself—the right thing by that little lad in Ireland. My first marriage must be proven, and the young one come to his rights. You are provided for in any case, as my richly dowered widow, and your boy will have a younger son's portion. But the one in Ireland, poor Maureen's boy, is the heir, mark that.'

"I knelt beside him, Terry, listening to this dreadful revelation, frozen with a horror too intense for words or tears. I have loved Eric from the day of his birth I think with fourfold mother love; he has all I had; his father did not share my heart with him, as is the happy case of most mothers. He was all I had on earth—all; and now I was called upon to stand aside, to take him with me, and give his title and estates to another woman's son. Terry," she cried out "he asked more than human nature could give."

Her voice broke in that fierce, hysterical, sobbing cry. Dennison took both her hands in his and held them in that strong but gentle clasp.

"I think he did," he answered sadly.

"He died as I knelt there," she went on, "his glazing eyes fixed threateningly on my face to the end.

"'Mind,' he said to me, 'that you see justice done. I couldn't do it; you must. I won't rest easy in my grave unless you promise. Promise me you will seek out this boy,

8

and see him righted before the world. Promise.' They
were his last words. But the promise was never gi ven—I
couldn't speak—not to save his life as well as my own. I
knelt there stunned, stupefied, dazed, soul and body. While
he still looked at me the awful death rattle sounded. His
eyes were fixed in ghastly threat on my face when the film
of death sealed them. I remember no more. Some one,
after a time, came to me, and I fell back and all was darkness.

"They buried him, and Eric and I went to the funeral as
chief mourners ! They put black on my boy ; I tore it off
in horror. Mourning for the father who had so bitterly
wronged him—no ! I wore it, but there was no mourning,
only fierce rebellion and passionate anger, in my heart.
They put up a marble tablet recording his social and
domestic virtues, and under the glowing record, '*His works
do follow him.*' Ah, yes, they followed him—in bitterness
and remorse and shame. I could have laughed aloud at the
hollow satire of it all. I believe my mind to a certain degree
gave way, my health began to fail. I had a horrible dread
of this man, dead in his grave ; that night and its revela-
tions haunted me like some ghastly nightmare. I could not
—would not obey. I trembled with horror at refusing, it
seemed so awful to deliberately disobey a dying command.
He couldn't rest easy in his grave, he had said, if I disobeyed.
A sickening, superstitious fear that he might rise from that
unquiet grave and pursue me, nearly froze me at times with
terror. I believe the struggle would have ended in insanity
if it had gone on, but the medical men ordered me to Italy
for change of air. I went to Galway instead, and found you.
The rest you know. I compromised with my conscience,
paltered with the truth. As my own son you should be reared
and educated ; share all his advantages—all but my affection. That, my poor Terry, much as you deserved it, I
could not give. The horror and hatred I was wicked enough
to feel for your father I was wicked enough to feel for you.
One day I thought, perhaps when I was dying myself I
would tell you ; meantime your life should be as easy and
pleasant as money could make it. When we are wronged,

not knowing we are wronged, our loss is nothing. Eric should never give up his title and estates to you, the son of an Irish peasant girl—his life should never be blighted at the dying command of a cruel, and selfish, and sensual father. I would *not* tell the truth.

"I have said that ten thousand times, Terry, and the years have gone on, and you are both men. His majority comes in a few days; France is to be his wife, the girl in Lincoln-shire yours. I vowed I would not tell, and I am telling. I have prayed passionate, rebellious prayers, wearied Heaven with them, to know the right, and be given strength to do it. That strength has been given to me at last—my duty is done. You know the truth—how shamefully all your life-long you have been wronged and cheated. Here are the papers Lord Dynely left; I am prepared to repeat the story in any court in England. All that seems easy, but—when I think of Eric, it breaks my heart."

Her voice died away in a choking sob. She knew so well Eric's passionate anger, his fierce rage and protest; how he would do battle to the death with his interloper; how he would, in his stormy, selfish wrath, curse the father and hate the mother. Hate her! Ay, his life long; your weak and selfish men are good haters always. Why had she not held her tongue?—how dared she speak?—what were the cowardly dying fears of ten thousand fathers to his birthright? Was this her pretended love for him? Let it end how it might he would never forgive her, never see her face again. She knew what would follow as well as she knew that she sat here.

She placed a packet in Terry's hand. He loosened his clasp of hers and took it in dead silence. Even he, she thought in her bitter despair, was turning against her already. And this is what it was to do one's duty.

"There is no more to tell," she said, in a stifled voice. "Go away, Terry, and leave me alone."

He arose, but lingeringly, and stood looking at her. In the deep darkness that now filled the room he could see but the outline of her figure and the white, rigid gleam of her face.

"I don't know what to say yet," he began, in a con-strained voice, that did not sound like Terry's. "I feel stunned and stupefied. My head is in a muddle. It is all so strange. You will give me to-night to think it over—will you not?"

"What have I to do with it?" she answered, huskily. "All is in your own hands now. You are master. You are Lord Dynely."

"You are not angry with me?" he asked, wistfully, still hesitating.

It was a question he had asked her many times in his life, when her look of half-concealed dislike had repelled and chilled him, and he had wondered timidly what he had done to vex her. Its wistful, boyish pathos and simplicity went to her heart now.

"Angry with you!" she said, with a sob. "Oh my Terry! you never gave me cause for anger in all your life."

"I am glad of that," he said, simply; "I hope I never will. And, Lady Dynely," hesitating again, "my opinion cannot matter to you, of course; but I hope you feel, I want you to feel, that I don't blame you in all this. I understand how you must have felt—it was too much to ask of any mother—you would have been more than mortal to have acted as he commanded you."

She only looked up at him in the darkness with sad, hope-less eyes. "*You* would have done it, Terry," she said.

"No—I don't know. I am not very heroic, and it requires heroism to do these things. I am an awkward, blundering sort of fellow, not much like Eric, but I think I could more easily die than deliberately wrong any one I cared for to gratify myself. You know what I mean, Lady Dynely. Don't grieve too much over this; I can't bear to see you in trouble. All will go well yet. Eric—Eric does not know, of course?"

"Not yet! oh, not yet! *That* will be the hardest to bear of all."

He knelt on one knee, and for the first time in all his life touched his lips to her cheek.

"Mother," he said, and love made Terry's voice like an

angel's, "mother, the best friend, the truest, man ever had, don't grieve. All will go well. To-night I will think it over—to-morrow we will make an end of it forever."

Then he arose softly and left her.

CHAPTER IX.

THINKING IT OUT.

HAT night, for the first time in the four-and-twenty years of his life, Terry Dennison set up until the " wee sma' hours ayont the twal," and thought. Thought!—of all novel experiences, this surely was the most novel in this supremely thoughtless young man's life. The good or the evil of Terry's life, and there had been much of both, had alike been unpremeditated ; in all things he had acted naturally and involuntarily, and without thinking of it beforehand. Now in a moment he was called upon to settle the destinies of four lives—his own, Eric's, Lady Dynely's and little Crystal's. A sort of smile came over his face as he thought of it—he the arbitrator of brilliant Eric's whole future life—he, Terry.

But the smile quickly faded as he entered the room and laid the little packet her ladyship had given him down upon the table, and looked at the yellow paper, the faded writing. The father who had wronged him so greatly, who had so irreparably wronged his mother, and written this—had striven to do him justice when that justice could no longer annoy himself. He had served Satan all his life, and would make his peace with Heaven at the last, at any sacrifice to those left behind. He had lived a life of sin and sensualism, and would offer the dregs of that bad life to his Creator. There was more a feeling of disgust in Terry's breast than any other as he looked at the faded writing and thought of him who had written it, dust and ashes years ago.

" And his works do follow him ! "

He sat down and looked blankly before him. He was Lord Dynely's elder son ; no longer plain, impecunious

Terry Dennison, a dependant on a great lady's bounty, but
Viscount Dynely, with estates and mansions in half a
dozen counties, a villa at Ryde, a rent-roll as long as his
lineage. And he could make Crystal, Lady Dynely. His
face flushed for a moment at that. All that might be spread
before him, a glittering vista. He was one of the least
mercenary of men, but he had lived too long in the world
not to know the great and utter change it would make in
his life. One of the oldest titles in the United Kingdom,
one of the noblest incomes—that is what he was called
upon to claim or resign to-night. For a moment, as he
thought of it, his heart beat quick. He was very human
after all, and this was no child's toy he must lay down or
take up. Men called Terry Dennison a good fellow—
rather a simple soul, perhaps, but a good fellow all the
same. He had few enemies and many friends, but in their
liking for him there was more or less blended a slight
shade of contempt. He was one of them, but not of them.
His manners and habits were primitive to a degree. He
wasn't a "plunger," as they were to a man; didn't drink, to
speak of; didn't gamble at all; hunted down no woman,
married or single, to her own destruction. He was behind
his age in all these things, in a most remarkable degree.
Still men liked him, and laughed with Terry, and at Terry,
and never carried their laughter too far. He was the soul
of good-nature, but there was that in his six feet of stature,
his trained muscles, and scientific British way of "hitting
out straight from the shoulder," on occasions, that commanded respect. In the annual battles between "Town
and Gown," at Oxford, Dennison had ever been a host in
himself. In all athletic and field sports he stood his own
with the best of them. He was a "mighty hunter before the
lord," down in the shires ; but in the ball-room and the boudoir, at court and at courting, Terry was decidedly a failure.
He never lost his heart for barronne or ballerina, duchess or
actress ; he ran away with no man's wife, wasn't a fascinating sinner of any sort. He had his failings, they were many
—he had his virtues, they were many too, and generosity
stood chief among them. To give pain to a woman, to *any*

woman—to a woman he loved and venerated, as he did
Lady Dynely, would have been impossible to him; and in
asserting this claim before the world he would simply break
Lady Dynely's heart.

Wrong had been done.   Yes; but, to Terry's mind, hardly
by her.   She loved her handsome son, as few sons ever deserve to be loved, and Eric Hamilton certainly did not.
How, then, loving him, could she deliberately, and at the
command of a selfish and cowardly husband, hand over his
birthright to a stranger, and blight his whole life?   Lord
Dynely had asked too much; it was not in frail human
nature to do it.   He had been wronged, but not by her.
Why, she might have left him all his life in that Irish cabin
by the wild Galway coast, to drag out the wretched, unlettered life of a peasant.   Who then would have been the
wiser?   But she had come for him, and in all things done
by him as her own son.   And now, at last, she had told him
all, and, at all cost to herself, was ready to prove the truth
of her words.   Then his thoughts drifted to Eric.   He saw
Eric's rage and fury as plainly as he saw the paper on the
table, the blue eyes lurid with rage, the fair, womanish face
crimson with anger and rebellion.   Eric would do battle to
the death, would contest every inch of the ground.   The
sympathy would be with Eric; possession, the "nine points
of the law," would be with Eric; the glory and the power
were Eric's;—what chance would he stand?   There would
be an endless chancery suit, the kingdom would ring with
the scandal, the informal Irish marriage would be contested;
perhaps in the eye of the law, proven no marriage at all.
And, meantime, Lady Dynely would have broken her heart
at the shame and publicity, and ended her part of the tragedy.   No, had he been ever so inclined, as selfishly bent on
his own interests as Eric himself, the thing was impossible
on the face of it.   But he was not.   It was really very little
of a sacrifice to him.   He had no ambition whatever—he
was, I have said, a most commonplace young man.   Life as
he held it contented him.   With his commission, his five
hundred a year, and Crystal for his wife, the world might
wag; he asked no more of fate.

With a long-drawn breath he broke from his reverie ; with a motion of his hand he seemed to dismiss the whole thing at once and forever.

He lit a cigar, opened the little packet and looked at the papers. The marriage certificate, the record of his baptism, his father's brief, terse confession of his own marriage to the Galway girl, under the name of Dennison. He read them all gravely and tied them up again.

"Poor soul," he thought, "it was hard lines on *her*. No, my Lord Dynely, you did harm enough in your lifetime ; we won't let you do any more in your grave."

He rose up, went to the open window and smoked away meditatively. What was Crystal doing? Ah, asleep no doubt, little darling, his ring on her finger and thoughts of him in her heart. He would go down to-morrow, and tell her what had been in *his* heart so long. He could see the dear little face, dimpling and smiling, and blushing, hear the dear little voice faltering forth its tender confession, and Terry's whole soul was in one glow of love and gratitude and rapture. How happy he would make her life, how devotedly he would cherish his little stainless lily, how sweet it would be to care for her, and devote his whole existence to her. Yes, to-morrow he would go down, and before Christmas they would be married, and then—well, Terry was not imaginative—and then they would live happy forever after.

Mr. Dennison was not an early riser. The early bird that catches the worm was no kin of his. All the clocks and watches of Dynely were sharply marking the hour of one, when, in freshest morning toilet, shaven and shorn, he presented himself before Lady Dynely.

"My dear Lady Dynely," he began, and there stopped.

Good Heaven ! what a ghastly, terrified face he saw. White with a pallor like death, lips blue and parched, eyes haggard and hopeless. She had slept not at all—she had spent the whole night in fevered pacing to and fro, half maddened at the thought of what she had done, of what might be. The world would know. Eric would know— there lay the bitterness of death. Terry was generous, but

8*

to her the generosity that would hide this 'from the world looked more than mortal.

She stood up and confronted him, one hand holding by her chair, her haggard eyes fixed upon his face. So might look a terrified woman waiting for sentence of death. She tried to speak—her dry lips trembled, only a husky sound came.

He was by her side in a moment, holding both hands fast in his, full of pity and remorse. How she had suffered. Why had he kept her in suspense even for a single night? How little she knew him, when she could fear him like this. It gave him a pang of absolute pain.

" Lady Dynely—my dearest mother—you did not think I could ever use the secret you told me last night? If you did, then you have certainly wronged me. I loved you too well, Eric too well, ever to dream of such shameful, selfish ingratitude. Look here ! "

He drew out the packet, took a match, struck it, and touched it to a corner of the paper, then threw it in the grate.

She uttered a gasping cry—a cry he never forgot—then stood spellbound.

With fascinated eyes both watched the paper shrivel, then blaze up, then a cloud of black drift floated up the chimney, and the record of the Irish marriage was at an end.

"With that ends our secret," Terry said. " Living or dying, a word of what you told me will never pass my lips."

She fell heavily forward, her arms around his neck, her face on his shoulder, shaking from head to foot with dry, hysterical sobbing. He held her close; neither spoke a word, and there were tears big and bright in Terry's round blue eyes. Then very gently he put her back in her chair and knelt down before her.

" Don't," he said, pleadingly ; " it hurts me to hear you. How could you think I would do what you feared? What a wretch you must have thought me."

" A wretch ! Oh, my Terry, my Terry ! You are more an angel than a man ! "

Terry laughed. It was all very solemn, but the idea of Terry Dennison in the rôle of angel, tickled the dragoon's lively sense of the ludicrous, and that merry schoolboy laugh of his pealed forth.

"I beg your pardon, Lady Dynely," Terry said, struggling manfully with that explosion ; "that's a little too good. You are the first, I give you my word, who ever accused me of angelic qualities. And I don't deserve it—oh, I assure you I don't—it isn't any sacrifice to me. I am not an ambitious sort of fellow, nor a clever fellow, nor a brilliant fellow, like Eric. As a dragoon, with five hundred a year and the dearest little girl in England for my wife, I am a round peg, fitting neat and trim in a round hole. As a nobleman, with title and estates, and the *noblesse oblige* business to do, I would be an object of pity to gods and men. Eric was born a darling of fortune ; I was born—plain Terry Dennison."

She looked at him with sad, yearning, wondering eyes. Her arms still loosely clasped his neck as he knelt before her.

"Plain Terry Dennison !" she repeated ; "Terry, you are the stuff heroes are made of. Eric is not like you—ah, if he only were ! Where did you get this generous heart, this great, grateful soul of yours ? You have your father's face—ay, you are like him to the very color of his hair. You have his face—Eric, I fear—I fear his heart."

"Oh, Eric isn't half a bad fellow," responded Terry, uneasily. He was uncommonly fond of Lady Dynely, but he was only a man, and the heroics were becoming a little too much for him. "Don't let's talk about it any more. Let all be as though you had never told, as though I were in reality what I have all along considered myself—a distant connection of a very grand family. If—," Terry's head drooped a little and his color rose—"if it makes you ever so little fonder of me, Lady Dynely, then, as the goody sort of novels say, ' I shall not have labored in vain.' "

She bent forward and kissed him, for the first time in her life, as fondly as she might have kissed Eric.

"Who could help being fond of you, Terry ? That girl

in Lincolnshire is a happy and fortunate girl, indeed I know you are dying to go back to her, but just at present I feel as though I could not let you out of my sight. My wonderful good fortune, your wonderful generosity, seem altogether unreal. If I lose you I shall doubt and fear, and grow wretched again. My nerves are all unstrung. Stay with me yet a few days, Terry—the happiness of your life is all before you—until I have learned to realize how blessed I am."

It was a far greater sacrifice, had she but known it, than the sacrifice he made in resigning all claim to title and fortune. But he made it promptly and gratefully.

"I will remain a week," he said; "as I have waited so long, a few more days will not signify."

He wrote down to Lincolnshire. A week would pass before he could be with them, but he was surely coming, and meantime he was " Hers devotedly, Terry."

The order of release came at last. Armed with his ring, a half-hoop of diamonds to fit the dearest little engagement finger on earth, Mr. Dennison started, one bright August morning, on his way. The birds were singing, the sun was shining, the grass was as green as though it had been painted and varnished, the sky was without a cloud. So was his sky, Terry thought; and in faultless summer costume, looking happy and almost handsome, his long limbs stretched across on the opposite cushions of the railway carriage, he was whirled away to Starling vicarage.

> " A frog he would a wooing go
> Whether his mother would let him or no,"

hummed Terry, unfolding that morning's *Daily Telegraph*. " I wonder what my precious little girl is about just now! And, by the bye, I should like to know why Eric doesn't come home. Egad! I should think France wouldn't like it—home for an evening and off again, and stopping away over two weeks. Is he at Carruthers' still, and what's the dear boy's little game now, I wonder? "

What, indeed ?

ITH that brilliant light of the August afternoon pouring down over everything like amber rain, Mr. Dennison opened the little wicket gate and made his way into the vicarage. It was all ablaze with double roses, and honeysuckle, and verbena, and geranium, and fuchsia, and the summer air was sweet with drifts of perfume. All the windows and doors of the vicarage stood open, but a Sabbath silence reigned. As his lofty six feet darkened the parlor doorway, the only occupant of that apartment looked up from her sewing with a little surprised scream. It was the eldest and scraggiest of the three elder Misses Higgins.

"Lor !" cried Miss Higgins, "what a turn you gave me. Is it you, Terry? Who'd have thought it? Come in. You see I wasn't expecting anybody to-day, and all the rest are off but Belinda and me, and—"

"Off !" cried Terry, blankly ; " off where, Arabella?"

"Off to the picnic. Oh, I forgot, you don't know. Sir Philip Carruthers, Lord Dynely, and some of the gentlemen stopping at the Court, have organized a picnic, and all the rest have gone. I and Belinda were invited, but some one must stay home and do the work, while the others gad. Belinda's in the kitchen, making jam—I'm sewing for Crystal. It's always the way," said the elder Miss Higgins, bitterly ; " ' this little pig goes to market, and this little pig stays at home.' I've been the one to stay at home all my life."

"Where's the picnic, Bella ?" asked Terry, briskly.

For a moment—a moment only—he had felt inclined to be disappointed at this contretemps ; now it was all right again.

" At Carruthers Court, of course," Bella answered. "They
have had no end of water parties, and garden parties, and
croquet parties, and junketings since you went away. Crystal's growing a regular gadabout, and so I tell mamma. A
chit of a child like that ought to be in the nursery for the
next two years, instead of flirting and carrying on with gentlemen in the way she does. I never did such a thing when
I was a—oh, he's off. Another of little missy's victims, I
suppose. What fools men are."

The eldest Miss Higgins, aged thirty-five, was not vicious,
as a rule, but the blind neglect of mankind during the last
fifteen years had rather soured the milk of human kindness
in her vestal bosom. She went back to her sewing, and
Terry went to the picnic.

The walk was a long one, the afternoon, as I have before
remarked, hot. The summer fields lay steeped in sunshine,
the scarlet poppies nodding in the faint breeze. Terry's
complexion was the hue of the poppies by the time he
reached the festal ground. Tents and marquees everywhere
dotted the sward ; the military brass band discoursed sweet
music beneath the umbrageous foliage ; archery, croquet,
dancing and other sports, in which the youthful and frivolous
mind delights, were going on. Girls in white, girls in blue,
girls in pink, girls in lilac and green, dotted the velvet sward
like gorgeous posies, but the girl of his heart Mr. Dennison
could nowhere behold.

" Ah, Terry, my lad," said the Rev. Samuel Higgins, ex-
tending one clerical hand in a black thread glove, "how are
you ? When did you come ? "

" Just now. Where's—I mean where are the girls ? "

"Amelia, and Josephine, and Emiline are yonder, engaged in archery ; Cornelia and Victoria are playing croquet ; Evangeline is with her mother, and Elizabeth Jane
was with me a moment ago. Arabella and Belinda are at
home," answered calmly the Reverend Samuel.

" I saw Bella. Where's Crystal ? " asked Mr. Dennison, in
desperation.

" Crystal is—ahem ! " said the Reverend Mr. Higgins,
looking meekly about through his spectacles. " I don't

see Crystal. Elizabeth Jane, my child, where is Christa
bel?"

"Crissy's gone off for a sail with Lord Dynely, pa," answered in a pert tone the seventh Miss Higgins, with a sharp
glance at Mr. Dennison. "If you want to find them, Terry,
I'll guide you."

Elizabeth Jane took Mr. Dennison's arm and led him
briskly across meadows, down woody slopes, to where, between two sloping hills, a broad mere, a miniature lake, lay.
And there, half-way out, went floating a little white boat like
a great water lily, and in that boat a young gentleman and a
young lady sat.

"That's Criss," said Elizabeth Jane, sharply, "and that's
Lord Dynely. I don't know what Lord Dynely's intentions
may be, but if I were pa I would ask."

Terry's face flushed. He turned suddenly and looked at
her with a sharp contraction of the heart.

"What do you mean, Lizy Jane?"

"This," said the seventh and sharpest of the Misses Higgins, "that Lord Dynely comes a great deal too often to the
vicarage, and pays a great deal too marked attention to our
Criss for an engaged man. He is an engaged man, isn't he,
Terry?"

"Yes—no—I don't know—Elizabeth Jane, you don't
mean to say that Crystal has—has"—his ruddy complexion turned white—"fallen in love with Lord Dynely?"

"I don't know anything about it," retorted Elizabeth Jane,
still sharply; "I don't go mooning about myself, reading
novels and poetry books, week in and week out; I have my
district visiting, and Bible society, and Dorcas meetings to
attend. I don't know anything about falling in love and
that sentimental rubbish," says Elizabeth Jane, her black
eyes snapping; "but I do know, if I were pa, I'd not have
a gay young nobleman loafing about my house from morning until night, flirting with my prettiest daughter, taking
moonlight rambles, and sunlight rambles, and early morning
rambles, and lying on the grass at her feet for hours at a
stretch, reading Meredith and Tennyson, and holding skeins
of silk for 'her, and singing duets with her, and—bah!" says

Elizabeth Jane, with snappishness, "if pa had three pairs of glasses he wouldn't see what goes on under his nose."

"And they carry on like this!" Terry asked, in blank dismay.

"Like this! You ought to see them. You can't so much as mention his name to Crystal but she blushes to the roots of her hair. I've told pa, Bella's told pa—what's the use? 'Tut, tut, tut, children; let the little one enjoy herself. He's only a good looking boy, she's only a child.' That's what pa says. Queer sort of child's play, I think. And ma, she's worse. We all know what ma thinks, that she'll have a 'my lady,' for her daughter. I've no patience with such folly!" cries the practical and matter-of-fact Miss Elizabeth Jane Higgins.

Terry stands dead silent. The ruddy heat has faded out of his complexion, leaving him very pale. He looks with blank eyes at the shining water. The little white boat has turned a wooded bend and disappeared. Crystal is singing now.

Her sweet voice comes to them where they stand. The clear tenor tones of Dynely blend presently with hers. They stand silent both, until the last note of the music dies away.

"Come," says Elizabeth Jane, looking up in Terry's face, and not without a touch of compassion in her own. She likes Terry; she is engaged to the Rev. Edwin Meeke, her father's curate, whose name but faintly sets forth his nature, and can afford to be sisterly and practical, and her liking for the big dragoon is beyond reproach. "Only if you're a friend of Miss France Forrester and our Crystal, drop Lord Dynely a hint to make his vicarage visits more like angels', few and far between."

She leads him back. But the glory has gone out of the heavens, the beauty from the earth. The sun no longer shines, or if it does, it shineth not on Terry. For the first time in his life he is jealous. Elizabeth Jane does with him as she pleases. She holds his arm and leads him about, and talks to him in her sharp little staccato voice of the house "Mr. Meeke" is furnishing—of the poor of the parish—of her schools and societies, and it all falls dead flat on Terry's ears. He hears as he might hear the drowsy ripple of a mill stream—he comprehendeth not. "Crystal and Eric—Eric and Crystal," these united names ring the changes over and over and over again in his dazed brain.

"There they are!" cries Elizabeth Jane, with another vicious snap of the little dark eyes. "Pretty pair, aren't they?"

The seventh Miss Higgins did not mean it in that sense, but they *were* a pretty pair. They came together over the grass. Eric, tall, languid, elegant, handsome, in faultless summer costume, a straw hat pulled over his eyes; Crystal, in pale rose-pink gauze, a little straw flat tilted over her pretty Grecian nose, and a bunch of big fragrant water lilies in her hand. It was a specialty of the prettiest Miss Higgins that you rarely saw her except covered with floral decorations. They espied Elizabeth Jane and her escort, and Crystal gave a little nervous start and gasp for breath.

"Oh!" she said, in that frightened whisper, "it is Terry!"

"Ah, ya-as—so it is, Terry," drawled Lord Dynely, putting up his eye-glass. "Where did he drop from? I say, little 'un, how are you?"

He sauntered up to Terry with the words, and held out one languid hand. Terry took it, and dropped it, as if it burned him. For the first time the sight of Lady Dynely's son gladdened neither his eyes nor his heart.

"Didn't expect you, you know. Glad to see you all the same. Awfully warm work travelling it must have been. Just come?"

"Just come," Terry responded, coldly, his eyes fixed on Crystal's face. That face was flushed and drooping; the shy, averted glance, the shy, reluctant hand, smote him to the heart.

"You are well, Crystal?" he said. "You received my letter?"

"Oh, yes, thank you."

It is always Miss Crystal's formula when greatly embarrassed, and then she stood blushing and downcast, tracing figures on the grass with her white parasol.

"You don't ask after them at home, Dynely," said Terry, looking at him ; "your mother or Miss Forrester ? "

"Don't I ? It's too warm to ask for anything or any-body at an August picnic. Thanks for your reminder. How are my mother and Miss Forrester ? "

There was a certain defiance in the coolly insolent glance of Eric's blue eyes, a certain defiance in the lazy drawl with which he repeated Terry's words.

"They are well—wondering a little though what can keep you so long in foreign parts. You were to be back in a week."

"Was I ? I find my constitution won't stand the wear and tear of a perpetual express train. And really, on the whole, I think I prefer Lincolnshire to Devonshire."

Then he turns and says something in a lower tone to Crystal, at which she laughs nervously, puts her hand within his arm, and turns to go.

"Ta, ta, Terry !" he says. "Amuse yourself well, only don't make your attentions to Elizabeth Jane too marked, else the Reverend Edwin, lamb-like as he is, may turn jeal-ous. And jealousy is a frightful monster to admit into the human heart."

They saunter away together as they came, and Elizabeth Jane's black eyes snap again as they look after them.

"There !" she says, " what do you think of that ? "

"I think I shall go and have some claret cup, if there is any going," is Dennison's response. "I see Mr. Meeke coming, 'Liza Jane. You'll excuse me, won't you ? "

He hardly waits for 'Liza Jane's stiff "Oh, certainly." He rushes off, takes a long draught from the iced silver tankard, but all the claret cup that ever was iced will not cool the fire of love and jealousy that is raging within Terry. He wanders away, he doesn't know where—anywhere, anywhere out of the world. Presently he finds himself far removed from the braying brass band, and sight and sound of the picnicers, and flings himself face downward in the warm scented summer grass.

He has lost Crystal!

Ay, lost her; though Eric should be playing his old game of fast and loose with girls' hearts, wooing them this hour with his charming grace and debonnaire beauty, to throw them away the next, Crystal is lost to him all the same. If her heart has gone to Dynely or any other man, then she goes with it. The heart that comes to him for life must have held no other lodger. And she loves Eric—it has ever been an easy thing for all women to do that—he has seen it in the first glance of her eyes, in the first flush of her cheek. And Eric—what does Eric mean?

" By heaven!" Terry thinks, his eyes flashing, "he shall not play with her, as he has done with so many. He shall not win her love only to fling it contemptuously away; he shall not woo her, and tire of her, and spoil her life, and break her heart as he has done with others. I'll kill him with my own hand first."

The day wanes, the sun sets, the stars come out, the evening wind arises. Terry gets up cold and pale, and looking as unlike Terry as can well be conceived, and returns to the merry-makers. Dancing is going on by the white light of the stars, in the great canvas tent, the band blares forth a German waltz, and little Crystal is floating round and round like a whiff of eider-down in Lord Dynely's practised arms. He sees Terry, and smiles a curious sort of smile to himself. If Terry's purpose in coming were printed on his forehead it could not be plainer reading to Lord Dynely. He has seen his state from the first, he knows as well as the dragoon himself, that he has come down to Starling Vicarage to woo and win the flower of the flock. And Eric's arm tightens around Crystal's slim, pink waist, his blue eyes look with an intolerable light of triumph down into her fair, childish face.

" She shall never belong to him—to any man but me," he thinks. " I will speak to-night, or that over-grown dragoon will to-morrow."

His fancy for Crystal has never cooled, never for a moment. He loves her—or thinks he does—with his whole heart. She will not be half so creditable a wife as France, he feels that he will tire of that sweet, shy, dimpling baby face a month after marriage; still—have her he must and shall. Opposition and a rival have but fired him; come what will, this little village beauty shall be his wife. This very evening he will speak.

The waltz ends; he draws her away with him, from the dancing booth, out into the white, star-gemmed twilight. She is ever willing to go—to ends of the earth, so that he leads the way. She has been living in a trance of bliss ever since she saw Lord Dynely first.

"Oh, what a day it has been!" she sighs, swinging her hat by its rosy ribbons, and looking up at the star-studded sky; "I never enjoyed myself so much in my life."

"Particularly since Terry Dennison has come!" puts in his lordship.

"Oh, Lord Dynely!—Terry! as if I cared for Terry!" Crystal says, with a pretty, petulant gesture.

"No? You are sure, Crystal? You don't care for Terry?"

"Lord Dynely, you know I don't."

"Then you do care for some one else. Who is it, little one? Such hosts of lovers you have. You don't know how madly jealous I have been before now."

She glances up at him quickly, almost angrily, to see if he is in earnest. Eyes and lips are smiling—he is looking at her with a gaze she cannot meet. She flushes rosy red and shrinks from him ever so little. Then all at once he speaks.

"I love you, Crystal," he says; "I want you to be my wife."

*   *   *   *   *   *   *   *   *

It is an hour later. The picnicers are beginning to disperse. Lord Dynely is to drive Miss Crystal home in his phaeton. Everybody is thronging to their carriages when they return to the starting spot.

What a face Crystal wears! transfigured with bliss. Lord Dynely is, as he ever is, cool, languid, self-possessed, and outwardly at least, a trifle bored. But in the phaeton, alone with Crystal, he is not in the least bored.

"I shall speak to the dear old dad to-morrow," he is saying. " Of course we know what the answer will be. And I must get you an engagement ring. Let's see ; give me this little blue and white concern as a guide."

" Oh ! " Crystal cries, a sudden pain in her voice, " Terry gave me that ! "

" Did he ? " said Dynely, coolly, abstracting it and putting it in his waistcoat pocket; " then we'll return it to Terry, and he can give it to Victoria, or Evangeline, or Josephine, or any of the rest he fancies. You wear no man's ring but mine henceforth forever."

CHAPTER XII.

HEY spend a very pleasant evening at the vicarage and end a delightful day in a very delightful manner. Delightful at least to Crystal and her lordly lover. They show little outward sign of the rapture within; but Crystal's eyes keep that radiant light of great joy, and there is a half smile of exultation and triumph in Eric's. They drink tea out of their egg-shell china, and partake of lemon cakes and thin bread and butter, and Crystal trips down to the gate, by her lover's side.

"I will be here to-morrow as early as common decency will allow, little one," he says, taking the pretty dimpled face between both his hands, "for that private interview with papa. Good-night, 'queen rose of the rosebud garden of girls,' and dream of me."

Will she not? She watches him out of sight. How handsome he is! A very king among men! How noble, how great, how good! So far above her, yet stooping in his wonderful condescension to love her and make her his wife. Oh, what a thrice-blessed girl she is! Surely some beneficent fairy must have presided at her birth that she should be thus chosen the elect of the gods.

Then she is aroused from her reverie, for the Rev. Edwin and Elizabeth Jane are crunching over the gravel behind her.

"Are you going to stay mooning here all night, Crystal?" sharply inquires the elder sister. "Do you know that the dew is falling, and that your dress is grenadine? Where is *he*?"

"Lord Dynely has gone," Crystal answers, gently. "Good-night, Mr. Meeke," and then she lifts two lovely, compassionate eyes to Mr. Meeke's face.

Poor little fellow, she thinks, what a life Elizabeth Jane will lead him, and how different her life is ordered from poor, plain Elizabeth Jane's. She feels a great pity for them both, so hum-drum and commonplace their wooing is ; a great pity for the whole other eight, so far less blessed than she.

"What have I ever done that I should be so happy ? " she muses. "What can I ever do to prove how thankful and grateful I am ? "

She stops and recoils, a swift flush of pain and shame darkens her lily-leaf face, for, tall and dark, Terry looms up before her.

"I've had no chance to say a word to you all day, Crystal," he says, trying to speak cheerfully. "You have been so completely monopolized by Dynely. It is a lovely night—let us take a turn around the garden ? "

"What—at twelve o'clock ? Oh, Terry !" she laughs, "I am dead tired besides after the picnic. Some other time. Good-night."

She flies up the stairs lightly, a small roseate vision, kisses her hand to him from the upper landing, and disappears.

The Rev. Mr. Higgins' nine daughters are paired off two by two. It is Crystal's misfortune to be billeted with Elizabeth Jane. And when Elizabeth Jane comes up, half an hour later, and finds her " mooning" again, sitting, leaning out of the window, heedless of dew and grenadine, the window is closed with asperity, and Miss Crystal ordered peremptorily to "have done fooling and go to bed."

She goes, she even sleeps, but she wakes early, to find the sun of another lovely day flooding her chamber, and a hundred little birds trilling a musical accompaniment without, to Elizabeth Jane's short, rasping snores within. Again Crystal thinks of the Rev. Edwin, and laughs and shudders as she looks at Elizabeth Jane asleep, with her mouth open, and pities him with unutterable pity. Yesterday's bliss comes back to her as she springs lightly out of bed and dresses. To-day he is coming to ask papa—in two or three hours at most he will be here. She sings softly as she dresses, for very gladness of heart, and flies lightly down the stairs, and out into the fresh, sweet summer morning.

All within is still and asleep, all without is awake and full of jubilant life. The roses turn their crimson, pink and snowy faces up to that cloudless sky, a hundred choirs of birds pour forth their matin song ; over all the sun rises in untold Summer splendor. Involuntarily Mendelssohn's Hymn of Praise rises to her lips—" Let all that hath life and breath sing to the Lord."

She runs down to the gate and leans over it, still singing. Her song reaches another early riser, lounging aimlessly against an elm near by, smoking a matinal cigar. He starts, flings the cigar away, and crashes through the dewy Lincoln-shire grass to join her. It is Terry. Who else in that house-hold of women smokes regalias at five in the morning ?"

Terry has not slept well—has not slept at all—and looks haggard and anxious in this brilliant morning light. He pulls his straw hat farther over his eyes to exclude the dazzling sun, and sees Crystal's sweet face cloud, and hears her glad song die away as he joins her. A nervous, troubled look fills the gentle eyes, the loveliest, he thinks, on earth.

" You were always an early riser, Crystal," he says, with a faint smile. " I see you keep up your good habits. I hope you have quite slept away yesterday's fatigue."

" Oh, yes, thank you," replies Miss Crystal. " I hope your dreams were pleasant, Terry ? "

" I neither slept nor dreamed at all," Terry answers, gravely.

She glances up at him shyly, then turns away and begins pulling nervously at the sweetbrier growing over the gate. He takes one of the little destructive hands and holds it fast, and looks at the finger upon which he had placed the pearl and turquoise ring. " It is gone," he says, blankly.

She snatches her hand away, half-frightened, half-petulant, and says nothing.

" You promised to wear it, Crystal."

" I beg your pardon, Terry, I did not. You put it there, and I wore it until—"

" Until—go on, Crystal." ·

But she will not, it seems. She turns farther from him and tears the sweetbrier sprays wantonly.

"Until when, Crystal? Answer me."

"Until last night, then."

"And what became of it last night?"

He tries to see her face, but she holds it low over the fragrant blossoms, and is silent again.

"Crystal! Crystal!" he cries out; "what does it all mean? Who removed my ring?"

Then all at once she turns at bay and looks at him full.

"Lord Dynely took it last night. He had a right to take it. I can wear no man's ring but his all the days of my life. I will give it to you back to-day. I—I don't want to hurt you, Terry, but—I love *him*."

Her courage dies away as quickly as it came. She grows crimson all over her pearl-white face, and returns once more to the suffering sweetbrier.

For Terry—he stands as a man who receives his deathblow—white, mute. And yet he has expected it—has known it. Only that does not seem to make it any the easier now.

The silence frightens her. She steals a look at him, and that look frightens her more.

"Oh, Terry, don't be angry," she falters, the ready tears springing to her eyes. "How could I help it? How could I—how could any one help loving him?"

"No," Terry answers, a curious stiffness about his lips, a curious hardness in his tone; "you could not help it. I might have known it. You are only a child—I thought you a woman. You could not help it; but he—by Heaven, he's a villain!"

She started up—stung into strength by that.

"It is false!" she cried out, passionately. "How dare you, Terry Dennison! You say to me behind his back what you dare not say to his face. He is the best and noblest man that ever lived."

He turned and looked at her. He caught both her hands, and the blue eyes looked up fearless and flashing into his own.

"You love him, Crystal?"

9

"With my whole heart—so well that if I lost him I should die."

"And he—he tells you he loves you, I suppose?"

"He tells me, and I know it. I know it as surely and truly as I stand here."

He dropped her hands and turned from her, leaning his folded arms across the pillar of the gate.

"He tells you, and you know it! I wonder how many score my Lord Dynely has told that same story to in his one-and-twenty years of life? We live in a fast age, but I doubt if many men go quite so fast as that. I wonder what France Forrester will say to all this?"

The angry color faded out of her face, the angry light died out of her eyes. She stood looking at him, growing ashen gray. She had utterly forgotten that.

"Miss Forrester!" she responded, slowly; "I forgot! I forgot! And last night he told me—he told me——"

"He told you nothing about her, I'll swear!" Dennison said, with a short, mirthless laugh: "that it has been an understood thing from his boyhood that he was to marry her; that he returned home three weeks ago to ask her to be his wife; that he *did* ask her, beg her, entreat her, and that she sent him down here out of the way, pending her final answer; that if that answer be favorable they are to be married next spring in London. His mother told me. Whatever he told you last night, Crystal, I am quite sure he did not tell you this."

"No," she said, in a voice like a whisper, her very lips blanched—"he did not tell me this."

"There is one fortunate circumstance about it," the young man went on; "he is a villain, but he won't break her heart. Incredible it may seem to you, but all the beauty and attraction of your demi-god are quite thrown away upon her. She doesn't care for him. She knows him to be weaker and more unstable than water—the frailest of all broken reeds for any woman to lean on—and will rejoice accordingly at being rid of him. But for you, Crystal—you're not the first, nor the hundred-and-first, he has sworn undying love to; and you'll not be the last, that *I* swear, if you give him a chance. If you care for Lord Eric Dynely, and want to keep him, why, then, marry him out of hand—strike while the iron is hot."

She said not a word. White and still she stood, all life and color stricken out of eyes and face by his words.

As he looked at her the bitterness died out of his own soul in compassion and remorse.

" Oh, Crystal, forgive me ! " he said. " I-am a brute ! I ought not to say such things to you. But—I loved you so —I have loved you all my life. I trusted you, and I trusted him."

It was more than she could bear—her own pain and his. She turned hastily away, down one of the garden paths, and vanished.

The day was six hours older—the vicarage clocks were striking eleven—as Lord Dynely dismounted from " his red roan steed " at the vicarage gate, and flung his horse's bridle over that very gate-post. Before he could reach the house, a slim, white figure came gliding out of one of the garden paths and beckoned him to approach.

" You, my darling," he said, gayly, "and on the watch for your devoted knight's coming. I'm not late, am I ? But early rising, as you understand the term in this primitive wilderness, is *not* my most prominent perfection."

" Eric," she said, faintly. " I have something to say to you. Last night when we were talking—when you told me you cared for me, you—you said nothing of Miss Forrester."

His face flushed, his blue eyes flashed with the quick angry light ever so ready to rise.

" Who has been talking to you ? " he demanded. " But I need hardly ask. Mr. Terrence Dennison, of course."

" I have known it this long time," she returned, shrinking from his angry looks, trembling like a nervous child, yet resolute to go on, "only 1 forgot it yesterday. Oh, Lord Dynely ! You were very cruel to say such things to me, and all the time engaged to marry her."

She broke down utterly for the first time with the words, and covering her face with her hands, sobbed hysterically.

"Why did you ever come here—why did you make me love you—how could you deceive me so? I knew I was not worthy of you. I was happy before you came; I—"

"You would have married Dennison, and lived happy for ever after? Is that what you are trying to say, Miss Higgins? Terry has been pleading his own cause this morning, I see, and slandering me. Common gratitude from the dependant of my mother's bounty might have kept him silent, if nothing else ; but gratitude is an obsolete virtue. Since you are so easily influenced by him, it would be a pity to take you from him. Here is his ring—let me replace it on your finger, and take back all the nonsensical things I said to you last evening."

She uttered a cry like a child under the lash. At that sound all anger died out within him, he caught her hands and held them in a fierce, close clasp.

"I will never let you go," he said. "I swear it. My wife you shall be, and no other's. You are mine—mine alone, and as mine I claim you. I deny all Dennison's slanders. I am not engaged to Miss Forrester or any other living woman. Miss Forrester is no more anxious to marry me than I am to marry her. It is all my mother's doing and her guardian's—they made the compact, but we will not ratify it. You I love, and you I will make my wife. Where is your father?—in his study? Then I will go to him at once, and make an end of all doubt."

He strode away, and, looking handsome and haughty, was admitted into Mr. Higgins' private sanctum. In few and somewhat insolently authoritative words he made known his errand. He loved his daughter Crystal, he wished to make her his wife. Then he sat still, and looked at the clergyman. If he expected the Vicar of Starling to be overpowered by the honor he was doing him, he was mistaken.

Mr. Higgins sat aghast, literally aghast, and pushing his spectacles up his forehead sat helplessly staring at the young wooer.

"My daughter! My daughter Crystal. *You* want to marry her, Lord Dynely. Oh, impossible! impossible!"

"And why impossible, sir, may I ask?" haughtily and angrily.

"Because—Lord bless my soul! because she's too young to marry any one; because when she's two or three years older we're going to marry her to Terry Dennison. It's been an understood thing always, always, that Christabel was to marry Terry."

"And may I ask again, Mr. Higgins," cried Lord Dynely, still more angrily, still more haughtily, "if you prefer Dennison to me?"

"Well—well—well, don't be angry, my dear young gentleman, don't be angry. Bless my soul! *you* marry Crystal! Upon my word and honor, I never thought of such a thing —never! Prefer Dennison! well, in a worldly point of view, you're the best match of course, but, then, we know Terry, and he's one of the family, and he's a good lad—oh, a very good lad! and I shouldn't be afraid to trust my little one to his keeping."

"And you *are* afraid to trust her to mine!" said lordly Eric, pale with passion.

"No, no, not that either! Bless my soul, don't be so quick to jump at conclusions. It's only this—I know him better than I do you—I trust him entirely, and then it's been an understood thing always. Crissy has no right to play fast and loose with Terry. Besides, there's your cousin—no, she's not your cousin, I suppose, but it's all the same. I mean, of course, Miss France Forrester."

"Well, sir," demands the exasperated young lord, "and what of Miss France Forrester?"

"Why, this—you've been engaged to her, or so I have been told."

"Then, Mr. Higgins, you've been told an infernal lie," retorted Lord Dynely, too utterly overcome with rage and exasperation to much mind what he said; "I never was engaged to France Forrester or any one else. Am I to understand that you decline to accept me as the husband of your daughter?"

"Oh, dear me," said Mr. Higgins, in a troubled tone, "I don't know what to say, I'm sure. You've taken me so much by surprise—I always looked upon her as belonging to Terry—"

This was growing more than Lord Dynely could bear. He rose to his feet, exasperated beyond endurance.

"Oh, don't," said the vicar, piteously ; "wait a little, my lord. What does Christabel say ? She is in love with you, I suppose ? "

"She does me that honor, Mr. Higgins."

"It's a brilliant match for her, and yet," in that troubled tone, "I do believe she would be happier married to——"

"Mr. Higgins, you insult me ! I decline to listen longer. Good-morning."

"I beg your pardon, Lord Dynely. I had no intention of insulting you, I am sure. If Crystal wishes it, and you wish it, why then—why then I have no more to say. Only this, obtain your mother's consent. No daughter of mine shall enter any family that considers her beneath them or is unwilling to receive her. Obtain your mother's consent and you shall have mine. Only "—this in a low voice and with a sorrowful shake of the head—"I would rather it had been Terry."

Lord Dynely, quite pale with haughty surprise and anger, bowed himself out. Opposition was crowding upon him, and he set his teeth, and swore he would have her in spite of a thousand imbecile vicars, a thousand match-making mothers. And Mr. Higgins sat blinking in a dazed way in the sunshine, full of vague, apprehensive regrets.

"He's a fine young man—a handsome young man, well-born, well-bred, titled and rich ; and yet I am afraid of him. It's these brilliant young men who break their wives' hearts as easily as I could my pipe-stem. It will be a great match for one of my girls, but I would rather it were Terry."

Leaning against the vine-clad porch, Lord Dynely came face to face with Terry himself. He paused and looked at him, his blue eyes lurid with anger and defiance.

"Well, little 'un," he said, with an insolent laugh, "you've heard the news, I suppose ? I'm to marry Crystal. Con-

his efforts were not in vain, his dress always looked as though it were a part of himself.

He looked up gayly at Dennison's approach. He was in high good humor this morning—at peace with all the world. Yesterday's irritation had entirely passed away. Crystal's father might be exasperating to the last degree, but Crystal herself was entirely satisfactory. And when Crystal was his wife he would take care the Vicar of Starling and his family saw uncommonly little of her. For Terry—well, looking at it dispassionately, after an excellent dinner and a prime Manilla, he was forced to admit that Terry, poor beggar ! *had* some little cause of complaint. Something very like foul play had been done on his part, something the codes of his order and his honor would hardly recognize. Still, what was done, was done. Crystal he would resign to no man living, and Dennison must make the best of it. This unexpected opposition had but strengthened his passion ; he had never been so thoroughly in earnest before about any love affair in his life. He was going to see his mother to-day and bring her to reason. She would prove a little restive on his hands at first, on France's account, but he would speedily bring her around. For France—well, he winced a little at the thought of meeting France. To be laughed at was horrible, and he could see France's dark, mischievous, satirical eyes, France's cynical little laugh, hear France's sarcastic, cutting speeches. "Who was she ? " indeed. The girl must be a witch. Your sharp girl, your clever girl, was an outrage on nature. Women were made for man's use, benefit and pleasure ; why, then, were half of them as man didn't like them? Crystal, without two ideas in her pretty head and loving heart, was his ideal of womankind. Yes, he would bring his mother round, fetch her down here to see Crystal, have the marriage arranged to take place before Christmas, all on the quiet, and spend the Winter rambling about sunny Italy. And next season Lady Dynely would burst upon London the loveliest thing out, a pride to her husband, an honor and credit to his taste.

All this in rambling, disconnected, self-satisfied fashion, Lord Dynely had thought over last night. Now he lay rolling

6*

up a cigarette, with white, practised fingers, a smile on his lips and in his handsome blue eyes as he looked up at Mr. Dennison.

"How are you, Terry?" he said, genially. "Come in ; knock those things off the chair, and sit down. I'm in the midst of an exodus, you see—off to Devonshire. Any commission for France or the madre?"

"I will send a note by you to Lady Dynely," Terry answered. He was looking very grave, and rather pale, Eric could see at second glance, his mouth set and stern under his tawny beard and mustache. "It may be some time before I see her in person. I join my regiment this week at Windsor."

"Ah! leave of absence expired? Be off, Norton, and order round the trap. Only ten minutes to starting time now. Very inhospitable of me, Terry—you don't pay morning calls at Carruthers Court often—but I really must cut it short. Twenty-five minutes to starting time, and you know what the drive to the station is."

"I won't detain you," Terry answers, setting his lips still harder under his leonine beard. "I came to say a few words about Crystal."

Lord Dynely's cigarette was quite ready now. He looked up at his companion with that slow, indolent smile of his that had so much of latent insolence in it, struck a fuse and lit up.

"About Crystal? Let us hear it, Terry. You couldn't choose a more interesting subject. How is the little darling this morning?"

"I won't say anything about your conduct in this matter, Lord Dynely," Terry began ; "you know best whether it has been the conduct of a man of honor or not. Crystal, perhaps, is not to blame."

"How magnanimous! 'Crystal is not to blame.' You have never asked her to marry you, and because she honors me by her preference and acceptance, she is not to blame. And don't you think—as her friend, now, Terry—she makes a rather better match in marrying Lord Dynely than she would in marrying Terry Dennison?"

That angry gleam was lighting again Eric's sleepy eyes,

but his soft, slow tones never rose as he spoke. He watched Terry from behind the wreaths of scented smoke, and saw the flush that arose and overspread his whole face.

"Yes," Terry answered, after a pause, in a slow, strange voice, "you are right ; she makes a better match in marrying Lord Dynely than in marrying Terry Dennison. As I had never, in so many words, asked her to be my wife, whatever may have been understood, I repeat I hold *her* blameless in this. She loves you—she never did me. I might have foreseen, but—I trusted you both."

"Don't seem to see it," Lord Dynely drawled, looking at his watch. "Only seven minutes, Mr. Dennison ; very sorry to cut it short, I repeat, but—"

"But you shall hear what I have come to say," Terry exclaimed, turning upon him. "It is this : I know how you hold women—I know how it is you have treated them—I know you hold it fair sport to win hearts and fling them away. What I have come to say is—don't do it here. She has no brother or father capable of protecting her. I will be her brother, if I may be no more. For your mother's sake, you are the last man on earth I would wish to raise my hand against, but this I say, this I mean—if you trifle with Crystal as you have trifled with others, Eric, you shall answer to me !"

He brought his clenched hand down upon the inlaid table, the veins of his forehead swollen and dark, with the intensity of feeling within him. Lord Dynely laughed softly, and flung his cigarette out through the open window.

"Bon ! But would it not be well to intimate as much quietly. You do it very well, my dear boy, for an amateur ; but one gets so much of that kind of thing at the theatre, and they do it better there. You mean well, I dare say— sentiments do you honor, and all that ; but this tremendous earnestness is in such deuced bad form—in August, of all months, particularly."

"I have said my say," was Dennison's response. "It is part of your creed, I know, to make a jest of all things ; jest if you like, but hear and remember. As surely as we both stand here—if there is any foul play in this business, your

life shall answer it. You shall not play with her, fool her
and leave her, as you have done with so many. You shall
not break her heart, and go unpunished of God and man.
If all is not open and above board here, you shall pay the
penalty—that I swear."

"Time's up," said Eric, looking at his watch again. He
replaced it, arose to his feet, and laid his hand on Terry's
shoulder, with that winning smile of his that made his face
so charming.

"Look here, Terry," he said, "I am not such a scoundrel,
such a Lovelace, such a Don Giovanni, as you try to make
me out. I'm ready to go with little Crystal to the St.
George's slaughter-house, or the little church down among
the trees yonder, this very morning if I might. You're a
good fellow, and, as I said before, your sentiments do you
honor, and so on. You feel a little sore about this business,
naturally—I would myself, in your place ; but all's right and
on the square here. I never was in earnest before—I am
now. I'm going up for my mother—she must come here
and receive Crystal as her daughter. And when the wedding comes off, you shall be the best man, 'an' ye will,'
Terry—that *I* swear, since swearing seems the order of the
day. And now, dear old man, don't lecture any more ; it's
too hot—give you my word it is, and I want to reserve all
my strength for the journey. Here's seltzer and sherry.
Compose your feelings with that liquid refreshment, and dash
off your note to the madre while I get into my outer garments."

There was no resisting Eric in this mood, it was not in
human nature. The charming smile, the charming voice,
the affectionate, frankly cordial manner, would have moved
and melted a Medusa.

"No, Crystal was not to blame," Terry thought, with a
sigh, glancing over at their two images in the glass—it was
in the nature of things that women should fall in love at
sight with Eric.

He scrawled off the note in a big, slap-dash sort of hand,
each long word filling a whole line ; folded, sealed it, and
gave it to Eric just as he sprang up into the trap.

"Bye-bye, old boy," he said, gayly. "When shall I tell the madre to expect you? Not before Christmas? Oh, nonsense! She couldn't survive without you half the time. Well, as you won't be here when I return, adieu and au revoir. Love to everybody."

The groom touched the horses. They sped down the avenue like the wind, and Terry was alone.

* * * * * * * * * * *

"It is very odd we don't hear from Eric—that he doesn't return. I can't understand it at all. It is three weeks since he left; he was to be back in one. There's something very singular about it, to say the least."

Thus petulantly Lady Dynely to Miss Forrester. They were together in the drawing-room—her ladyship reclining upon a sofa, a book in her hand. Miss Forrester looking charming in palest amber tissue and white roses, lying back in a vast downy arm-chair before the open window, putting the finishing touches to a small sketch.

"The house is like a tomb since he and Terry left. It is most incomprehensible indeed, Eric's staying all this time. If you understand it, France, and feel satisfied, it is more than I do. My dear child, do put down that tiresome drawing and listen. Ever since Mr. Locksley's advent, I believe you have given yourself wholly to art."

The color rose in Miss Forrester's clear, dark face. She looked up from her drawing at once.

"I beg your pardon, Lady Dynely. What was it you said?"

"About Eric. It's three weeks since he went away—he was to be back in one. And he never writes to me at least. Perhaps he treats you better—France, what are you laughing at? Eric has written to you?"

Miss Forrester's musical, merry laugh chimed out.

"Oh, yes, *ma mère*, Eric has written to me."

"And you never told me. What does the wretched boy say?"

"I don't think he is wretched. It was a very pleasant letter. He merely wrote to give me up."

"France!" in horror.

"Yes, mamma—he came to his senses down in Lincoln-shire. Couldn't think of forcing my inclinations—if the proposed alliance of the noble houses of Dynely and Forrester were distasteful to me, then, at any cost to himself and his own lacerated heart, he resigned me. It read like one of Lord Chesterfield's masterpieces—was a model of polite and chivalric composition."

"Good Heaven! and you—France, what did you say?"

Again Miss Forrester's laugh rang out.

"I answered in three words, mamma—terse, pithy, and to the point. I wrote, 'Dear Eric: Who is she?' That epistle he has not done me the honor of answering. I think I see his face when he read it."

And then France lay back and went off into a prolonged peal of merriment.

Lady Dynely rose up on her sofa, her delicate cheeks flushing with vexation.

"You wrote that, France—to Eric?"

"I wrote that, mamma, to Eric. I understand Eric better than you do, and I'm not the least afraid of Eric, and you are. I could not have written anything more to the point, if I had tried for a month. He might have answered, though; I should like to know who my rival is this time."

"France, do you really believe—"

"That Eric has fallen in love in Lincolnshire, for the one-millionth time? Yes, Lady Dynely, as firmly as that I sit here. Now, who do you suppose she can be? There are no ladies in Sir Philip's household, and I don't think he would bestow his heart's best affections upon the cook."

"Miss Forrester, if you consider this a theme for jest—"

"Please don't be dignified, mamma, and please don't call me Miss Forrester. Don't I say, I don't believe he would. It must be one of Terry's family—you know what I mean—one of the Council of Nine—one of the nine Misses Higgins! It would be comical if Terry and he were brothers-in-law after all, both married on the same day, in the same church, in the same family, by the same pastor and papa. Quite a pastoral idyl altogether."

Miss Forrester laughed again. Of late, since the receipt

of Lord Dynely's letter, the whole world had turned rose-color to the heiress of Caryllynne. The portrait painting business was still going on ; but not even to herself would Miss Forrester admit that that had anything to do with it.

Tears actually sprang to Lady Dynely's pale blue eyes.

"You are cruel, France ; you don't mean to be, perhaps, but you are. I have set my heart, my whole heart, on see-ing you Eric's wife, and you treat the matter like this. You despise him—you must, since you hold him and his feelings so lightly and contemptuously."

France laid down her drawing, went over, knelt beside the elder lady, and gave her a kiss.

"Now, mamma mine, look here," she said, coaxingly, "it's just this. You love Eric, and love is blind ; you don't see him as he is. I'm not in love with him, and couldn't be if he lived in the same house for the next hundred and fifty years, and I do see Eric as he is. He's very handsome, and very brilliant, and very charming, but he is as unstable as water. He has no back-bone ; and if I married him, and he didn't break my heart the first year, I should henpeck him to death, or—the divorce court. For the rest, you'll see I'm right. Some new face caught his fickle fancy down there, and hence that magnanimous letter. I don't blame him , he was born so, I suppose, and can't help it. Hark !"

She started to her feet and ran to the window. A fly from the railway was just stopping, and a young gentleman in a light gray suit in the act of leaping out. Again France laughed.

"'By the pricking of my thumbs,
Something wicked this way comes,'

as Hecate says. Speak of the angels and you hear their wings. Here's Eric now."

Eric it was. He came in as she spoke, and met her laugh-ing, roguish glance, that seemed to read his inmost thoughts.

"At last ! Just as your mother and I were turning our thoughts to crape and bombazine. We had given you up for lost, Eric, and here you come upon us like a beautiful

" I don't know.   This girl is the sister of the girl Terry is going to marry ? "

" No, madame," said her son, coolly, filling another glass of sherry ; " not her sister, but herself."

" What ! "

" What an amount of talking these things seem to involve," Eric said, pathetically, " and how inexcusably void of comprehension people appear to be.   I repeat, my dear Lady Dynely, the young lady I intend to marry is the young lady Mr. Dennison honored with his preference, and intended to transform into Mrs. Dennison.   Unfortunately for him, ' I came, I saw, I conquered.'   She preferred me to the big dragoon, and I left ; Terry exclaiming, like Francis First at Pavia, ' All is lost but honor.' "

He paused.   His mother had risen to her feet, every trace of color leaving her face, her eyes fixed in a sort of horror upon her son.

" Eric," she said, huskily, " you tell me—you mean to tell me that you have taken from Terry the girl he loved ? "

Eric lifted his blonde eyebrows in weary resignation.

" If you put it in that sentimental way—yes, mamma."

She stood and looked at him.   She tried to speak—no words came.   The baseness of this, after all Terry had resigned, the noble self-sacrifice he had shown—was too much.   He had given up his birthright to Eric, and this was Eric's return.

" Mother," Eric cried, rising to his feet, aroused to something like alarm by the pale horror of her face.   " What is the matter now?   Why do you take Terry's affairs so much to heart?   Isn't he big enough and old enough to look after himself?   Am I to blame, is she to blame, if she prefers me to him?   I expected to be taken to task on France's account, but, gad ! I certainly didn't expect to on Terry's."

" You don't know—you don't know—" she said in a broken voice.

" No, I don't know," Eric answered, with an impatient frown, " but I should uncommonly like to.   What is Dennison that I should let his feelings stand in my way ?   He hadn't spoken, so he has no reason to complain. Here is a note from him, by the way, to you."

He presented her the letter, and sat watching her while she read it, lying back among the cushions of his chair. It was short:

"DEAREST LADY DYNELY:—Eric has told you all by this time. If he loves her, and is good to her, I ask no more, If he is not, then, as I have told him, he shall answer to me. She loves him with all her innocent heart, and she is so dear to me, that I would die to save her a moment's pain. Let him look to it, if he tires of her, and tries to throw her over. For you, if I have any claim whatever upon you, I ask this favor of you in return. Come here, take her to your heart as your daughter, and I shall consider myself more than repaid. Ever yours,

"TERRY."

She sank back on her sofa, crushed the letter in her hand, laid her face against the cushions, and burst into an unrestrained passion of tears. Eric arose angrily to his feet.

"I don't understand this," he said. "What is Dennison that his interests should be nearer to you than mine? What has he said in the letter?"

"Nothing that concerns you to see," Lady Dynely said, proudly lifting her head. "Have you anything more to say, Eric, before I go to dress?"

"This, that it is my wish you accompany me to Lincolnshire to-morrow, and formally receive Crystal as my betrothed wife."

He stood haughtily erect before her—a young Sultan issuing his sovereign commands to his womankind.

"I will go," she answered briefly. "Is there anything else?"

"'That you will tell France—I don't wish any chaffing on this subject; it is a weakness of Miss Forrester's to chaff a fellow, and is very bad form. Tell her at once, and have done with it."

The youthful autocrat must be obeyed. With a weary sigh Lady Dynely sought out Miss Forrester, and found her

dream once more. And now, while you tell her all the news
of your sojourn, I will run away and dress for dinner."

She left the room, almost disconcerting Eric by her last
saucy backward glance. Almost, not wholly—nothing earthly
ever entirely put his lordship out of countenance.

"Really, Eric," his mother began, pettishly, "I don't see
how France can treat your desertion of her so lightly. In
my days such conduct would have been considered unpardonable."

"Ah! but we don't live in the dark ages now," Eric responded, first ringing the bell, then sinking into France's
vacated chair. "And my desertion of France—please trans-
late that, mother mine; I don't understand."

"It is easily understood. You asked France to marry
you before you left, did you not?"

"I—I believe so. It is three weeks ago, and a man may
naturally be pardoned if his memory is somewhat hazy at
that distance of time."

"You asked her to marry you," pursued his mother, over
looking this persiflage, "and she told you to come for her answer in a week—did she not?"

"My dear mother, what an admirable counsel for the
prosecution you would make. Yes, she did. Sherry and
seltzer," to the footman who entered.

"And you never came," Lady Dynely said, her eyes
flashing angrily. "Eric, is that the conduct of a gentleman
—a lover—a man of honor?"

"It was the conduct of a man of sense.

"'If she be not fair for me?
What care I how fair she be?'

It would have been an act most unbecoming a gentleman to
force a lady's inclination. So France gave me to understand; and so, upon sage second thought, I came to see.
I didn't come for the answer; I wrote for it."

"You did?"

"I did," said Eric, filling himself a glass of sherry; "I
wrote, renouncing her unless she came to me of her own free

will. It was a most honorable, manly and high-toned letter, I consider myself."

"And she said?" eagerly.

"She said," said Eric, laughing at the recollection, "'Who is she?' I believe Miss Forrester must be a sorceress. I haven't taken the trouble to tell her who she is, but I have taken the trouble to return here to-day to tell you."

"Eric," his mother cried, starting to her feet, "you mean to tell me—"

"Mamma," Eric said, plaintively, "do sit down. Don't excite yourself. Good Heaven! where's the use of everybody taking things so seriously in this way—getting steam up to such a height for nothing? I mean to tell you that I have met a girl I like a thousand times better than France Forrester; that I have asked her to marry me; that I have asked her father for his consent, and that he has given his consent, contingent upon yours. There is the whole matter for you in a nutshell."

His mother dropped back, stunned.

"In three weeks," she murmured, in a dazed voice, "all this in three weeks' time."

"We live in a rapid age, mother," responded the young man, coolly. "Time is precious; why waste it? Strange it may seem, but no less strange than true. And truth is stranger than fiction. It is an accomplished fact."

"Who is she?" Lady Dynely asked, helplessly.

"France's question over again. She is Miss Higgins."

"Higgins!"

"Yes, poor child. It's not a distinguished appellation, and a rose by any other name does not smell as sweet. 'Christabel—twenty-first Viscountess Dynely, *née* Higgins,' will not look well in Debrett. However, there is no rose without its thorn, they tell me. She is the Vicar of Starling's eighth daughter."

"France said so," murmured her ladyship, still in that helplessly stunned tone.

"Did she? Then we ought to have France burned as a witch. Terry hasn't been writing to her, has he?"

quite dressed and looking very handsome, sitting gazing with dreamy eyes at the sun setting over the green Devon woods.

"Well, *ma mère ?*" she asked.

"It is all as you said, France," my lady answered; "he fell in love in Lincolnshire."

Miss Forrester laughed, and yet with a touch of feminine pique too.

"I knew it. I felt it in the uttermost depth of my prophetic soul—

"'Oh, my cousin, shallow-hearted,
Oh, my Eric, mine no more.'

Who is she ? One of the nine Misses Higgins ?"

"One of the nine Misses Higgins."

"And Terry and Eric will be brothers-in-law, as I said. What a capital joke, Lady Dynely."

"No, France—not brothers-in-law. It is—"

But France started impetuously to her feet.

"Lady Dynely don't say it. Don't say it is the particular Miss Higgins Terry wanted. Don't make me think so badly of Eric as that."

But Lady Dynely sat sorrowful and mute, and France read all the truth in that sad face.

"It is, then. Oh, this is too bad ! too bad !—too bad of her, too bad of Eric. It reminds one of the Scripture story of the cruel man who took his neighbor's one ewe lamb. My poor, good Terry !"

She sat down, her eyes flashing through bright tears.

"I knew him weak and fickle," she said; "I never thought him dishonorable. For her," contemptuously, "she never could have been worth one thought from Terry Dennison."

"I have had a letter from Terry," Lady Dynely said, sadly. "Poor fellow ! he makes no mention of coming back. He wishes me to accompany Eric to Lincolnshire and for mally countenance the engagement."

"You will go, of course ?"

"I can do nothing else. And you, France—you care wholly on Terry's account, I am sure, not at all on your own."

"Not in the least on my own," France said, holding her handsome head high, her dark eyes still full of indignant fire. "But Terry loved this girl, and Terry—I must say it, though I offend you, Lady Dynely—is worth two hundred Erics. Oh, it is a shame—a shame!"

They met at dinner. Miss Forrester's greeting was of the coldest and most constrained. Eric was his own natural, languid, charming self, at his best. His mother's sad, pale face he would not see, France's flushed cheeks and angry eyes he overlooked.

"It takes two to make a row," Eric thought; "you won't make a row with me."

Once France spoke of Terry—her bright, angry eyes fixed upon his face, her own wearing a very resolute look. Where was Terry? How had he left him? Where was he going? When did he mean to return? Eric bore it heroically.

> "Io pæan,
> Terry! Terry!"

he laughed. "How you ring the changes on that classical name. I don't know anything of Terry's outgoings and incomings. Am I my brother's keeper? Your solicitude does Mr. Dennison too much honor."

She turned from him.

"He has no heart," she thought; "no sense of remorse; no feeling for any human being but himself. I pity Miss Crystal Higgins."

The evening brought Mr. Locksley, the artist.

"So he comes still," Eric thought, watching with sleepy, half-closed eyes his mother and the artist playing chess, while France sat at the piano and sang softly. "I wonder —I wonder if this is the secret of your queenly indifference, Miss Forrester, to me."

Next day Lady Dynely and her son departed. France watched Eric out of sight with a smile, the fag end of an old ballad on her lips:

> "'Lightly won and lightly lost,
> A fair good-night to thee.'"

CHAPTER XIV.

"ONCE MORE THE GATE BEHIND ME FALLS."

N that·pleasant upper room of Dynely Abbey, set apart as Mr. Locksley's studio, and sacred wholly to that artist and his painting goods and chattels, Mr. Locksley himself stood on the morning of the day that took Lady Dynely and her son to Lincolnshire. He stood with folded arms and a darkly thoughtful look, gazing at his own work. As he stood there, tall, strong, erect, the soldierly air that told of his past calling was more manifest than ever.

This portrait was a gem—something more than an ordinary portrait—as a work of art, worthy of Reynolds or Romney. It had been a labor of love, heart and soul had been in the work, and the result did what the works of master hands seldom do, satisfied himself.

From a darkly misty background the face of France Forrester shone vividly out, startlingly life-like in coloring and expression. He had caught her very look, that mischievous sparkle of eye and smile, that brightly mutinous turn of the graceful head, as she leaned forward from the canvas. Those darkly laughing eyes looked up at the artist now from beneath that floating chevelure of rich, waving hair, the perfect lips smiled upon him saucily, as though they understood his sombre thoughts and mocked at them.

"As she would, most likely," he thought, "if she knew all. But no—that is not France Forrester. Proud she is, proud of the name she bears, the lineage that lies behind her and the place she holds in life, but to laugh at any mortal pain is not in her. I can see the first flush of haughty anger and amaze at the nameless painter's presumption—then the soft womanly compassion for his suffering, that would make gentle and tender her parting words. And yet I have thought that if she knew all, the whole truth "—he paused suddenly and turned impatiently away towards the window. "What a fool I am," he muttered, half-aloud. "She loves that handsome dandy, of course—he is the sort of gilded fop womankind make idols of. Could I not see it in her face last night?"

He stood staring out at my lady's carefully kept Italian garden, all ablaze with gorgeous August flowers. It was a sultry, overcast day—sunless, windless, gray. Early in the morning the sun had come out with a dazzling brightness, only to vanish again and leave behind a low, leaden sky, frowning with drifting cloud.

The great house was very still. My lord and lady had gone ; Miss Forrester's clear voice, and the light, silken rustle of her garments were nowhere to be heard. She was not to sit to Mr. Locksley any more ; the last sitting had been given a week ago, and though he still came daily it was but to add the few last finishing touches to his perfected work. He dined with the two ladies at intervals, and spent occasional evenings at the Abbey when there were no other visitors. From general society he shrank ; but he never refused my lady's cordial invitations when she and her ward were alone. It might have been wiser if he had. They were growing dangerously dear to him, these long tête-à-tête evenings with the heiress of Caryllyne ; perilously precious, this standing beside her, turning over her music, listening to the old ballads she loved to sing, watching the white, flying fingers, the tender, lovely, spirited face—how dear, how precious, he was finding out now to his cost.

He turned from the window and began pacing impatiently up and down the long, lofty room. In spite of the wide open window the atmosphere was almost painfully oppressive. So sultry, so airless was the leaden day, that it was only by an effort one could breathe. The physical suffering blended with the mental. He loosened the strip of black ribbon at his throat, as though even that suffocated him. He was facing for the first time the bare truth to-day. He had shut his eyes wilfully to his own danger ; the moth had seen the lighted candle, and intoxicated by its brilliancy, had still flown headlong in. Was the moth to be pitied, then, let him singe his wings ever so badly?

" I will go ! " he said to himself, abruptly, " I will go to-morrow. Flight is one's only safeguard in these things. If I stay, if I see any more of her I will commit the last crowning act of folly, and tell her all. My work is finished—there is no cause to linger. Yes, I will go—I will start for Spain to-morrow, and explore it from the Escurial to the Alhambra, and in painting dark-eyed Morisco maidens and bull-fights I will forget this summer's fooling."

He looked at his watch—two o'clock. Three was his dinner hour—it would take him the hour to walk to the village. He made his headquarters at the " Kiddle-a-wink " in the village of Dynely, and slept in that upper chamber wherein sixteen years before, one summer night, Alexis Dynely lay dying.

As he passed out from the house into the sultry afternoon, he glanced up at the sky. It was growing darker every instant—a faint, damp rain was beginning to fall. It was doubtful, good walker though he was, if he would outstrip the storm and reach the inn before the summer rain fell. He looked around as he walked rapidly away, to catch a glimpse of a gauzy dress, to hear a girl's sweet voice singing, to see a graceful head bent over a book or a drawing. Miss Forrester, however, was nowhere to be seen. It was as well so, perhaps.

" I will call this evening and make my adieux to both ladies," he thought, and, pulling his hat over his eyes, strode rapidly on his way.

Yes, he would leave England on the morrow—for good and all this time. Where was the use of coming back, where the sight of the familiar places, the familiar faces that knew him no more, brought nothing but pain? He would make Rome his headquarters for life, and give himself up utterly to his art. A boy's mad folly, a woman's base deceit had wrecked his life sixteen years ago. He had been thrust out from his mother's home and heart with scorn and bitter words, his birthright given to a stranger. It

never occurred to him to sue for commutation of that
sentence. With the past he had nothing to do; he had
deserved his fate, he had disgraced his name; his mother
had done rightly; in the future the art he loved was all he
had left him. He would start upon his second exile to-morrow. This time there should be no looking back, this time
it should be life-long. To return to England meant returning to see her the happy wife of Lord Dynely; to return
and sue for his mother's favor, meant to oust her from her
fortune, to rake up all the old dead-and-gone scandal, to
bring the shame from which that mother, the haughtiest
woman in England, had fled sixteen years before, back to
her in its first force. No, there was nothing for him but
silence and exile to the end.

"Mr. Locksley?"

The clear sweet voice made him look up from his moody
reverie with a start. And then, like a vision, France Forrester's brightly smiling face, set in a ravishing bonnet, beamed upon him. Miss Forrester, with a tiny groom
behind her, drove a low, basket phaeton and a pair of
spanking little ponies. She drew up the ponies in dashing
style, and turned to the artist with that bewitching smile of
hers.

"Are you going home, Mr. Locksley—I mean to the inn?
Pray don't go just yet. Let me offer you this vacant seat.
I have something to say to you."

Was fate pursuing him when he meant to fly from danger?
He took the seat beside her, and Miss Forrester with a
touch of her parasol-whip, sent the little steppers briskly
ahead.

"I am alone to-day—do you know it? And as I didn't
expect even your society, Mr. Locksley—I came away.
They left by the early train this morning."

"They—who?"

"Lady Dynely and Eric. Oh, you don't know, then—I
thought perhaps she had told you over your chessmen last
evening. Yes, they started for Lincolnshire this morning—
to be gone a week at the least; and I am queen regent,
monarch of all I survey, until their return. The first use I

10

make of my liberty is to spend a whole long day at dear old
Caryllynne. It is not nearly so ancient nor so stately as the
Abbey, but I love it a hundred times more. Have you ever
been there, Mr. Locksley?"

She looked up at him, half wondering at the dark gravity
of his face.

"I have been there, Miss Forrester."

"Indeed! Strange that Mrs. Matthews, the housekeeper,
told me nothing about it."

"I have not been in the house."

"Then you have missed an artistic treat. The Caryll
picture gallery is the pride of the neighborhood; there is
nothing like it in the whole country. Mrs. Caryll, as I have
told you, is really a devotee of art, and always was. There
are Cuyp's, and Wouvermain's, and Sir Joshua's portrait,
and sunsets by Turner, and sunrises by Claude Lorraine, a
gallery of modern and a gallery of Venetian art. Oh, you
really must see it, and at once. I shall drive you over and
play cicerone. Nothing I like so well as showing the dear,
romantic old Manor."

"You are most kind, Miss Forrester," he said, with a sort
of effort, "but it is quite impossible. I mean," seeing her
look of surprise, "that as I leave Devonshire to-morrow, I
will have no time. Wandering artists don't keep valets, so
I must attend to the packing of my own portmanteau, and that,
with some letters to write, will detain me until midnight."

He was not looking at her, else he might have seen and
possibly understood the swift, startled pallor that came over
her face.

"You are going away?" she said, slowly.

"The portrait is finished, my work here is done. I owe
Lady Dynely and you, Miss Forrester, many thanks for your
kind efforts to render my sojourn agreeable."

"If Lady Dynely were here," Miss Forrester answered,
her color returning, and in her customary gay manner, "she
would say the thanks were due you, for helping to while
away two poor women's long, dull evenings. Isn't it rather
a pity to go before she returns? She will regret it extremely,
I know."

"If I had known of this sudden departure, I would have made my adieux to her ladyship last night. May I further trespass on your great kindness, Miss Forrester, and charge you with my farewell?"

She bent her head and set her lips a little as she cut the ponies sharply with her whip. It had come upon her almost like a blow, this sudden revelation, but her pride and thorough training hid all sign.

"Artists are like gypsies—ever on the wing—that I know of old. And whither do you go, Mr. Locksley? Back to the green lanes and rural quiet and the inspiring surroundings of old Brompton."

"Farther still," he said, with a smile; "to Spain. I have roamed almost over every quarter of the habitable globe in my forty years of life, but Spain is still a terra incognita. I have had an intense desire ever since I gave myself up wholly to art to make a walking tour over the country. One should find a thousand subjects there for brush and pencil."

"To Spain," she repeated, mechanically; "and then?"

"Well, I can hardly say. I shall devote a year at least to Spain, and then most probably I shall return to Rome and make it my headquarters for life."

There was dead silence. The ponies bowled swiftly along; the road that led to the village had long been passed. Neither noticed it. The thoughtful gravity had deepened on his face. Her hands grasped the reins tightly, her lips were set in a certain rigid line. Her voice, when she spoke again, had lost somewhat of its clear, vibrating ring.

"You picture a very delightful future, Mr. Locksley; I almost envy you. Oh, no need to look incredulous—the Bohemian life is the freest, brightest, happiest on earth, but it is not for me. What I waylaid you for—to return to first principles—is this. I have had a letter from my dear old guardian, Mrs. Caryll, and she begs me to send her a duplicate of my portrait. She has one, but that was painted five years ago, and I have been chanting the praises of your handiwork until she is seized with a longing for a copy. You flatter me so charmingly on canvas, Mr. Locksley, that I really should like to gratify her if it were possible to procure her the copy. But I suppose all that is out of the question now."

"Mrs. Caryll shall have the copy. I trust she is well. I saw her so often in Rome," he said, half apologetically, "that I take an interest in her naturally."

"She is as well as she is ever likely to be," France answered, rather sadly, "and so lonely without me that I think of throwing over everything and going back to join her. I should infinitely prefer it, but she will not hear of it and neither will Lady Dynely. I must remain, it seems, and run the round of Vanity Fair whether I wish it or not. I ought not to complain—I *did* enjoy last season. Come what will," with a half laugh, "I have been blessed."

"Mrs. Caryll has no intention then of returning to England?"

She will never return. It is full of bitter associations for her. It would break her heart to see poor old Caryllynne."

"She still takes her son's wrongdoing so much to heart—she is still so bitter against him? Pardon me, Miss Forrester, I have heard that story, of course."

"There is no apology needed. You will wonder, perhaps when I tell you, you remind us all of him. That is the secret of Lady Dynely's interest in you from the first."

The clear, penetrating, hazel eyes were fixed full on his face. That trained face never moved a muscle.

"As to being bitter against him," pursued France, "it is just the reverse. It is remorse for her own cruelty that drives her nearly to despair at times. For she was cruel to him, poor fellow, when he came to her in his great trouble and shame—most cruel, most unmotherly. He came to her in his sorrow and humiliation, and she drove him from her with bitter scorn and anger. *That* is the thought that blights her life, that has preyed upon her health, that makes the thought of home horrible to her. She drove him from her into poverty and exile here, and here she will never return. A thousand times she has said to me, that, to look upon his face once more, to hold him in her arms, to hear him say he forgave her, she would give up her very life, give up all things except her hope of Heaven."

"She has said that ?"

She was too wrapped in her subject to heed his husky voice, to mark the change that had come over his face.

"Again and again. The hope of seeing him once more is the sole hope that keeps her alive."

"She thinks that *he* is still living ?"

"She thinks it. Every year since that time, with the exception of the two last, he has sent her some remembrance. A line, a trinket, a flower, a token of some sort to let her know he still exists. Those tokens have come to her from every quarter of the globe. India, Africa, America, and all countries of Europe. There is never an address—merely the post-mark to denote whence they came, and his name in his own familiar hand. Ah ! if we but knew where to look for him—where to find him, I believe I would travel the wide earth over, if at the end I could find Gordon Caryll."

"Miss Forrester ! you would do this?"

"A hundred times more than this ! He was my hero, Mr. Locksley, as far back as I can remember. There is no one, in all the world, I long so to see."

"And yet the day that finds him robs you of a fortune."

She looked up at him indignantly, impetuous tears in her eyes, an excited flush on either dusk cheek, more beautiful than he had ever seen her.

"A fortune ! Mr. Locksley, do you think no better of me than that ? Oh ! what would a million fortunes be to the joy of seeing him once more—of restoring him to his mother ! Caryllynne is not mine—only held in trust. One day or other, I feel, Gordon Caryll will return, and then ' the king shall have his own again ! ' "

What was it she read in the face of the man looking down at her ? Something more than intense admiration surely, though she read that there plainly enough. It brought her down from her heroics, from cloudland to earth, from romance to her sober senses. She pulled up the ponies sharply.

"We must go back," she said, in a constrained tone. "I have passed the turning to the village. As you insist upon going at once to the inn, I suppose a ' wilful man must have his way.' "

He touched the reins lightly with his hand, and checked her in the act of turning.

"Excuse me, Miss Forrester; I have changed my mind. I resist no longer. Since you are so kind as to be my guide, I will gladly go with you to Carryllynne and see the picture."

She looked at him again—rather haughtily it seemed.

"You are quite sure it is your wish, Mr. Locksley, and not a matter of politeness? You are quite sure it will not inconvenience you at all?"

"Quite sure, Miss Forrester. I wish to go."

She turned without a word and drove on. The distance was short. In a few minutes the great Manor gates were reached, and not an instant too soon. The summer storm, threatening all day, was upon them at last. As they passed beneath the lofty arch of masonry, two great drops splashed upon their faces.

They sped up the avenue, beneath the dark waving trees, at full speed. A groom came out to take the horses. Two or three old servants, on board wages, still kept up the place. Not an instant too soon; the rain was beginning to fall heavily and fast, and a sharp flash of blue lightning cut the dark air.

"Hurry! hurry!" was Miss Forrester's cry, as, laughing and breathless, she ran up the steps. "Welcome to Caryllynne, Mr. Locksley!"

He removed his hat with a certain reverence, as though he stood in a church; emotion on his face she could not read. She led the way into the vast tiled hall, the black and white marble flooring covered with skins of wild beasts.

Mrs. Mathews, the housekeeper, came forward to receive her young lady.

"We have come to see the pictures, Mrs. Mathews," Miss Forrester said, "and, as we appear to be storm-bound for some hours, I think I must ask you to give us some lunch. This is Mr. Locksley, and as Mr. Locksley has not dined, pray give us something that will serve as a substitute."

Sixteen years ago Mrs. Mathews had been housekeeper here. She bowed deferentially, her eyes fixed upon Mr.

Locksley with a curiously intense gaze. As she turned away she met her daughter, also domesticated here.

"Who is it, mother?" the girl asked. "Who is the gentleman? Lord Dynely—Mr. Dennison?"

"Neither," her mother answered. "His name is Mr. Locksley; and if ever I saw one man's eyes in another man's head, he has the eyes of Mr. Gordon Caryll."

CHAPTER XV.

"STAY."

MISS FORRESTER ran lightly to cne of the upper rooms to remove her bonnet and lace scarf. It was but a moment's work. Her guest awaited her below; but she made no haste to rejoin him. She stood by one of the windows looking down blankly at the rain-beaten garden, and trying to realize what she had been told. He was going away—going away the first thing to-morrow—never to return to England more.

She lingered, leaning against the window, while the rain lashed the clear glass, and beat down the tall ferns and grasses and flowers, heedless of how the moments passed.

All at once she awoke—as one might from a dream— broad awake. Why was she lingering? To-morrow was still to-morrow; to-day was here and he with it. He was her guest, in this house by her invitation; the duty of hospitality called her to his side. The rôle of love-lorn damsel was a rôle entirely out of her part in the drama of life. She would put off all thought of what to-morrow must bring until to-morrow came.

She found Mr. Locksley loitering through the long drawing-room, looking at the few pictures it contained, mostly family portraits, examining the curiously carved ebony chairs and cabinets, the sandalwood caskets, the great porcelain jars filled with roses and lavender, and touching tenderly, as though they were sensitive things, the curious, old china, the quaint, pretty trifles scattered everywhere, just as Mrs. Caryll's hand had placed them last.

"Isn't it a darling old room," France said. "Everything old-fashioned, and quaint, and queer, and faded, with no modern newness or splendor anywhere, and yet twice as beautiful as any of the grand recently-fitted up rooms of the Abbey. Everything is just as it was left when she went away—this room and her room. In Gordon's too, poor fellow, nothing has been changed."

Mr. Locksley looked at her—a curious smile on his face, a curious expression in his eyes, half cynical, half sad.

"What an interest you seem to take in Gordon Caryll, Miss Forrester—this black sheep of a spotless flock, this one scapegoat of an irreproachable family. Was he worthy of it."

"Most worthy of it, I am sure. He was unfortunate, Mr. Locksley; he ruined himself for a woman's sake. It's not a common act of folly—men don't do that now-a-days, they're not capable of it. I think I should like them a little better if they were. There's a sort of heroism, after all, about a man who deliberately throws up all his prospects in life for a woman."

"Very doubtful heroism, Miss Forrester, it seems to have been in his case. He took a leap in the dark, and awoke to find himself in a quagmire of disgrace, from which all his life long he can never arise. What a pretty garden."

He joined her at one of the windows and stood looking down. The Caryllynne gardens covered in all some half-dozen acres, utterly neglected of late years, and running wild, a very wilderness of moss-grown paths, tangled roses and honeysuckles, clematis and syringa, fallen statues, empty marble basins, where fountains once had been. Over all, to-day, the wildly sweeping rain and vivid play of summer lightning.

"Ruin and decay everywhere," France said, with a sigh. "It is plain to be seen no master's eye ever rests here. The gardens of Caryllynne, years ago, Mr. Locksley, were the glory of the place. This was Mrs. Caryll's; it has never been kept up since she went away."

"But you, Miss Forrester, I should think that—"

"Nothing shall be changed—nothing altered by me. As Gordon Caryll left, so he shall find it when he comes back."

"You are so sure he will come back, then."

"As sure as that I stand here. I don't know why, but

10*

ever since I have been old enough to hear about him and think about him I have known that he will come back."

"And that return will really make you—really make his mother happy ? "

"It will be new life to his mother. It will make me hap-pier than anything," she paused a moment and her color rose—"*almost* happier than anything on earth."

"Then in spite of the past Gordon Caryll ought to be a happy man. You have never seen him—this forgotten exile in whom you take so deep an interest ? "

" I have never seen him, but I have seen his picture and have heard of him from my earliest childhood, and when-ever and wherever we meet I shall know him."

He gave a quick start, flushed slightly and laughed. She looked up at him in surprise.

" You will know him—you who have never seen him—you think that, Miss Forrester ? "

" I think that, Mr. Locksley."

" But he will have changed—sixteen years and more is a tolerable time. No, Miss Forrester, you might meet him face to face, talk to him, clasp hands, and still be as strangers. Time and trouble change men ; sixteen years knocking around the world, leading the sort of life he has led, a free companion, a soldier of fortune, will change any man. Miss Forrester, believe me, when you meet, if ever you do meet, you will not know Gordon Caryll."

He paused abruptly. The dark, penetrating eyes were watching him with a suspicious intentness he did not care to meet.

" Mr. Locksley," she said quickly, "*you* were a soldier of fortune—you fought in India. about the same time, or so Terry Dennison has told me. Did you ever meet Gor-don Caryll ? "

His face flushed again, dark red. There was an instant's silence—then once more he laughed.

" You are a sorceress, Miss Forrester. What have I said to make you think so ? "

" You have said nothing. And yet—Mr. Locksley, if you know anything tell me. I would give half my life to know."

"Well, then—yes," but the answer was given reluctantly, "I think I once met Gordon Caryll."

She clasped her hands together, and stood looking at him breathlessly.

"In India?" she asked.

"In India I met a man that I judge may have been the man you mean. He was not called Caryll—how was it he called himself? And yet I know from certain things he told me of his history that he was the man."

Her eager eyes were fixed upon him, her eager lips were apart, the sensitive color coming and going in her face.

"Go on," she breathed.

"I have very little to tell. He told me his story one night as we lay beside our bivouac fire—the story of his terrible mistake—of his terrible awakening—of his divorce from the woman who had so utterly deceived him—of his return to England—of his sentence of outlawry and exile. I know he had no intention of ever trying to have that sentence revoked—he felt that he deserved it. It was simple justice; he bowed his head and accepted his doom. He had dishonored a name never approached by disgrace until he bore it; he had broken his father's heart and brought him to the grave; he had driven his mother forever from the home and the country he had resigned. What return—what earthly redemption, could there be for him?"

"And yet there is—there is!" she broke forth vehemently. "From first to last he was more sinned against than sinning. He loved that woman—that wicked, wretched woman, whose memory I hate—and he would have given up all things for love of her, had she not been the wretch she was. He came to his mother in his trouble, and she thrust him forth. She has repented—oh, how bitterly—and the only happiness life can hold for her is to make atonement, to receive and forgive him again. Oh, Mr. Locksley, if you know anything of him now, if you can aid me in finding him, help me. Bring him back to us, to his mother, to his home, and the whole gratitude of my life will be yours."

She stretched forth both her hands to him. He took them, very pale, and held them in his.

"He will rob you of a noble inheritance. Have you any right to throw it away? What will Lord Dynely say to that?"

"Lord Dynely!" She looked at him in angry surprise. "What has Lord Dynely to do with this!"

"Much, since he has to do with you. The day that re· stores Gordon Caryll to his mother, robs you of half your fortune."

"You spoke of that before, Mr. Locksley. Never speak of it again. What are a thousand fortunes compared to the right?—to seeing her, my best and dearest friend, happy, and him restored from wandering and exile to his own?"

"And as Lady Dynely you can afford to be magnanimous —a fortune more or less can concern you little."

She looked at him still haughtily, but with a heart beginning to beat fast. If he cared nothing for her, why this bitter tone, this pale, stern face?

"As Lady Dynely. There is some mistake here, Mr. Locksley. I don't know what you mean."

"I beg your pardon, Miss Forrester. It is presumptuous, no doubt, in me to allude to it, but as your engagement to Lord Dynely is no secret, I may—"

"My engagement to Lord Dynely! Who says I am engaged to Lord Dynely? I am nothing of the sort. Lord Dynely is engaged to a clergyman's daughter in Lincoln· shire."

He stood still, looking at her, his head in a whirl, wonder, incredulity, blank amaze in his face.

"There was some sort of foolish compact between Mrs. Caryll and Lady Dynely," proceeded Miss Forrester, "to marry us when we grew up—a compact in which I have had no part—and which we never could ratify. Eric and I have grown up as brother and sister—more than we are now we never will or could be to each other. With the ordering of my life or fortune, *he*, at least, has nothing to do."

There was a moment's pause—a most awkward and uncomfortable pause for Miss Forrester. Mr. Locksley stood still, so petrified by this sudden revelation that his very breath seemed taken away.

"I thought—I thought," he said, "you loved him."

She made no answer.

"I thought you loved him," he went on. "I thought you were engaged to him. And last night, when he returned, I fancied I read new happiness in your face—that his coming had brought it, and it was more than I could bear. I had done with loving—or so I thought—done with women for-ever, and yet I accepted Lady Dynely's invitation and came down here. And I thought you were to be his wife, that all your heart was his, and I—"

"Resolved to run away to Spain, and in painting dark-eyed Spanish donnas, forget France Forrester."

She laughed as she spoke. Her dark face was flushed, but the old, gay, mischief-loving spirit was back. She could not look at her lover, but she could laugh at him.

"Yes," he said, moodily, "there are some dangers from which flight is the only safeguard. You, a wealthy heiress in your first youth—I, a man of forty, poor, unknown, an artist whose brush brings him the bread he eats. You can-not realize more fully than I do, how insane my love for you is."

"Have I said it was insane?"

"France!" he cried.

She did not speak.

"France," he cried again, "can it be possible that you care for me! Speak my fate in one word—shall it be go, or stay?"

She turned toward him, the dark eyes full of radiant light, and answered :

"Stay !"

CHAPTER XVI.

EN minutes have passed. All that it is necessary to say has been said ; the first delirium is over, and reason has resumed her sway.

"But what will Lady Dynely say ? " Locksley asks. "How am I to go and tell her that the impecunious artist whom she brought down here, to paint her ward's picture, has had the presumption to fall in love with his sitter, and declare that presumptuous passion? And what will your guardian in Rome say—Mrs. Caryll ? "

"I don't know that it matters very greatly what they say," France laughs. "Mrs. Caryll I should like to please certainly, but since I am not to marry Lord Dynely, I do not think her objections will be very difficult to overcome. For Lady Dynely, I am under her care for the present, but to control my actions in any way she has no right whatever. I shall be of age in two years, and then "—she looks up into the eager face above her, still laughing—" and then, so you are pleased, it won't matter very greatly what all the world together says."

"'That means you will be wife. France—am I to believe it—that one day I may claim you as my own ? "

"If you care to have me. And, meantime, I suppose you will give up your idea of rushing out of the world, and remain here like a reasonable mortal, and paint that duplicate picture for dear old grandmamma Caryll."

"I will do anything you say—I will paint a thousand duplicates—I will stay here and face an army of guardians if necessary, and be branded as a fortune-hunter, an adventurer. For a fortune-hunter they will call me, and believe me to be."

"Not in my presence, at least," France answers ; "no one, not those I hold nearest and dearest, shall speak ill of you and remain my friend.   And speaking of fortune, I hope you have no objection to my restoring to Gordon Caryll, should he at any time return, all the inheritance his mother bequeathes me.   I hold it in trust ; and let him appear to-morrow, or thirty years from now, I will still return it."

Locksley laughed.

"I object !   Not likely !   Still—I hope he will not come !"

"Mr. Locksley !"

"I decline to answer to that name any longer to you. I have another, though the idea does not seem to have occurred to you."

"What is it?   I have seen G. Locksley at the bottom of your pictures.   What is it?   George?   Godfrey?   Geoffry? What?

"None of these—my name is——"

The dark, luminous eyes were lifted to his face.

"Is—well?"

"My name is Gordon."

"Gordon !" a startled expression came over her face for a moment—her eagerly wistful eyes looked at him.   But he met her gaze with his curiously imperturbable smile.

"It is a favorite cognomen of yours, I know.   There are other Gordons in the world beside Gordon Caryll, who as I said before, I hope will never return."

"And why?"

"Because I am mortally jealous of him.   He has always been your hero, by your own showing—is so still—and I feel in the depths of my prophetic soul that he is destined to be my rival.   If it were not for that, I might be tempted to—" a smile and a provoking pause.

"Well, to what?" she cries with that pretty imperiousness of manner that was one of her chief charms.

"To find him for you.   It ought not to be an impossible task.   I think I could accomplish it, if I were quite sure your hero of the past would not become your idol of the future.   To bring him here with a halo of romance envelop-

ing him would be a dangerous experiment. I had made up my
mind to go and surrender you to Lord Dynely ; to surrender
you now to Mr. Gordon Caryll—no, I am only human—I
could not do that.   Lord Dynely would be a dangerous rival
for any man living, with the youth and the beauty of a Greek
god ; but Gordon Caryll must be old and as battered as myself.   To be ousted by him—"

He paused ; she had clasped her hands, her lips were
apart, her eyes were dilated.

"Mr. Locksley—"

"Gordon—Gordon—I told you my name."

" Gordon, then—do you think—*do* you think you can find
him ? "

" Caryll ?   Why, yes.   I can try at least.   I dare say he is
as anxious to return as you are to have him back.   Only tell
me, France, that when he is found he will never come between you and me ? "

She looks at him, an indignant flash in her eyes—an indignant flush on her cheeks.

"Neither Gordon Caryll nor any man on earth can do
that.   I belong to you.   Only I want him back for his own
sake, for his mother's, for mine.   He has suffered enough,
been in exile long enough, for what at no time was his fault,
but his misfortune.   Fetch him back, if you can—it is all
that is needed to complete my perfect happiness now."

The name of her lover does not come fluently from her
lips yet.   "Gordon."   It is an odd coincidence, she thinks,
that he should resemble the exiled heir of Caryllynne, and
bear the same name.   Some dim, vague suspicion is beginning to creep over her, some shadow of suspicion rather ; for,
as yet, the truth is too wildly unreal and improbable to be
thought of.   He knows more of Gordon Caryll, she thinks,
than he will tell, and the dark eyes look up at him wistfully,
searchingly.   Something in Locksley's face makes her think
the subject distasteful to him.   He stands there understanding her thoroughly, and with a half-repressed smile on his
lips.   They have changed places it would seem ; she is no
longer the haughty, high-born heiress—he no longer the ob-

scure, penniless artist, and soldier of fortune. It is his to rule, hers to obey.

"What a wretched expression of countenance, Miss For-rester," he said laughing. "Are you regretting your hasty admission of five minutes ago? Are you sorry already you bade me stay? If so—"

Her clasped hands tighten on his arm. Sorry she bade him stay! Her radiant eyes answer that.

"Then it is solely on Gordon Caryll's account. Be at peace, my France, ask no questions; we will talk of ourselves, not of him. Only be sure of this—he shall return to his home, to his mother, and to you."

She lays her happy face against his shoulder in eloquent silence. So they stand—looking out at the leaden summer afternoon, listening to the soft, dark rush of the summer rain.

"How will we get back to Dynely Abbey if this lasts?" France says at last.

"It is not going to last," Mr. Locksley answers; "it is lighting already in the west yonder. In two hours from now, *ma belle*, you will drive me back to the village through a perfect blaze of sunset glory. Meantime we have the house to see, luncheon to eat, and, by the same token, I wish your old lady would hurry. It may seem unromantic, Miss Forrester, but——"

"You have had no dinner and are famished," laughs France. "Here comes Mrs. Mathews now, to announce that our banquet is ready."

Mrs. Mathews enters, unutterably respectable to look at, in her stiff, black silk, and widow's cap. Yes, luncheon is ready, and as Mrs. Mathews makes the announcement, she gazes with strange intensity into the face of the tall, bearded stranger. She remembers her young master as though she had seen him but yesterday, and *how* like this gentleman is to him none but Mrs. Mathews can realize. His eyes, his expression, the very trick of manner with which he shakes back his thick brown hair. Her master returned! It cannot be, else surely Miss France must know it; and yet-- and yet — the house-keeper's eyes followed him as one fascinated.

She waits upon them. It is a very merry little repast. In spite of love's delirium they both enjoy the creature com-forts provided. Mr. Locksley is really hungry—does the *grande passion* ever impair a healthy man's appetite? It does France good to see him eat. And then, luncheon over, they saunter away to look at the rooms.

Locksley's prediction concerning the weather is already beginning to be fulfilled. The afternoon has lighted up once more—the sun, behind its veil of clouds still, will be out in full splendor presently; the rain falls, but gently. The swift August storm is spent.

"We shall have a delicious drive home," France says, as they wander through long suites of rooms, drawing-rooms, library, and picture-gallery. "What an eventful day this has been. How little I thought, when I started forth 'fetter-less and free' this morning, that I should wear captive chains before night; I am glad Lady Dynely is away—she would be certain to read all my wrongdoing in my guilty face upon my return, and to sit down and tell her in cold blood so soon, I could not. It would seem a sort of desecration."

You are sure you will never repent?" Locksley asks, un-easily. "You have made but a miserable bargain, France. With your youth and beauty, your birth and fortune, the offers you refused in the season, to end at last with a free lance, an obscure artist, whose youth is passed, who can give you nothing but an unknown name, and a heart that you took captive at sight, in return. My darling, the world will tell you, and tell you truly, you have made but a sorry bargain."

'The world will never tell it to me twice. Why do we talk of it? I love you; with you I am happy—without you I am miserable—all is said in that."

There is silence for a time. They look at the pictured faces of dead-and-gone Carylls, and do not see them. At last—

"And so you take me blindfolded?" Locksley says. "You ask nothing of the forty years that lie behind me? You give me yourself, without one question of what my life has been? How are you to tell I am worthy of the gift?"

She looks at him and her happy face pales suddenly. All at once there returns to her the memory of Eric's words, the memory of that hinted at, hidden away, "obnoxious wife."

"I have a story to tell you," he says in answer to that startled look; "you shall hear it before we quit this house —you shall know all my life as I know it myself. How many more rooms have we to see? Whose is this?"

"It is—it was—Gordon Caryll's."

They pause on the threshold. The sun has come from behind the clouds and fills the room with its slanting, amber glory. The rain has entirely ceased—a rainbow spans the arch of blue sky they can see from the tall window.

"Nothing has been altered," France says softly; "everything is as he left it. Books, pictures, pipes, whips, guns, —all!"

They enter. What a strange expression Locksley's face wears, the girl thinks, as he looks around. She does not understand, and yet those vague, shapeless suspicions are floating in her mind. They touch nothing—they stand together and look, and the yellow sunshine gilds all. The books in their cases, the handsomely framed proof engravings of dogs and horses, the pipes of all nations, the side-arms of all countries—dirks, cimetars, swords, bowie knives, the gaudy robe de chambre, now faded and dim, thrown over a chair back—all as Gordon Caryll had left them.

They quit this room presently and enter the next. It was Mrs. Caryll's sitting-room, in those long gone days, the room in which, as the twilight of another August day fell, she stood and banished her only son from her side forever.

The bright yellow sunshine floods all things here too; the chair in which she used to sit, the work-table and work-box upon it, her piano in the corner, the velvet draperied oratory beyond; and over the chimney, one picture with its face turned to the wall. "It is a portrait of Gordon Caryll," France says, almost in a whisper, for something in her companion's face startles her strangely; "she placed it so on that last cruel evening when she drove him from her. So it has hung since."

"Turn it," Locksley commands briefly, and she obeys. She stands upon a chair and turns the pictured face to the light. It is covered with dust. Spiders have woven their webs across it. She glances around for a cloth, finds one, wipes dust and cobwebs together off, and the boyish face of the last Squire of Caryllynne smiles back upon her in the sunshine.

"Was he not handsome ? " she asks, regretfully. "Poor Gordon ! brave and generous and beloved of all—to think he should pay for one mistake by life-long exile and loneliness."

She looks down at her lover. She pauses suddenly ; a wild expression comes over her face. She springs from her perch and glances from the pictured face of the boy to the living face of the man gazing gravely up.

She sees at last—neither years, nor bronze, nor beard can deceive her longer. She gives a little cry, and stands breathless, her hands clasped, her color coming and going.

He sees he is known, and turns to her with the very smile the pictured face wears.

"My France," he says, "you know at last that I am Gordon Caryll."

CHAPTER XVII

THROUGH THE SUNSET.

S O ! The truth is out at last—the desire of her life is gained. Gordon Caryll stands there before her —her lover !

She hardly knows whether she is glad or sorry, she hardly knows even whether she is surprised. She has turned quite white, and stands looking at him in a silence she is unable to break.

Gordon Caryll laughs—the most genially amused laugh she has heard yet.

"If I had said, 'I am his Satanic Majesty, horns, hoofs and all,' you could hardly look more petrified, more wildly incredulous. My dear child, do come out of that trance of horror and say something."

He takes both her hands, and looks smilingly down into her pale, startled face.

"Look at me, France—look at that picture. *Don't* you see the resemblance ? Surely you don't doubt what I have said ?"

"Doubt you ! Oh, Gordon ! *what* a surprise this is. And yet—I don't know—I don't really know—'As in a glass, darkly,' I believe I must have seen it from the first."

"And you are sorry or glad—which ? You told me that the desire of your heart was Gordon Caryll's return. Gordon Caryll stands before you—your heart's desire is gained, and you look at me with the blankest face I ever saw you wear. Are you sorry, then, after all ?"

"Sorry ! Ah, you know better than that. Why," with a laugh, "the romance of my life was that Gordon Caryll would return, and that I should be the one to console him for the bitter past—that I should one day be his wife. And to think —-that my dream should come true. Yet still—"

"Well—yet still."

"Yet still—more or less it is a disappointment. I had hoped to be the good genius of your life in all things--that my fortune would be your stepping stone to fame. Now I can do nothing ; I am not going to marry a struggling artist and help him win his laurel crown. The heir of Caryllynne need owe nothing to his wife. My romance of love in a cottage, while you won a name among the immortals, is at an end."

"Not so. After all it will be due to you the same—I take Caryllynne from you. And I would never have taken off my mask, and shown myself to the world as I am, but for you."

"Not even for your mother's sake ? "

"Not even for my mother's sake. How, but for you would I ever have known that my mother desired it, that I was forgiven, that she longed to take me back ? It makes me happier than I can say now that I know it; but of my-self I never would have discovered it. What was done, was done ; I meant to have walked on the way I had chosen to the end. But you appeared, and lo ! all things changed."

"It is like a fairy tale," she said ; "I *cannot* realize it. Oh ! what will Lady Dynely, what will Eric, what will your mother, what will all the world say ?"

"I don't think it will surprise Lady Dynely very greatly," Caryll answered coolly. "She recognized me the first day —I saw it in her face—only she took pains to convince herself it was an impossibility. I had been gone so long it was impossible I could ever come back ; that was how she reasoned. For Eric, well it would be dead against every rule of his creed to be surprised at anything. He will open those sleepy blue eyes of his for a second or two, and lift his blonde eyebrows to the roots of his hair."

"Very likely," says France ; "he has not far to lift them."

"I wonder you did not marry him, France. He's a hand-some fellow, and a gallant. As unlike a battered old soldier such as I am as—as the Apollo is unlike the Farnese Her-cules."

"And yet there are many people, of undoubted taste too, who prefer the Hercules as the true type of manliness to the Apollo. Eric is very handsome—absurdly handsome for a man ; the wife of a demi-god must have rather a trying time of it. I don't care, besides, to share a heart that some scores of women, dark and light, have shared before me. 'All or none,' is the motto of the Forresters. Are you sure, sir, I may claim all in the present case?"

"All—every infinitesimal atom. I offer you a heart that for the past seventeen years has had no lodger. Before that," he drew a deep breath and looked at her. "You know that story."

"Yes, I know it—Lady Dynely told me. She is dead?"

"Would I ever have spoken to you else? Yes, she is dead."

He dropped her hands suddenly and walked over to the window. Beyond the green hill tops the sun was dropping into the sea—the whole western sky was aflush. The sparkling drops, glittering like diamonds on roses and verbenas, were all that remained of the past storm.

She stood where he had left her, looking after him wistfully, with something that was almost a contraction of the heart.

"Nineteen years have passed," she thought, "since they parted. Does the very memory of that time still affect him like this?"

She remembered the story Lady Dynely had told her—of how passionately he had loved that most worthless wife. Could any man love like that twice in a lifetime. The wine of life had been given to that dead actress—the lees were left for her.

"France!"

She was by his side in an instant—ashamed of that unworthy spasm of jealousy of the dead.

"Am I to take this day as emblematic of my life? Have the rain and the darkness passed forever, and will the end be in brightness such as this? It has been a hard life sometimes, a bitter life often, a lonely life always, but the darkest record you know. The story of the woman I married and who was my ruin."

She glanced up with that new-born shyness of hers into his overcast face in silence.

"Let me tell you all to-day, and make an end of it," he said. "It is something I hate to speak of—hate with all my soul to think of. You know the story—Lady Dynely has told you, you say. You know then how I was divorced, how our united names rang the changes through England and Canada; how the name of Caryll, never dishonored before, was dragged through the mire of a divorce court. You know how I came to England and saw my mother and Lucia. Saw Lady Dynely, told her all, and bade her good-by upon that other August night nineteen years ago—the very night her husband died. All that you know?"

"Yes, I know," she said. "Go on."

"I had left my old regiment and exchanged into one ordered to India, and in India the next twelve years were spent. It was hot and exciting work at first; little time to think, little time to regret. The horrible mutiny, of which you have heard, with whose bloody and sickening details all England was ringing then, when women and children were butchered in cold blood, was at its height. Who could stop and think of private woes when the whole British heart was wrung with agony. It was the best discipline that could possibly have befallen me—for my life I was reckless, the sooner a Sepoy bullet ended a dishonored existence the better. But the flying Sepoy bullet laid low better men and passed me. I carried a sort of charmed life—I passed through skirmish after skirmish, hot work too with the fierce black devils, and never received a scratch. At last our slaughtered countrymen were avenged and the mutiny was over.

"Of the life that followed in India I have little to say. It was the usual dull routine of drill and parade ; of Calcutta and Bombay—of hill parties, of up-country excursions, of jackal shooting, and pig sticking. Of a sudden I grew tired of it all. India became insupportable, a sort of homesickness took possession of me. I must see England. I must see my mother once more. I sold out and came home, and came here, and heard all about my people. My mother had quitted Caryllynne forever, and taken up her abode at Rome. She had adopted General Forrester's only child as her daughter and heiress, Miss Forrester being then at a Parisian convent. Lady Dynely was a widow—she too was abroad—she too had adopted an orphan lad, who was now with her son and heir at Eton. That was what I learned from the village gossips, and then once more I left England.

"This time I went to America. There I remained, rambling aimlessly about the country, trying to decide what to do with my future life. Suddenly it occurred to me to ascertain for certain what had become of the woman who had been my wife. Was she living or dead? I never thought of her at all when I could avoid it, but that thought had often obtruded. Now was the time to know for certain.

"I went to Canada—Quebec, to the place where I had seen her last. The lonely house on the Heights, which she had chosen as her home, stood silent and gray, desolate and uninhabited. I returned to the town, hunted up the man who had been its owner thirteen years before, who was its owner still.

"'Could he tell me anything of the lady—Mrs. Gordon— who had been his tenant in that past time?' He pushed up his spectacles and looked at me curiously.

"'Humph!' he said, 'that is a very long time ago. Mrs. Gordon! Do I remember her? I should think so, indeed —no one who ever saw *that* face was likely to forget it in a hurry. Perhaps—would I mind telling him?—perhaps I was Mr. Gordon—the gentleman whom he had the honor of speaking to once before?'

"'It can matter nothing to you,' I answered, 'who I am. I am interested in Mrs. Gordon's ultimate fate. Can you tell me where she is now?'

"He laughed in a grim sort of way.

"'Well, no—seeing there is no telegraphic communication between this world and the next. Mrs. Gordon is dead.'

"'Dead!' Whether we hate or love, the abrupt announcement of the death of any one we have intimately known

11

must ever come upon us with something of a shock.
"Dead !' then I was free ! I drew a long breath—a breath
of great relief. 'Will you tell me how she died?' I asked
after a moment.

"'It was a very shocking thing—oh ; a very shocking
thing, indeed. She was killed.'

"'Killed.'

"'I don't wonder you look startled. Yes, poor soul—
killed in a railway accident. Wait a moment—I have the
paper somewhere—I generally cut out such things and keep
them.'

"He ransacked in his desk—produced a Montreal paper
of four years before, and pointed out a paragraph. It gave
a detailed account of a very terrible collision on the Grand
Trunk Railway, of the loss of life, the list of the wounded
and killed. Among the killed I read the name of Mrs. Gordon.

"'Is that all your proof?' I said to him. 'That is nothing. Gordon is a common name.'

"'Ah, but look here.'

"He turned over the paper and pointed to another place.
'The Mrs. Gordon whose name is recorded in another
column as among the number killed, was a lady with a history of more than ordinary interest. She was of a beauty
most remarkable, by profession an actress of more than
ordinary talent. Her history must still be familiar to our
readers, as the heroine of the celebrated divorce case of
nine years ago. A young English officer of family and
wealth, named Gordon Caryll,' etc., etc. In short, the
whole miserable story was given of the actress, her accom-
plice, and her dupe. 'Since that time,' the record went on
to say, 'she had returned to the stage and was rising rapidly
to fame and fortune when this most melancholy disaster ended
her brilliant career.'

"I sat with the paper before me. And this was the end
—the end of all that beauty that, among all the women I
had met since or before, I had never seen equalled. The
voice of Mr. Barteaux aroused me.

"'Every year from the time she left, she returned for a

flying visit of a few days, to settle accounts with Joan Kennedy and to see the child. A fine little girl now, and her
mother's living image.'

"I stared at him in blank amaze. 'The child!' I said.
'What child?'

"He pushed up his spectacles once more, and scrutinized
me over them.

"'Then you are not Mr. Gordon, after all? Mr. Gordon
Caryll, of course; I mean the gentleman who married her,
and who divorced her. I give you my word, I thought you
were.'

"'It can't matter to you who I am, my good fellow.
Only I want to know to what child you allude.'

"'To Mrs. Gordon's child, to be sure. Born in the
House that Wouldn't Let, a few weeks after your last visit
here, and left by Mrs. Gordon in charge of Joan Kennedy,
when she went away.'

"A child! I had never known of that—never thought of
that. I sat for a moment quite still trying to realize what I
had heard.

"'She named the little one Gordon, after its papa, I suppose. She couldn't take it with her very well, so she left it
with Joan when she went, and had ever since paid liberally
for its support. Once a year, too, she came to visit it, and
it was returning from that ill-starred visit this year she had
met her terrible end.'

"I rose up, startled beyond all telling by this new revelation.

"'Where does this Joan Kennedy live?' I inquired. 'I
must see her at once, if possible.'

"'It is not possible,' returned Mr. Barteaux. 'I know
nothing of Joan Kennedy now. Three years ago she married a man named McGregor, and left with him for the
Western States. She took Mrs. Gordon's child with her.
She could not have been more attached to it had it been
her own. Since then I have seen or heard nothing of her.'

"'Can I not obtain her address?'

"'Not here, sir—no one knows where they went. Mc-
Gregor had no particular location in view. You might ad-

vertise in New York and Western papers, and see what
will come of it.'

"I followed his advice—I did advertise, again and again,
but with no result. I wanted intensely to find that child. I
travelled West, I inquired everywhere—in vain. Then the
civil war broke out, and I joined the army. Two more
years passed, and then in one of the great battles I received
a wound that was so nearly mortal as to incapacitate me
from further fighting. The moment I could quit hospital,
I returned to Europe—went at once to Rome, and took to
painting, as the one last ambition and love of my life. In
Rome I saw you, saw my mother many times, but I held
aloof. I only knew I had driven her from England, that
my dishonor clung to her like a garment. I had no thought
but if I came before her I should be spurned once more.
That I did not choose to bear. Then my restless familiar
again took possession of me—I came back to England. I
painted that picture, sent it to the Academy, and there, one
sunny May afternoon, met my fate and you. "

"And that picture," France said, speaking as he paused
and looked fondly down upon her, "'How the Night Fell,'
was your parting with *her*, was it not ?"

"It was."

"Poor soul ! Ah, Gordon ! she was to be pitied, after all.
She loved you and lost you. I can think of no bitterer fate."

"Don't waste your pity, France. Of love, as you understand it, she knew nothing. Good heavens ! what an
utterly vile and cold-blooded plot it was ! and what an easy
dupe she and that scoundrelly old major found in me !
Don't let us talk about it. I have told you—so let it end.
I never want to speak of her while I live again. Only—I
should have liked to find that child."

They stand silently, side by side. The sun has set, but
the sky is all rosy, and purple and golden, with the glory it
has left. France pulls out her watch.

"Seven. How the hours have flown. I should have
started long ago—it will be quite dark before I reach the
Abbey now. Do order round the phaeton, Gordon, whilst I
run up and put on my hat."

She quits his side and runs lightly up the polished oaken stairs, singing as she goes for very gladness of heart. She has always loved the dear old house ; she will love it now more than ever, since in it she has been so supremely happy.

She adjusts the coquettish little bonnet and returns.

The lord of the manor, stately and tall, a very man of men, France thinks, awaits her and assists her in. He gathers up the reins as one who has the right, and drives her at a spanking pace away from Caryllynne. The broad yellow moon is lifting her luminous face over the pearl and silver sky, the rose and amethyst splendor is fading tenderly out of the west. She sits beside him in silence, too happy to talk much. All her life dreams are realized. Her artist lover is hers—and he and Gordon Caryll are one. She has been wooed and won as romantically as the most romantic girl could desire. His voice breaks the spell.

" I start for Rome to-morrow."

"To-morrow !" She looks up for an instant. " Gordon ! so soon ? "

" She has waited sixteen years," he answers. " Can I go too speedily ? Yet if you—"

" Oh, no, no ! It is her right, it is your duty. You must go. Only you will not stay very long ? "

The nightingales are singing in the woods of Caryllynne— they alone may hear his answer.

He drives her to the Abbey gates—he will not enter. He will walk back to the village, he tells her ; he needs a walk and a smoke, to calm his mind after all this.

" Shall I see you to-morrow before you go ? " she asks.

" I think not—no, I will leave by the first train—it would be too early. Our parting will be to-night. Tell Lady Dynely ; and let wonder be over before I return."

Then under the black shadows of the chestnut trees they clasp hands and say farewell.

CHAPTER XVIII.

KILLING THE FATTED CALF.

THE golden summer days are over. September is at an end—the sharp crack of the fowling-pieces no longer rings the long days through, as the doomed partridges wheel in the sun. The ides of October are here—the steel-gray mornings, the frost-bound nights, the stripped branches of the tossing trees, the shrill wild winds. It is October, the last week of the month, the last hour of the day ; and the night which the white chill moon is heralding even now, is to be a grand field night at Dynely Abbey. For my lady gives a ball, the first for many a year ; half the county are invited, and all invited are coming. Has not the news spread ;—has not Gordon Caryll, the black sheep of the flock, the "hero of a hundred battles," whose life reads, so far as they know it, like a chapter from some old romance, returned to claim his own, and are they not to behold him to-night ? It has been something more than the ordinary nine days' wonder, this story that has been told of him ; these good people in a circuit of twenty miles have talked of nothing it would seem since it came out first. They can recall him well, scores of them—a tall, fair-haired, handsome lad, a dashing young trooper before he left for that transatlantic world, where he met the siren who has been his doom. It all comes back to them, the first dark whisperings of that terrible scandal that broke his haughty father's heart, that drove his mother into exile forever. Then the full details of the story—the public shame, the divorce, the return, the decree of banishment. They had all thought him dead, and France Forrester the heiress of Caryllynne, and lo ! he starts up all in a moment, a distinguished and popular artist, and the accepted lover of his mother's heiress. He has been in Rome all these weeks, visiting that mother herself; publicly and joyfully recognized and received by her, and to-night he returns, and they will see him face to face at Lady Dynely's. At Lady Dynely's! Why, in the days that are gone, when he was but the merest lad, there was an old story that he was his cousin's lover. She has not seen him yet in his new character—it will be curious to watch them, the friends and neighbors maliciously think. And France Forrester is to marry him. Is the actress wife dead then, they wonder? They had thought Miss Forrester and Lord Dynely were engaged, and now it comes out that Lord Dynely is to marry a clergyman's daughter in Lincolnshire—a Miss Higgins. Miss Higgins is to be present also to-night—she and her father and one of her sisters are expected this evening. Certainly a treat is in store for them—not one who is invited will miss coming.

As the last light of day fades out and the white starry moonlight floods earth and sky, Lady Dynely comes out of her dressing-room. In the clustering waxlights she looks pale, pale even for her who is always pale, but fair and youthful and elegant in her trailing violet velvet, her priceless point lace, and the Dynely diamonds flashing on slender throat and wrists and hands. The very first of her guests will not arrive for a full hour yet, but she has dressed early, and stands quite alone, glad to be alone for a little before it all begins. Up in her room France is dressing—in theirs Crystal and Crystal's sister are dressing likewise—Eric is in his—Terry in his. For Terry has broken through his resolution of not putting in an appearance before Christmas, and run down for a night. Lady Dynely has ordained it so, and Terry knows no will of his own where she wills otherwise. The first sharp, cruel pain of loss is not even yet obliterated —all his life long, though he lived to be a hundred, no other woman will ever be to him quite what little Crystal Higgins has been. In no way is she at all remarkable ; pretty, but scores he sees every day are as pretty ; not brilliant, not wise, not clever, and yet—she will stand alone among all womanhood forever and ever to Terry Dennison. He has not met her yet. She reached the Abbey early in the afternoon, he not half an hour since, and he looks forward to the meeting with nervous dread that half unmans him. She is Eric's now—well, so that Eric is loyal, so that Eric makes her life happy, he can forgive even him. On New Year's eve she is to be Eric's wife, and he is bidden to the wedding. He has had an interview with Lady Dynely—of necessity very brief. All his generosity, all Eric's disloyalty is in her mind as she comes forward to meet him, and takes his hand in hers and holds it tight, and looks with pale imploring eyes up in his face—a face that is just a thought graver and more·worn than she ever saw it before.

"It is all right," he says, simply, knowing by intuition what she would say. "So that Eric makes her happy, all the rest is nothing. I don't blame him much—her not at all. Who would look at me twice beside Eric?"

And then he kisses her cheek gently and goes up-stairs to his own old room, and meets France on the upper landing on her way to dress.

"Dear old Terry," Miss Forrester says, giving him both hands; "it is like water in the desert to see you again. Go where I will, meet whom I may, there is but one Terry Dennison."

"And but one Mr. Locksley—no, I beg his pardon, but one Gordon Caryll. So your hero has come at last, France. All your life you have been worshipping him from afar off, now your demigod has plumped from the clouds at your feet. You have thrown over Eric and are going to marry Caryll."

"'Thrown over Eric!" Miss Forrester retorts, forgetting grammar in indignation. "I like that way of putting it, when everybody knows he threw over *me*. A case of love at sight, wasn't it, Terry? and, amazing to relate, it seems to last. I suppose you know she's here."

"Yes, I know. Do you like her, France? But you do, of course."

"I don't perceive the of course. She is pretty enough— oh, yes, I don't deny her pretty Grecian features and pink and pearl complexion; but, like her —that's another thing. Little idiot!"

"And why little idiot, Miss Forrester?"

"She jilted you, Terry, for him—a man for a mannikin. She led you on, and would have married you if he had not come ; and, at the first sight of his ambrosial curls and little amber mustache and girl's complexion, she goes down at his lordly feet. Bah ! I've no patience with her."

"But you'll be good to her, France, all the same. Poor little Crystal ! It looks a very brilliant match, and yet——"

"And yet she would be ten thousand-fold happier as your wife. The woman who is lifted to the honor and bliss of being my Lord Viscount Dynely's bride, bids fair, once the honeymoon is ended, to win the martyr's crown. The handsomest peer in the realm, the most notorious male flirt in Europe, is hardly likely to be held long by the pretty, innocent, baby face of Crystal Higgins. It was awfully good of you, Terry, to come at all."

"Her ladyship wished it," is Terry's quiet answer, as though all was said in that, and Miss Forrester shrugs her imperial shoulders.

"As the queen wills ! You should have been born of the Dynely blood and race ; the motto of the house suits you—' *Loyal au mort.*' You would be faithful to the death, Terry, I think. It certainly does not suit Eric—it is not in him to be faithful to any human being."

"I wish he heard you, France."

"He has heard it a thousand times. By the bye, Terry, it occurs to me to ask exactly what relation are you to Eric ?"

The clustering wax lights shed their lustre full upon Terry's face, and, as she asks the heedless, impulsive question, France sees that face turn dark red from brow to chin. The swift abruptness of the simple demand strikes him mute. The truth he may not tell—may never tell, and falsehoods never come trippingly from Terry's tongue. Miss Forrester lays her slim ringed hand on the young man's arm.

"I beg your pardon," she says, hastily. "I know, of course—Eric's distant cousin ; but, as you stood there, on my word you looked sufficiently like him to be his brother. I have often noticed a vague resemblance before, in height and bearing ; but never, I think, so markedly as now."

11*

The dark, painful flush deepens on Dennison's face. He looks at her with startled eyes. She is wonderfully acute in her surmises. Has some inkling of the truth come to her? But no—the smiling face that meets his is supremely uncon- scious. She pulls out her watch.

"Past seven. I should have been under the hands of Pauline an hour ago. Ta, ta, Terry; run away, my dear boy, and make yourself beautiful forever."

She trips past and vanishes in one of the upper rooms; and Terry, drawing a long breath, goes more slowly to his.

"No," he thinks; "it was but a random shot that struck home. I am Eric's distant cousin. She suspects nothing."

But Mr. Dennison was mistaken. It had been a random shot; but, as the red light of guilt flamed out in the dra- goon's face, the first suspicion of the truth that had ever come to her broke upon her then. She had heard that vague story of distant kinship—she had heard, years ago, that Lady Dynely had made a pilgrimage to some wild region of western Ireland and brought Terry back, a little uncouth waif and stray; she knew how zealously she had cared for him since—she knew of Terry's boundless love and grati- tude, in which to her there was always something almost pa- thetic; but she never dreamed there might be more on the cards than met the eyes. "Sufficiently like Eric to be his brother." She had heard what manner of man the late Right Honorable Viscount Dynely had been—Eric's light- headed fickleness was as hereditary as the title. Who was to say that Eric and Terry were not brothers, after all? Yes, that was the secret of Lady Dynely's compassionate care—of Terry's humble, patient devotion.

"Poor fellow!" she thought, "it is hard lines on him. The name, the rank, the wealth, the love—all to the youn- ger; to the elder brother nothing. Ah, well! as poor Stephen Blackpool says, 'Life's aw a muddle.'"

She sits musing for a while under Pauline's practised hands, then her thoughts shift away from Terry Dennison to Gordon Caryll. He will be here to-night, and under the silk, and flowers, and laces her heart gives a glad leap. Since that happy evening under the moonlit limes and chestnuts they have not met ; to-night he will be with her once more. How strange, how romantically strange it all has been, she thinks. From earliest childhood she has heard of him, set him up as a hero, and loved him in her girlish, romantic way, without any hope of ever seeing him. And now he is back —her own, forever.

"Hurry, Pauline—hurry, my child," she says in French.

It wants but an hour until his arrival, and she must be the first to meet him. Already wheels are crashing over the gravel, and the guests are beginning to arrive.

There is a tap at the door.

" Please, Miss Forrester, may I come in ? " says a timid little voice.

France breaks away from Pauline's hands, opens the door, and sees Crystal standing there dressed and ready to go down and trembling with nervous dread of the ordeal. She has been but little accustomed to society—until the coming of Lord Dynely and her fairy fortune she has been looked upon as a baby at home. To-night she must do credit to Eric's taste —Eric, the most critical and sensitive of mankind—must face half a county and be criticised, and see Eric's mortification in his face if her country manners fail. She loves him so wholly, that the thought of his displeasure is as death.

Two great, imploring, blue eyes look up to Miss Forrester, shy, humble, deprecating—the gaze of a very child. She is afraid of this stately, dark-eyed heiress, but not half a quarter as she is of Eric.

" Please, Miss Forrester, may I come in and wait until you are dressed, and go down with you ? " she falters.

France takes her suddenly in her arms, all her prejudices fading away at sight of that pathetic, baby face, puts back the feathery, flaxen hair, and kisses her.

"You pretty little baby," she says ; "come in and let me look at you. My dear, I had no idea you were half so lovely."

" Oh, Miss Forrester "—Crystal's pearly face flushes rose-pink with pleasure—" do you think I am pretty ? Do you think I will do ? Do you think Eric will not be ashamed of me ? "

"Ashamed of you ? Well, Eric is tolerably fastidious,

tolerably hard to please, but I think even he would find it difficult not to be fully satisfied to-night.   No, little vanity, I won't flatter you, I won't tell you what I think of your looks.   Only you are more like the queen of the fairies, or a ' lily in green covert hiding,' than any ordinary mortal I ever saw.   Pauline, what do you think ? "

Thereupon Pauline bursts forth into a vehement French outpouring of praise and admiration, that brings smiles, and dimples, and blushes to Crystal's shy face.   " Like a lily in green covert hiding ? "   Yes, the poetic simile is a true one. With her filmy, gossamer dress of palest green, her pale pearl ornaments, her paler floating, flaxen hair, her pure, pale face, her large, shy eyes, she looks like some water spirit, like Undine herself—a lake lily in its green array.

Ten minutes more complete Miss Forrester's toilet.   Dark, and stately, and tall, entirely self-possessed and at her ease, a greater contrast than the two could scarcely be found as they descend to the already filled rooms.   A blue, silvery silk sweeps behind her, silver lilies trail in the rich darkness of her hair, looped with diamond stars, a cluster of fragrant white blossoms in her hand.   So Miss Forrester and Miss Higgins dawned upon the view of the best county society.

Eric is watching for his lady love—Eric, looking extremely patrician, and elegant, and his eyes light as they fall upon his betrothed.   Truth to tell, he has been dreading this ordeal almost more than she has ; his vanity is so thin-skinned—so much stronger than any other passion of his life.   What if she does not do him credit to-night?   What —good Heaven !—what if she appears looking rustic, or countryfied, or dressed in bad taste ?   He has been turning alternately hot and cold for the last fifteen minutes as he stands here, when he sees her enter the rooms on France Forrester's arm.   And then doubting and fearing are at an end.   His heart gives an exultant leap, his eyes light, a smile comes over his lips, he draws a long breath of intense, unutterable relief.   Rustic, countryfied, dressed in bad taste !   Why, she is lovelier than he has ever seen her, and her dress is the very perfection of good taste.   Yes, the country parson's daughter will do credit to Lord Dynely to-night.

He advances and takes possession of her, stooping his fair, tall head to whisper something that lights up Crystal's soft, sweet face. The worst is over now, she feels she can face all England, all the United Kingdom, in a body. Eric, the sovereign lord and ruler of her life, is deigned to be pleased with his lowly handmaiden.

Miss Forrester is surrounded immediately, she is besieged with petitions for the next waltz, but she declines. It is her intention not to dance at all before supper, and she takes Terry Dennison's arm, and clings to him as her rock of refuge.

"I'm engaged to you for the next waltz, Terry," she says imperiously; "not to dance it though—you understand?"

"I understand," Terry gravely responds. "We are waiting for the hero of the piece to come on, and we want to be disengaged to meet him, looking cool and lovely, and our very best. That is a very delicious thing in the way of dresses, Miss Forrester—misty, silvery blue, a sort of moonlight color that is vastly becoming to your dark complexion. Being in love agrees with you, I think—I never saw you looking so well as to-night. Give you my word there's nothing half so handsome in the house."

Miss Forrester bows her acknowledgment.

"Monseigneur, 'you do me proud.' The first compliment I ever received from Mr. Dennison in my life! But you haven't seen all in the house—you haven't seen Miss Crystal Higgins. Look yonder."

Terry looks. Sooner or later he knows it must come, and he has schooled himself to meet her. His sunburnt face pales a little as he sees her leaning on Eric's arm, lovely as a dream, happy as it is ever given mortals here below to be. He pulls his tawny whiskers and tries to laugh.

"Bliss is a wonderful beautifier—knocks all Madame Rachel's cosmetics into thin air. Handsome couple, aren't they?—look as though they were made for each other, and all that. Shall we go up and pay our respects?"

"You may—I have none to pay; and Lady Dynely beck-ons—I think she wants you, Terry. When you've spoken to Crystal, you had better join her."

So Terry goes up, and Crystal lifts those imploring, innocent eyes of hers in humble appeal to his face, and the look goes through Terry's heart of hearts. Ah no; she is not to be blamed. She has done as eleven girls out of twelve would have done—there are not many like France Forrester to look upon Eric, with undazzled eyes. He pays his respects and makes his greetings in frank, brotherly fashion enough, and requests the honor of a waltz. The turquoise eyes glance timidly up at Eric as if seeking his permission. For, earlier in the evening, Eric has issued his princely ukase that his affianced wife shall waltz with no one but himself.

"I don't choose to see my promised wife gyrating round the room with every fellow in the county who chooses to ask her. Remember, Crystal, you dance round dances with me only!"

She is very willing. If he had ordered her to sit in the remotest corner of the room until morning dawned, she would have obeyed willingly, gladly, so that his sultanship deigned but once or twice to smile upon her in her exile. But Terry Dennison, Terry, who is almost like a brother, will not Eric make an exception in his favor? Eric, who is to have so much—Terry, who has lost all. But Eric's blonde brows knit themselves ever so slightly; to Terry he is not disposed to yield an inch.

"Crystal only waltzes with me, Terry. Scratch your initials down for a quadrille, old boy, if you do that sort of idiotic performance, and do it quickly, for our waltz begins."

Terry does that sort of idiotic performance, scratches his initials accordingly, then seeks out Lady Dynely. Lady Dynely merely wants him to make himself useful all night, in finding partners for unpartnerable elderly girls, and lead the forlorn hope himself.

"It is what Eric should do," her ladyship says, "but Eric won't do it. If he dances at all, it will be with the youngest and prettiest girls present, so, Terry, I look to you."

"'England expects every man to do his duty,'" laughs France Forrester, passing him, and giving him a perfumed blow of her fan. "My poor Terry! Some men are born martyrs. Some have martyrdom thrust upon them; I begin to think you are one of the latter."

But Mr. Dennison pulls on his kid gloves a little tighter, braces himself for the battle, and looks about him undismayed. Old or young, handsome or ugly, it is all the same to Terry. Since Crystal is not for him, all the rest doesn't much matter. The most venerable virgin present, the scraggiest matron, are the same to him for this night as the Venus herself.

"Let's see," he says; "there's Belinda Higgins—I'll lead off with her. After that I'll take 'em as they come—one down, t'other come on."

Mr. Dennison goes and with polite empressement asks the eldest Miss Higgins but one for that waltz. Eric and Crystal float past them as perfect in their waltzing as in their beauty. Eric whispers something in her pretty pink ear that makes her look at Terry and her bony elderly sister and laugh. It is the unkindest cut of all, but Terry bears it manfully. Let them laugh. He is pleasing Lady Dynely, he is making, for the time, poor old Belinda happy—he asks no more.

Miss Forrester is not dancing. She is growing impatient. Her restless eyes wander ceaselessly to the door. He should have been here a full hour ago; the train was due at eight, it is ten now. Can anything have happened? Can he not be coming, after all? He telegraphed this morning he would be with them by the eight o'clock train. Why does he not come?

"Will she dance?" Dance! No, she could as soon think of flying. She gets away from Prince Di Venturini, who is present, and who dances like a little yellow Italian angel; makes her way from the warm, brilliantly lit, brilliantly filled saloon, to the cloak room, throws a heavy wrap over her shining ball-dress, and goes out into the chill October night.

A wild autumnal gale is blowing, the trees rock in the stormy moonlight that floods earth and sky and distant sea. She goes down the portico steps and stands alone on the white, cold terrace. The stone urns gleam like silver; Ajax in marble stands with his face uplifted to the purple sky, defying the lightning. Above the roaring of the gale she can hear the deeper, hoarser roar of the far-off sea, above all the sweet ringing of the German waltz music within. The old stone Abbey is lit to the roof—countless figures flit past the windows like shapes in a magic lantern. She stands here alone, wondering why he does not come. Suddenly, over the soughing of the wind, the tossing of the trees, there comes a sound that makes her heart spring, her eyes light—the rapid roll of the wheels up the drive. The carriage was sent two good hours ago to meet him ; all is well, he is here at last.

She leans eagerly forward. Yes ! the tall form of her lover leaps out and approaches. He sees the solitary figure standing on the terrace—the pale, expectant, eager face upon which the white moon shines. He is by her side in a moment, and France's perfect hour has come.

"What ! waiting for me ?" he says ; "getting your death out in the cold. Come into the house immediately. How long have you been here ? "

"Not long—ten minutes or more. I must confess to feeling just a trifle uneasy. You are two hours behind time."

"And you took it for granted that perishing in a ball-dress on the terrace would fetch me the sooner," growls Mr. Caryll, but he takes her happy face between both his hands, and his frown changes to a smile. "Yes, we're two hours behind time ; got shunted off—misplaced switch, something wrong with the road—I was asleep at the time, and knew nothing about it until we were under way again. High jinks going on within, aren't there ? Awful bore to go and dress and face them all."

"You would rather face a regiment of Sepoys, I dare say ; but a brave man never shows the white feather, be the danger what it may. Will you go to your room at once ? —the dear old *atelier* where my portrait was painted—"

"And the unhappy painter hopelessly done for."

"Has been fitted up for your use," goes on Miss Forrester. "So run up at once, get into regulation costume, and come down to be looked at."

"Is there a *very* great crush, France?" Caryll asks, in dismay.

"Three hundred, if one; and as Miss Higgins has been stared at until they can stare no more, you will be the cynosure of all; every eye will be concentrated upon you."

She laughs at his blank face, slips her hand through his arm, and leads him into the house.

"How is grandmamma?" she asks; "and what did she say? Tell me everything."

"Tell you everything! They talk of the labor of Hercules; but to tell you everything 'grandmamma' has said in the past seven weeks would be a Herculean task indeed. She says this, for one thing—that you are to join her in Rome next week, or a week after, at latest."

"What! with you?"

"Forbid it, Mrs. Grundy. Oh, no! we don't outrage the proprieties in that fashion. With Lady Dynely, of course. She will chaperone you—will she not?"

"Are you going back, Gordon?"

"Naturally. We part no more. My poor mother! It is something to be loved as she loves me."

"She knew you at once?"

"At once—the moment we met. She neither fainted nor screamed—it is a wonderful old lady!—she just came forward and took me in her arms, and not one word was spoken on either side. Outwardly all those years have changed her little less than they have done me; she is very feeble. She would have come with me if she had been able. Not being able, and longing to see you, she bids me bring you and Lady Dynely when I go back. Will you come, France?"

"Will I not?" she answers, lifting her happy eyes. "But my stay must be a short one. Eric's wedding takes place on New Year's Eve, and I am to be first bridesmaid."

"Bridesmaid for the last time, then," says Gordon Caryll. "Pity we can't make it a double wedding. I don't see the sense of waiting, myself; and I promise you this, I don't mean to wait long. When will it be, France? January?"

"No, sir; not January, not February, not March, nor

April; not a day sooner than May. And then, in the height
of the season, with flying colors, if you insist upon it, we will
march to St. George's, and you shall be made miserable for
life. No, it's of no use putting on that imploring face;
when my decree is issued, all the eloquence of men fails to
move me. Go up to your room—you have not a moment
to spare, you are shamefully late as it is."

She releases herself, and hastens back to the ball-room.
Near the entrance she meets Eric on his way for ices and
orangeade, and in her face he reads the truth.

"'Lo! the conquering hero comes!' and Miss Forrester's eyes light up their lamps, and Miss Forrester's cheeks
fling out the flag of welcome. I had about given up the hero
of the night as a laggard in love; but better late than never."

Half an hour passes, and then into their midst, so quietly
that but few find it out for the first hour, the "hero of the
night" enters. He makes his way to Lady Dynely's side,
and she who has met him daily but seven short weeks before, greets him as though she had never looked upon him
since that August night by the lake.

"It is like a fairy tale," she says; "I cannot realize it.
I thought you dead, in spite of all of France's hopes, in
spite of the yearly gifts to your mother. And to think that
we have you with us once more. But you are greatly, wonderfully changed."

"Well, yes," Caryll answers; "a dozen years' campaigning
is apt to change a man. Still, I think you half-recognized
me that day at the Academy."

"You see, I could not realize it," her ladyship answers,
leaning on his arm, and making her way slowly through the
rooms. "The voice was the same, and the eyes; but I had
made up my mind so entirely never to look upon you more,
that I wouldn't admit the likeness. Still, it drew me to you.
It was for the sake of that likeness I wished you so much
to accompany us here."

"I came to my destiny!" he laughed. "But for that
journey, France and I would never have arrived at an understanding, and I should have gone down to my grave
'Gordon Locksley.'"

" France will make you a charming wife, Gordon. I congratulate you, with all my heart. After all, you have not done so badly with your life. You have won a name for yourself, with your sword, and with your brush, and you nave won France Forrester's whole heart—such a great, generous, loyal heart! I had thought to see her Eric's wife ; but you know how that has ended."

" Happily for me—yes ; happily for him, I trust, also. Is that little green-and-white fairy on his arm, with the apple-blossom face, the bride elect ? What a model for Undine ! Present me, Lucia, will you ? "

Mr. Caryll is presented and begins the business of the night by dancing with the bride elect. As France has laughingly predicted, people stare, in a well-bred way, until even curiosity is satiated. The hero and heroine of the evening, meandering through the Lancers, are the observed of all observers. France dances, too, with her lover, with Eric, with Terry, whom she rescues from an elderly-young lady, with unpleasantly prominent shoulder blades, and unpleasantly prominent rouged cheeks. With the Prince Di Venturini last of all before supper. As this dance ends Mr. Caryll advances to claim his property, and the Neapolitan prince renews his acquaintance and presents his congratulations.

" Madame Felicia has been deploring her loss in your gain, monsieur," the prince says; "she fears now she will never receive what you promised her—the companion picture to ' How the Night Fell.' "

" Did I promise her ? " says Caryll, carelessly. " Then let madame be at rest. If it affords her any pleasure she shall yet have the companion picture. What shall we call it ? ' How the Morning Broke ? ' "

He looks at France with a smile that says the dawn has come with her.

" A charming title," cries Di Venturini. " May I ask has monsieur ever seen Madame Felicia ? "

" Never," Caryll responds. " She was playing in London last season, I am aware, and I naturally heard a great deal about her, but I never had curiosity enough to go and see her. I was very busy, and I had long lost my relish for theatre-going."

His face clouds a little. Di Venturini looks at him with small, keen, glittering eyes.

"Pardon, monsieur, but I inferred from what I have heard Madame Felicia say, that she certainly knew you."

"Impossible, prince. To my knowledge she never met me in her life."

"Ah! my mistake then, of course. She will be charmed to learn that she is to have the companion picture."

He bows himself off, and France and Caryll go into supper together. That pleasant banquet is prolonged. When it is over, a little knot of Miss Forrester's admirers press around and plead with her to sing. She yields and is led to the piano, still on Gordon Caryll's arm.

"Sing 'Ay Chiquita,'" some one says.

She points to a pile of music, and Mr. Caryll tosses it over to find the song. He places it upon the piano, and Frances' slim fingers float over the keys in tender prelude. He is replacing the loose sheets as he found them, when all at once he stops still—stops with one of the pieces in his hand and stares at it as though it were a ghost. He is gazing at the outer page, not at the music, with a face from which every trace of color slowly fades out. The song begins—Miss Forrester's sweet, vibrating voice fills the room. He never hears, he never heeds. Every feeling of sight and sense, and hearing, seems concentrated in that fixed rapt gaze on what he holds.

It is a waltz. "The Felicia Waltz," composed by Prince Di Venturini, and dedicated to Madame Felicia. Below the title is a colored vignette of madame herself, leaning smilingly forward—*en buste.* It is a beautiful face— even this highly-colored lithograph cannot make it otherwise—and eyes and lips flash back their brilliant smile on all beholders.

So long he stands there holding it, that the song ends. There is a murmur of pleasure and thanks from the group about the piano, but the singer turns from all for a smile of praise from him. His face is averted, he is bending over a piece of music, and does not speak a word.

"What is it you have there, Gordon?" she asks, gayly, "that holds you so enchained?"

"Monsieur honors my poor composition with his closest attention," says the voice of Di Venturini; "or is it madame's fair face that holds him spell-bound?"

Their words arouse him. He lays down the sheet and turns away, but his face still keeps that startled pallor under its bronze.

"A fair face indeed, prince, and one I have surely seen before, though the name is new to me. In America, or Canada probably—madame has been there?"

He listens for the reply with an intensity of eagerness his outer quietude does not betray. Prince Di Venturini looks at him with quick, suspicious eyes.

"But no, monsieur—Madame Felicia has never crossed the Atlantic in her life."

"You are sure, prince?"

"I am very sure, monsieur. I have it from madame's own lips. She detests everything transatlantic."

"I have been mistaken then," Caryll says, calmly; "I really thought I had seen that pictured face before. It is merely one of those chance resemblances we meet sometimes. I once knew a person who looked very like that."

He offers his arm to France and leads her away. No more is said on the subject, but through all the hours that follow the pale gravity never quite leaves his face. And once, when all are dancing and the music-room is entirely deserted, he goes back, tears off the page that has the pictured face of Madame Felicia, and conceals it quietly in one of his pockets for further inspection.

The chill October morning is gray in the east when the last carriage rolls away from the great gates of Dynely Abbey, and the spent household betake themselves to their rest. But for full an hour after, Gordon Caryll sits in his room, that picture spread out before him, gazing steadfastly down at the gaudily-colored portrait of the French actress as though it held him by some sorceress' spell.

"Her eyes, her smile, her every feature," he says under his breath. "Can there be two women on this earth so much alike? Years older, but the same. Had she a sister, or—has the grave given up its dead? H.. *re* come back from Hades itself to torment me?"

CHAPTER XIX.

'T is the night of the 31st of December, and the vicarage of Starling is bright with lights, gay with people, merry with music, and festive with feasting. The eve of the old year is going merrily out in "babble and revel and wine." And to-morrow is pretty Crystal's wedding-day.

They are all down—Lord Dynely, his mother, France, Terry. They have been here two days now, and to-night a score of guests, intimate friends all, crowd the quaint, low-ceilinged, comfortable old vicarage to repletion, to welcome in right merrily the blithe new year.

Gordon Caryll is not here—he is the only absentee of the family. He is back with his mother under the genial Roman sky. She is not able to travel, not able to bear the rigor of an English winter, and she grows more and more exigeante in her old age, and cannot bear her restored idol out of her sight. So he is with her greatly to Miss Forrester's regret.

She and Lady Dynely have but just returned from Italy for this wedding ; they go back for the winter when it is over. The first week in May she and Gordon are to be married, and, after their bridal tour, settle down at Caryllynne. Already the workmen are busy there, beautifying and putting it in order. Eric and his wife will take up their abode at the Abbey, his mother going to her jointure house, Dynely Hall. That is the programme.

The vicarage rooms are full—the gayety is at its height. A set of "Sixteen Lancers" are pounding away over the drawing-room carpet to the piping of the eldest Miss Higgins, who adorns the piano stool. They will support nature presently on lemonade and negus. Eric leads off the revellers ;

looking happy and handsome, and in the wildest of wild high spirits. It is a difficult thing to believe, but on this eve of his wedding he is as deeply in love as he was the day of the memorable picnic. It may possibly not last—but it is intoxicatingly delicious while it does last, and little Crystal is ready enough to take the glitter for purest gold. For Crystal—well, she is at her brightest and fairest, too, to-night. There are hot red roses in her cheeks, a streaming light in her blue eyes; her sweet, foolish little laugh rings out in her joyous excitement. Even now, on the eve of her wedding, she can hardly realize her own bliss. Surely it is the most wonderful freak of fortune that gives this darling of the gods to be her very own to-morrow morning at eleven o'clock. It is eleven at night now—twelve more hours, and earth and all its powers will never be able to separate her from him more. She lifts her little peach-bloom face to her partner and talks and laughs. As a rule, she has but little to say, but she can always talk to Terry, and never half so gayly as to-night. Terry is her partner, and, whatever he may feel, no one outwardly is happier there.

Miss Forrester is not dancing. She is flitting restlessly about, here and there and everywhere. The rooms are garlanded with holly, and ivy, and mistletoe; glorious fires are burning, and in the dining-room a long table is set out, to which the gay company will sit down presently to toast the New Year in. No room is vacant; sentimental couples sit spooning in spoony little nooks, go where you will. The vicar and Lady Dynely, a portly dowager and Sir John Shepperton, the nearest magnate, sit at whist. So the moments fly.

Presently France steals away, and leaving the hot, bright rooms, goes out into the porch. It is a dazzling winter night; the earth lies all white, and sparkling and frozen, under the glittering stars; the leafless trees stand motionless, their black branches sharply traced against the steel blue sky. Far off the village bells are ringing—bells that ring out the dying year. One hour more and the new year will have dawned. It has been a very happy year to the girl who stands there, in her white dress and perfumy roses, and the new year is destined to be happier still. Her heart is full of a great unspoken thankfulness, and ascends to the Giver of all good gifts in eloquent, wordless prayer.

Presently the dancing ends, and, flushed and warm, the dancers disperse themselves about, eating ices and drinking lemonade. Terry leads Crystal to a cool nook, and Eric, his fair face flushed, joins them, and flings himself on a sofa by his bride's side.

"Lend me your fan, Crystal," he says. "Look upon me and behold an utterly exhausted, an utterly used-up man. Did you see my partner—did you see that stall-fed young woman who has been victimizing me for the past half hour? It was the most flagrant case of cruelty to animals to ask that girl to dance. I saw her eying you, Dennison—there's your chance, old fellow, to take fortune at its flood. She's two hundred and fifty avoirdupois, and she has seven thousand a year, so I am told, to her fortune. Go in and win, Terry; you'll never have such another chance."

The young lady alluded to had sunk into a capacious arm-chair at the other end of the room, her face crimson, her fleshy chest heaving, her fan waving after her late exertions.

"You see her," says Eric, "the sylph in green silk and pink roses, quivering like a whole cascade of port wine jelly."

"Yes," answers Terry, looking at the shapeless florid mass of adipose good-nature, with sleepy, half-closed eyes; "only, you see, it requires courage to marry so much, and I don't set up for a hero. How she does palpitate—reminds one of the words of the poet: 'A lovely being scarcely formed or molded—a'—France, what's the rest?"

"'A peony with its reddest leaves yet folded,'" supplements France, gravely. "Terry, what will you do through life without me by your side to tell you what you mean? I am sent here to order you gentlemen to take somebody down to supper. I suppose you're booked, Eric, for the green-silk young lady?"

"Not if I know it," Eric answers, drawing Crystal's hand within his arm. "A lifetime of bliss, such as I look forward to, would hardly compensate for another hour like the last."

12

"Then you take her, Terry," commands France, and Terry obeys, as usual, while Sir John offers his arm to Miss Forrester, and Lady Dynely takes the place of honor by the vicar's side.

It is a very long table, and the party is not so large, even counting the nine daughters of the house, but that they all find seats. For it is not a " stand-up feed," as Terry says, where every chicken wing and every glass of wine is fought for *à outrance*. And then the battle begins—the fire of knives and forks and plates, the sharp shooting of champagne corks, the chatter and clatter of laughter and talk, of toasts and compliments. The boar's head that has grinned as the centrepiece with a lemon in its jaws, is sliced away, raised pies are lowered, wonderful pyramids of amber and crimson jellies are slashed into shapeless masses, and lobster salads vanish into thin air.

The moments fly—the last hour of the old year is fast drawing to its close.

"Ten minutes to twelve," cries Lord Dynely. " Here's to the jolly New Year. Let us drink his health in the good old German way, to the one we love best."

He filled his glass, looked at Crystal, and touched his to hers.

"The happiest of all happy New Years to you," he says, "and I am the first to wish it."

And then a chorus of voices arises. " Happy New Year ! " cry all, and each turns to somebody else. Lady Dynely stretches forth her hand to her son with a look of fondest love ; Terry Dennison leans over to her with the old wistful light in his eyes. The vicar and his wife exchange affectionate glances. France turns to no one ; her thoughts are over the sea, with one absent.

Then they all rise, and as by one accord throng to the windows to see the New Year dawn. White and clear the stars look down on the snow-white earth ; it is still, calm, beautiful. From the village the joy-bells clash forth ; the old year is dead—the new begun.

"Le roi est mort !—vive le roi ! " exclaims Lord Dynely. "May all good wishes go with him."

The piano stands by his side. He strikes the keys with a bold, skilled touch, and his rich tenor voice rings spiritedly out :

> " He frothed his bumpers to the brim—
> A jollier year we shall not see ;
> And though his eyes are waxing dim,
> And though his foes speak ill of him,
> He was a friend to me !
>   Every one for his own.
> The night is starry and cold, my friend ;
> And the New Year, blithe and bold, my friend,
>   Comes up to take his own."

"My pale, my pensive France," he says, "why that mournful look ? The old year has been a good friend to you also, has he not ? As Tennyson says, ' He brought you a friend and a true, true love.' "

" ' And the new year will take them away,' " finishes Lady Dynely, with a smile. " An ominous quotation, Eric. Let us hope for better things. And now, my little bride elect, as you are to be up betimes to-morrow, I propose that you go to bed at once, else that pretty peach face of yours will be yellow as any orange at the altar to-morrow."

So it is over, and the new year is with them. The guests not stopping at the vicarage say good-night and go, the others disperse to their rooms. There is a farewell which no one sees between the happy pair, then Eric saunters out into the white starry night to smoke one last bachelor cigar, and Crystal is kissed by mamma and Lady Dynely and France, and takes her candle and goes off to her room singing softly to herself as she goes :

> " You must wake and call me early, call me early, mother dear,
>   For to-morrow will be the happiest day of all the glad New Year."

The morning comes, sparkling and glimmering with frosty sunlight, and the vicarage is all bustle and gay confusion, a very Babel of tongues. Nine ; coffee—ten—dressing ; eleven —carriages at the door, everybody down stairs, and *the* supreme hour has come.

Up in her "maiden bower," the bride stands robed for

the altar. The hot red roses of last night have died out, she is paler than the white silk she wears. The chilly nuptial flowers are on her head, the filmy veil shrouds her like a mist. Silent, lovely, she stands in the midst of her maids, not crying, not speaking, with a great awe of the new life that is beginning overlying all else.

She is led down, she enters the carriage, and is whirled away through the jubilant New Year's morning to the church, There the bridegroom awaits her. The church is full; villagers, friends, guests, charity children, all assembled to see the vicar's prettiest daughter married. There is a mighty rustling of silks and moires as the ladies of the family flock in, a flutter of pink and snowy gauze as the six bridemaids take their places. France is at their head, and divides the admiration of the hour with the bride herself. As usual the bridegroom dwindles into insignificance—the one epoch in the life of man when he sinks his lordly supremacy and is, comparatively speaking, of no account. Terry Dennison is there, looking pale, and cold, and miserable, but who thinks of noticing *him?* Only France's compassionate eyes look at him once as he stands, silent and unlike himself, with an infinite pity in their dark depths.

It begins—dead silence falls. The low murmured responses sound strangely audible in that hush. It is over—all draw one long breath of relief, and a flutter and a murmur go through the silent congregation. They enter the vestry—the register is signed—they are back in the carriages, whirling away to the wedding breakfast, and bridegroom and bride are together, and the Right Honorable Lord Viscount Dynely is " Benedick, the Married Man."

After that the hours fly like minutes. They are back at the vicarage. They are seated at breakfast, champagne corks fly, toasts are drunk, speeches made and responded to. The bridegroom's handsome face is flushed, his blue eyes glitter, all his feigned languor and affected boredom, for the time being, utterly at an end. By his side his bride sits, smiling, blushing, dimpling, most divinely fair. Opposite, is Terry Dennison, trying heroically at light talk and laughter, that he may not be the one death's head at the feast, but his face keeping all the time its mute, cold misery.

The breakfast is over. The newly-made Viscountess hurries away to change her dress. They will travel by the afternoon express to London—thence to Folkestone. The honeymoon will be spent in Brittany—the first week of February will find them in Paris, there to remain until the London season is fairly at its height.

White satin splendor, nuptial blossoms, virginal veil, are changed for a travelling suit of pearl gray, that fits the trim little figure to a charm. From beneath the coquettish round hat and gossamer veil, the sweet childish face looks sweeter and more childlike than ever. In the hall below the impatient bridegroom stands—at the door the carriage waits. She is trembling with nervous excitement from head to foot; she is but a frail, sensitive little creature at best. Her mother is weeping audibly—her father coughs, takes off his glasses and wipes them incessantly. France Forrester stands with dark, tender eyes, and in her heart a vague feeling of pity, which she cannot define, for this fragile looking child-wife.

"Oh, Eric!" she says, laying her hand on his shoulder and looking up at him with those dim, dusk eyes, "be good to her! take care of her, love her always. You hold that child's very life in your hands; if you ever neglect her, if you ever grow cold to her, as surely as we both stand here, she will break her heart."

He laughs—nothing irritates him this thrice happy day, and *this* is really a most stupendous joke.

"*I* neglect her! I cold to her! When I am either, I pray Heaven I may die!"

She shrank back, something in his words, something in his look, frightened her.

"He will neglect her, he will turn cold," some inward, prophetic voice whispered; "and the doom he has invoked may fall."

One other heard those impassioned words—Dennison. He paused a moment, caught Eric's hand, and wrung it hard.

"Look to yourself, Dynely," he said, in a hoa:se, hurried voice, "if you ever forget that vow!"

Then he ran rapidly up the stairs and disappeared.

Lord Dynely looked after him, shrugged his shoulders slightly, and laughed again.

"Poor old Terry!" he said, "'the ruling passion strong in death.' As much in love with Lady Dynely as he ever was with Crystal Higgins. Ah, well! time blunts these things. Let us hope he will have lived down his ill-starred madness before we meet again."

The bride's door opens—a flock of pink and white, and sky blue nymphs flutter out. The bride for an instant remains alone. Indifferent to what may be thought, may be said, Dennison enters, goes up to the new-made peeress, takes both her hands in his, with a clasp whose cruelty is unconscious, and looks down with gloomy eyes into the startled, milk-white loveliness of her face.

"Crystal," he says, his voice hoarse and hurried still, "I must say one word to you before we part. If, in the time that is coming, you are ever in trouble, if you are ever in need of a friend, will you send for me? All our lives we have been as brother and sister—by the memory of that bond · between us let me be the one to come to you if you ever need a friend."

She looked up at him. To the day of his death that look haunted him—so radiantly, so unutterably happy.

"*I* in trouble! *I* in need of a friend!" she repeated in a slow, rapturous sort of whisper. "*I*, Eric's wife! Ah, Terry! dear old fellow, dear old brother, that can never be. I am the happiest, happiest creature on all God's earth!"

"Yet, promise," he reiterates, in the same gloomy tone. "Who can foresee the future? *If* trouble ever comes—mind, I don't say that it ever will—I pray it never may—but if it comes and you need help, you will send for me? Promise me this."

"It is treason to Eric to admit any such supposition," she laughs; "I *don't* admit it, but if it will please you, Terry," the radiant brilliance of her eyes softens to pity as she looks at him, "I promise. It is a promise you will never be called upon to redeem—remember that. No trouble can ever touch me. Eric loves me and has made me his wife. Let go, Terry—he is calling."

He releases her hands, she holds out one again, with that tender, compassionate glance.

"Good-by, Terry," she says, softly. "If I have ever given you pain I am sorry. Forgive me before I go."

"There is nothing to forgive," he answers, huskily. "No man on earth could help loving you, and all women seem to love *him*. Good-by, little Crystal, and God in heaven bless you!"

It is their parting. She flies down the stairs to where her impatient possessor stands.

"I—I was saying good-by to Terry," she falters, trembling already, even at that shadow of a frown on his god-like brow. But at sight of her the shadow changes to brightest sunshine.

"Good-by! good-by! good-by!" echoes and echoes on every hand.

The bride is kissed, and passed round to be kissed again, and there is crying and confusion generally, and in the midst of it Miss Forrester's wicked black eyes are laughing at Eric, who stands inwardly fuming at all this "confounded scene," mortally jealous, and longing to tear his bride from them all and make an end of the howling.

It does end at last; he hands her into the carriage, springs after, slams the door, the driver cracks his whip, and they whirl off from the door. A shower of slippers are hurled after them—then the carriage turns an angle and disappears, and all is over.

* * * * * *

The guests begin to disperse, some at once, some not until next day. A gloomy silence falls over the lately noisy, merry house—it is almost as though there had been a death. Reaction after so much excitement sets in, everybody, more or less, looks miserable. Terry Dennison is the first to go —he rejoins his regiment. Lady Dynely, dowager, and Miss Forrester are the next, they return for the winter to Rome; and Miss Forrester makes no secret of her eagerness to be off.

The next day dawns, sleety, rainy, chill, a very winter day. The last guest has left the vicarage by the noon train, and the depression and dismalness is more dismal than ever. The eight remaining Misses Higgins wander, cheerless and miserable of aspect, through the lately-filled rooms, setting to rights and taking up the dull thread of their dull gray lives once more.

When night falls, shrouded in sleety rain, the dark old vicarage stands sombre and forlorn, despite the presence of those eight bright creatures, under the inky, dripping, Lincolnshire sky.

PART THIRD.

———•••———

CHAPTER I.

HOW THE NEW YEAR BEGAN.

 RAW and rainy February evening—the first week of the month. Over London a murky, smoke-colored sky hung, dripping wet, miserable tears over the muddy, smoke-colored city. The famous "pea-soup atmosphere" was at its very pea-soupiest—figures flitted to and fro through the murk, like damp spectres, shrouded in great-coats and umbrellas. The street lamps, that had been lit all day, winked and flickered, yellow and dismal specks in the fog.

The streets of the city were filled with noisy, jostling life—the streets of the West End were silent and deserted. The deadest of all dead seasons had come; the great black houses were hermetically sealed; the denizens of Belgravia and Mayfair had flitted far away; even the brilliant, gas-lit emporiums of Regent Street were empty and deserted this foggy February evening.

At the bay-window of one of the great club houses of St. James Street, a man stood smoking a cigar and staring mood-ily out at the dark and dismal twilight. The wet flag-stones glimmered in the pallid flicker of the street lamps, few and far between; drenched and draggled pedestrians went by. Now and then a hansom tore past, waking the grue-some echoes. These things were all the man at the bay-win-dow had to stare at; but for the last hour he had stood there

12*

motionless, his moody eyes fixed upon the rain-beaten glass. The solitary watcher, stranded upon Western London at this most inhospitable season, was Terry Dennison. Terry Dennison who yesterday had obtained a fortnight's leave, and who, this dreary February evening, found himself in the old familiar quarters—why or wherefore, he hardly knew. There were numbers of country houses—bright, hospitable houses, to which he held standing welcome—houses where a " southerly wind and a cloudy sky proclaimed it a hunting morning," but he had thrown over all, and was here as utterly alone, it seemed to him, as though he had been wrecked on a deserted island.

The five weeks that had passed since Christabel Higgins' wedding day had made but slight outward alteration in Terry. He was looking haggard, and jaded,—the honest blue eyes kept the old kindly, genial glance for all things, but they look out with wistful weariness to-night. Where are they this wretched, February evening, he wonders—where is *she*, what is she doing ?

Are she and Eric doing the honeymoon still in the leaf-less groves of Brittany, or have they gone to Rome to join the Gordon Caryll party, where Lady Dynely and Miss Forrester also are ? An unutterable longing to see Crystal once more fills him—it is folly, he knows, something worse than folly, perhaps, but before these two weeks of freedom expire he must stand face to face with Viscount Dynely's bride.

The last gleam of the dark daylight is fading entirely out as a hansom whirls up to the door and deposit sits one passenger. The glare of the lamp falls full upon him, and Dennison recognizes an old acquaintance. As the man enters he turns and holds out his hand.

"What ! *you*, Dennison? My dear fellow, happy to meet you. I saw a face at the window and thought it was Macaulay's New Zealander come before his time, to philosophize over the desolation of London. Beastly weather, as usual. How three millions of people, more or less, can drag out existence through it—"

The speaker flings himself into a chair and gives up the problem in weary disgust.

"I thought you were in Greece, Burrard," says Terry,

throwing away his cigar, and depositing himself in a second easy-chair.

"Was, all January. Gave it up and came to Paris, to have what our transatlantic neighbors call 'a good time ;' and just as I was having it (Felicia's there, you know), came a telegram from Somersetshire, summoning me home. Governor—gout in the stomach—thinks he's going to die, and wishes to have all his offspring around him. It's the fifth time I have been summoned in the same way," says Mr. Burrard, in a disgusted tone, "and nothing ever comes of it. It's all hypo on the governor's part, and the family know it ; but as he'll cut us off with a shilling if we disobey, there's nothing for it. It was beastly crossing the Channel, and I'm always seasick. It's an awful nuisance, Terry—give you my word," Mr. Burrard gloomily concludes.

"Hard lines, old fellow," laughs Terry. "Let us hope this time that your journey will not be in vain. So Paris is looking lively, is it ? No February fog there, I suppose ? I shouldn't mind running over myself for a few days. Many people one knows ? "

"Lots," Mr. Burrard sententiously replies ; "and, as I said before, la belle Felicia at the Variétés, younger, and lovelier, and more fatal than ever. Gad ! Terry, the divine art of *petits soupers* will never die out while that woman exists. She's a sorceress and enchantress, a witch. She must be five-and-thirty at the very least : and last night, as I sat beside her, I could have taken my oath she wasn't a day more than seventeen."

"Hard hit as ever, dear boy," Terry says, lighting another regalia. "I thought that was an old story—over and done with ages ago—that you were clothed and in your right mind once more, and about to take unto yourself a wife of the daughters of the land. Have one ? "

He presents his cigar case and box of Vesuvians, and Burrard gloomily selects and lights up.

"You know Felicia, Terry ? " he asks, after a smoky pause.

Terry nods.

"*You* never were one of her victims though, were you," the other pursues.

"Not I, old fellow," Terry laughs good-humouredly. "The rôle of quarry to any woman's hawk is not in the least my line. And I never could see, for the life of me, what there was in belle Felicia, that men should go down before her, like corn before the reaper. She's a monstrous fine woman for those who admire the swarthy sort, which I don't, and knows how to use those two black eyes of hers ; but that dancer has never danced—were it the daughter of Herodias herself—who could quicken my pulses by one beat."

"You're a cold-blooded animal, Dennison, I'm afraid," responds Mr. Burrard. "Your insensibility to all womankind has passed into a proverb. You always had the entree, too, when Felicia was in London."

"I had the good fortune to be of some slight service to her on one occasion, and, like all women, she magnified a mole-hill into a mountain. So she is still as fatal as ever— who is the last unhappy devil who has fallen into her clutches ? "

"Their name is legion. There are two American millionaires over there, ready to blow each other's brains out about her. There is an Austrian archduke, with five-and-twenty quarterings, an empty purse, and the bluest of sang azure, ready, they say, at a moment's notice, to make her his wife. There is Prince Di Venturini, who has come to his own again, since the young Italy party took the reins—that affair is old and settled ; it's an understood thing if she behaves herself she is to be Madame la princess. And last, but by no means least in the fair Felicia's eyes—since the bracelets, and rings, and rubbish of that sort he gives her, they say would fill a Rue de la Paix jeweller's window—is young Lord Dynely."

Terry has been lying back in his chair, dreamily watching the clouds of smoke curl upward, and taking but a languid interest in the conversation. At this name he sits suddenly upright, staring with round, startled blue eyes.

"Who ? " he asks, sharply and suddenly.

"Dynely—know him, don't you ? Oh, by the bye, yes— you and he are connections, aren't you ? Married at Christmas—country parson's daughter, didn't he, all on the quiet ? Well, my word, he's going the pace now, I can tell you."

" Burrard, do you mean to say Dynely is in Paris ? "

" Been there the past three weeks. Went to Brittany or Normandy, or somewhere for the honeymoon—so I was told ; found love among the roses, a week after matrimony, awfully slow work ; most men do in like case, poor devils ; set the proprieties at defiance—couldn't serve out his sentence ; came to Paris, and fell, like the greenest of all green goslings, straightway into the talons of that bird of paradise, Felicia. By the bye, birds of paradise haven't talons, I daresay, but you know what I mean."

The color has faded out of Terry's face, leaving him very pale. Mr. Burrard, with whom the handsome dancer is evidently a sore subject, and who is also suffering evidently from an attack of the green-eyed monster, goes aggrievedly on :

" Never saw a fellow so far gone in so short a time—give you my honor, Dennison ! He's mad, stark mad, running after that piratical little demon. It's early days to leave the pretty wife alone in their big hotel. All Paris is talking about it, *sotto voce*, of course. Did you know her, Terry ? "

Burrard's sleepy, half-closed eyes, look across at him, and note for the first time the sudden, startled pallor of his face.

" Yes—I know her," he answers slowly. " How is she looking, Burrard ? "

" Never met her but once, and that was before the Felicia had gobbled her husband up body and bones. I met them driving in the Bois, and I remember everybody was turning to stare at the little blonde beauty. She appeared also one night at an embassy ball, and was the talk of the clubs for the next three days. It was her first and last appearance. She's there still, but invisible to the naked eye. While he follows Felicia like her poodle or her shadow, the little one mopes at home. I wouldn't say all this, Dennison, you understand," says Mr. Burrard, fearing he has gone too far, " but it is public talk in Paris. Dynely's infatuation is patent to all the world."

The face of Terry has settled into an expression Horace Burrard has never seen on that careless, good-humored face before. It is set and stern, the genial blue eyes gleam like steel. But he speaks very quietly.

"And the Prince Di Venturini allows her to carry on like this? Wide latitude for a future princess, you must own. Accommodating sort of Neapolitan, the prince."

"Understand me, Terry," says Burrard, answering this last sneer rather earnestly. "I don't mean to say Felicia goes much further than some of our own frisky matrons do. A flirt she is *à outrance*—she would flirt with her own chasseur if no better game offered. Beyond that, scandal goeth not. Di Venturini is most assuredly a man who can take care of his own, a dead shot, and a noted duelist. Madame is also most assuredly his *fiancée*. She has an *ame damnée*, who goes about with her everywhere—the widow of an English curate, and propriety itself in crape and bombazine. But she takes men's presents, fools them to the top of their bent, cleans them out, and throws them over, with as little remorse as I throw away this smoked-out cigar. 'One down, t'other come on,' that's the fair danseuse's motto."

There was some bitterness in Burrard's tone. Evidently he was one of the "cleaned out and thrown over." He arose as he spoke and looked at his watch.

"Have you dined, Dennison? Because I have ordered—"

"Thanks—I dined two hours ago. Don't let me detain you, Burrard, and good-night."

He went slowly up to his room, his face keeping that set, stern look.

She has no father, no brother to take her part; I may be that to her, if I may be no more. If Burrard's story be true, then it is high time some one went to the rescue."

His own words came back to him. Had the time come already for him to defend her against the husband she loved, and for whom she had jilted him? He knew Eric well—knew how recklessly, insanely, he tore every passion to tatters—knew how little hold principle or fidelity had upon him, knew him weaker, more unstable than water, selfish to the core. regardless of all consequences where his own fancies were concerned. And into the keeping of such a man as this, little Crystal's whole heart and life had been given.

"If he is false to her," Terry ground out between his set teeth, "I'll kill him with my own hand. Only one short month his wife, and neglected, forsaken already. Oh, my little Crystal ! My little, pretty, innocent Crystal ! "

He remembered his words to her on her wedding-day : "If you are ever in trouble—if you ever need a friend, promise to send for me." She had not sent, poor child ! but she had not forgotten those words, he knew. He would go to her—go at once. While Eric was kind she had not needed him—Eric had tired of her, was on with another love before the honeymoon had waned—she needed him now. Yes, he would go at once—to-morrow—by fair means or foul, Eric must be made to quit Paris ; and that painted sorceress, who wrought men's ruin, must be forced to give back his allegiance to his wife. He should not neglect her and break her heart with impunity.

That night Terry Dennison spent tossing feverishly on his bed, listening to the lashing rain, and chilly, whistling, February wind. Before the dark, murky day had fairly broken he was at the London bridge station—at nightfall he was in Paris.

* * * * * . *

The February weather, so bleakly raw in London, is brilliant with sunshine, sparkling with crisp, clear frost here in Paris. The great avenues of the Bois and Champs Elysées may be leafless, but the hoar frost sparkles in the early sunshine like silver, the icicles glitter like pendant jewels, and the bright, glad life, that never under the Parisian sky grows dull, is at its brightest.

On this night that brings Dennison to Paris, gaslight has taken the place of sunlight, and seems to his eyes, accustomed to London fog and dreariness, no whit less dazzling. The bright streets are thronged—the huge front of the Hotel Du Louvre is all a glitter of gaslights as his fiacre whirls up, and deposits him and his portmanteau at the entrance.

"Can he have a room ? " he asks the gentlemanly clerk.

And "*Mais oui monsieur,*" is the answer ; "there is one
room at monsieur's service, but it is *au cinquième numéro
quatre-vingts douze.*"

Monsieur does not care ; he prepares to mount, turns
back and asks :

"Lord and Lady Dynely are here ? "

"Certainly, monsieur.   Their apartments are *au premier*,
lately vacated by his Serene Highness M. le Duc ——."

Terry ascends to his cockloft, with a gravely meditative
face.   Are they at home he wonders ? is she ? and how
will Eric receive him ?   If what Burrard says be true, it
does not much matter—his and Eric's day of reckoning will
have come.

At that very hour, in one of her gorgeous suite of rooms,
Lady Dynely sits, quite alone.   Alone ! ah, poor Crystal ! when
is she not alone now?   She sits, or rather crouches, on the
wide velvet-cushioned window sill, overlooking the brilliant,
busy quadrangle below, where flowers bloom in great tubs,
and tall palms stand dark under the glass roof, heedless of
how she crushes her pretty dinner dress of blue silk, the hue
of her eyes.   The soft blonde hair falls loose and half curled
over her shoulders.   What does it matter ?   Eric is not here
to see—Eric is never here now it seems to her.   What she
wears, how she looks, have ceased to interest Eric.   He
cares for her no more—after the deluge.

Her very attitude as she sits, huddled up here, is full of
hopeless, pathetic pain.   The street lamps flare full upon
the pretty, youthful face—youthful still, childish no longer.
She has eaten of the tree of knowledge, and its fruit has been
bitterer than death.   All the sweet, childlike, surprised innocence of the soft fair face, that made half its charm, is
gone—its peach-like, dimpled outline has grown sharp, the
pearly fairness has turned to fixed pallor—its delicate wild
rose bloom has entirely faded—the tender, turquoise eyes
have taken a look of patient despair, very sad to see.   Not
six weeks a bride, and the wife's despair shining from the
sad, sweet eyes already.

Her cheek is pressed against the cool glass ; her hands—
from one of which her wedding-ring slips, so wasted it has

grown—are loosely clasped in her lap ; her tired eyes watch listlessly the crowds that pass, the many vehicles that flash up to the great doorway, and flash away again. Her mind is as listless as her looks. She has been alone for two hours —two weeks it seems to her. She does not care to read, she cannot go out, she cannot call in her maid and talk to her, and there is no one else she knows. For Eric—well, the largest of the small hours will bring Eric home—perhaps.

Suddenly she starts. From a fiacre that has just drawn up a man leaps out. The lamp light falls upon him for a second, and Crystal's heart gives a leap. Big, broad-shouldered, ruddy, bearded, in the familiar round hat and suit of tweed—how much it looked like Terry. Oh ! to see Terry once more—dear old, ever kind Terry ! oh, to see any of them from home—even sharp Elizabeth Jane or snappish old Belinda. What a long, long time it seems since her wedding day !

Her wedding day ! It is only six weeks—six little weeks, and how happy she had been ! That day, with all its details, returns to her with a pang of remembrance that pierces her heart. She recalls Terry's parting words with strange vividness now—in all these weeks she has never thought of them before.

" If in the time that is coming, you are ever in trouble, if you ever need a friend, will you send for me ? All our lives we have been as brother and sister—by the memory of the past, let me be the one to help you if you ever stand in need."

She had laughed in her happy incredulity then—ah, how true his words had come. But she could never send for him, or for any one on earth ; her trouble was a trouble she could only take to the good God. He alone could befriend her here. How had the change come about ? —was she to blame? She could not tell. Her mind went over, in a dazed, helpless sort of way, all her brief married life, and the fault had not been hers—that she knew. They had been so happy in Brittany, so intensely happy —with a happiness that, as a quaint English writer says, " Spread out thin, might have covered comfortably their

whole lives." They had been happy—intensely—for one
week; happy in a more moderate degree, on Eric's part,
the second. The third set in with steady drizzling rain,
and wild wintry winds, and before its close the bridegroom
was yawning in the face of the bride. He was as fond of
Crystal as ever, no doubt, but four days of incessant rain in
a dull Breton town are apt to be trying to the frivolous masculine mind.

"Oh, I say, Chris," Eric said, with a prolonged yawn,
"this is awfully slow, you know. I can't stand much
more of St. Malo and this infernal weather—upon my word
I can't. It's a beastly dull hole at any time ; a fortnight's
as long as any rational being could survive it. I say, let's
go to Paris."

If Eric had said, "Let us go, like Hans Pfaal, up to the
moon in a balloon, and live there," Crystal would have
looked up in her lord's handsome, bored face, with blue
eyes of adoring delight, put on her things, and gone. Paris,
or St. Malo, or the moon, were all alike to this worshipping,
little three weeks' wife. Next day they came to Paris.
and Crystal's troubles began. The first four days all was
well. He drove with her in the Bois, his vanity tickled
by the profound admiration her delicate blonde loveliness
everywhere excited. He took her to the Louvre, to the
Tuileries, to a ball at the English Embassy, to a dinner at
the Earl of Albemarle's.

The fourth evening was windy and wet ; she had a slight
headache, and could not go out. Eric was to dine at the
Jockey Club, of which he was a member. After dinner,
with a couple of friends, he went to the Varieties to see
Felicia in her new piece, "The Golden Witch." He went,
and Crystal's doom was sealed.

"It's rather odd," Eric said, as he and his friends took
their places in the stalls, "that I've never seen this celebrated Felicia. She had finished her engagement and left
London before I came. Is she really the great irresistible
she's called ?"

"Ah ! wait until you see," one of his companions answered. "If you are made of anything like the inflamma-

ble materials I wot of of old, one flash from her black eyes will finish you."

Eric laughed.

"We have changed all that, *mon ami.* I have outlived my taste for black beauties, and can defy all the sorceresses that ever bounded before the footlights."

There was a glow at his heart as he said it. A vision rose up before him, of the pure, sweet face, crowned with its halo of pale gold hair, that he had left at home. Ah yes! these dark daughters of the earth had had their day—he was his little white wife's forever now. Then the curtain rose, and the " La Sorcière d'Or," in a triumphant burst of music, bounded before them. The lights flashed up, a thunder of welcome shook the house, their favorite was smiling and kissing hands to her friends. Eric Dynely looked with critical eyes. Her scant drapery was as if woven of cloth of gold— she seemed robed in a sunburst. Her magnificent black hair fell in a rippling shower to her slim waist, clasped back with brilliants. The great, dark Southern eyes seemed to outflash the diamonds. Whatever her age, under the gas-lights she did not look a day over eighteen.

"By Jove!" Eric said, his breath fairly taken away; "she's handsome, Argyll!"

Argyll smiled.

"Look out for your counter-charm, old fellow. The fair Felicia slays, and spares not. She is handsome—yes as a tigress or panther is handsome—and as merciless."

She danced—it was the very poetry of grace and motion. She sang—and her magnificent contralto filled the building. It was the merest trifle of a play, but she threw herself with wonderful *abandon* and passion into her part, carrying her audience with her. At the close, when the "Golden Witch" is tried, condemned, and found guilty of witch-craft, when she is sentenced to be bound to the stake, when the sacrificial fire is kindled about her, when, with wild agony and despair in the beautiful, ghastly face, she chants her own weird death song, a silence that is pain-ful and oppressive fills the house. The mimic flames mount high- -the death song dies out in an unearthly wail of anguish as the curtain falls. The "Golden Witch" has been burned alive.

"Best thing they could do with her," growls Argyll; "it's a thousand pities they don't try it in reality. There are a good many *belle dames sans merci* in this one city, but I'll take my oath she's the wickedest woman in Paris. Wake up, Dynely. On my word, the fellow's in a trance!"

The theatre shook with its thunders of applause. "Felicia! Felicia!" a hundred voices called. She came, gliding out before them, smiling and bowing once more, with a serpentine smoothness of motion, a supple grace, that *was* very pantheresque. A shower of bouquets were flung upon the stage—then with a last brilliant smile she vanished, and everybody arose to go.

"Will you come behind and be presented, Dynely?" his friend said; "you rather look as if you'd like it. I have the *entrée*. There's to be a supper, and Felicia's little suppers are things to dream of. She and I are old acquaintances," he laughs as he lights his cigar; "any friend of mine is sure of a welcome."

To turn from the voice of the tempter was an act of self-sacrifice Eric had never striven to do in his life. He did not strive now. Certainly he would go and be presented to the adorable Felicia.

"By Jove! Argyll, old fellow, she *is* a stunner and no mistake," he said.

So they went, and the lovely Felicia, all smiles and darkling, sparkling glances, proffers her hospitality to Mr. Argyll's friend. Eric accepts. For one instant the pale slumbering face of his wife rises before him reproachfully, but he puts the thought impatiently away. She is asleep long ago—what odds will an hour or two make to her to-morrow. It is, as Argyll says, a *chef d'œuvre* of a supper—the cuisine, perfection—the guests the wittiest, cleverest men, the most beautiful and successful actresses in Paris. And in a state of wild intoxication, that comes more from Felicia's smiles and looks than her sparkling wines, Eric reaches his rooms as the new day grows gray in the east. Next morning—is it by chance?—they meet in the Bois—Lord

Dynely on horseback, Felicia in a fairy chariot, drawn by two coal-black Arabs, handling the lines like " Four-in-hand Fossbrooke " himself. The brilliant smiles and glances are showered on Lord Dynely once more in dazzling profusion—he becomes her attendant cavalier, and they take the Bois in dashing style, the observed of all observers. In a delicious bonnet—a work of art in itself—behind a flimsy dotted veil, madame still looks eighteen—no more. Her violet velvets, her rich sables, set off her dusk beauty well ; all eyes follow her, very audible French exclamations of admiration reach her gratified ears. Hats fly off at her approach—gentlemen innumerable salaam before her, and the graceful head bends like a queen's to it all. Ladies look on the other side, it is true—but what will you ! She is a dancer, and men adore her—two unforgivable sins in their eyes ; a coquette of the first water—farther than that slander itself will not go. The sheep dog—the demure-faced curate's widow—occupies the other side, as they fly along, down the great wooded drive of the Bois de Boulogne.

And little Crystal's doom was sealed ! Neglect, coldness, impatience—there was nothing left for her but these. Evening after evening, upon one pretext or another, he was absent ; evening after evening she sat while the long, dragging, miserable hours wore by, and waited, waited, waited, for one who did not come. Many madnesses of this sort had held him before, but none so utterly, recklessly mad as this. What did it mean ? What had she done ? She could not understand the change in him. Was Eric growing tired of her already ? The childish blue eyes would lift to his face in bewildered, pathetic questioning, the childish lips would quiver. He could not meet those glances. He avoided her more and more—her meek, uncomplaining patience was the keenest reproach she could make. Then the bewildered questioning died out of the eyes, and a dark despair took its place. Even to her, secluded as a nun, vague rumors of the truth came. Eric had tired of her—another woman had caught his eye and fancy. All was over for her. " Milor's " infatuation for the actress was the gossip of the very servants, the magnificent presents he gave her, his constant attendance upon her; and in some way it all floated to Crystal's ears. Her own maid looked upon her with pitying eyes—all Paris knew that she was a bride forsaken before the honeymoon had waned. She uttered no word of complaint—no reproach, only the color died out of her face, the light from her eyes—to her it was death—her life had come to an end—just that.

She sits alone this evening as usual—she is always alone now. She accepts no invitations—she receives no visitors. But there is a visitor for her to-night, however, a tall gentleman, at whom Marie, the maid, casts glances of admiration as she announces him. Crystal rises, bewildered, from the window—she has not caught the name. Under the light of the chandelier her visitor stands, and a great cry of amaze and delight fills the room.

"Terry!" she cries; "oh, Terry!"

She rushes forward, and fairly flings her arms around his neck. She is so utterly lonely, so homesick and desolate, poor child, and Terry is the big brother who has always been so good to her—nothing else.

His face flushes under the swift caress. Then she recollects herself, and lets him go, and puts back her loose, falling hair in blushing confusion.

"I——it was so sudden, and I—I *am* so glad to see a face from home. Sit down, Terry. When did you come, and how are they all?"

Her fingers lace and unlace nervously. Her lips tremble like the lips of a child about to cry. She has grown nervous and hysterical of late from being so much alone with her misery, and the sight of Terry has unnerved her.

"All well," he answers cheerily; "at least I've not been down at the Vicarage, but I had a letter from Linda a week ago. I told them I was going to cross over and look you up, and they sent no end of love and all that."

Then there is a pause—a painful one. The color has faded out of her face, and it looks bluish white against the crimson velvet back of her chair. Good heavens! Terry thinks, with a thrill of pain and anger, how changed she is, how thin, how worn, how pallid. But he makes no mention of her looks, he only asks in a constrained sort of voice :

" Eric is well, I hope ? "

" Oh, yes, thank you ! "

Her voice falters as she repeats the old formula. Again there is silence. Terry is not a good one for making conversation, and silence is little Crystal's forte.

" Is Eric not at home ? " he ventures after that uneasy pause.

" No," she answers, her eyes fixed on the rings she is unconsciously twisting round and round ; "he is dining out. It—it is a bachelor party. He could not take me."

" And what business has he at bachelor parties *now* ? " rises to Terry's lips, but he represses it. She is going to say something, he sees—the sensitive color is coming and going in her face—something that she finds hard to say. It comes out at last hurriedly."

" Terry ! I wish you would take me to the theatre to-night."

" Crystal ! "

" To the Variétés. I—I want to go. I must go ! " She lifts her eyes to his, and they flash for a moment. " I have wanted to go all this week. Will you take me to-night ? "

He sets his lips. She has heard then. He asks no questions—he makes no reply.

" Don't refuse me, Terry," she pleads, and the sweet lips tremble. " You never did refuse me anything—don't begin now. I want to go—oh, so much ! I want to see—that woman."

The wifely hatred and jealousy she feels for " that woman " are in the bitterness with which she pronounces the two words. It is hard to refuse her—but Terry sits silent and troubled still.

" I would do anything for you, Crystal," he says at length ; " but this—is this best ? "

" I want to go—I *will* go," she says, passionately, turning away. " I did not think you would refuse, Terry Dennison."

" I have not refused, Crystal," he answers gently. " Or

course I will take you, with pleasure, since you wish it,
There is plenty time, too.   While you put on your mantle
and gloves, I will go and secure a box—if one is to be had."
    She gives him a grateful glance.
    "You were always good to me, Terry," she repeats
softly.
    He sighs to himself as he leaves her.   So changed! so
changed! and she is as dear to him as ever.   The hottest
anger he has ever felt against any living man, he feels to-
night against Lady Dynely's son.
    She dresses without the aid of her maid—dresses hurriedly,
and stands all ready as Dennison reappears.
    "It is all right, Lady Dynely," he says in his cheery
voice ; "by great good luck there was one unoccupied box,
and I got it.   Our fiacre is at the door."
    She slips her gloved hand within his arm and goes down ;
she is trembling with nervous excitement, he can feel.
She has never seen this beautiful, wicked actress, who has
charmed her darling from her—she has never dared speak of
her to Eric, and he has never offered to take her anywhere.
He may be angry when he hears of this—she has no intention of concealing it from him—but she must see her, she
must.   She must look upon the face fair enough to take the
bridegroom from his bride before the honeymoon is at an
end.
    The house is full when they reach it—a glittering horse-
shoe of faces, and toilettes, and gaslight, and perfume
and fluttering fans.   She sinks into her seat and draws
back behind the curtain.   The play has begun, and "*La
Sorcière d' Or*," in her dark, insolent, triumphant beauty,
and dazzling raiment, is on the stage, electrifying the
audience by her passionate power.
    Crystal looks at her and turns sick, sick at heart, sick with
despair.   Yes, she is beautiful—terribly, brilliantly beautiful
—insolently, demoniacally beautiful, it seems to her.   Her
voice is like silver, her eyes like dusk stars ; and Eric worships beauty in all things, and this woman—this, is her rival.
She turns away in sick, mute despair as the curtain falls.
What power has she to hold him against a glittering enchan-

tress like this. At that moment a party of gentlemen enter the box opposite; she gives a quick gasping cry—one of them is her husband.

He has been dining and wining evidently. His fair, girl's complexion is flushed—his blue eyes glitter with passionate excitement. He leans back and sweeps the house with his glass—she shrinks tremblingly farther from sight. Terry, too, draws back—Terry, whose face wears a look Crystal has never seen it wear before.

The curtain rises on the second act. Lord Dynely's double-barrels turn from the people to the players. *She* is on the stage once more—his opera glass devours her. He lies back and stares immovably all through the act. When at its close loud plaudits ring through the house, his primrose-kidded hands applaud to the echo. She comes—floral showers, as usual, rain upon her. Crystal does not look at her now —her fascinated eyes are riveted upon her husband. She sees him lean forward, a smile on his handsome face —sees him take a little bouquet of fairy roses and geranium leaves from his button-hole and fling it to the actress. Crystal gives a little gasping cry of sheer physical pain. *She* formed that little bouquet—*she* pinned it into his button-hole as she kissed him good-by four hours ago. And now the actress lifts it—lifts it from amid hosts of others, presses it to her lips—flashes one lightning glance at the fair-haired Englishman in the box above, and disappears.

"You stand well with the Felicia, Dynely," one of the party, a compatriot of Eric's, says, with a loud laugh. "She selects your bouquet from all that pyramid. Lucky beggar! We poor devils stand no chance against such a curled darling of the gods."

The third act finishes—the golden witch dies at the stake, singing her wondrous funeral song. The play is over.

"And I'd like to be the one to fire the fagots, by —," Terry grinds out between his set teeth. Then he leans over and speaks to his companion. "Are you tired, Crystal? You look pale," he says—so gently he says it.

She is more than pale; her very lips are colorless; but

13

she lifts her grateful, hopeless eyes, and repeats the old foolish formula:

"Oh, no, thank you."

"The 'Golden Witch' is finished.   There is a grand new ballet—do you care to wait to see it?" he asks again.

"I will wait, Terry, if you please."

She does not care for the ballet ; she will not see it at all, very likely ; but Eric is yonder—her Eric—her husband— and while she can sit and watch him, this place is better than any other in Paris.

But presently Eric gets up, leaves his box, and goes away. There is rather a long interval before the ballet.   People chat, flirt, laugh, discuss the play and Felicia, and presently there is a stir, and a bustle and a sensation amid them all.

Every glass in the house turns to one box as the cur- tain rises and the new ballet begins.   Terry and Crystal look, too.

In that stage-box the star of the night sits.   Madame Felicia, in elegant full dress, ablaze with diamonds, lies back in her chair, wielding a fan with the grace of a Castilian donna, and listening, with a smile on her perfect lips, to the whispered words of the man who bends over her.   He stoops so low that his blonde hair mingles with her jetty tresses.   The little knot of fairy roses nestle in these ebon locks ; and the tall cavalier who bends so closely, so devotedly, is Eric, Lord Dynely

Crystal can bear no more.   With a great sob, she turns to Dennison, and holds out her hands.

"Oh, Terry," the poor child says, "take me home!"

He does not speak a word.   He rises, wraps her cloak around her, draws her hand within his arm, and leads her out of the theatre.   In the fiacre she falls back in a corner and hides her face from the pitiless glare of the streets.   No word is spoken all the way—what is to be said?   Both know the worst.

He conducts her to her own door, still dead silent.   There he pauses, takes both her hands and holds them in his strong, friendly clasp, while he looks down in the drooping, heart- broken face.

"Keep up heart, little Crystal," he says ; "I'll fetch Eric home in an hour."

She lays her cold cheek down for a second on the warm, true hands.

"Dear old Terry !" she says, softly.   Then he lets her go, and the velvet-hung door closes behind her.

CHAPTER II.

"LA BELLE DAME SANS MERCI."

ND this is how it has ended. Only five weeks married—and he has wearied of her already—a newer, more brilliant beauty has won him from her. Terry has known it would come—known it from the first, but not so soon—good Heaven! not so soon. He takes his way into the street, the hottest, fiercest wrath he has ever felt against any human being, burning in his heart against Eric Dynely. How she has changed—what a pale shadow of the lovely, happy face she took to the altar last New Year's day. What a pitiful, crushed, heart-broken look the sweet, childish eyes wear. If she could have loved him—if he could have won her—if Eric had never come between them, how happy he could have made her! He would have made her life so blessed, she would have been all his own in time, beyond the power of any man to come between them. With a sort of groan he breaks off. His she is not, his she can never be. Eric must return to her or she will die—the whole story is told in that.

"He shall return to her," Terry says inwardly, setting his teeth, "or I will know the reason why."

He does not pause a moment—he hurries at once to the theatre. The ballet is but just ended—the people are pouring forth, but nowhere among them does he see Eric. At length in the crowd he espies a man he knows, one of the four who first entered with him he is seeking, and he makes his way to him and taps him familiarly on the shoulder.

"Boville, old boy," he says with the Briton's customary curt greeting, "how are you?"

Mr. Boville looks over his shoulder and opens two small, sleepy-looking eyes.

"What, Dennison! what, Terry! you here! thought you were at Aldershot. Awfully glad to see you all the same."

"I'm looking for Eric," Terry responds, plunging at once into his subject. "He came in with you. Where is he now?"

"Yes, he came in with me," Boville says, with a faint, weary little laugh. "Where is he now? In much pleasanter company, dear boy—driving home with Madame Felicia. Intoxicating creature that—eh, Terry? And weally, on my word, you know," lisps Mr. Boville, raising his white eyebrows, "Dynely is altogether the spooniest fellow!"

"Where does Madame Felicia live?" Terry growls, with a flash of his eye, cutting Mr. Boville's drawl suddenly short.

The slow, sleepy eyes open again. Mr. Boville looks at Mr. Dennison with a curious little half smile. But he gives Madame Felicia's address readily enough, and watches the big dragoon out of sight with a shrug.

"Is Eric to be brought to his senses, and is Terry deputed to do it, I wonder?" he thinks. "If so, then Terry has quite the most difficult task before him that heavy dragoon was ever called upon to do."

Yes, Terry was going to bring him to his senses—going to bring him to his wife; and without a moment's hesitation, he hails a fiacre, gives the address, and is whirled away through the noonday gaslit brilliance of the boulevards.

"There's to be a supper, no doubt," he thinks. "Is not Felicia famous wherever she goes for her after-theatre suppers? Well, fortune stands my friend this time—I hold the open sesame to *her* doors, and though I have never availed myself of it before, by Jove! I will to-night."

His mind goes back to a certain day two years before, when he had in all probability saved Madame Felicia's life, or at least what was of equal account to her, her beauty. It was the old story of runaway horses—the lady rescued in the nick of time. Madame's passion for spirited ponies had, on more occasions than one, placed her pretty neck and graceful limbs in jeopardy—on this occasion the runaways had become altogether unmanageable, the reins had been jerked from her hands, and with heads up and eyes flashing, they had rushed madly along. The gates of a great park ended the road—if those gates were open madame still stood one chance, if they were closed—she shuddered, intrepid little Amazon as she was, and sat still as death, and white as marble, straining her eyes through the whirlwind of dust as they flew along. The park came in sight—the gates were *closed!* It was just at that moment Terry Dennison, on horseback, came in view. He took in the situation in an instant. To a tempt to check the horses in their mad career would have been useless now ; they would wrench his arms from the sockets before they could be stopped. He galloped up, hurled himself off his horse, and with the agility of a circus rider and the strength of a latter-day Samson, lifted the lady sheer out of the carriage. The horses went headlong at the closed gates, shivering the frail phaeton to atoms, and Madame Felicia fainted quietly away in Lieutenant Dennison's arms.

That was the story. Terry never made capital of it, but the actress did. She was profoundly and greatly grateful, and to show that gratitude, made every possible effort to captivate her preserver and break his heart. For once she failed. Mr. Dennison was invulnerable. All her cajoleries, all her fascinations, all her beauty and *chic*, fell powerless on this big dragoon's dull sensibilities. He saw through her and laughed at her quietly in his sleeve. What the deuce did the little, gushing dancer mean making eyes at him? Terry wondered. He wasn't an elder son ; he didn't keep an open account at Hunt & Roskell's ; he had never given any one a diamond bracelet in his life. She knew it too—then what did she mean? It was madame's way of showing her deep gratitude to the preserver of her life—simply that. But for Terry she would have been smashed to atoms with the phaeton, her beauty ruined, her symmetrical limbs broken, her occupation gone. She shuddered when she thought of it ; death would have been preferable to that. She *was* grateful, deeply and truly grateful, and gave Mr. Dennison carte blanche to come and go as he pleased from henceforth forever. It was a privilege for which royalty itself was sighing just then, but with the dull insensibility that had always characterized him in these things, Dennison treated it and her with the calmest, utterest indifference. He liked her as a dancer, but as a woman, and in private life, not any, thanks. Terry did not go in for dancers. In short Mr. Dennison would *not* be numbered among her victims, would not lose his head for her; and madame saw and laughed good-naturedly, and gave it up and respected him accordingly. It would be a refreshing novelty to have a masculine friend, a friend pure and simple, who would never be a lover, and so she liked Dennison as honestly, as a more honest woman might, and still kept her doors open to him. He came at times to those pleasant, post-opera suppers, where the cleverest painters, the most distinguished novelists, the handsomest actresses in London were to be met, and was ever warmly welcomed.

He had known she was in Paris—he had not met her for seven months, but he had not had the faintest intention of calling upon her here. And now he was whirling along rapidly to her rooms. Of his welcome from her, at all times and in all places, he was sure; his welcome from Eric was much more to the point just at present; and of that he was not at all sure.

"Hang her!" Terry thought, with an inward growl; "hang all such confounded little pirates, cruising in honest waters, and raising the devil wherever they go. Still if one goes there at all, one must be civil, I suppose.

Civil accordingly, Mr. Dennison was when ushered into the gem-like drawing-room of Madame Felicia.

A chandelier, blazing like a mimic sun in the frescoed ceiling. made the room one sheet of golden light. The walls were lined with mirrors, the windows hung with satin and lace, the air heavy with pastilles. Half-a-dozen elegantly dressed and exceptionally handsome women reclined in every species of easy-chair, with attendant cavaliers. On a low fauteuil reclined the great Felicia herself, robed 'n a billowy cloud of translucent white. As a rule she affected costly moires, stiff brocades, heavy velvets; to-night, crisp, white gossamer floated about the perfect form, rich est lace draped the arms and shoulders, diamonds and opals glittered about her, and pale, perfumy, yellow roses nestled in the dead-blue blackness of her hair. By her side, Lord Dynely sat, gazing at the dusky, languid, slightly-bored, warmly-lovely face, as if he could never gaze enough. All started and stared as the new-comer was announced. Unknown to all but two—most unlooked for by them—Terry yet advanced with that ease that the utter absence of all vanity, of all self-consciousness, gives.

" I only reached Paris to-night," he said, "and unorthodox as is the hour, I could *not* resist the temptation to call. It is seven months since we met, madame, and you will recollect that in your goodness I hold permission to visit you in season and out of season."

Quite a lengthy and diplomatic speech for the speaker, but he had prepared it in the fiacre. When one deals with serpents one must be subtle. The yellow-black eyes turned upon him, a light of real pleasure in them ; she half arose and held out her hand. She was cordially pleased to see Terry.

" Mr. Dennison knows he is always more than welcome —one does not easily forget such service as he rendered. How very nice of you to call. Let me introduce you to Lord Dynely ; but you know him, perhaps?"

She looked doubtfully at his lordship. Know him? Surely ! for on Lord Dynely's face an unmistakable scowl has arisen.

" What the devil brings you to Paris, Dennison?" he bluntly demands ; "when did you come?

" To-night, *mon cher*—have you not heard me say so? Delighted to see me does he not look?" Terry says gayly, turning to madame.

" Where are you stopping?" Eric asks, still with a scowl.

" I honor the Louvre with my patronage on this occasion, my lord."

Then there is a pause. The two men look at each other —one straight, level, searching glance—angry and sus picious on Eric's part—stern and resolved on Terry's. Eric is the first to turn away, with a shrug, and a slight contemptuous laugh.

" John Bull is ubiquitous! Go where you will he crops up when you least expect him. It is one of the great drawbacks of our civilization."

" Was monsieur at the Variétés to-night?" madame asks, coquettishly. She is not French, but she affects the French language as she affects French cookery, French toilettes, and French morals.

" I have had that pleasure," Terry responds. " Madame is irresistible in all things, but she out-does herself in '*La Sorcière d'Or.*' Shall we see you in it at the Bijou next London season?"

Felicia laughs softly, and glances up from under her black lashes at Lord Dynely's gloomy face.

" Ah—who knows? Next London season—it begins in a month or two, does it not? but who knows what may happen in a month or two? One may be a thousand miles away from your bleak fogs, and easterly winds, and dull phlegmatic stalls by that time. *Mon ami,* how sulky you look," striking Dynely a blow with her perfumed fan. " As you say in your country—a penny for your thoughts."

" They are worth much more—I was thinking of *you,*" he answers rather bitterly.

" Lord Dynely does me too much honor. Judging by his tone they must be pleasant. May I ask what?"

" I was wondering if there will be *any* Madame Felicia to enchant the sleepy British stalls of the Bijou next season. I was wondering if by that time it will not be Her Excellency, Madame La Princesse Di Venturini."

She laughs a second time. His angry, jealous tone, which he cannot conceal if he would, amuses her vastly.

" Who knows?" is her airy answer; " such droll things happen! I am not sure, though, that it would be half so pleasant. They are announcing supper. Mr. Dennison, will you give me your arm? Lord Dynely, the most delightful of men, the most gallant of gentlemen on ordinary occasions, yet falls a prey at times to what I once heard a

13*

countryman of his call *the doldrums.* And I cannot endure people who have the doldrums!"

She laughs once more, softly and musically, and shows dazzlingly white teeth. She is a trifle vulgar, this peerless Felicia—her most ardent admirers admit that. She smokes, she drinks a great deal of her own champagne—she has even been known to swear at times. But she laughs well—it is one of her most telling points—languidly, sweetly and very often. What her nationality is no one seems exactly to know. English she is not—French, Italian, Spanish, German, she is not. There are people who hint at Yankee extraction ; but this madame herself denies, furiously and angrily denies. She has never crossed the Atlantic in her life, and never, *never* will. She hates America. The lazy, topaz eyes flash as she says it. She will never play in America in her life.

The ruby velvet portières were drawn aside, and they filed in by twos into the adjoining dining-room. Here too the light was vivid as noonday, and beneath the mimic sun of gas a table glittered that was a vision. Tall epergnes of frosted silver, filled with rarest hot-house flowers, slender glasses of waxy camellias from the greenery of a duke, rarest, costliest grapes, peaches and pears.

There was a brief pause in the gay hum of conversation as they sat down. Felicia's cook was a *chef* of the first water—his works of art were best appreciated by silence. For her wines—was not every famous cellar in Paris laid under contribution? —nothing finer were to be met at the table of imperial royalty itself. Presently, however, the first lull passed, gay conversation, subdued laughter, witty sallies, brilliant repartees flashed to and fro. Perhaps of all the clever company assembled, the hostess herself was least clever. As a dancer she was not to be surpassed—as a beauty she was without peer—as a brilliant, a witty conversationalist, she was nowhere. She ate her delicate *salmis,* drank her famous clarets and sparkling Sillery, laughed softly at the gay sallies going on around her, and watched Lord Dynely, her *vis-à-vis,* with a mocking smile in the languid depths of her topaz eyes. He sat, like herself, almost entirely silent through all the bright badinage going on around him, his brows bent moodily, drinking much more than he ate—a sort of "marble guest" amid the lights, the laughter, the feasting and the flowers.

Terry's sudden coming had completely upset him. Something in Terry's eyes roused him angrily and aggressively. What business had the fellow here? What business in Paris at all? Through the unholy glitter, his wife's face rose be·fore him as he had left her hours ago, pale, patient, pathetic. The tiny knot of roses she had given him gleamed still amid the blackness of Felicia's hair—Felicia, who, lying back, eating an apricot, seemed wholly engrossed by her conversation with Dennison. The broad band of gold and diamonds on her perfect arm blazed in the light. Only yesterday he had given it to her, and now she had neither eyes nor ears for any one but this overgrown, malapropos dragoon.

"*Mon ami,*" Felicia said to him, with a malicious laugh, as they arose to return to the drawing-room, "you remind one of the *tête de mort* of the Egyptians—wasn't it the Egyptians who always had a death's head at their feasts as a sort of *memento mori ?*—and the rôle of death's-head does not become blonde men. For a gentleman whose honeymoon has not well ended, that face speaks but illy of post-nuptial joys."

"Ah, let him alone, madame!" cried Cecil Rossart, a tall, pretty, English singer, with a rippling laugh. "You know what the poet says—what Byron says:

> " ' For thinking of an absent wife
> Will blanch a faithful cheek.' "

His lordship is thinking of the lecture her ladyship will read him when he returns home."

"If late hours involve curtain lectures," cried Adele Desbarats, shrilly, "then, *ma' foi !* milor should be well used to them by this. To my certain knowledge, he has not been home before three in the morning for the last two weeks."

"Let us hope my lady amuses herself well in his ab-

sence !" exclaimed Miss Rossart, flinging herself into a
Louis Quatorze fauteuil, and rolling up a cigarette with white,
slim fingers—"no difficult thing in our beloved Paris."

Eric glanced from one to the other at each ill-timed jest,
his blue eyes literally lurid with rage. Dennison's face
darkened, too, so suddenly and ominously, that Felicia, not
without tact, saw it, and changed the subject at once.

"Sing for us, Adele," she cried imperiously, lying luxuriously back in her favorite dormeuse. "Mr. Dennison has
not heard you yet. Have you heard Mademoiselle Desbarats, *mon ami ?*"

"I have not had that pleasure, madame."

The vivacious little brunette went over at once to the
open piano, and began to sing. The others dispersed themselves to smoke and play bezique. Madame's rooms were
Liberty Hall itself. Lord Dynely leaned moodily across
the piano, a deep, angry flush, partly of wine, partly of jealousy, partly of rage at Dennison, partly of a vague, remorse-
ful anger at himself, filled him. For Terry, madame cleared
away her billowy tulle and laces, and made room for him beside her, with her own enchanting smile.

Immediately above the piano — immediately opposite
where they sat, a picture hung, the broad yellow glare of
light falling full upon it. It was the picture that had created the furore last May in the Academy. "How the Night
Fell."

"I have always had a fancy, madame," Terry said, doub-
ling his hand and looking through it at the painting, "that
the woman in that picture is excessively like you. I never
saw you with such an expression as that—I trust I never
may ; still the likeness is there—and a very strong one too.
Do you not see it yourself?"

"Yes. I see it," madame answered, with a slow, sleepy
smile.

"It's odd too, for Locksley—Caryll I mean—never saw
you. I asked him myself. He had a dislike to theatre-
going it seemed, and never went near the Bijou."

The slow, sleepy smile deepened in madame's black
eyes, as they fixed themselves dreamily on the picture.

"He never went to the Bijou—never saw me there? You are sure of that?"

"Quite sure. Told me so himself."

"Ah! well, his dislike for theatres and actresses is natural enough, I suppose, considering his past unlucky experience. Quite a romance that story of his; is it not? Is she alive still?"

"No," Terry answered gravely, "dead for many years. Killed in a railway accident in Canada, ages ago."

The sleepy smile has spread to madame's lips. She flutters her fan of pearl and marabout with slim jewelled fingers.

"Mr. Locksley—I mean Caryll—promised me a companion picture to this. I suppose I may give up all hope of that now. I really should like to make his acquaintance; I have a weakness for clever people—painters, poets, authors—not being in the least clever myself, you understand. No, I don't want a compliment—there is no particular genius in being a good dancer. For the rest," with a faint laugh, "my face is my fortune. Where is Gordon Caryll now?"

She speaks the name as though it were very familiar to her—with an undertone—Terry hears but does not comprehend.

"In Rome, with his mother."

"Does he ever come to Paris?"

"He is expected here almost immediately, I believe."

"Ah!" she laughs. "Well, when he comes, Monsieur Dennison, fetch him some night to see me. Will you?"

"If he will come. And when he hears you have wished it, I am quite sure he will," says Terry.

There is a pause. Madame's eyes are fixed, as if fascinated, on the picture beyond.

"I presume, after Mr. Caryll's first unlucky matrimonial venture, he will hardly thrust his head into the lion's jaw again. I have heard a rumor—but I can hardly credit it—that he is to be married again next May."

"It is quite true."

"To a great heiress—to that extremely handsome Miss Forrester I saw so often with you last season in the park?"

Terry bows. He does not relish France's name on Madame Felicia's lips.

"It is a love-match, I suppose?"

"A love-match, madame."

She tears to pieces a rose she holds, watching the scented
leaves as they flutter and fall.

"But there is a great disparity of years. She nineteen,
he almost forty. I wonder"—she says this suddenly, flashing
the light of the yellow-black eyes electrically upon him—
"if the first unlucky Mrs. Caryll were *not* dead, only divorced—if Miss Forrester would still marry him?"

"I am quite sure she would not," Dennison responds;
"but there is no use speaking of that. The woman is dead
—dead as Queen Anne—was killed in a railway accident,
as I say, and a very lucky thing too for all concerned."

There is a flash, swift and furious, from the black eyes, but
Terry does not see it. The ringed hands close over the
pretty fan she holds with so savage a clasp that the delicate
sticks snap.

"See what I have done!" she laughs, holding it up;
"and Lord Dynely was good enough to give it to me only
yesterday. Well—it has had its day—he must be content."
She flings the broken toy ruthlessly away, and looks up at
her companion once more. "Does Miss Forrester accompany Mr. Caryll to Paris in this expected visit?"

"They all come together—his mother, Lady Dynely (the
dowager Lady Dynely I mean), Miss Forrester and Mr.
Caryll," Terry answers, uneasily, longing to change the subject but hardly knowing how.

She smiles a satisfied kind of smile and is silent. Her
eyes rest on Lord Dynely's moody, sullen face, as he stands
by the piano, heedless of the song and the singer, and she
laughs.

"Your coming seems to have had a depressing effect upon your kinsman. By the bye, he *is* your kinsman, is he
not? He was in the wildest of wild high spirits before you
entered. Is this romantic Mr. Caryll not a relative also?"

"A second cousin. You do Gordon Caryll the honor of
being interested in him, madame," Terry says brusquely.

Madame laughs again and shrugs her smooth shoulders.

"And you are sick of the subject ! Yes, he interests me —one so seldom meets a man with a story nowadays—men who have ever, at any period of their existence, done the 'all for love, and the world-well-lost' business. Shall we not call over poor Lord Dynely and comfort him a little ? He looks as though he needed it. *Très cher,*" she looks to· wards him and raises her voice, "we will make room for you here if you like to come."

"I shall make my adieux," Lord Dynely answers shortly. "You are being so well entertained, that it would be a thousand pities to interrupt. It is one o'clock, and quite time to be going. Good-night."

He turns abruptly away and leaves them. Again madame laughs, and shrugs her graceful shoulders at this evidence of her power.

"What bears you Britons *can* be !" she says ; "how sulkily jealous, and how little pains you take to hide it. Why did not your Shakespeare make Othello an Englishman ? What, *mon ami !*—you going too? "

"For an uninvited guest have I not lingered sufficiently long?" Terry answers carelessly, and then he hurriedly makes his farewells, and follows Eric out.

He finds him still standing in the vestibule, and lighting a cigar. The night has clouded over, a fine drizzling rain is beginning to fall, but Eric evidently means to walk. The distance to the Hotel du Louvre is not great.

"Our way lies together, old boy," Terry says, linking his arm familiarly through Eric's, "so I cut it short and came away."

"What an awful cut, for Felicia," Eric retorts, with an angry sneer. " Let me congratulate you, Terry, on your evident success ; I never knew before that you went in for that sort of thing."

" If by going in for that sort of thing, you mean flirtation with danseuses, I don't go in for it," is Terry's reply. " If I did I should certainly choose some one not *quite* old enough to be my mother."

" What do you mean ? " Dynely asks, savagely.

"I mean Felicia, of course—thirty-five if she's a day. Oh, yes, she is—I've heard all about her. She wears well, but she's every hour of it. And the most dangerous woman the sun shines on."

"I wonder, then, you fling yourself into the jaws of the lioness," Eric retorts, with another bitter sneer. "You make a martyr of yourself with the best grace possible—make love *con amore* as though you enjoyed it, in fact."

"I didn't come to see Felicia," Terry says, quietly. "I came to see *you*."

Eric's eyes flash fire. He turns to speak, but Dennison stops him.

"Wait one moment," he says, in the same quiet, resolute tone. "You are angry, and excited, and jealous. Jealous! faugh! of such a woman as that! Do you know that your infatuation for her—your neglect of your wife—is the talk of Paris—the talk of London?—for in London it reached me."

A furious oath is Eric's answer as he wrenches his arm free.

"And you came after me as my keeper, as a d— spy!" he cries, hoarse with passion.

"I came after you as your friend, as *hers*," Terry answers, his own eyes kindling. "It is early days, Dynely, to neglect your bride—to leave her there, utterly forsaken and alone, to break her heart in solitude, while you fling gifts in the lap, and sit at the feet of a Jezebel like that. I do not set up as your keeper—as any man's—but I will not stand by and see *her* heart-broken, her life blighted, while I can raise my voice to prevent. Eric! if you had seen her as I did, three hours ago, pale, crushed, heart-broken—"

"'Thou shalt not covet thy neighbor's wife!' My wise Terry, my virtuous Terry, my pink and pattern of all morality, did you ever hear *that?* You're as much in love with Lady Dynely as you ever were with Crystal Higgins. I only wonder you took the trouble to come. Would it not have been pleasanter to have stayed behind and soothed her sorrows with your pathetic and pious conversation?"

Terry looks at him—at the flushed, furious face—at the blue eyes lurid with rage, in wonder—almost in horror.

"Good Heaven!" he says, "is *this* Eric? If any other living man had said as much, or half as much, I would have knocked him down. But I see how it is ; that devilish sorceress has turned your brain. Well—she has turned stronger brains, but she shall not make an absolute fool of you. Eric ! dear old man, I'm not going to quarrel with you, if I can help it. You don't know what you are saying. I promised little Crystal to fetch you home in an hour. It's awfully lonely in that big hotel for her, poor child, and she was never used to being alone, you know."

His voice softened. "Ah, poor little Crystal!" he thinks, with a great heart-pang, "if your married life begins like this, how in Heaven's name will it end!"

"So!" Eric says between his set teeth, "*she* sent you after me, did she ?—a naughty little boy to be brought home and whipped! Perhaps she also told you where to find me ?"

"She told me nothing—nothing, Eric, and you know it," Terry answers, sternly. "Is it likely she would discuss her husband with any one ? It wasn't difficult to find you. The very street gamins could have told me, I fancy, so well is your new infatuation known, Eric, old fellow, we have been like brothers in the past, don't let us quarrel now. Keep clear of that woman—she's dangerous—awfully dangerous, I tell you. She has ruined the lives of a score of men—don't let her ruin yours. Don't let her break Crystal's heart—Crystal, whose whole life is bound up in yours. Pity *her*, Eric—poor little soul—if you have none for yourself."

Again Eric laughs harshly and long.

"Hear him, ye gods! Terry Dennison in the rôle of parson ! Is your sermon quite finished, old boy ?— because here we are. Or is this but a prelude to a few more to come ? How well the patronizing elder-brother tone comes from you—you, of all men—the dependant of my mother's bounty. *She* comes to Paris next week—what fine stories you will have to tell her—what eloquent lectures you can prepare together. Let me tell you this, once and for all, Dennison," he says, white with anger, his blue eyes aflame—" I'll have no sneaking or spying on my actions—I'll be taken to task by no man alive, least of all by *you* /   Let there be an end of this at once and forever, or by—you'll repent it ! "

Then he turns, dashes up the wide stairway, and Terry is alone.

CHAPTER III

IN THE STREETS.

ERRY stands for a while irresolute. One by one the clocks of the great city chime out the hour after midnight; a few belated pedestrians, a few fiacres fly past. Even Paris is settling itself for its night's sleep, but Dennison has no thought of sleeping. It is of no use mounting to his cock-loft under the eaves in his present disturbed state of mind—sleep and he will be strangers for hours to come. Eric has robbed him of more than one night's rest since last September—since that eventful day of the Lincolnshire picnic, when all that was brightest and sweetest in his life went out of it forever. Well, so that he had been true, so that he made her happy, Terry could have borne his pain with patient heroism to the end; but to-night, the old, half-healed pang comes back sharp and bitter as ever. Only six weeks a bride—six weeks, and neglected, outraged already—his brief, hot fancy dust and ashes—Felicia, the actress, preferred before Crystal, the wife.

"He's a villain," Terry thought, savagely; "he's worse than a villain—he's a fool! Yes, by Jove! as they say over here, a fool of the fourth story."

He glanced up at the window where four hours ago Crystal had wistfully sat. Lights still burned there. Was Eric taking her to task for what *he* had done—little Crystal, to whom no one ever spoke a harsh word! He could not stand there with the thought in his mind—he turned, and without knowing or caring whither, made his way through the now almost silent city streets.

The drizzling rain that had begun to fall at midnight was falling still, not heavily, but with a small, soaking persist-

ence, that showed it meant to keep it up until morning.
Smoking as he went, his hands thrust deep into the pockets
of his overcoat, Dennison strolled on and on, quite heedless
where he went, or how far. His thoughts were still with
Crystal—what should he do for her? how help her? It
was useless, worse than useless to remonstrate with Eric—
no one knew better than Terry how hopelessly and utterly
obstinate opposition made him. If he could only induce
him to quit Paris. His mother was coming; but Terry
knew how little influence his mother had over him where the
gratification of his own fancy was concerned. For Eric himself it did not so much matter—he could afford to spend a
few thousands in bracelets and bouquets for the dark-eyed
dancer, until his feverish fancy burned itself out as so many
scores of other feverish fancies had done; it was Crystal
who was to be considered—Crystal, who lived but in his
love, who drooped already like a broken lily—whose heart
he was breaking as thoughtlessly and as surely as ever careless child broke the toy of which it had wearied.

"I'll speak to Felicia herself," Terry thought, with a last
desperate impulse; "she can't be *all* bad—no one is, they
say, and I have heard stories of her lavish generosity to the
poor, and all that. Even so insatiable a coquette as she is
may spare one victim. I'll go to her to-morrow and tell her
how it is, tell her of the poor little girl-wife he neglects for
her, and ask her to shut the door in his face. She told me
once, I remember, after that runaway scrape, to ask any
favor I chose, 'though it were half her kingdom,' and I
should have it. I never wanted anything of her before—let's
see if she will keep her promise to-morrow."

The idea was a relief. His train of thought broke—much
thinking was not in Terry's line—he paused suddenly and
looked about him. For the first time he became aware that
he had lost his way, that the night was advancing, that it
was black, chill and rainy, and that the sooner he retraced
his steps the better. As he turned, a cry, faint and far off,
reached his ear—a cry of pain or fear—then another, then
another. It was a woman's voice, a woman in trouble. Instantly Terry plunged in the direction, running full speed.

The cry was repeated, nearer this time—a shrill, sharp cry of affright.   He made for the sound, turned a corner, and found himself in a narrow, dark street, high houses frowning on either hand, and a woman, flying, panting, and crying out, with two men in hot pursuit.

" Hallo ! " Dennison cried, sending his strong, hearty, English voice through the empty, silent street, "what the deuce is to pay here? "

With a shrill scream of delight the flying figure made for him and clutched his arm, panting for breath.

" Oh, sir, you are English," she gasped, in that language ; "save me from those horrid men ! "

Terry passed his right arm around her.   One of the men, a beetle-browed, black-bearded Frenchman, came insolently up, and without further parley Mr. Dennison shot out his left in the most scientific manner, and laid him on the pave-ment.   His companion paused a second to see his fellow's fate, and then precipitately fled.

"And unless we want the gendarmes to come up and march us to the station, we had better follow his example, I think," said Mr. Dennison to his fair friend.

He looked down as he spoke with some curiosity.   An Englishwoman alone and belated at this hour, in the streets of Paris, was a curiosity.   The light of a street lamp fell full upon her.   A woman ! why, she was a child, or little better, a small, dark, elfish-looking object, with two wild black eyes set in a minute white face, and a dishevelled cloud of black hair, falling all wet and disordered over her shoulders.

"Who are you?" was Dennison's first astounded ques-tion.

The wild black eyes lifted themselves to his face—two small hands clutched his arm tightly.   Where had he seen eyes like those before ?

"Oh, sir ! don't leave me, please !   I am so afraid !   it is so late."

" Late !   Egad, I should think so.   Rather late for a little girl to be wandering the streets of any city, French or Eng-lish.   You *are* a little girl, aren't you ? " doubtfully.

"I am sixteen years and six months—and I didn't want

to wander the streets.   I lost my way," was the answer, somewhat angrily given.

"Who are you?"

"I am Gordon Kennedy."

"And how do you come to have lost your way, if I may ask, Miss Gordon Kennedy?"

The big black eyes lifted themselves again to his face in solemn, searching scrutiny.   Evidently the gaze was reassuring; she drew a long breath of relief and clung confidently to his arm.   But again Terry was nonplussed—*where* had he seen some one like this before?

"I came from Scotland—from Glasgow," the girl answered, with a certain old-womanish precision.   "I came in search of a person residing in Paris.   I reached here in the train to-night.   I have very little money, hardly any, and I was foolish enough to try and find the person I wanted on foot, instead of in a cab.   I lost my way naturally; and I know so little French, and speak it so badly that I could not make myself understood.   I did not know what to do; I wandered on and on; it grew dreadfully late; I thought I would stay in a church porch until morning out of the rain. While I was looking about for one, those two dreadful men followed and spoke to me.   I ran away and they pursued.   I screamed for help and you came.   And I am very, very much obliged to you, sir," concluded Miss Gordon Kennedy, with another solemn, upward, grateful glance of the lustrous eyes.

"And how do you know whether I am any better than the two men you fled from?" Terry asked, with a half-laugh.

"Ah, sir, you are English, and you have a good face.   I am not afraid of *you*," the girl answered, with a second profound sigh of relief.

"Thank you," Terry said, still laughing; "it is the highest compliment ever paid me in my life.   Well, Miss Kennedy, it is getting on for two o'clock, and is raining, as you see.   Shall I look you up a convenient church porch, or what shall I do with you?   Even a church porch in Paris on a wet night is not altogether a desirable lodging for a young lady of sixteen.   Where shall I take you?"

"I don't know," the girl answered, with an air of anxious distress. "If it were not so late, so dreadfully late, I might try to find *her*. Tell me, sir, are all the theatres closed yet?"

"Closed two hours ago. You don't think of exchanging the church porch for a theatre, do you, mam'selle?"

"Don't laugh at me," she returned, with a sudden flash of the black eyes; "there's nothing to laugh at. I want to find a person who belongs to a theatre—a lady, an actress. She plays at the Varieties."

"At the Varieties?" Terry repeated, a little startled. The flashing black eyes had once more discomfited him by their resemblance to other eyes he had somewhere seen. "I know some of the ladies who play at the Varieties. May I ask what is her name?"

"It is Madame Felicia."

They were walking swiftly along through the rain. At these words Dennison suddenly stood still. The girl looked up at him in surprise. Again, by the glare of the street lamps, that strange, striking resemblance flashed upon him. Madame Felicia! Why, this child was sufficiently like Madame Felicia to be her own daughter. Well—Terry suppressed a whistle, and still stared blankly down at his little companion.

"Well," she cried, impatiently, "what is it?—Why do you look at me so? Have I said anything strange? Do you know," with a sudden glow of hope, "Madame Felicia?"

"Come on," was Terry's answer; "you'll get your death standing here in the rain. Do I know Madame Felicia? Well—a little. Do you know her?"

"No."

"You don't! Then, why—if I may ask—"

The dark eyes look up at him again with another petulant flash.

"No, you may not ask! I can't tell you. I want to find Madame Felicia—the actress who plays at the Varieties. That is all I intend to tell you. I have come all the way from Glasgow alone to find her. I *must* find her—to-night, if possible. She is the only friend I have in the world. Oh, sir, you have been very good to me. You have done me a

great service—I know you have a kind heart ; take pity on
me and, if you know her, take me to her."

'Does she expect you ?" Terry asked, staggered.

" No, sir, she does not ; but all the same she will take care
of me."

" You are quite sure of that ? "

"Quite sure, sir."

" Have you ever met Madame Felicia ? "

"Never to remember her, but I know what she is like.
It is a great many years since she came to see me.   We
lived in Canada then."

" We—whom ? "

" Joan and me.   Joan is my foster-mother, and she is
dead.   But I have no right to tell you this.   I *won't* tell
you !" with a child's impatient petulance again.

" You speak of Madame Felicia visiting you in Canada,"
Terry went on, taking no notice of the brief outbreak of
anger ; " you must make a mistake, mademoiselle.   The
Madame Felicia I know was never in Canada in her life."

" Look here ! " cried the girl, excitedly.   She disengaged
her arm, and produced a photograph from the pocket of
her dress.   " Look at this !   Is your Madame Felicia anything like this ? "

They pause again—again beneath a street lamp—and he
looks at the picture.   Madame Felicia, sure enough—to
the life—a softly tinted, perfect likeness.

" Well ? " the girl impatiently demands.   He hands it
back and looks at her with strongest curiosity.

" That is my Madame Felicia.   There is but one such
face as that on earth.   And, I repeat again, she never was
in Canada."

" And I repeat she *was !* " she flashed out angrily.
" Why do you contradict me ?   I know better !   It is very
impolite !   She *was* in Canada !   she was !   she was !   She
lived there—I was born there—"

She paused.   In her excited vehemence she had betrayed
herself.   She clasped her hands and looked up at him wildly.

" I—I—didn't mean that ! " she gasped.   " I—I—didn't
mean anything ! "

"No, of course not," Dennison responded, unable to re-press a smile. What a child she evidently was, what a passionate, excitable, wilful child !

"Oh, take me to her!" she cried, with a sort of sob. "It is so late, so cold, so wet ! I never was out at this time of night with a strange man before. What would Joan say ? Ah, poor Joan !"

She sighed bitterly and clung to him, looking about at the unfamiliar scene, her eyes dusk with bewilderment and terror.

"Joan was your mother?" Terry insinuated ; "no, by the bye, your foster-mother ? "

"It does not matter to you what she was !" retorts Miss Kennedy, with a sudden return to sharpness. " Will you take me to Madame Felicia, or will you not ?—there ! "

"My dear child, Madame Felicia will be in bed."

"She will get up when she hears who I am. Oh ! please take me to her house—only to her house. She will let me in. She will take care of me when she hears who I am."

"When she hears who you are," Terry thought, looking at the dark, passionate, pleading, upturned face—at the large, dilated black eyes. "*She* was in Canada, and you were born there ! There is a story in the past, then, that madame keeps as a sealed book. I always thought so—I always thought there was more in her hatred of America than met the eye."

"Will you take me to her—say?" cried the girl, giving his arm an angry, impatient shake, "or are you a wicked man after all, like the Frenchman you knocked down ? "

"A wicked man ?" Terry repeated, laughing, and with a sort of pity in his face for this unsophisticated child. " My dear little girl, no. I am the incarnation of every do-mestic and Christian virtue, and I will take you to Madame Felicia instanter. We are near her house now—I only hope she will take you in. If she will not, some one else shall. Gracious powers !" he thought, "if this outspoken child had fallen into other hands."

The girl drew a long breath, and gave the arm she had so lately shaken a little, grateful squeeze.

14

"You *are* good. I am sorry I was so cross with you, but I hate to be contradicted. She will take care of me ; don't you be afraid, and she will thank you too. What is your name ? "

" Terry, mademoiselle."

" Terry what ? "

"Terry Dennison ; and yours you say is Gordon Kennedy? An odd name for a young lady."

"Yes, isn't it ? But the Gordon was after my father, and the Kennedy was after Joan. Joan always called me Donny, for short."

"The Kennedy was after Joan, was it ? That's odd too. Had your father no other name than Gordon ? Was that his family name ? "

"I wish you wouldn't ask so many questions ! " was Miss Kennedy's answer, with still another return to sharpness. "It is awfully impolite to ask questions. My name is Gordon Kennedy, and I want to go to Madame Felicia—that's enough for you to know."

"I beg your pardon, mademoiselle," Terry said, laughing ; "I stand rebuked. I won't offend again. Here we are at Felicia's, and lights are burning yet. Stand here ; I will inquire at the *loge* if madame is to be seen."

He left her and hastened to make inquiries. The household of madame had not yet retired—madame's chasseur, in gorgeous livery, was produced, who in voluble French declared it to be utterly impossible to disarrange madame at that hour.

"Call madame's maid," Dennison said, authoritatively ; "it's a matter of the utmost importance to madame herself. I will explain to her."

The maid was reluctantly summoned. Dennison hastened back to his waiting protégée.

"Have you anything—a note, a token to send to madame that will prove your identity ? She will not see you else," he explained.

The girl produced from her pocket a small sealed packet, and put it confidently in his hand.

"Joan gave me that before she died," she said. "She

told me to give it to Madame Felicia when I met her. You send it to her, and all will be right."

The femme de chambre appeared, sleepy and sulky. Madame could see no one at such an hour. Madame had already retired—she could not dream of disturbing madame. Monsieur's business must wait until to-morrow. Monsieur cut short the flow of French eloquence by slipping a glittering Napoleon in one hand and the packet in the other.

"Give madame that, with Mr. Dennison's compliments. Tell her that the young lady—Gordon Kennedy—is here, just arrived from Scotland, and waiting to see her."

The Frenchwoman vanished. In silence, Dennison and the young girl stood and waited. How would it end?

Would madame receive her? Or would she treat her as an impostor, and send her away? His own pulses quickened a little with the suspense. Five, ten, fifteen minutes, and the maid did not appear.

"Are you cold?" Terry asked very gently, as the girl gave an irrepressible shiver from head to foot.

She looked at him, with those sombre, spectral dark eyes, so like, yet so unlike Felicia's own.

"I am *afraid,*" she answered, her teeth chattering. "I don't know! what if she will not receive me after all? She is a great lady—I am so poor, so wretched. She may not want me. Oh, if she does not, what will become of me?"

"I will care for you," he answered kindly. "My dear child, don't tremble so. Ah! here comes the woman now."

The maid returned, curiosity painted on every feature of her face.

"Madame would see mademoiselle. Mademoiselle was to come to madame at once."

With a little cry of joy the girl sprang forward.

"I knew she would! I knew she would!" she said, with a sob. Then she reached out both hands to Dennison. "You were so good! I will never forget you—never! I thank you with all my heart!"

He pressed the little cold hands kindly, and watched her out of sight. Then he started at a rapid pace for his hotel.

" So ! " he thought ; " an odd adventure, surely ! I seem destined to be mixed up in Madame Felicia's affairs. Will she be grateful, or the reverse, for this night's work, I wonder ? That girl's maternity is written in her face—although, of course, she might be Felicia's sister. I wish I could get a hold upon her of any sort, yes, of any sort, that would make her hear to reason about Dynely. Come what may, I don't care how, *he* must be freed from her thrall."

He had reached his hotel. It was past two now. But few lights burned—Eric's rooms were in darkness.

Rather fagged, Terry made his way to his own sky-parlor, and soon forgot his first eventful Paris evening in sound, fatigued sleep.

CHAPTER IV

HE departure of Lord Dynely and Dennison was
the signal for the departure of the rest of madame's
guests.   Half an hour later and the lights were
fled, the garlands dead, and Felicia was alone in
her own pretty, rose-hung, gas-lit drawing-room.   She lay
back in the soft depths of her fauteuil, a half-smile on her
lips, too luxuriously indolent as yet even to make the exer-
tion of retiring.   The picture "How the Night Fell" was
the object upon which her long, lazy eyes rested, while that
well-satisfied smile curled her thin red lips.

"So he is coming," she was thinking; "and he is to be
married.   To be married to France Forrester, one of the
very proudest girls in England, as I have heard.   She knows
all about my story, no doubt.   And she thinks, and he thinks,
and they all think, I was killed in that railway accident so
many years ago.   Her mother was a French Canadian; and
she is of her mother's religion, so they tell me; and even if
her pride would permit, her religion would forbid her to
marry a man who is the husband of one living divorced wife.
And this, then, is the form my vengeance is to take after all.
I have wondered so often, so often—it seemed so impossible
my ever being able to reach him, my ever being able to
make him suffer one tithe of what he has made me.   But,
'I have him on the hip' now.   Through his love for
this girl I will stab him to the heart.   I will part them
and stand between them—ay, even if I have to make my history patent to the world.   If I have to confess to Di Venturini,
to whom I have lied so long.   I will prevent *his* marriage if
I have to do it by the forfeit of my own."

She paused a moment to roll up and light a rose-scented
cigarette, her face clouding a little at her own thoughts.

"It will be a sacrifice too, if I *should* have to make things public, to confess to the prince. He knows nothing of my past life, except the pretty little romance I invented for his benefit. At my worst he believes me to be an outra-geous coquette with more head than heart, not in the least likely to be led astray by the tender passion, and with no false pride to stand in the way of my accepting costly pres-ents. Indeed, in the very fishy state of the prince's own exchequer since I have known him, the diamond bracelets, etcetra, were not at all obnoxious in his sight." She lifted her dusk, lovely arm, and looked with glittering eyes at the broad band of yellow gold, ablaze with brilliants. "What a fool that boy lordling is!" she thought, contemp-tuously; "so great a fool that there is really no credit in twisting him round one's finger. And he has a bride of six weeks' standing, they tell me—neglected and alone for *me*—at the Louvre. Ah! these brides!" with a soft laugh. "She is not the first whose bridegroom has left her to spend the honeymoon at my feet. He is a relative of Caryll's, too. Will his neglect of her, and besotted admiration of me, be another dagger to help stab him? If there were no bracelets in question I think that motive would be strong enough to make me hold fast."

She flung away her cigarette and began abruptly drawing off the many rich rings with which her fingers were loaded. On the third finger of the left hand, one—a plain band of gold, worn thin by time—alone remained—the only one she did not remove. She lifted her pretty, dimpled brown hand, and gazed at it darkly.

"I wonder why I have worn you all this time?" she mused. "My wedding ring! that for sixteen years has meant nothing—less than nothing. And yet by day and by night, I have worn you in memory of that dead time—of that brief five months, when I was so happy, as I have never, in the hours of my greatest triumph, been happy since. Di Venturini says it is not in me to love. He is in love, poor little old idiot! If he could have seen me then!"

Her hands fell heavily in her lap, she sighed drearily.

"How happy I was! how I did love that man! what

a good woman I might have been if he would have but forgiven and trusted me. But he spurned me, he drove me to
desperation, to death nearly. What did he care? I vowed
my turn would come—for sixteen years I have waited, and it
has not. But the longest lane has its turning, and my hour
is now."

She arose and walked up and down, her floating muslin
and laces sweeping behind her. Once she paused before the
picture, leaning over the back of a chair, and looking up at
it·with a curious smile.

" What an agonized face he has painted," she said softly ;
"what anguish and despair in those wild eyes. Did I
really look like that, I wonder? and what was there in him
that I should wear that tortured face for his loss. Good
Heaven ! if it comes to that, what is there in any man that
women should go mad for their loss or gain—selfish, reckless
fools, one and all ! Even he is ready to paint his own folly
and madness of the past, to make money of it in the
present."

She turned away with an impatient, scornful last glance
and slowly left the room. Up in her own chamber, she rang
for her maid, and with a yawn resigned herself into her hands
for the night.

"If I can only make it all right with the prince," she
mused, as the Frenchwoman brushed out her thick, black
hair. " I don't want to lose him, particularly now, as he has
come to his own again. Madame la Princesse Di Venturini !
My faith ! a rise in life for the little beggarly singer of the
New York concert hall, for poor old Major Lovell's accom-
plice, for Gordon Caryll's cast-off wife. No, I must not lose
the prize if I can, and he is most horribly jealous. Let the
truth reach him—that I have had a husband, that I have a
daughter, and much as he is infatuated, I really and truly
believe he will throw me over."

Her thoughts wandered off into another channel, suggested
by the incidental remembrance of her daughter.

"What shall I do with the girl ?" she thought, ''now
that Joan is dead, and Joan's boor of a husband does not
want her. He will be sending her to me one of these days

if I do not take care. I must answer his insolent letter to-
morrow, and tell him at all risks to keep her from coming
here. From what Joan has written of her, I believe her to
be quite capable of it."

Madame's *toilette de nuit* was by this time complete. The
maid had departed, and madame was in the very act of depositing her loveliness between the lace and linen of the
rose-curtained bed, when the woman suddenly and excitedly
reappeared, the packet in her hand. In a dozen voluble
sentences she related the cause of the disturbance.

"A tall, blond English monsieur—Deens-yong—it was
impossible to pronounce the name, but one of the English
gentlemen who had been present this evening, and a young
lady with him, who insisted upon seeing madame, and Monsieur Deens-yong, with his compliments, had sent madame
this."

"Mr. Dennison," madame repeated, aghast, "and a young
lady." She looked at the superscription and turned white.
"Mon Dieu!" she thought, in horror, "Joan's writing!
Can it be possible *she* is here?"

It was quite possible—the contents of the little packet left
no doubt. It was a rare thing for madame to turn pale,
but the dusk complexion faded to a sickly white by the time
she had finished the letter.

"I will see this young person, Pauline, mon enfant," she
said carelessly, feeling the needle-like eyes of the waiting
woman on her. "Show her up here at once, and wait until I ring; I may need you."

The woman departed, marvelling much. And Felicia,
throwing a dressing-gown over her night robe, and thrusting
her feet into slippers, sat down to await the advent of her
daughter.

It was two o'clock—what an hour to come, and with Terry
Dennison, of all men. What did it mean? How did the
girl come to be in Paris at all, and what should she do with
her, now that she was here? She had not seen her for ten
years. Although Joan and her husband had removed to
Scotland—she had never felt any desire to see her. From
what Joan wrote of her, she was a wilful, headstrong, pas-

sionate creature, whom love alone could rule, upon whom discipline of any kind was lost, reckless enough if thwarted for any desperate deed. And now she was here. What *should* she do with her? If the truth reached the ears of Di Venturini! No, it must not—at any hazard it must not. She must win the girl over by kindness, by pretence of affection, and, when opportunity offered, get rid of her quietly and forever.

And then the door opened, and Pauline ushered her in. For an instant there was silence while mother and daughter looked at each other full. A very striking contrast they made—the mother in her mature and well-preserved beauty, her loose robe of violet silk, her feet in violet velvet slippers, elevated on a hassock, lying indolently back in her chair, the lamplight streaming across her rich dark beauty. The daughter draggled and wet, her black hair disordered, her pale, pinched face bluish white, her great dusk eyes half shy, half defiant.

"Come here, child," said the soft silky tones of Felicia.

The girl advanced, still with that half-shy, half-defiant air and attitude, ready to be humble or fierce at a moment's notice. Madame stretched forth her hand, drew her to her, and kissed her cold, thin cheek.

"You are Gordon Kennedy?"

"And *you* are my mother!"

She made the answer with a certain defiance still—prepared to fight for her rights to the death.

"Hush-h-h!" madame said, with a smile; "*that* is your secret and mine. No one knows it here—no one must know it as yet. My marriage was a secret in the past, is forgotten in the present. I was divorced long ago. But you know all that."

"Of course I know; Joan told me everything. Look here."

She pushed up her sleeve, and showed on the upper part of her arm the initials "G. C." in India ink.

"*You* did that, Joan said," went on the girl still defiantly. "She told me to show it to you, and remind you of the day you sent her away and did it yourself."

"I remember very well," Felicia said, still smiling, still

14*

holding the girl's cold hand. " My child, how chill you are, how wet. Here, sit down on this hassock and tell me how in the world you come to be in Paris at this unearthly hour, and in charge of Mr. Dennison."

Gordon Kennedy obeyed. The defiance was gradually melting out of her face, but there was a visible constraint there still. With straightforward precision she narrated her adventure of the night.

"I ran away from Glasgow," she said, boldly. "Joan died, and I hated *him*. He was a brute, and he tried to beat me. I threw a plate at his head and cut one cheek open. It was a horrid gash," said this young virago, with a shudder; "but I didn't care; he *was* a brute; I had to run then, and I came here. I had some money; Joan gave it to me; I have some yet, and might have taken a cab when I got to Paris as well as not, and gone to your theatre, but the streets were so bright and dazzling, the shops so splendid, I thought I would walk. I was a fool for my pains. I don't know what would have happened, only Mr. Dennison came. Ah, I like *him*—he was awfully good."

" But surely, surely, child, you did not tell him who you were ? " madame cried in horror, as she listened to this outspoken confession.

"I told him nothing," Gordon answered, proudly, "only my name, and where I came from, and how I got lost, and that I wanted to find you. He said he knew you, and would take me to you, and here I am."

"It is the most extraordinary thing I ever heard of," madame said, bewildered; "and you are the most extraordinary child. Surely there is a Providence that watches over children and fools."

" I am no child, and I am no fool. I'll thank you not to call me either," cried little spitfire, blazing up.

"No, no, certainly not. Why, child, will you be angry with me, your own mother? " madame said, in her sugarest tone.

"You don't look very glad to see me, if you are my mother," retorts Miss Kennedy, sulkily.

"You have surprised me so much, don't you see, and I

don't want it known that you *are* my daughter. It would be a very bad thing for me, and create no end of talk."

"You are ashamed of me, I suppose?" the young girl cried. "I knew you would be. You are a fine lady, and I am—yes, look at me. I am a miserable, draggle-tailed object, am I not?"

"What a temper you have," madame said, still smiling, still holding her hands. "Don't speak so loudly. I am not in the least ashamed of you. Properly dressed you will be quite like me."

The black eyes lit.

"Do you think so," eagerly; "Joan always said I was like you, but you are so beautiful, and I am so thin, and black, and pale. You will let me stay with you, then, will you?"

"Certainly—that is for the present. I think I shall send you to school. You would like to go to school, would you not, Gordon. By the bye, I would rather not call you that."

"Joan called me Donny."

"Donny be it, then. I will dress you properly and send you to school, and you are not to say a word—no, not a whisper—about our relationship. You can keep a secret, I think, by your face."

"Try me," the girl said, proudly. "I'd die before I'd tell, if I promised not."

"And you *do* promise. It would never do for me, Donny, at least not just yet, to acknowledge you. People here do not know I ever was married."

"If you wish it—yes, I promise," the girl said, a wistful light in the great eyes.

"Then for the present you shall remain here—for a few days, that is. You shall sleep in my dressing-room, and I will tell my maid and the rest that you are my cousin—yes, a cousin from Scotland. And now, as it is late, and have been travelling and are tired, I will see you safely in bed myself."

"And may I see *him* again—the gentleman who was so kind to me?" the girl asked, only half satisfied after all.

"Mr. Dennison? Oh, well—yes—I suppose so. Tell him you are a cousin, and I will indorse your story."

"I hate telling lies," Donny muttered, rather sullenly ; but madame prudently took no notice. In her own mind she had resolved that long before Prince Di Venturini's return to Paris, this obnoxious daughter should be safely out of sight for good and all.

With her own hand she led her to the dressing-room, helped her to arrange the little lace-draped bed there, and saw her safely in it before retiring to her own room.

It had been a very unexpected and rather disagreeable ending to a pleasant evening. Contretemps will occur, and must be made the best of. Madame had reached that age when we learn the folly of disturbing ourselves for trifles. A composing draught of wine and spices stood on the table. She rang for her maid, and dismissed her, drark her sleeping potion, and went calmly to bed.

CHAPTER V

WHAT LOVE'S YOUNG DREAM SOMETIMES COMES TO.

T is twelve o'clock, more or less, by all the clocks and watches of Paris—high noon by the broad brightness which is pouring a flood of golden light through the blue silk curtains, over the glass, and silver, and china of a dainty breakfast-table set for two, over two blonde English heads—Lord and Lady Dynely.

They are breakfasting *tête-à-tête*, and in profound silence. His lordship hides a very sulky, dissatisfied and conscious face, behind that day's *Moniteur*. Her ladyship, on the other side of the big shining urn, droops over her teacup, pale as the dainty cashmere robe she wears, with blue eyes that look jaded and dull from want of sleep. She has not slept all night, and it tells upon her not used to " tears o' night instead of slumber." In the garish morning sunshine, the pretty little face looks wofully wan and piteous, poor child, and he sees it ; how can he fail to see it, and is in a fine rage with her and with himself in consequence. No words have passed between them concerning last night —no words as yet. That pleasant conjugal debate is still to come. He had found her feigning sleep, the tears undried upon her cheeks, so peachily plump only five weeks ago —then like the heart of a blush rose—now paler than the palest lily. This morning only monosyllables have been exchanged, but the tug of war is to come, and although he dreads it horribly—as he dreads and hates all things unpleasant to his own super-fastidious selfishness—his lordship throws down the paper at last and begins.

" I suppose," he says, in a voice he tries not to render harsh, but which *is*. " I suppose you know Dennison came last night ? Confounded meddling prig ! I suppose you know, or will know, he followed me, and tried to play parson for my benefit. I wonder now I did not knock him down for his impertinence—I will, by Jove, if he tries it again. I hope, Crystal, you did not send him?"

She shrinks and shivers away at his tone—at his words. He sees it, and the sting of remorse that follows and tells him he is a brute, hardly tends to add to his good-humor.

Did you send him?" he angrily repeats.

She lifts her eyes for an instant to his irritated face, then drops them, shrinking into herself more and more.

"I sent no one," she answers, in a voice so low as to be hardly audible.

"Oh," Eric says, in a grumbling tone. "You saw him though. He was here?"

"He was here—yes."

"How did he know so well where to find me then? I told you I was going to dine with some fellows at the Café de Paris."

"Yes, you told me," she repeats, in the same faint voice. Then she looks suddenly up at him and her blue eyes flash. "We went to the theatre, Eric," she says, boldly.

"To the—," so astounded is Lord Dynely that the last word fails on his lips.

"To the theatre—yes," Crystal goes on quickly and gaspingly. "I wanted to go—it wasn't his fault, poor fellow—I asked him to take me—I made him take me."

"And may I ask," says his lordship, with labored politeness, and turning quite white with anger, "which theatre you honored with your preference? *Les Italiens*, no doubt?"

"We went to the Varieties. We saw that woman. We saw *you*," she answers in the same gasping tone.

His lips set themselves with slow, intense anger—his blue eyes gleam with a dangerous light.

"You saw *that* woman! Be more explicit, if you please, Lady Dynely. You saw what woman?"

"That actress. That wicked, painted, dancing woman. And we saw you. You threw her the flowers I gave you. She wore them in her hair. And then you were in the box with her—as if—as if—"

But Crystal can say no more. At the recollection of his looks as he bent over that woman, she breaks utterly down, covers her face and bursts into passionate weeping.

He is white to the lips now—white with an anger that has something quite deadly in it. She is his bride but six weeks, and she sits yonder sobbing her heart out, but he never softens or relents. Who is to gauge for us of the capabilities of evil that are within us? All his life Lord Dynely had been taken by superficial observers for a kind-hearted gentleman, free of hand and large of heart, who would not willingly injure a worm—all his life he had taken himself to be a good-natured fellow—tender-hearted, indeed, to a fault ; and now he sits watching his wife with a glance that is absolutely murderous. With it all he is so astounded that it is a moment before he can speak.

"You did this?" he says at last, in a slow, cruel, suppressed sort of voice. "You played the spy upon me— *you !* You gave your old lover the cue, did you—you dragged him after me to the theatre to spy upon me. You're a fool, Crystal ; and, by Heaven, you'll live to repent it !"

She gave a gasping cry. He arose from his seat, flung down his paper, and stood before her, white with rage.

"It is a thousand pities," he says with a sneer, that for the moment blots out all the fair Greek beauty of his face, "that I did not let you marry Dennison. He's in love with you yet—no doubt your old penchant too is as strong as ever. *It was not his fault, poor fellow.* May I ask where you and Mr. Dennison are going together to-night ?"

She looks up at him—her eyes all wide and wild, with a bewildered sort of horror. Eric has insulted her—*insulted* her. She tries to speak, but only a gasping sound comes. Something in her eyes—in her face frightens even him, in his blind fury, into remorse and relenting.

"Don't look like that," he says with a strident sort of laugh. "I didn't quite mean what I said ; but when a man finds his wife running about to theatres in his absence, with her old lover—Well, sir ! what do you want ?"

For a servant has entered with a card upon a salver, and

presents it with a bow. Lord Dynely takes it up and utters an exclamation.

"Miss France Forrester!" he exclaims. "The plot thickens. *They're* here, too, are they? Where is the lady?" he demands of the man.

"In the salon, my lord."

"Very well, tell her we will be there in a moment." The man salaams and departs. "Go to your room, Crystal," he says, less harshly; "and, for Heaven's sake try and get rid of that face. You look like a galvanized corpse. You will have them thinking here I adopt the good old British custom of beating my wife. Put on rouge—anything—get your maid to do it, only don't fetch that woe-begone countenance to France Forrester's sharp eyes."

With this pleasant and bridegroom like adjuration he leaves her and goes to the salon to receive their guest. He is humming a popular Parisian street song as he goes, a half smile on his lips, all his old sunny debonnaire self once more:

"Ma mère est à Paris.
Mon père est à Versailles,
Et moi je suis ici,
Pour chanter sur la paille—"

he sings as he enters. France sits in a great ruby velvet chair, charmingly dressed, looking fresher, fairer, more brightly, saucily handsome, Eric thinks, than he has ever seen her. "How blessings brighten as they take their flight." *What* did he see in his faded, *passée*, pallid little wife, to prefer her to this brilliant, dark beauty? For my lord's taste has changed, and "black beauties" are decidedly in the ascendant again.

"My dear France," he says, holding both her hands, "this is an astounder. We knew you were coming, but not so soon. When did you arrive, and where are you located?"

"We arrived late last night, and have apartments in the Faubourg St. Honore, near the British Embassy. And with my usual impetuosity, and my usual disregard of *les contenances*, I ran the risk of finding you still asleep, and rushed away immediately after breakfast. You *are* up, I see, for which, oh, be thankful. And now where is Crystal?"

"Crystal will be here in a moment. How well you are looking, France," he says, half-regretfully; "being in love must be a great beautifier—better than all Madame Rachel's cosmetics."

"Must be!" she laughs; "you don't know from experience then? I can return the compliment—you are looking as if life went well with you—

> " His 'and was free, his means was easy,
> A finer, nobler gent than he,
> Ne'er rode along the shons Eleesy,
> Or paced the Roo de Rivolee!"

quotes France, after her old fashion; "but then, of course, we are in the height of our honeymoon, and see all things through spectacles *couleur de rose.*"

Eric laughs, but rather grimly. He is thinking of the honeymoon-like *tête-à-tête* her coming ended.

"And how are they all?" he inquires—"the Madre and Mrs. Caryll? Mrs. Caryll is here, I suppose?"

"Grandmamma is here—yes. And better than you ever saw her. And your mother is well and dying to see you, and how matrimony agrees with you. Do you know, Eric," laughing, "I can't fancy you in the *rôle* of Benedick the married man."

He laughs too, but it is not a very mirthful laugh.

"Caryll is with you?" he says, keeping wide of his own conjugal bliss; "Of course he is, though—lucky fellow! I needn't ask if *he* is well?"

"You need not, indeed," France says, and into her face a lovely rose light comes; "but you will soon see for yourself —they will all call later. What does keep Crystal—I hope she is not so silly as to stay and make an elaborate toilet for me?"

"No, no—she will be down in a moment. She has a headache—is rather seedy this morning—late hours and dissipation will tell on rustic beauty, you know. By the bye, apropos of nothing, do you know Terry Dennison is here—

at this hotel ? We are quite a family party, you see,' he
laughs again rather grimly.

"Terry here ! dear old Terry ! how glad I shall be to see
him. When did he get over ? "

"Last night also. It appears to have been a night of
arrivals. Ah, here is Crystal now."

He looks rather anxiously as he says it. He knows of old
how keen Miss Forrester's hazel eyes are—he feels that she
has already perceived something to be wrong. That she has
heard nothing he is quite sure. Her manner would certainly
not be so frankly natural and cordial if one whisper of the
truth had reached her.

Crystal has done her best. She has exchanged her white
wrapper for a pink one that lends a faint, fictitious glow to
her face. The suggestion about rouge she has not adopted
—rouge, Crystal looks upon as a device of the evil one.
Something almost akin to gladness lights her sad eyes as she
comes forward and into France's wide, open arms.

" My dear Lady Dynely ! My dear little Crystal !" and
then France stops and sends her quick glance from her face
to Eric's, and reads trouble without a second look. She is
honestly shocked, and takes no pains to hide it.

Eric winces. *Has* Crystal so greatly changed then for the
worse ? All his selfish, unreasoning anger stirs again within
him.

"You have been ill ? " she says, blankly. "You—you
look wretchedly."

" I told you she had a headache," Eric interrupts, irritably.
"I told you late hours and Paris dissipation will tell upon
rustic beauty. There is nothing the matter. Open your
lips, oh, silent Crystal ! and reassure Miss Forrester."

" I am quite well, thank you," Crystal says, but no effort
can make the words other than faint and mournful. Then
she sits down with her face from the light, and leans back in
her great carved and gilded chair, looking so small, and fragile, and childish, and colorless that a great compassion for
her, and a great, vague wrath against him, fills France's heart.
She does not know what he has done, but she knows he has
done something, and is wroth accordingly. Why, the child

has gone to a shadow—looks utterly crushed and heart-broken. Is he tired of her already?—is he—but no, *that* is too bad to think even of fickle Eric—he cannot be neglecting her for a rival.

Her cordial manner changes at once—a constraint has fallen upon them. All Eric's attempts at badinage, at society small talk, fall flat. He rises at last, looks at his watch, pleads an engagement, and prepares to go.

" I know you and Crystal are dying to compare notes," he says, gayly, " and that I am in the way. Only Crystal's notes will be brief, I warn you, France ; she has not your gift of tongue. Lady Dynely is the living exemplification of the adage that speech is silver, and silence is gold."

"Shall you be in when your mother and Gordon call, Eric?" France asks, rather coldly. "If not, I am commissioned to tender an impromptu invitation to dine with Mrs. Caryll."

" Awfully sorry," Eric answers, " but we stand pledged to dine at the Embassy. *I* must put in an appearance, whether or no, and Crystal will also—headache permitting. Crystal rather shrinks from heavy dinner parties and goes nowhere."

" I thought late hours and Paris dissipation were telling on her," retorts France, still coldly. And Eric laughs and goes, with a last severe, warning glance at his wife—a glance which says in its quick blue flash :

" 'Tell if you dare ! "

It is a needless warning—Crystal has no thought of telling —of complaining of him to any one on earth. She lies back in her big chair, her little hands folded, silent and pale, while the sounds of ringing life reach them from the bright, gay boulevard below, and the jubilant sunlight fills the room.

" How thin you have grown, Crystal," France says at last, very gently. " Paris does not agree with you I think. We must make Eric take you home to Dynely."

Her eyes light eagerly—something like color comes into the colorless face. She catches her breath hard.

" Oh ! " she says, " if he only would ! "

France is watching her intently.

" You don't like Paris, then ? "

" Like it ! " the gentle eyes for an instant flash. " I hate it."

There is a pause. France's heart is hot within her. Fickle, unstable, she had always known Eric to be ; selfish to the core and cruel in his selfishness ; but an absolute brute, never before.

" Do you go out much ? " she asks.

" No—yes." Crystal falters. She hardly knows which answer to make in her fear of committing Eric. " I don't care to go out—dinner parties *are* a bore—I never was used to much society, you know, at home."

" I am afraid you must be very lonely."

" Oh, no ! that is—not very. I read and play—a little—and then, Eric—"

But her voice breaks, it is not trained to the telling of falsehoods, and the truth she cannot tell.

" Yes," France says quietly, " Eric is out a great deal naturally—he is not a domestic man ; but once you return to Dynely all that will be changed. We must try and prevail upon him to take you home at once.

The sad blue eyes give her a grateful glance. Then a troubled, frightened look comes into them.

" Perhaps—perhaps you had better not," she says ; " he will think you are dictating to him, and he cannot bear to be dictated to. He likes Paris—I am sure he will be angry if he is urged to go."

" We can survive that calamity," Miss Forrester answers, cynically ; " and your health—and, yes, I will say it—happiness, are the things to be considered first."

" But I am happy," cries Crystal, in still increasing alarm, "indeed I am. How could I be otherwise so soon ? "

Her traitor voice breaks again. France looks at her in unutterable compassion.

" Ah, how indeed ! " she answers, " you poor little pale child ! Well, I must go—they really don't know where I am, and we are all to go sight-seeing to the Luxembourg. Do come with us, Crystal ; you look as though you needed it."

But Lady Dynely shakes her small, fair head.

"I cannot," she says. "Eric may return, and be vexed to find me out."

"Eric! Eric!" thinks France, intolerantly; "I should like to box Eric's ears!"

"Besides, sight-seeing tires me," Crystal goes on, with a wan little smile, "and I don't think I care for pictures. We visited the Luxemboug, and the Louvre, and the Tuileries, and all the rest of the show places, when we first came, and I remember I was ill all day with headache after them. I like best to stay at home and read—indeed I do."

France sighs.

"My little Crystal! But you will be lonely."

"Oh, no. Eric *may* come to luncheon—he often does—and Terry will drop in, I dare say, by and by. You know Terry is here?" interrogatively.

"Yes; Eric told me. I wish I could take you with me all the same, little one. I hate to leave you here in this hotel alone. It is a shame!—a shame!" says France, in her hot indignation.

But Crystal lifts a pained, piteous face.

"Please don't speak like that, France. It is all right," she says, with a little gasp; "I—I prefer it."

"Do come!" France persists, unheedingly. "We will leave you at home with grandmamma Caryll, while we do the sight-seeing. You will love her, Crystal—she is the dearest, best old lady in Europe. Then we will dine comfortably together, *en famille*, and go to the Varieties in the evening, to see this popular actress Paris raves about—Madame Felicia."

But, to France's surprise, Crystal suddenly withdraws her hands and looks up at her with eyes that absolutely flash.

"I will never go to the Varieties!" she cries; "I will *never* go to see Madame Felicia! She is a wicked, wicked woman, and I hate her!"

She is trembling from head to foot with nervous passion as she says it. France stands petrified. Then all in an instant Crystal recollects herself, and piteously clasps her hands.

"I did not mean to say that!" she cries; "it is very wrong of me. Please don't think anything of my angry words—I did not mean anything by them—indeed I did not."

France stoops and kisses her as a sister might, holding her close for a moment; and a little sob she cannot wholly repress breaks from the poor, jealous child, as she lays her head on France's breast.

"My darling," France whispers, in that warm kiss, "keep up heart. Eric shall take you out of this wicked, tiresome' Paris before the week ends, or I will know the reason why."

Then, with profoundest pity for this poor little girl bride, she goes, her own day's pleasuring totally spoiled.

"This is what Eric's love-match comes to," she think sadly. "Ah, poor little Crystal!

> " ' I have lived and loved—but that was to-day ;
> Go bring me my grave-clothes to-morrow.' "

CHAPTER VI.

AT THE VARIETIES.

T is close upon luncheon hour when Miss Forrester returns to the Faubourg St. Honore. As she enters the drawing-room, still in her street dress, she sees her lover sitting in an arm chair by the open window, smoking a cigar, and immersed in the art criticisms of the *Revue des Deux Mondes.* He throws down the paper and looks at her with lazily loving eyes. Happiness and prosperity certainly agree with *him*—as Gordon Caryll, the accepted suitor of Miss Forrester, he looks ten years younger than did Mr. Locksley, the impecunious portrait painter. Handsomer, nobler, France thinks, than Mr. Locksley, it is impossible for mortal man to grow.

"Well," he says, "you have returned. My thoughts were just turning seriously to the idea of having out the detective police, and offering a reward for your recovery. Is it admissible to ask, my child, where you have been?"

She comes behind him, lays her little gloved hands on his shoulders, and looks down into the gravely smiling face resting against the chair back. They are not demonstrative lovers those two, but now, rather to Mr. Caryll's surprise, Miss Forrester impulsively stoops and leaves a kiss on his forehead.

"And to think," she says, drawing a tense sort of breath, "that I *might* have married him!"

Mr. Caryll opens his handsome gray eyes. Both the kiss and the irrelevant exclamation take him rather aback.

"You might have married him! You might have married whom? You have not been proposing to any one this morning, have you? What are you talking about France?"

"About Eric," she answers, absently.

"And with the most woe-begone of faces. Melancholy has evidently marked you for her own this morning. You are regretting you threw Eric over for me—is that it, my dear?"

"Nonsense!" is France's energetic answer. "I hate to have you say such things, even in jest, Gordon. Thank Heaven, no! I liked Eric, certainly—one could hardly fail to do that; but, I always had a most thorough-paced contempt for him all the same. And if I had married him—but no, I never would, I never could, if there had been no Crystal Higgins, no Mr. Locksley, in the scheme of the universe. Gordon, I have been to see them this morning."

"So I inferred, my dear, from your very energetic language. And you found them well, I hope?"

"Eric is well," France says, resentfully; "he will be, to the end of the chapter. But, Crystal—"

"Yes?" Mr. Caryll says, interrogatively. "Crystal is well also, no doubt?"

"Well!" France cries, and then stops. "Ah! you should see her—wait until you do. I never saw any one so changed in my life."

"For the better?"

"For the worse. She is the shadow of herself—poor little soul! Her sad, heart-broken face and voice haunt me like a ghost. Eric is a brute!"

"Indeed! Husbands invariably are, are they not? What has Eric done?"

"I don't know what he has done," Miss Forrester answers, indignantly. "I only know he is breaking his wife's heart. Why don't you say 'husbands invariably do'? I daresay it is true enough."

Mr. Caryll takes one of the gloved hands and gives it an affectionate little squeeze.

"My dear child, don't excite yourself. I intend to prove an exception. Seriously, though, I am very sorry for little Lady Dynely. I am afraid the rumors I have been hearing must be true."

"Rumors? What rumors? I never heard you allude to them."

" No ; one does not care to talk about that sort of thing, and I knew it would annoy you, and make his mother unhappy. But as you seem to be finding out for yourself, well they *do* say he neglects the little one, and runs about with—."

" With Felicia, the actress ! Gordon, I am sure of it ! With Felicia, the dancer !"

" With Felicia, the dancer. But take it calmly, my love. How do you know it ?"

" I know it from Crystal herself. That is what she meant when I asked her to come with us to the Varieties to see Felicia."

" Ah, what did she mean ?"

"She said she hated the Varieties, she hated Madame Felicia ; that she was a wicked, painted woman. And you should have seen those dove-eyes of hers flash. My poor, dear little Crystal !" The dark, impetuous eyes fill with tears and fire with indignation. "Only six weeks married !" she says passionately. "Gordon, I hate Eric."

" Now, France," he says gravely, "don't make yourself unhappy about this. Lady Dynely must have known she ran no ordinary risk in marrying Dynely—the most notorious male flirt in Europe. If she had had one grain of sense in that pretty flaxen head of hers she must have known that matrimony would work no miracles. A flirt he is by nature —there is not a grain of constancy in his whole composition ; and as she has taken him, so she must abide by her bargain."

" He is a brute !"

" So you said before," answers Mr. Caryll, a half-smile breaking up the gravity of his face. " Still, allowance must be made for him. He has been spoiled all his life—he has never been thwarted—to wish has been to have, and ladies have petted and made much of him for his azure eyes, and golden curls, and his Greek profile, all his life long. Time *may* cure him. Meanwhile, neither you nor I, Miss Forrester, can help Crystal. And they say this Felicia plays the deuce with her victims."

" Have you ever seen her, Gordon ?"

15

" Nevei. I was too busy last year when she was at the Bijou, and besides, I had an aversion to theatres and theatre-going. I shall see her to-night, however."

" She bought your picture, 'How the Night Fell,' didn't she ? "

" Yes. Di Venturini purchased it for her. By the bye, I promised at the time a companion picture. They say she's to marry Di Venturini immediately upon his return from Italy."

" Marry him ! *That* woman !"

" My dear France," Caryll says, laughing, " with what stinging scorn you bring out *that* woman ! There is nothing said against ' that woman ' except that she is a most outrageous coquette."

" But she is a dancer, and he is a prince."

" That goes for nothing. The best blood of the realm takes its wife from the stage in these days. I shouldn't fancy it myself, but you know the adage, 'A burnt child dreads the fire.' "

" Poor little Crystal !" sighs France.

" Poor little Crystal, indeed. Rumor says he is altogether infatuated. Let us hope rumor, for once, is wrong. Are they coming to dinner ? "

" No. Eric pleads a prior engagement, and she does not seem to have heart enough left to go anywhere. Here is Lady Dynely. By the bye, I forgot to tell you Terry is in Paris."

" Terry ? Terry Dennison ? " cries Lady Dynely, eagerly ; "is he, really. Where, France ? "

" At the Hotel du Louvre. I stole a march upon you this morning, and made an early call upon the happy pair."

Her ladyship's eyes light eagerly.

" And you saw them ? You saw Eric ? "

" I saw Eric, mamma."

" How is he looking ? Will they dine with us ? "

" Eric is looking well—never better. And they dine at the Embassy this evening. No doubt, though, Eric will call."

" Here he is now," Caryll interrupts, looking from the window, and France disappears like a flash. She feels in no mood at present to meet and exchange pleasant commonplaces with the Right Honorable the Lord Viscount Dynely.

She goes to her room, throws off her bonnet and seal jacket, and pays a visit to grandmamma Caryll, in her own apartments. Paralysis has deprived her of the use of her limbs. She sits in her great invalid chair the long days through. But in her handsome old face a look of great, serene content reigns.

The restless, longing, impatient light that for years looked out of her eyes has gone—she has found what she waited and watched for. Her son is with her—France is to be his wife—she asks no more of earth.

The luncheon-bell rings. Mrs. Caryll's is brought in, and France descends. To her great relief, Eric has gone, and Terry is in his place. Terry, who is changed too, and who looks grave and preoccupied.

" You were at the Louvre this morning, France," he says to her as they sit side by side. " You saw *her* ? "

" Yes, Terry," and France's compassionate eyes look at him very gently. " I saw her."

" And you have heard ——"

" Everything—poor little Crystal. Terry, Eric must take her to England, and at once."

" Ah, if he only would," Terry says with a sort of groan, "but he will not. That is past hoping for. He is killing her—as surely as ever man killed woman. And when he does," Terry sets his teeth like a bulldog, "*my* time of reckoning will come."

" You must accompany us this afternoon, Terry," Lady Dynely says, after the old imperious fashion. "France is quite as much as Gordon is capable of taking care of. *I* want you."

Terry falls into the old groove at once. In his secret heart he is longing to be at the hotel with Crystal, to cheer her in her loneliness ; but that may not be, may never be again. So he sighs and goes. They spend the long, sunny, spring-like afternoon amid the lions of Paris, and return to dine, and dress for the theatre.

" The whole duty of family escort will fall upon your victimized shoulders, Dennison," says Mr. Caryll, looking up from a letter that the post has brought him. " This is a note from General McLaren—I served under him at the beginning of the American civil war. He is at the Hotel Mirabeau ; and as he leaves Paris to-morrow, begs me to call upon him to-night. You won't mind, I suppose ; and I will look in upon you about the second act."

" I always told Terry he was born to be a social martyr," France says. " The fetch-and-carry, go-and-come, do this and that *rôle*, has been yours from your birth, my poor, boy."

So it chances that when the curtain goes up, and the " Golden Witch" begins, Gordon Caryll does not make one of the party of three who look down from the front of their box, amid all the glittering " horse-shoe " of gaslight and human faces. The pretty, bright theatre is very full ; there is an odor of pastilles, a flutter of fans, a sparkle of jewelry. Felicia is in great form to-night—she has heard from Lord Dynely himself of the family party coming to view her with coldly-critical, British eyes. They have laughed together over it in her little dusk-shaded, perfumed, luxurious drawing-room, where his lordship has made a much longer morning call than he made immediately before in the Faubourg St. Honore.

She glances up now, swiftly and eagerly, as she comes forward to the footlights, a golden goblet in her hand, her long hair floating loosely over her shoulders, singing some wild bacchanalian, Theresa-like ditty. She is gloriously beautiful in her scant drapery, and her rich voice fills the theatre superbly. But as she tosses off her goblet, at the end of her drinking song, she sees that the man she looks for is not in the box.

Will he know her ? He has never seen her since that long, far-off night when they parted in the darkening day by the shore of the lonely Canadian river. He thinks her dead. Will he know her ? A wild, fierce delight fills her soul, flames up in her eyes, and burns in her cheeks. Will he know her ? She will sing to-night (if he comes) the song she ever sang for him, that first evening in the cottage of

Major Lovell. It will run very well with this play—that is much more song and dance than drama. If he doubts her identity, surely, surely, he will remember *that.*

She is wild with excitement, she surpasses herself. The audience applaud to the echo—she flings herself into her part with a reckless abandon that sweeps her listeners along with her. And still she watches that box, and still he does not come. Will he not come at all? Amid a storm of excited applause, amid a shower of bouquets, the curtain falls upon the first act.

"How well she plays." "How magnificently she is looking." "Never saw her dance half a quarter so well in my life before." "By Jove! you know, *what* a voice Felicia has." These and a hundred such exclamations run the round of the theatre.

"She is beautiful!" France exclaims, "with a *beauté du diable* I never saw equalled. And she dances and sings like a very Bacchante."

"Wish to Heaven they would burn her as a witch," growls Terry, under his ruddy beard. "Such a woman should no more be let run loose than a leopardess."

"She sings very well," Lady Dynely says, languidly; "but there is something fierce and *outré* about her, is there not? I don't like this sort of exhibition. A ballet is bad enough—this kind of thing is positively indelicate. What is she looking at our box for? I caught her more than once."

"She is looking for what she does not see. There is Eric yonder in the stalls," says Miss Forrester, in a tone of stony resentment.

"Is he, really?" Eric's mother puts up her glass and leans forward. "So he is, and quite alone. Where is Crystal, I wonder?"

"Crystal is at home, and *quite alone* also, you may be very sure," answers France, still in that tone of strong, suppressed indignation.

"I wonder if he sees us? Oh, yes, he does. There he is rising. No doubt he will call upon us directly. France, why don't you look? He is bowing to *you.*"

But France's bright, angry eyes are fixed steadfastly upon

the rising curtain—she will *not* see Lord Dynely. And Lord Dynely looks away from her, feeling he has been snubbed, and knowing very well the reason why.

He has come to the theatre to-night, partly because he cannot stay away, partly out of sheer bravado.

What ! shall he stay away because he is afraid of Terry Dennison, and France Forrester ? Is he still a child in leading-strings, to be dictated to ? Not if he knows it. So he leaves early the ambassador's saloon, and goes to the Varieties, and sits out all the second act, directly under the lorgnettes of the Gordon Caryll party.

Again madame surpasses herself—again the whole house rings with applause—again bouquets are showered upon her. Lord Dynely adds his mite to the rest, a bouquet of scarlet and white camellias. Again and again, the black, fierce, restless eyes, flash their feverish light to that one box. And still the man for whom she looks does not come.

He comes as the curtain falls for the second time, and France's eyes and smile welcome him.

"Am I *very* late?" he asks. "McLaren and I had a thousand things to say, and time flew. I say, France, how do you like it ?"

"Not at all ! She fascinates one, but it is a horrid and unhealthy sort of fascination. Her mad singing and dancing throw me into a fever."

"Is there much more of it ?" he says, standing behind her chair. "Is it all over ?"

"There is one more act. She is to be burned alive, Terry tells me, and I want to wait and see her. I shall try to fancy the burning real, and enjoy it accordingly."

"By Jove !" he says, and laughs, "what a blood-thirsty spirit we are developing ! Ah ! Dynely, *you* here ?"

For the door opens, and Eric, languid and handsome, saunters in.

"How do, Caryll ? Late, ar'n't you ? Well, France— well, *ma mère*, how do you like it ? Superb actress, isn't she ?"

He looks at France. With a certain defiance, she sees and accepts.

"If dancing mad jigs, singing drinking songs, and capering about like a bedlamite, go to constitute a fine actress, then yes. A little of Madame Felicia goes a long way."

His eyes flash, but he laughs.

"There is no accounting for tastes. She seems to please her audience, at least."

"Where is Crystal ? " France abruptly asks. " I thought you were to dine at the Embassy."

"Crystal is at home. And you thought quite right ; we *were* to dine at the Embassy." The defiant ring is more marked than ever. " I have dined there, and on my way home dropped in here, knowing I would have the pleasure of being in the bosom of my family."

He looks at her steadfastly, and France turns her white shoulder deliberately upon him. Her lover is leaning over the back of her chair—ah ! how she loves him, how she trusts him—how different he is from this shallow-brained young dandy, with his Greek beauty, and callous heart ! How differently her life will be ordered from Crystal's, when she is his wife.

As she thinks it, the curtain goes up for the third time, and the "Golden Witch" bounds on the stage.

She is singing as she springs to the footlights, a gleeful hunting chorus this time. A troop of followers in green and gold come after, and join in the chorus. Her costume is of green and gold also ; a green hunting cap, with a long white plume, is set jauntily on her raven tresses. She is dazzling in the dress, she is radiant as she sings. Again her sweet, high voice, rings to the domed roof. And it is the very song Rosamond Lovell sang for Gordon Caryll, seventeen years ago, in the Toronto cottage.

She flashes one fierce electric look up at their box.

Yes, he is there at last—at last. Thank Heaven for that ! if she can thank Heaven for anything.

He hears her, he sees her ; recognizes the song. He knows her.

Her hour of triumph is complete. Her excitement reaches its climax. As she never played before, she plays to-night. She holds the multitude breathless, spellbound. She sings her own death-song, wild, wailing, weird, unearth-

ly, so ghastly in its tortured agony, that France shudders
and turns pale. The mimic flames arise—surround her,
her uplifted face is seen above them, as the curtain falls
down, her ghastly death-song dies wailing away.

For a moment, so rapt and petrified are the audience,
that they cannot applaud. *Then*—such a storm of clapping,
of calling, shakes the walls of the theatre, as never shook it
before. "Felicia! Felicia!" they shout, as with one voice.
She comes out smiling and kissing hands. Another tempest of applause and delight breaks forth. Then flashing up
one last look, straight into Gordon Caryll's face, she disappears.

There is a stir and commotion, an uprising and shawling
of ladies.

"Ugh!" France says, with a shudder; "it is diabolical!
it is like the nightmare. I shall never come to see this *outre*
spectacle again. Do *you* like it, Gordon?"

She leans back, and looks up at him. He does not seem
to hear her, he does not seem to see her—he is staring at
the stage like a man stupefied.

"Gordon!" she cries.   .

His eyes turn slowly from the blank, green curtain to her,
but his face still keeps that dazed, stunned look. His
bronzed skin, too, has turned of a dead ashen gray.

"Gordon," France says once more, this time in terror,
"what is it?"

Her question seems to break the spell. He makes an
effort—a mighty effort, she can see, and answers her.

"Nothing. Will you come?"

His very voice is changed—it is hoarse and low. He
offers her his arm mechanically, and watches her arranging
her opera-wrap, without trying to help her. She takes it
and goes with him out, and all the while he keeps the dazed
look of a man who is walking in his sleep.

"Oh, Gordon!" she cries out, "*what* is it? Do you
know that woman?"

He wakes then—wakes to the whole horrid truth.

"For Heaven's sake, don't ask me," he says, "to-night.
Wait—wait until to-morrow."

Her eyes dilate. They are out under the frosty, February stars. He puts them into the carriage—Lady Dynely and France—but he makes no effort to follow them. Eric and Terry make their adieux and turn away.

"Are you not coming, Gordon?" Lady Dynely asks in surprise.

"No," he answers, still in that low, hoarse tone. "Home," he says to the coachman. And as they whirl away, France leans yearningly forward, and sees him standing under the street lamps, quite alone.

15*

CHAPTER VII.

"AFTER MANY DAYS."

E knows her! From the first moment in which his eyes rested on her, from the first instant he has heard her ringing voice, he knows it is his wife. The song she sang for him in Major Lovell's dim drawing-room so many years ago, she is singing again for him to-night, for him—he knows that, too. His divorced wife stands yonder before him—this half-nude actress—his divorced wife whom for the past ten years he has thought dead. He knows it in that first moment of recognition as surely as he ever knew it in the after days.

She has hardly changed at all—in the strong, white lime light, she does not seem to have aged one day in seventeen years. The dusk, sensuous beauty is riper and more of the "earth, earthy;" the delicate outlines of first youth have passed, except that she is even more beautiful in her insolent, voluptuous womanhood than in her slim, first girlhood. He thinks this in a dazed, stupefied sort of way as he stands and looks at her. And this is Rosamond Lovell—the woman who was once his wife.

His wife! his wife! The two words echo like a knell through his brain, set themselves to the wild, sweet music that is ringing about him, fit themselves in time to her flying feet. His wife! Yonder creature, singing, dancing in that dress, that *undress* rather—gaped at by all these people. His wife!

The lights, the faces, the stage, seem to swim before him in a hot, red mist. He grasps the back of the chair he holds, and sets his teeth. Great Heaven! is the Nemesis of his mad, boyish folly to pursue him to the end?

And then France's cool, sweet voice falls on his ear.

"Do you like it, Gordon!" she is asking, with a smile. The fair pure face, the loving, upturned eyes, the trustful smile, meet him and stab him with a pang that is like death. He has forgotten her—in the first shock of recognition and dreadful surprise, he has forgotten her. Now he looks down upon her, and *feels* without thinking at all, that in finding his divorced wife he has lost his bride.

He cannot answer her—his head is reeling. He feels her wondering, startled eyes, but he is beyond caring. He tries to answer, and his voice sounds far off and unreal even to his own ears. .

It ends. The curtain is down, the blinding stage-light is out, she is gone. He can breathe once more now that fatal face is away. The whole theatre has uprisen. Lady Dynely is moving out on the arm of her son—France is clasping his and gazing up at him with eyes of wistful wonder.

They are out under the cool, white stars—he has placed them in their carriage, seen them roll away, and is alone.

Alone, though scores pass and repass, although dozens of gay voices and happy laughs reach him ; although all the bright city is still broad awake and in the streets. He takes off his hat and lets the cold wind lift his hair. What shall he do, he thinks, vaguely ; what ought he do first ?

Rosamond, his divorced wife, is living—he has seen her to-night. And France Forrester will marry no man who is the husband of a wife. They have spoken once on the subject—gravely and incisively—he recalls the conversation now, word for word, as he stands here.

"If she had not died, France," he had asked her, "if nothing but the divorce freed me—how then ? Would you still have loved me and been my wife ? "

And she had looked at him with those clear, truthful, brave eyes of hers, and answered at once :

"If she had not died—if nothing but your divorce freed you, there could have been no '*how then.*' Loved you I might—it seems to me I must ; but marry you—no. No more than I would if there had never been a divorce. A man can have but one wife, and death alone can sever the bond. I believe in no latter-day doctrine of divorce."

They had spoken of it no more, he had thought of it no more. It all comes back to him as he stands here, and he knows he has lost forever France Forrester.

And then, in his utter despair, a wild idea flashes across his brain, and he catches at it as the drowning catch at straws. It is *not* his wife—he will not believe it. It is an accidental resemblance—it may be a relative—a sister; she may have had sisters, for what he ever knew. It is not Rosamond Lovell—the dead do not arise, and she was killed ten years ago. Some one must know this Madame Felicia's antecedents; it is only one of these accidental resemblances that startle the world sometimes. He will find out. Who is it knows Madame Felicia?

He puts his hand to his head as this delirious idea flashes through it, and tries to think. Terry Dennison—yes, he is sure Terry Dennison knows her, and knows her well. He will be able to tell him ; he will follow at once.

A moment later and he is striding with a speed of which he is unconscious in the direction of the Hotel du Louvre. He finds his man readily enough. Terry is standing in the brilliantly-lit vestibule, smoking a cigar. Eric is *bon garçon*, and has run up at once to his wife. A heavy hand is laid on Terry's shoulder, a breathless voice speaks :

"Dennison ! "

Terry turns round, takes out his cigar, and opens his eyes.

"What ! Caryll ! And at this time of night ! What's the matter ? My dear fellow, anything wrong ? You look—"

"There's nothing wrong," still huskily. " I want to ask you a question, Dennison. Come out of this."

He links his arm through Terry's, and draws him out of the hotel entrance into the street. Terry still holds his cigar between his finger and thumb, and still stares blankly.

"There must be something wrong," he reiterates ; "on my word, my dear fellow, you look awfully."

"Never mind my looks," Caryll impatiently cries. "Dennison, you know Madame Felicia ? "

At this unexpected question, Dennison, if possible, stands more agape than ever. Then he laughs.

"What! You, too, Caryll! Oh, this is too much—"

"Don't laugh," Caryll says, harshly. "Answer me. You know this woman?"

"Well, yes."

"Intimately?"

"Well, yes, again. 1 suppose I may say tolerably intimately."

"What is her history?"

"What?"

"Who is she? Where does she come from? What is her real name?" Caryll asks, still in that same hoarse, breathless haste.

Mr. Dennison's eyes dilate to twice their usual size. He altogether forgets to resume his newly-lit cigar.

"My dear fellow——"

"The devil!" Gordon Caryll grinds out between his set teeth. "Answer me, cannot you?"

No jesting matter this, evidently, and Terry, slow naturally, takes that fact in.

"Who is she? Where does she come from? What was the rest?" he demands helplessly. "Good Lord! Caryll, how should I know? I'm not Felicia's father confessor."

"You told me you knew her intimately."

"I know her as well as most people know most people, and that goes for nothing. What do we, any of us, know of any one else? Don't grow impatient, old fellow; all I know I'm willing to tell, but it's precious little. Now begin at the beginning and cross-examine. You shall have the truth, the whole truth, and nothing but the truth. Only don't keep the steam up to its present height, or you'll go off with a bang!"

There is a second pause. Terry resumes his cigar, thrusts his hands in his coat pockets and waits. Gordon Caryll comes to his senses sufficiently to make a great effort and calm down.

"I beg your pardon, Terry," he says, more coherently than he has yet spoken; "but this is a matter of no ordinary importance to me—a matter almost of life and death."

Again Terry's eyes dilate, but this time he says nothing.

"I never saw Madame Felicia before to-night," goes on Caryll ; "and she bears the most astonishing, the ir ost as. tounding resemblance to another woman, a woman I have thought dead for the past ten years. I want to know her history, and I have come to you."

"Go on," says Terry, calmly.

"Was Madame Felicia ever in America?—ever in "—a pause—"in Canada?"

"She *says* not," is Terry's answer.

"Says not? Then you think—"

"I think she was. She has always been so vehement in denying it that I have suspected from the first she lied. And since last night I felt sure of it."

"Since last night—"

"I don't know that it's quite fair to tell," says Terry; "but I don't see that I'm bound to keep Felicia's secrets—I owe her no good turn, and if it's of any use to you, Caryll—"

"Anything—everything connected with that woman is of use to me," Caryll answers, feverishly.

Without more ado, Terry relates the episode of last night —the rescuing the girl in the street, her inadvertent words, and the bringing her to Felicia.

"She asseverated again and again that Felicia had been in Canada. She said she herself had been born there, in such a way, by Jove ! that you could only infer Felicia to be her mother. And she looked like Felicia. And she had Felicia's picture. And Felicia received her at once. And I believe, upon my soul, that she is Felicia's daughter."

Gordon Caryll listened dumbly. Felicia's child and — his. He knew there had been a child—a daughter—had not Mr. Barteaux told him? And she too was here.

"She called herself— ?" he began.

"She called herself Gordon Kennedy. *Gordon !* By Jove !" For the first time a sudden thought strikes Terry— a thought *so* sudden, and *so* striking that it almost knocks him over. "By Jove !" he repeats again, and stares blankly at his companion.

There is no need of further questioning. Assurance is made doubly sure—Felicia and Rosamond Lovell are one, and this girl picked up adrift in the Paris streets is his daughter. No need of further questions, indeed. He withdraws his arm abruptly and on the spot.

"That will do," he says. "Thanks, very much. And good-night."

Then he is gone, and Terry is left standing, mouth and eyes open—a petrified pedestrian. It all comes upon him —the story of Gordon Caryll's Canadian wife—the actress— the picture—the puzzling resemblance to Felicia—her eager questions about him the evening before. Terry is dumbfounded.

"By Jove!" he says again aloud, and at the sound of that dear and familiar expletive his senses return. "By Jove, you know!" he repeats, and puts his cigar once more between his lips, and in a dazed state prepares to go home.

Gordon Caryll goes home too. He sees France's face at the drawing-room window as he passes, looking wistful and weary, and at the sight he sets his teeth hard. He cannot meet her. He goes up to his room, locks the door, and flings himself into a chair to think it all out.

He has lost her—forever lost her. To-morrow at the latest she must know all, and then—he knows as surely as that he is sitting here—she will never so much as see him again.

It is no fault of his—she will not blame him—she will love and pity him, and suffer as acutely as he will suffer himself. All the same, though, she will never see him more. And at the thought he starts from his chair, goaded to a sort of madness, and walks up and down the room.

The hours pass. He thinks and thinks, but all to no purpose—not all the thinking he can do in a lifetime can alter facts. This woman is his divorced wife—and France Forrester will marry no divorced man. The law can free him from his wife, but it cannot give him France. The penalty of his first folly has not been paid—and it is to be paid, it seems, to the uttermost farthing. His exile and misery are to begin all over again.

He suffers to-night, it seems to him, as he has never suffered in the past. And as the fair February morning dawns, it finds him with his face bowed in his hands, sitting stone-still in absolute despair.

The first sharp spear of sunshine comes jubilantly through the glass. He lifts his head. Haggard and pallid beyond all telling, with eyes dry and burning, and white despair on every line of his face. His resolve is taken. All shall be told, but first that there may not be even a shadow of mistake, he will see this woman who calls herself Madame Felicia—will see her and from her own lips know the truth.

Early as it is he rings for his man, and has a cold bath. It stands him in the stead of sleep. He makes a careful toilet, has a cup of coffee and a roll, and goes out of the house before any of his womankind are stirring.

The bright sunshine and bustle of the streets help him. He smokes, and that soothes him. As eleven chimes from all the city clocks, he is altogether himself again, the excitement and agitation of last night over and done with. He is very pale—beyond that there is no change in him.

He feels no anger against the woman he is going to see—he is just enough for that. The fault has been all his—all his also must be the atonement. But he will see her, and then—

He cannot quite think—steady as he has forced himself to be—of what will come after. It is very early yet to make a call, but he cannot wait. It is not difficult to discover the address of the most popular actress in Paris; he does discover it, walks steadfastly there, and encounters madame's tall chasseur in his gorgeous uniform of carmine and gold.

Madame sees no one at this hour, monsieur is politely told ; it is doubtful if madame has arisen.

But madame will see *him*, monsieur is quite certain. Will this Parisian "Jeames De La Pluche" be good enough to forward monsieur's card to madame.

The chasseur looks doubtful, but something in the English monsieur's face causes him to comply. The card is passed onward, and inward, until it reaches the hand of madame's maid, and by madame's maid is presented to madame.

Madame has arisen—early as is the hour, has even breakfasted. She lies back in her dusk-shaded drawing-room, looking rather fagged after last night's unusual excitement, with deep bistre circles surrounding her eyes. Her lady companion sits near reading aloud. She lies back with closed eyes, not listening, but thinking of Gordon Caryll's face as she saw it last night looking down upon her.

" A visitor for madame—a gentleman," Pauline announces.

" I can see no one, it is too early," madame says crossly ; "is it M. Di Venturini ? "

" No, madame. An English gentleman, tall and fair—who has never been here before."

Madame sits suddenly up, and seizes the card. Her pale face flushes dark red as she reads the name. She does not quite know what she has expected—certainly not this. For a moment her heart beats fast.

" I will see the gentleman, Pauline," she says. " Mrs. Hannery, you must be tired of that stupid book. The morning is fine—suppose you take Pandore [the poodle] and go for a walk. It will do you both good, and I shall not need you."

Thus dismissed, the lady companion rises and goes; madame turns to her maid :

" Where is my new protégée ? " she asks. " Miss Donny."

" In her room, madame, reading."

"See that she does not leave it then, see that she does not enter here. Now show the gentleman up."

The maid departs. Madame springs up, darkens the room yet a little more, looks at herself in one of the full-length mirrors, and is back in her seat with drooping, languid eyes before the door re-opens. But her heart is beating fast, and her topaz eyes are gleaming savagely under their white-veiled lids.

The door opens, and he comes in. And so again, after many years, this man and woman, once husband and wife— are face to face.

The first thing he sees in that twilight of the room is his own picture. It hangs directly opposite the door, and the sunshine, as it opens, falls for a moment upon it. Like that they parted, like this they meet again ! He stands for a second motionless, looking at it, and she is the first to speak.

" A very good picture, and very well painted; but I don't
think, I can't think, I ever wore *such* a face of despair as
that. You ought to know, though, better than I."

The slow, sweet voice was as smooth and even as though
the heart beneath were not throbbing at fever heat. A cruel,
lingering smile was on her face, and the yellow, stealthy eyes
were watching him greedily. He turned as she spoke and
looked at her.

" Rosamond ! "

She started at the name, at the low, even gentle tone, in
which it was spoken. The blood rose again over her face,
and for a second she found no voice to answer. Then she
laughed.

" Ma foi ! " she said, " how droll it sounds to hear that ! I
had almost forgotten that once *was* my name, so long is it since
I have heard it ? Ah, *Dieu /* how old it makes one feel."

A real pang went through her heart. Growing old !
Yes, surely, and to grow old was the haunting terror of this
woman's life.

" You have changed," she said, looking at him full,
" changed more than I have. You do not resemble very
greatly the slender, fair-haired stripling I knew so long ago
in Toronto. And yet I should have known you anywhere.
Mon ami, will you not sit down ? "

" Thanks," he answered in the same low, level voice, " I
will not detain you but a moment. Last night, for the first
time since we parted at Quebec, I saw you—"

" And the sight was a shock, was it not, monsieur ? " she
gayly interrupted.

" It was," he replied gravely, " since I thought you dead.
Since I was sure of it."

" Ah, yes ! that railway accident. Well, it was touch and
go—I never expect to be so near death, and escape again.
But I did escape, and—here I am ! "

She looked at him with her insolent smile, her eyes gleam-
irg with evil fire.

" Here I am," she repeated with slow, lingering enjoy-
m·nt ; " and it spoils your life for you—does it not ? As
· ı spoiled mine for me *that* night."

She pointed to the picture—the vengeful delight she felt shining in her great eyes.

"You were merciless that night, Gordon Caryll, and I vowed revenge, did I not? Well the years have come and the years have gone; we both lived, and revenge was out of my reach. I never forgave you and I never will; but what could I do? Now we meet, and I need do nothing. The very fact that I am alive is vengeance enough. It parts you from her—does it not? Ah, you feel that! Monseigneur, I wonder why you have come here this morning? It is certainly an honor I did not expect."

"I came to make assurance certainty," he answered. "I *had* no doubt, and still—"

"And still you would stand face to face with me once more. Well—there is no doubt, is there? I am Rosamond Lovell—Rosamond Caryll—the girl you married, and whose heart you so nearly broke, seventeen years ago. Oh, don't look so scornful! I mean it! Even I had a heart, and I loved you. Loved you so well that if I had been able I would have gone down to the river and drowned myself after you left me that night. Fortunately I was not able. I could laugh now when I look back and think of my besotted folly. We outlive all that at five-and-thirty."

"You were not able," he repeated; "that means—"

"That my child was born twelve hours after we parted," she interrupted once more. "Did they tell you in Quebec that?"

"Yes, they told me. And the child is with you now."

"Who told you so?" she demanded, sharply.

"I know it—that is enough. You ask me why I came here to-day—one reason was to see her."

She laughed contemptuously.

"And do you fancy I will let you? Why, I meant that child from her birth to avenge her mother's wrongs. And she shall—I swear it?"

"You refuse to let me see her?"

"Most emphatically—yes. When the time comes you shall see her to your cost—not before."

He turned to go. She rose up and stood before him.

"What! so soon," she said, with a laugh, "and after so many years' separation? Well, then, go—actions, not words, are best between us. But I think, Gordon Caryll, *my* day has come. Miss France Forrester is a very proud and spotless young lady—so they tell me. Have you told her yet who Felicia the actress is?"

He made no reply. Without speaking to her, without looking at her, he passed out of the greenish dusk of the perfumed drawing-room into the sparkling sunshine, and fresh, cool wind of the fair spring day.

CHAPTER VIII.

A MORNING CALL.

T is just one hour later, and France Forreste: stands with hands clasped loosely before her at the window of Mrs. Caryll's invalid room, gazing with weary wistfulness at the bright avenue below, a strained, waiting, listening expression on her face. For since they parted last night so strangely at the entrance of the theatre she has not seen her lover, and when has *that* chanced between them before ? Something has happened ! Something wrong and unpleasant—she feels that vaguely, although she cannot define her own feeling. How oddly he looked last night, how strangely he spoke, how singularly he acted. Did he too know Madame Felicia ? Then she smiled to herself. Of course not—had he not said so a dozen times. Madame Felicia might have power over the weak and unstable, such as Eric Dynely ; over men of the stuff Gorden Caryll was made, no more than the ugliest hag that prowled Paris.

But why did he not come ?

Last night, long after the rest had retired, she had waited up in the salon wistfully anxious for the good-night she so rarely missed. And he had entered very late, and had passed on at once to his room, although he *must* have known she would wait. Had he not been belated times before, and had she ever failed to wait—had he ever failed to seek her out ? She had gone to bed vexed and disappointed. But she was not one easily to take offence, and it would be all right to-morrow. He *might* have looked into the salon, but he did not—and—there was an end to it. To-morrow at breakfast he would tell her, whatever it might be. So she rose happy and light-hearted, the fag-end of a tune between her lips, with no presentiment of all that was so neal shadowing her happy girl's heart.

Breakfast hour. She ran down eagerly. Gordon was never late. He was always to be found in dressing-gown and slippers reading Galignani at this hour. But his favorite arm-chair this morning was vacant, and only Lady Dynely met her across the crystal and the silver.

" Has Gordon turned lazy, I wonder ? " the elder lady said, carelessly ; " it is something new to miss his face at the end of the table. Eric and his wife are coming to-day. France and I had counted on Gordon for you. We are going to Saint Cloud, and if Gordon does not return—"

" In any case I do not think I shall go," France answered, rather wearily. " One grows so bored of perpetual sight-seeing. I shall stay at home with grandmamma Caryll."

She had no appetite for breakfast, and when it was over she ran up to say good-morning to "grandmamma." No, Gordon had not been there either—his mother's first question was for him.

" It is the very first day he has failed to pay me a before breakfast call," Mrs. Caryll said, with a half-laugh, and yet dissatisfied. " Can he have gone out, or where is he ? "

" I do not know," France answered, vaguely uneasy ; " he was not down to breakfast."

" Not down to breakfast ? "

" He was absent rather late last night," Miss Forrester said, speaking lightly ; " no doubt he has turned sluggard, and overslept himself. Susan," she said to Mrs. Caryll's nurse and maid, who entered at that moment, " do you know if Mr. Caryll is still in his room ? "

" Mr. Caryll went out three hours ago, Miss France," the woman answered. " So I heard his man Norton say."

There was a pause.

" How *very* strange," France was thinking, more and more uneasily ; " how very unlike Gordon. What can it mean ? "

But there was no solution of the enigma. The morning wore on, bringing Eric and Crystal—Eric handsome and de-bonnaire as ever, Crystal clinging to his arm, silent, shadowy.

And Lady Dynely alone was their companion in the day's pleasuring at Saint Cloud.

" I wish you were coming, France," Crystal said, in a wistful whisper. Somehow, in France's strength and sunny brightness, even this little wilted lily seemed to revive.

" Not to-day, darling," France answered, kissing her. " It will not do to leave grandmamma quite alone. Besides, Saint Cloud is an old story to me and rather a tiresome one. We will all meet at dinner and go to the Opera aux Italiens together."

" Has Crystal's eloquence prevailed, France ? " Eric says in his languid way, sauntering up. " No ? Then," with a slight, half-contemptuous laugh, " the case is hopeless indeed. When a woman won't, she won't. I suppose we must be resigned, although your absence spoils our excursion. Come, madre, come, *sposo mio.* By-by, France—'we meet again at Philippi.' "

And then they are gone, and France draws a long breath of relief. Gordon will be here presently, and they will have a long, delicious day all to themselves, and everything will be explained.

She goes up to Mrs. Caryll's room, takes a favorite book, seats herself by a window, whence no one can enter unperceived, and tries to read. But so many people come in and go out, so many carriages and fiacres whirl up and down, that her attention is perpetually distracted. How long the hours are—how the morning drags—will he *never* come ? Eleven, twelve, one ! Will he return to luncheon at two ? He hardly ever eats luncheon, but surely he will come. How dazzlingly bright the sunshine is—her eyes ache. She rises with an impatient sigh and closes the curtains. A brass band somewhere near is thundering forth its music. They are playing one of Felicia's popular airs. She wishes they would stop ; the noise makes her head ache. Mrs. Caryll is dozing in her chair. The brazen braying of the band is beginning to make France sleepy too. Just as her tired eyes close, and her head droops against the back of her chair, Susan taps softly and enters the room.

" Miss France." She has to repeat the name before the

girl looks up. "Miss France, there is a lady in the salon to see you."

"A lady." For a moment her heart had bounded. But, only a lady !

"Susan," she impatiently exclaims, "*hasn't* Mr. Gordon come yet ? Surely he must be in his room or—"

"No, Miss France, he hasn't come yet. And the lady is waiting in the salon—"

"Who is she ? Where is her card ? I am not dressed. I don't wish to see any one."

"She would not give her name ; she sent up no card. She said she wished to see Miss Forrester at once on very important business."

"Very important business !" Miss Forrester rises, opening her hazel eyes. "Important business !" Again her heart leaps—is it anything about Gordon ? "In the salon, you say, Susan ? I'll go down at once."

She goes. In the long, cool salon, the jalousies are half-closed, and in the dim, greenish light a lady sits. A lady very elegantly dressed—*over*-dressed, it seems to France, her face hidden by a close, black lace veil.

"You wished to see me, madame ?" Miss Forrester says gently, and marvelling who her veiled visitor can be.

The lady turns, rises. "Miss Forrester ?" she says, interrogatively, and Miss Forrester, still standing, bows.

"You wished to see me on important business—"

France does not finish the sentence, for the lady quietly removes her veil, and they stand face to face. A very beautiful and striking face France sees, and oddly familiar, though for the moment she cannot place it. Only for a moment, then she recoils a step.

"Madame Felicia !" she exclaims.

"Madame Felicia !" the actress repeats, with a graceful stage bow and a coolly insolently smile. "Now you know why I did not send up my name. You would not have seen me."

Miss Forrester has recovered herself. Surprised excessively she is still ; intensely curious she is also, but outwardly she is only calmly, quietly courteous.

" You mistake," she says, in the same coldly gentle tone ; " I would have seen you. May I ask to what I owe this unexpected visit ? "

She seats herself at a distance, near one of the windows, and glances at her watch as a hint to be brief. Madame Felicia takes the hint. The coolly insolent smile yet lingers round the full, red lips, the yellowish black eyes (like a cat's eyes, France thinks) have an exultant, triumphant light.

" I will not detain you long," she says ; " and I think what I have to say will not bore you. May I ask—although I *know* you have not—have you seen Mr. Gordon Caryll this morning ? "

France's heart gives one leap. It *is* something about Gordon after all. Her dark face pales slightly ; and she has to pause a second before she can quite steady her voice.

" And may *I* ask," she says, haughtily, " in what way that concerns you ? "

" It concerns me much more nearly than you think," the actress answers. " You shall hear presently. I know you have not seen him this morning, else you would not be sitting here with me now. I thought I would be beforehand with him, and I am. I thought he would hardly have the courage to come straight from me to you."

The blood rushes in a torrent to France's face, to her temples.

" From me to you ! " There is a great green tub of jessamines in full bloom standing behind her. Is it the sweet, sickly odor of the flowers that turns her so deathly faint now ? " From you to me," she repeats ; " I don't know what you mean."

" I am quite sure you don't. Mr. Caryll has not been visible here this morning because he has been with me. He left me just one hour and a half ago, and I dressed at once and came to see you. You should hear the story from me as well as from him. I was resolved I should have no more of your blame than was my due. I saw you in the box last night at the Varieties. I saw you often last spring in London. You looked good, and brave, and noble, and although I care little for the opinion of the world, of its women par-

16

ticularly," with a reckless laugh, "it is my whim to stand as well as possible with you. I felt sure I would be before him. Men do not hasten to tell such a story as he has to tell you."

Oh, the deathly faintness of these jessamine flowers. Oh, the horrible clashing, crashing of the band, whose braying seems to pierce her head. For a moment France turns so giddy and sick that she cannot speak. The actress half rises in alarm.

"Miss Forrester! you are going to faint—"

But France lifts her hand and motions her to be still.

"Wait," she says, almost in a whisper. "You have frightened me. I am all right again. Now go on."

She sits upright with an effort, clenches her hands together in her lap, and sets her teeth.

"Go on!" she says almost fiercely, and looks Madame Felicia full in the face.

The insolent smile, the exultant light, have died out of the dark face of the dancer. In its stead a touch of pity has come. After all, this girl is to suffer as she suffered once— and she remembers well what *that* means.

"Miss Forrester," she says, gravely, "did you notice nothing unusual in Mr. Caryll's looks or manner last night at the Varieties—last night, when he saw me?"

Did she? Did she not? The ashen pallor of his face, the husky tone of his voice, and his abrupt departure!

"Go on," she says, under her breath again.

"Let me ask you one other question," says Madame Felicia. "You are to marry Gordon Caryll?"

"I am."

She seems to answer by no volition of her own. Even at this moment it strikes her—what an odd thing that she, France Forrester, should be sitting here answering whatever questions this dancing-woman chooses to ask.

"You know his story, of course—that he had a wife, that he was divorced. You think, you all think, he is a widower."

"Yes," France says in the same mechanical way—slowly and dully, "he is a widower."

" He is *not* a widower," Madame Felicia cries, with one flash of her black eyes—"no more than I am a widow. *He* thought me dead, thought me killed in a railway accident. I was not. For seventeen years we have not met. Last night we did. Miss Forrester, I am Gordon Caryll's wife ! "

" His wife ! " France has known it before it is said. " His wife ! his wife ! " How oddly it sounds. She is conscious of no acute pain—her principal wish, as she listens almost dreamily, is that that horrible band would cease and that she could get away from the smell of these jessamines.

" You do not seem to understand, Miss Forrester," Felicia cries sharply. " I repeat, I am Gordon Caryll's divorced wife."

" I understand," France says, dreamily. " Go on."

" Does it not matter to you, then ? " madame cries still more sharply. " Would you marry a divorced man ? "

" No. Go on."

There is a moment's silence. It is evident her quietude puzzles madame. It cannot puzzle her any more than it does France herself. By and by, she feels dimly, she will suffer horribly. Just at present she feels in the hazy trance of the lotus eater, listening to the music of the band, looking at the sunshine lying in broad, golden bands on the carpet, inhaling the scent of the jessamine. To the day of her death those will turn her sick and faint.

" Go on," she says quite gently, unable to get beyond these two words, and madame incisively *goes* on.

" He recognized me last night," she says, her voice hardening as she sees how quietly the other takes it. " I had recognized him long before, since I saw his picture at the Academy, ' How the Night Fell.' Well—last night he saw me, and, naturally, knew me at once. I have not changed much—so they tell me."

There is a pause—madame watching her, half irritated by her profound calm. Miss Forrester watching the flickering bars of light on the carpet.

" Is it her training, or is it want of feeling ? " the actress wonders. " No, I think not that. They are all alike—these aristocrats—ready to stand like a red Indian and die game.

I fancy his slumbers were rather disturbed last night," she goes on, with a hard laugh; "he looked like it this morning when he came to me."

Miss Forrester lifts her eyes from the carpet, and looks at Felicia. "Why did he go to you?" she asks.

"Chiefly, I think, because he wanted to make certainty more than certain, partly because he knew his child—*our* child—was with me, and he wanted to see her."

A pang that is like a red-hot knife-thrust goes through France Forrester's heart. *Our* child! Yes, this woman has been his wife, is the mother of his child. She gives a little gasp.

"You—you let him see her?"

"I did *not* let him see her—I am not quite a fool. As I told him he shall see her one day to his cost. She is mine, and I mean to keep her. His name, he took from me—his child he cannot."

There is silence again. The pity has died out of Felicia's face; it is hard, and bitter, and relentless as she speaks again.

"All the evil he could work me he did. I loved him and he left me—he cast me off with scorn and hatred. I swore revenge; but what can a woman—even a bad woman—do? Look, here, Miss Forrester!" Her voice rose rapidly and her eyes flashed. "In marrying me he fell a victim to a plot, an unscrupulous plot, I don't deny. I was not Major Lovell's daughter; I was no fit wife for such as he—I was taken from the lowest concert-room of New York city. When I was a baby I was thrown upon the streets; I had to make my own living, and earn the crusts I lived on. I knew no mother, no father, no God. To make money—to wear fine clothes anyhow—that was my religion. Lovell came and took me, and Gordon Caryll saw and fell in love with me. He asked no questions—he married me. And I loved him with a love that would have been my earthly salvation, if he had let it. I was true to him, in thought, and word, and action; I would have given my life for him. Then Lovell died, and dying told his story. I fled, and hid myself from his first fury; I knew he would take my life if we met. And then, months after, he found me out, and spurned me as he would a dog, and showed me the decree of divorce, and left me forever. Miss Forrester, I was a fool, I know, but I fell down there on the sands where he quitted me like a dead woman. It would have been better for him and for you to-day," with another reckless laugh, "if I had died. But—here I am."

She broke off abruptly. In the dark eyes looking at her she read nothing but a great and infinite pity.

"Poor soul!" France said, softly, "you loved him, and were his wife. It was hard on you."

Madame shrugged her shoulders.

"I have survived it, you see. Men die and worms eat them, but not for love! That night my baby was born. There is the story. You have heard it often before, no doubt. He is divorced—I cannot stop your marriage. Do as you will—only I had to come and tell you this."

She arose as she spoke. France stood up, too, and drew a step nearer.

"Madame," she softly said, wistful wonder in her eyes, "do you—do you love him yet?"

Once more madame laughed.

"Love! Ma foi! it is years since I knew what the word meant. Only fools ever love. Not I, Miss Forrester! I hate him as I do—well, not the devil—for I have no reason to hate *him*. No, no! it would be strange, indeed, if I did; I finished with all that forever the evening we parted by the Quebec shore. I am to marry the Prince Di Venturini in a month; but marrying and loving—well, they are different things"

"Does *he* know of this?" France asked, hardly knowing why she did ask.

"M. Di Venturini? Not yet—not at all if I can help it. And I don't think he ever will. Mr. Caryll will not tell, and I am quite sure I shall not."

She moved to the door; on the threshold she paused.

"Are you angry with me for coming?" she demanded, abruptly.

"Angry?" France echoed, wearily. "Oh, no, why should I be?"

Angry! No, she was angry with no one. She felt tired and sick, and worn out—she would like to be alone, to darken her room and lie down, and get away from the distracting music of that ceaseless band, from the dazzling glare of the sunshine, from the heavy odor of the flowers. But, angry—no. A touch of pity crossed again madame's hard, insolent beauty.

"I am sorry for you," she said. "You look good and gentle—you deserve to be happy. Yes, I *am* sorry for you."

And then she had left the room, and her silks were rustling down the wide stairway, and France was alone.

Alone! She leaned her folded arms on the table, and laid her face down upon them and drew a long, tired sigh. It was all over; and the woman was gone, and out of France's life all the happiness was forever gone, too.

Gordon's wife! How strangely it sounded. *She* was to have been that—she never could be now. If he were dead and in his coffin, she could not be one whit more widowed than she was. There was a dull sort of aching at her heart —but no acute pain. She wondered at her own torpor.

The band was striking up another tune, She could *not* endure that. She arose and toiled slowly and wearily up the stairs to her own room. The great hotel was very still. She reached her chamber, lowered the blinds, threw herself face downward on the bed.

"Gordon's wife! Gordon's wife!" Over and over, like some refrain, the words rang in her ears. Then they grew fainter and fainter—died out altogether; and in the midst of her great trouble France fell fast asleep.

CHAPTER IX.

"THE PARTING THAT THEY HAD."

HE last amber glitter of the sunset was gleaming through the closed jalousies, and lying in broad yellow bars on the carpet, when France awoke. Awoke with a great start, suddenly, and broad awake, her horrible trouble flashing upon her with the vividness and swiftness of lightning. Gordon's wife was alive; *she* could never be that; she must give him up at once and forever. Then a passionate sense of desperation and misery seized her.

"I cannot! I cannot!" she cried out, clenching her hands and flinging herself face downward among the pillows. "Oh, I *cannot* give him up!"

The yellow light flickered, faded, grew gray. One by one the golden bars aslant the carpet slid out of sight. Ten minutes more and the closed room was almost dark. And slowly the wild tempest of hysterical sobs was subsiding, too violent to be long-lived, but France Forrester did not move. Presently it died away altogether, and kneeling by the bedside, her face bowed in her hands, she was seeking for strength to bear her bitter sorrow where strength alone can be found.

"Thou whose life was all trouble," France's soul cried, "help me to bear this!"

No thought had ever come to her that he was free—that legally she might become his wife to-morrow in all honor before the world. Her French mother had reared her in a faith which teaches that divorce is impossible—a faith which holds marriage a sacrament, too holy to be broken by law of man, in which, "until death doth ye part," is meant in the fullest and most awful sense of the words. His wife lived

—his wife, although she were Princess Di Venturini within the hour—and she and Gordon, even as friends, must meet no more. Friends ! Ah, no, they could never meet as that ; and so they must meet just once, and say good-by forever.

She got up at last, utterly exhausted in body and mind. How still the vast hotel was. How dark the room had grown. She drew up the blinds in a sort of panic and let in the gray light of evening. It was almost night. Perhaps Gordon had come and was waiting for her. She must go to him at once, at once.

"Oh, my poor dear," she thought, "you have borne so much—could you not have been spared this last, bitterest blow ? "

She went down stairs without pause. If he had returned at all, he would be in the salon ; he would not tell his mother until he had told her—that she felt. She never stopped to think of her white cheeks and swollen eyes ; he was alone and in trouble, and she must go to him.

Yes, he had come. As she softly pushed the door open she saw him. He was sitting where she had sat three hours ago.· Three hours ! was it only that ? Three years seemed to have passed since this morning. He sat, his folded arms on the table, his head lying on them—his whole attitude despairing and broken down.

He did not hear her as she entered and crossed the room, neither heard nor saw, until she laid one hand lightly on his shoulder and spoke.

"Gordon ! "

Then he looked up. To her dying day that look would haunt her, so full of utter, infinite despair. Those haggard, hopeless eyes might almost have told her the story, had Madame Felicia never come. Haggard and hopeless as they were, they were quick even in this supreme hour to see the change in her.

"You have been crying ? " he said.

In all the months they had been together he had never seen the trace of tears on France's happy face before. The sight of those swollen eyelids and tear-blotted cheeks struck him now as with a sense of actual physical pain.

"What is it?" he asked. "'Ill news travels apace,' but I hardly think," with a harsh sort of laugh, "mine can have reached you already. France, my own love, what is it?"

But she shrank away, drawing her hand from his grasp, and covering her eyes with the other.

"Oh, Gordon, hush!" she cried out; "I cannot bear it. I——," with a great gasp, "I know all."

"All!" His face turned of a dull, grayish pallor, his eyes never left her. "France, do you know what you are saying? What do you mean by all?"

"That—that——" No, her dry lips would not speak the words. "Madame Felicia has been here," she said, with a quick desperate gesture, and walked away to the window.

The bright street below was dazzling with gas-lights—golden stars studded the violet February sky. Carriages filled with brilliant ladies flew ceaselessly by—the brilliant life of the most brilliant capital of the world was at its height. And France leaned her forehead against the cool glass and wondered, with a dull sickness of heart, if only this time yesterday she had indeed been happier than the happiest of them all.

Gordon Caryll had risen from his chair and stood looking at her, actually dumbfounded by her last words. In whatever way she might have heard the loathsome truth, he had never thought of this—that *she* would have the untold audacity to force an entrance here.

"France!" he exclaimed, a dark flush of intense anger crimsoning his face; "do you mean what you say?—that woman has dared come here?"

"Yes," she said, wearily. "Ah, don't be angry, Gordon. What does it matter, since I must know it?—what difference who tells the tale? She is not to blame, poor soul, for being alive."

"Poor soul!" he repeats, in a strange, tense tone. "Do you mean Felicia—that utterly vile and abandoned creature? Is it possible you pity *her*?"

"With all my heart, Gordon—more, almost, than I pity myself, and I do pity myself," France said, with a wistful sort of pathos in her voice. "I was so happy—so happy!"

16*

He stood for a moment silent—struggling, it seemed, with his own rebellious heart. The angry glow faded from his face. In its place an infinite sadness came.

"When did she come? Will you tell me what she said?" he asked.

"She came this afternoon—about three. It seems like a whole lifetime ago, somehow," France answered, in the same weary way, passing her hand across her eyes; "and she told me she was your—your wife."

And then suddenly her strength breaks down, her voice falters and fails, and she clenches her hands together, and is silent.

"She is no wife of mine!" he says, fiercely. "Years ago the law freed me from the maddest marriage ever madman made. France, why should we sacrifice the happiness of our whole lives to her? Let us set her at defiance. She is no more to me—and you know it—than any of the painted women who danced with her last night. She shall *not* part us. She shall not blight your life as she has mine. France, I cannot give you up—don't look at me like that—I tell you I will not give you up. You shall be my wife."

She made no struggle as he held her hands. She stood and looked at him, in grave calm.

"Let me go, Gordon!" is all she says, and with a sort of groan, he obeys. "I can never be your wife now, and you know it. I am sorry for you, sorry for myself, sorrier than I can say; only if we are to part friends, never speak to me again like that."

He turned from her, his brows knit, his lips set.

"Forgive me," he said, bitterly; "I will not offend again. It is easy for you, no doubt, to give me up; I was but a doubtful prize from first to last—no one knows it better than I; but you see it is not quite so easy for me. I have grown to love you, in the mad and idiotic way in which I have done most things all my life; and that woman (whom you honor with your pity, by the way,) has made such an utter failure of the best part of it, that now, when hope and happiness were mine once more, it seems rather hard she should crop up to make an end of it all. I have earned my retribution richly, I am aware—all the same, it is bitter to bear."

She looked down at him with eyes of sorrowful wonder and reproach. Was this Gordon—her hero, her "man of men?"

"Easy for me!" she repeated, her lips quivering. "You were but a 'doubtful prize' from the first! Ah, I have not deserved that. I don't know whether hearts break— I suppose not, but I feel as if mine were breaking to-night. See, Gordon! I love you so dearly—so greatly, that there is nothing on earth I would not do for you, suffer for you, only—commit a crime. And to marry a man whose divorced wife lives, is to my mind one of the blackest, most heinous crimes any woman can commit. All my life I will love you—I could not help that if I would—all my life I will be true to you, all my life I will pray for you. Only don't say bitter and cynical things any more—it is hard enough to bear without that."

Her words, her tone, touch him strangely and tenderly. The anger, the fierce temptation—each dies out, never to return. There is even the shadow of a smile on his lips as he looks up.

> "'I could not love thee, dear, so much,
> Loved I not honor more!'"

he murmurs. "Forgive me, France; you are right, as you always are—you are all that is brave, and noble, and womanly. Only—that does not make the losing you any the easier."

And then there is silence, and both look out at the gaslit panorama below, while the heavy minutes pass. So long the silence lasts, that France grows frightened, and breaks it with an effort.

"You knew her last night?" she asks.

"At once," he answers, in a dull, slow way; "the very moment she appeared. France, do you recollect the night of Lady Dynely's ball last autumn? I saw her portrait that night—the vignette, you remember, on Di Venturini's waltzes; and I recognized the face. But I would *not* believe it—it seemed too horrible to be true. It was some one who resembled her, I said to myself—a relation, perhaps; but she was dead—dead beyond doubt. It is easy to believe what we wish to believe. I never thought of her again until she stood before me on the stage."

"I knew by your face something had happened," France says, softly, "but I never dreamed of that."

"How could you? Oh, my poor child, it is not alone that she spoils my life, but to think she should have power to spoil yours! To think that you should suffer for my sins at this late day."

"We all suffer for the sins of others," France says, and somehow says it bravely. "We might all safely take the battle-cry of the strong old Crusaders for our staff of strength, ' *God Wills It.*' It is inevitable—don't let us talk of it— since it is no longer a question of talking, but endurance. You saw her this morning?"

"I did. I wished to make assurance doubly sure, as they say, before I came to you. For I knew what you would say —that the decree of divorce, which freed me seventeen years ago, would be no freedom in your eyes. And, my darling, the thought of losing you was, and is, more bitter than the bitterness of death."

"Don't!" she says, with a gasp, "don't! don't!"

"I saw her," he went on, "and I knew all hope was at an end. The girl I had married seventeen years ago in Canada was before me—Madame Felicia. I lingered but a few moments—it was her hour of vengeance, and I think even she was satisfied. And the child is with her—did she tell you that?"

"Yes—she told me. Oh, Gordon! if she would but give her up."

"She *shall* give her up," Gordon Caryll said, his mouth setting hard and tense beneath his beard; "if not by fair means, then by foul. She is no fit guardian for any young girl. Terry Dennison will help me here; and, one way or other, my daughter shall come into my keeping."

"Terry?" Miss Forrester said, in surprise.

As briefly as possible Caryll narrated the odd manner in

which Terry had been instrumental in bringing the girl to her mother.

"Dennison can keep a secret—I know no man I would trust as I do him. You will not mind my telling him all, France? All?"

"No," she answered; "you may tell Terry, but—no' Eric."

"Eric!" Caryll repeated contemptuously; "Eric is a fool! And my mother must know."

"Your mother, of course. Ah, poor grandmamma! it will be a blow to her."

He caught at her words.

"Must I really go, France—really and truly—and leave you and my mother alone?"

"Gordon, you know you must."

"I don't know it," he said, recklessly; "if you cannot be my wife, at least we can be friends, and together—"

"We can never be together. You can do as you please," her head drooping, her voice faltering; "it is your place to stay with your mother, of course. I will ask Lady Dynely to take me back to England at once."

"Stay, France!" he said, rising hastily. "Forgive me once more. No, I will go—it will be best so; and immediately—to-morrow."

Then again silence fell, and both stood apart, neither able to speak the words that must come next. In five minutes they must say good-by and forever.

A carriage whirled up before the hotel. The door opened, and Eric, looking unutterably bored by his day's "on duty," got out and assisted his wife and mother to alight.

"Here they are," Caryll exclaimed, starting back. "I cannot meet them, any of them. Make my adieux to Lucia to-morrow; tell her, if you like, I shall not see her again. France—"

And then he was clasping both her hands hard, and looking in her face with that straining gaze we look on the face we love best the instant before the coffin-lid is shut down.

"Oh, Gordon!" she cried out, "where will you go?"

"I don't know, I don't care—what does it matter?"

"You will write to—to your mother?"

"Yes, I will write.   I will see her now and say good-by. I will see Dennison, too, before I leave Paris.   Oh, my France! my France! how can I give you up!"

There were footsteps and voices in the hall—on the stairs. One moment and the Dynelys would be upon them.

"Good-by, France! good-by! good-by!"

And then he was gone.   And France, breathless, and white, had fallen upon the sofa, feeling as though the whole world had come to an end.

CHAPTER X.

I F they would not come in, if she could be alone—that seemed the only thought of which France was conscious, as she lay there, utterly unable for the time being to speak or move, knowing, in a dazed sort of way, what a ghastly face the wax-lights would show them. Oh, to be alone—to be alone !

She had her wish. A swish of silk, a flutter of perfume, the saloon door flung wide, and Lady Dynely's voice saying, impatiently :

"All darkness, and coldness, and solitude. Where can they be? where is France ?"

"With Mrs. Caryll, mamma," Crystal's soft voice suggests. "It looks dreary—that great, gilded saloon; let us go up to your boudoir."

So they go, and France feels as though she had escaped some great danger. She rises, feeling stiff and strange, and gropes her way out through the darkness, and up to her own room. She has to pass Mrs. Caryll's door ; she pauses a moment, while a passionate longing to enter there, at all risks, to look on his face once more, even to bid him stay, seizes her. Her wedding day is so near—oh, so near—and they have been so infinitely happy together. What right has that wicked, dancing, painted woman to come and tear them apart? For a moment she listens to the tempter, then she clasps her hands over her eyes, and rushes up to her room. Lights are burning here ; she locks the door, and throws herself on the bed, there to lie motionless, sleepless, all the long night through.

The Dynelys dine alone. No one can tell, it seems, what has become of the Carylls and Miss Forrester. Mrs.

Caryll's room is forbidden—her mistress is ill to-night, the maid gravely tells Lady Dynely. Even she cannot be admitted. Miss Forrester's door is locked, and Miss Forrester may be deaf or dead for all the attention she pays to knocks or calls. It is really very odd, and Lady Dynely wonders about it, all through the rather dull family dinner, to her son and daughter.

Rather dull ! It is horribly dull to Eric. He forfeits a banquet at Francetti's this evening, with half a dozen congenial spirits, for this " bosom-of-his-family " sort of thing, and worse still, forfeits his stall at the *Variétés*, to do escort duty for his harem, to the Opera aux Italiens. But since he is in for it, he does it with tolerably good grace, and Crystal's wan, moonlight little face lights, and smiles come to the pale lips. She says little, but she is happy. Eric has been her very own all day—will be her very own until noon to-morrow. Beyond that she does not look—" unto the day, the day."

Dinner ends, and they go to the opera. Patti sings, and the grand opera house is brilliant with ladies in marvellous toilettes. If France were only here, Eric thinks, as he struggles manfully with his tenth yawn, it would not be so bad, but a man cast over wholly to the tender mercies of his mother and his wife, is an object of compassion to gods and men.

About the time the Dynely party take their places in their private box on the grand tier, Gordon Caryll opens the door of his mother's room, and passes out.

He goes up to his room, where his valet awaits him, and gives his few orders. A portmanteau is to be packed at once—he (the valet) is to follow with the rest to Liverpool, before the end of the week. That is all—and the man listens with an immovable, wooden face, outwardly, in direst, blankest wonder within.

" Blessed," he says, as his master departs, " if this here ain't a rum go ! I thought we was going to be married, at the British Hembassy ; and now we're up and hoff 'ot foot, with all our luggage, hover to Liverpool. I wonder where we go hafter that ? "

"We" were going to America once again—to California—
Nevada—Oregon—all the wild, new lands, whither "we" had
never set foot yet. .Not to forget—that could never be !
But life, it seemed, amid perpetual hardship and adventure,
amid wild regions and wilder men, would be more easily
dragged out without hope than elsewhere.

He had told his mother ; and she had listened in such
wonder, such pain, such pity, as words cannot tell. She
had set her heart on this match, and it was never to be.
Her whole happiness in life was wrapped up in her son,
and he was to be taken from her. He must go—since this
woman stood between him and France forever, better, far
better, they should part.

" I would rather go," he had said ; " not to forget, not to
suffer less—I do not hope that, I do not even wish it ; but
I cannot stay and face the wonder, the scandal, that will
ensue. I am a coward, if you like, but I underwent the
ordeal once, and—" he set his teeth hard and stopped.

"Yet, I will stay if you wish," he said, after a moment's
pause. "I will stay with you, and," another pause, "*she*
can return to England with Lucia Dynely."

But the mother, whose life was bound up in him, clasped
her arms about his neck, and answered :

"You must go, Gordon. France is right—she can never
be your wife, while that woman lives, and so parting is best
for you both. You must go, and may Heaven's blessing be
with you."

And then there had been a parting, so sad, so solemn,
last words so sweet, so motherly, a parting prayer so earnest,
so holy, that the fierce wrath and hot rebellion had died
out, and somehow calm had come. He had left the hotel,
very pale, very grave, a great sadness on his face, but otherwise unchanged.

He must see Dennison before he left. He went to the
Louvre and found him, providentially, lounging aimlessly
about, and looking bored.

" De do, Caryll," Terry began, abbreviating the formula,
and swallowing a gape. " Awfully slow work this. Haven't
seen a face I know since noon. Was at your place, and

found the family invisible—dead or sleeping. Eric is doing the *rôle* of Master Tommy Goodchild—trotting out the madre and Crystal, and making a martyr of himself, I know. But I say, old boy, anything wrong, you know? On my life, now I look again, you seem awfully seedy."

"We can talk in the street, I suppose?" Caryll answers, abruptly, and taking his arm. "I have something of importance to say to you. Come this way. Dennison, I'm off to-morrow!"

"Off?" Terry repeats the word and stares.

"Off for good and all—to return no more—to the other end of the world. It's all up between me and—Terry, can't you guess? I thought you did last night. Madame Felicia is my divorced wife."

There is a pause, a speechless, breathless pause. Mr. Dennison looks at the moon, the stars, the sky, the streets, the gaslights, the people, and all spin round. At last, "By Jove!" he breathes, and is still.

Caryll does not speak—his mouth is set rigid and hard behind his beard. They walk on, and the silence grows uncomfortable. Terry in desperation breaks it first.

"I thought she was dead," is what he says.

"So did I," Caryll answers; "so did they in Canada, so the papers said. She is not, however. Madame Felicia seventeen years ago was my wife; the girl you rescued on the streets two nights ago my daughter."

"Little Black Eyes! By Jove!" Terry aspirates again.

"I fancied you must have suspected something of this since last night. I recognized her at the theatre. I visited her this morning. There is not a shadow of doubt. The dancer, Felicia, is my divorced wife."

"By Jove!" once again is all Terry can say, in his blank amaze. "And France?" he asks, after a pause.

"All is at an end there. In France's creed there is no such thing as divorce. I am as much the husband of Felicia as though that divorce had never been."

There is another uncomfortable silence. What is Terry to say? Fluency and tact are at no time his. But silence is better than speech just now.

"So I am going away," Caryll resumes, steadily ; "and I leave my mother and France in your charge, Dennison. 1 go to-morrow. When does your leave expire ? "

" In a fortnight."

"There will be ample time, then. My mother proposes returning to Caryllynne ; you will escort her thither. For the rest, Lady Dynely will be told the truth, but no one else —least of all, Eric. There will be no end of conjecture, and gossip, and mystification, no doubt, but since none of us will be here to hear it, it won't greatly matter."

" But," Terry hazards, " will *she* keep the secret ? They say women never can, you know ? "

A cold smile lights Gordon Caryll's lips.

"Trust them when it is to their own interest. Felicia has fooled M. Di Venturini into offering to make her his wife. The wedding, I am told, is to take place soon. *He* has no idea that she has ever been married—she has lied to him from first to last. It is her interest to hold her tongue, and now that her revenge is satisfied she will."

" It's a deuced bad business, Caryll, old fellow," Terry says, gloomily. " I'm awfully sorry. Confound the woman ! she seems born to work mischief and deviltry to every man she meets."

"Another thing, Dennison," Caryll pursues, taking no heed ; "what I principally wished to speak to you about, is my daughter. By fair means or foul, she must be taken from her mother and given to me. And, Terry, for this I look to you."

"To me ? " Terry repeats, blankly ; "but how ? I can't go to Felicia and demand her, I can't watch my chance and steal her away. Hang it, no ! She's a female fiend, and I owe her no good turn, but still she is the girl's mother, and as such has a right to her. I suppose she is fond of her ? "

"She is not. Felicia never was fond of any human being but herself. She would send the girl adrift to-morrow, only it adds to her revenge to retain her. She will not treat her kindly, of that I am sure ; and before the week ends the poor child will need but the offer to fly. My mother will gladly receive and care for her. Terry, you must see her for

me. Let her know the truth. You have been of service to
her and she will trust you, Explain everything; tell her a
better home and kinder relatives than she has ever known
await her. She will go with you of her own free will—take
my word for that."

"Well, I'll try. I'll do my best," Terry said. "Hang it,
Caryll! there's nothing I *wouldn't* do for you and France. I
suppose they—your mother and Miss Forrester—are awfully
cut up."

"Naturally. Don't speak of it, Terry. I know I can
trust you ; and if anything could help me now, it would be
that knowledge. There is no more to be said, I believe.
Look after the mother and France—get the child away
from Felicia—make Eric leave Paris for his wife and mother's sake if you can. A multiplicity of tasks, dear boy, and
the last the hardest by far ; but I know it will be no fault of
yours if you fail. I will bid you good-by and good speed
here."

They clasped hands hard in silence, then, without one
word more, parted, and each went his own way. Terry lit a
cigar, and with his hands deep in his pockets made his way
gloomily back to the Hotel du Louvre.

"And if ever the fiend incarnate came on earth to work
mischief in human shape," Mr. Dennison inwardly growls,
"he has come in the form of Felicia the dancer. Devil
take her! is there no end to the trouble she is destined to
make?"

Next morning, Lady Dynely, to her surprise and annoy-
ance, finds herself breakfasting alone. Neither Gordon
Caryll nor France Forrester is to be seen when she enters.
She waits half an hour—still they fail to put in an appearance.
Lady Dynely hates solitary breakfasts, and rather pettishly
rings the bell.

"It's *very* odd," she thinks annoyedly ; "all day yesterday,
and now again this morning, neither Gordon nor France is
to be seen. And both are such preposterously early risers."

Her own maid answers the summons, and her ladyship
impatiently sends her in quest of the truants. Ten minutes,
and Simpson returns.

" Miss Forrester has not yet left her room. She is suffering from headache, and begs my lady to excuse her until
luncheon. For Mr. Caryll—Mr. Caryll, my lady, has gone.'

" Gone ! " my lady repeats with a blank stare.

" Yes, my lady. Norton, his man, received his orders last
night to pack up and follow him at once to England. Mr.
Caryll left the hotel himself late last evening, and has not
since returned."

Lady Dynely listens to this in dazed incredulity. France
ill !—Gordon gone ! Now what does this mean ? Her first
impulse is to go to Mrs. Caryll and inquire, her second to
eat her breakfast and wait quietly, until she is told. She
acted on the second, ordered in breakfast, and sipped her
chocolate as best she might for the devouring curiosity that
possessed her.

An hour later, and Miss Forrester came down. The
dainty morning toilet was as fresh and unexceptionable as
ever, the pretty rich brown hair as perfectly *coiffed*. But
out of the dark bright face all the color was stricken, out of
the clear brown eyes all the youthful gladness, all the loving,
happy light. She went to Mrs. Caryll's room. The elder
lady sat in her easy-chair, dressed for the day, waiting in an
anguish of suspense. As France came in she opened her
arms, and without a word the girl went in to them, and laid
her pale face on the motherly bosom with a great, tearless
sob.   ·

" My child ! my child ! "

She held her to her, and there was silence. The eyes
of Gordon Caryll's mother were full of pitying tears, but the
eyes of France were dry and burning.

" I sent him away—from you who love him so dearly.
Oh, mother, forgive me. I did it for the best."

She says it in a choked whisper, lifting her face for a moment. Then again it falls on the other's shoulder.

" It was like death, it was worse than death, but I told him
to go," she says, again, in that husky undertone.

" My dearest," Mrs. Caryll answers, " you did right.
Dearly as I love him, precious as your happiness is to me, I
would rather part with him forever, rather see you as I see

you now, than let you be his wife while that woman lives. *I* believe as you believe. No law of man can alter the law of God. If she was his wife seventeen years ago—my child, how you shiver! are you cold?—she is his wife still. It is right and just that he should have put her away—that I believe ; knowing her to be alive now, it is right and just also that you should have sent him from you. But, oh, my dear, my dear, it is hard on you—it is very hard on him."

"Don't," France says. "Oh, mother, not yet! I *can't* bear it. This day fortnight was to have been our wedding-day, and now—"

She breaks down all in a moment, and the tears come—a passionate rain of tears. The mother holds her almost in silence, and so on her bosom lets her weep her anguish out.

She is crying herself, but quietly. Great self-control has always been hers—is hers still. To part with her lately-found son has been like the rending of soul and body—more bitter than the bitterness of death ; but she has learned, in weary years of penitence and waiting, the great lesson of life—endurance. So she comforts France now, in a tender, motherly fashion, and France listens, as she could listen to no one on earth, this morning, but Gordon's mother.

· "It is not for myself," she says at last, after her old, impetuous fashion, "it is for him. He has suffered so much, atoned so bitterly in exile, and loneliness, and poverty, all the best years of his life for that mad marriage of his youth, and now, when I would have made him so happy, when he *was* happy, in one instant everything is swept from him—home, mother, wife—and he must go out into exile once more. Oh, mother! help me to bear it! It breaks my heart!"

The wild sobs break forth again. The mother's heart echoes every word. It is retribution, perhaps justice—none the less it is very bitter. They both think of him, leaving all things, and going back to outlawry and wretchedness ; they think of her in her insolent, glowing beauty and prosperity, the world going so well with her, glorying in her vengeance, and it requires all the Christianity within them to refrain from hating her.

But presently the storm of grief ends, and sitting on a low hassock, her head bowed on Mrs. Caryll's knee, France listens to her sad plans for the future—so different, oh, so different from all the girl's bright hopes of but a day before.

"We will return to England, France," Mrs. Caryll says, gravely; "to Caryllynne. It has been deserted long enough. There we will live quietly together, and hope, and pray, and wait—"

"Wait," France repeats with mournful bitterness. "What is there to wait for now?"

What, indeed! Both are silent. Unless this fatal woman dies—and in her rich and perfect health she is likely to outlive them all—what can her son ever have to hope for in this lower world? For France—well, as the years go on, the elder woman thinks happiness *may* return to her. She is so young, there may be hope for her—for him, none.

"Would you rather we went to Rome?" she asks, after a pause.

"No," France says. "Let us return to Caryllynne. It was *his* home; I shall be less wretched there than anywhere else on earth."

So it is agreed.

"Terry will take us," Mrs. Caryll says. "Terry knows all. And Lucia must be told, my dear—it is impossible to keep the truth from her."

"Yes, tell her," Miss Forrester assents, wearily; "the sooner the better. And ask her to spare me—to say nothing of altered looks, or of—him. I will return to my room, and you had best send for her at once. She was speaking of taking Crystal to Versailles—let her know all, and make an end of it before she goes."

Then France toils spiritlessly, cold and white, and wretched looking, back to her room, and Lady Dynely is sent for, and the miserable sequel to Gordon Caryll's early marriage is told her, as she sits surprised and compassionate, beside Gordon Caryll's most unhappy mother.

* * * * * * * * *

"Where is he now?" is France's thought, as she sits wearily down, and lays her head on the table, as though she

never cared to lift it again. He is whirling along in a
French express train—Calais-ward. To-night he will cross
the channel ; by the first Cunarder that quits Liverpool he
will sail for New York, and so begins the second exile to
which his fatal wife has driven him.

CHAPTER XI.

QUIET street near the Rue de la Paix. The hour, ten in the evening. Almost absolute solitude reigning—only at long intervals the footsteps of some passer-by awakening the echoes. Dim and afar off as it seems, the turmoil of the great city coming mellowed and subdued.

One house, large, unlighted, gloomy, standing in a paved quadrangle, has had a constant stream of visitors for the past two hours. They are all men—men who have a stealthy and furtive look, who pass on rapidly, who give a counter-sign to a waiting servant at the gate, who do not spend more than fifteen minutes within those gloomy precincts, who flit away and disappear, only to have others take their places. So it has been for the past two hours, so it is likely to be until perhaps midnight.

This house is the property of his Excellency Prince Di Venturini ; and M. Di Venturini is the leader and moving spirit of a secret political society. For upward of two months he has been absent on a mission of grave import; this is the evening of his return, and the members of the society—Italians all—have been summoned to their headquarters to report progress to their leader.

Outside the gloomy and secluded mansion is wrapped in profound darkness ; inside, halls and passages are dimly lit —one room only, that in which M. Di Venturini sits, being brightly illuminated.

He sits at a table strewn with papers, letters, pamphlets— small, spare, yellow, with black, glancing eyes, sharp as stilettos, and thin, compressed lips. One by one, his followers

27

come and go ; one by one, their reports are noted down and docketed.

With sharp, quick precision he conducts each interview, with imperious command he gives his orders, with scant ceremony he dismisses each man of them all. Business of a still more private and delicate nature awaits his attention— business purely personal to M. le Prince—and he rather cuts short the latest comers, and hurries the levee to a close.

A clock over his head chimes eleven. With an impatient gesture he dismisses his last client, flings himself back in his chair, pushes his scant black hair, thickly streaked with gray, off his forehead with a weary air, and then sits for some minutes lost in deep and anxious thought. His thick brows knit, his lips set themselves in a tight, tense line, then, with a second impatient motion, he seizes a silver hand-bell and rings a sharp peal.

"I shall speedily learn whether it is truth or slander," he mutters. "Paujol and Pauline watch her well, and they belong to me soul and body. I may trust their tale, and if she has played me false, why, then—let her look to herself!"

The bell is answered almost immediately by the servant who has stood on guard.

He bows and awaits.

"Have they all gone?"

"All, M. le Prince."

"Has Paujol come?"

"Paujol has been awaiting your excellency's commands, for the last hour."

"Let him enter."

The man bows again and disappears.

M. le Prince lies back in his chair and plays a devil's tattoo of ill-repressed impatience on its arm. Then M. Paujol enters—a very tall man, in a gorgeous uniform, no other, in fact, than Madame Felicia's huge chasseur in his robes of state.

"Ah! Paujol. You have been here for some time, Antoine tells me. Have you obtained leave of absence, then, from madame?"

"Madame is not aware of my absence, M. le Prince.

Madame departed one hour ago to the bal d'opera at the Gymnase—the instant she left the Varieties, in fact."

"Ah-h!" the interjection cut the air sharply as a knife; "to the bal d'opera at the Gymnase. With whom?"

"With the young milor Anglais—M. le Vicomte Dynely."

A moment's silence. An ominous flash, swift, dangerous, has leaped from the eyes of the Neapolitan—his cruelly thin lips set themselves a little tighter.

"It is true, then! all I have heard. He is the latest pigeon madame has seen fit to pluck, this green young British lordling! He is with her at all times, at all places. Paris rings with his infatuation—eh, Paujol? is it so?"

"It is the talk of Paris, monseigneur, of the clubs and the salons, of the streets and the theatre. Does your excellency wish me to tell you *what* they say?"

"All, Paujol. Word for word."

"They say, then, M. le Prince, that but the English noble has a wife already, madame would throw over your excellency and marry milor Dynely. They say that madame has fallen in love with his handsome face, and that while your highness will be the husband and dupe, *he* will still remain the favored lover."

The hand—thin, sinewy, strong—that clasps the arm of the chair, clutches it until the muscles stand out like cords. A fierce Neapolitan oath hisses from his lips—otherwise he sits and listens unmoved.

"Go on, Paujol," he reiterates. "Your report is most amusing, my friend. He is at madame's constantly, is he not?—he is her *cavalier servante* to all places?—his gifts are princely in their profusion and splendor?—again, is it not so?"

"It is so, Illustrissima—Pauline tells me the jewels he has given her are superb. He is her nightly attendant home from the theatre, he is at all her receptions, each day they ride in the Bois or the Champs Elysées, he spends hours in madame's salon each morning. To none of the many gentlemen whom madame has honored with her regard has she shown such favor as to M. le Vicomte Dynely. Madame Dynely, it is said, is dying of jealousy. All Paris laughs,

monseigneur, and when your excellency returns, wonders
how the drama will end."

"Paris will soon learn," monseigneur answers grimly.
An ominous calm has settled upon him, the devil's tattoo
has quite ceased now, his black eyes glitter diabolically.
"Thou hast watched well, Paujol, my friend; thou shalt
be well rewarded. Madame dreams not then of my return ? "

"She does not, your excellency. I heard her tell M.
Dynely only to-day that your highness would not return to
Paris for another week."

A smile curled the thin lips.

"It is well. And so safe in my absence, not dreaming
that her chasseur and femme de chambre are my paid and
devoted spies, she takes as her lover this pretty-faced English boy, and all Paris laughs at *me /* It is well, I say. But
I am not the husband yet, and the English say those laugh
best who laugh last. And so they assist at the bal d'opera
to-night ? Ah, what hour does madame propose returning,
Paujol ? "

"An hour after midnight, M. le Prince. She quits early
that she and M. Dynely may start early for Asnières, where
they spend to-morrow."

Again that threatening flash leaps from the eyes of the
prince.

"What does madame wear ? " he demands.

"A domino *noir,* with a knot of yellow ribbon on the left
shoulder."

"And, Monsieur ? "

"Monsieur goes in full evening dress, with a yellow rose
in his button-hole, and lemon gloves."

Di Venturini takes out his watch.

"Half-past eleven—ample time. A million thanks, friend
Paujol ! As I say, your fidelity shall be well rewarded. Is
your report made ? If so, you may depart."

"One moment, monseigneur. My report is not finished
—the most important part is yet to come. Is your excellency aware that madame has a daughter ? "

"What ! "

" That madame has a daughter—a tall English mam'selle of sixteen years, at present stopping with madame ? "

The yellow complexion of the Neapolitan fades to a greenish white. He sits and stares.

" Paujol ! A daughter ! What is it you say ? "

" The truth, M. le Prince. A daughter and a husband. The daughter is with her now, as I tell you ; the husband divorced her many years ago. The daughter was brought to the house late one night by an English gentleman, a friend of M. Dynely, Monsieur Dennison,"—Paujol pronounces the English names with perfect correctness—" and has remained ever since. Before you return, however, madame proposes sending her away. The husband came once, and once only. The interview was brief. Here is his card."

He draws it out and places it before him. " Gordon Caryll," Di Venturini reads. For a moment he is at a loss, for a moment his memory refuses to place him. Then it all comes upon him like lightning. The picture " How the Night Fell," the mysterious resemblance of the woman's face to Felicia, her determination to have it at any price, and the name of the artist—Gordon Locksley, then—Gordon Caryll afterwards. In common with the rest of the world he has heard Gordon Caryll's story—the mad marriage of his youth, the scandal, the divorce, the prolonged exile from home and country, and now—and now Paujol stands before him with an immovable face, and tells him gravely that Felicia, the woman he has honored with the offer of his hand, is that fatal divorced wife.

He sits for a moment, petrified, and in that moment he believes. Paujol never makes mistakes, never hazards rumors without proof. She had lied to him then from the beginning, duped him from first to last, and Prince Di Venturini could better endure anything than the thought that he has been fooled and laughed at by the woman he has loved.

" So ! " he says between his teeth, " this must be seen to ! Proceed, Paujol—you are indeed a treasure beyond price."

Thus encouraged, M. Paujol, still with a gravely immovable face, proceeds. In detail he narrates how Dennison brought to madame at midnight this waif of the streets, how madame at once received her, how Pauline faithfully did her part, overheard every word of the conversation that passed between mother and daughter, and faithfully repeated that conversation to him. He had taken it down in writing from her lips on the spot, and would read it aloud to monseigneur now.

He unfolded the document as he spoke, and slowly read it over, that momentous conversation, in which "Donny" had claimed Felicia as her mother, and Felicia had acknowledged her as her child—the pledge of secrecy between them, and the compact by which madame was to pass her off as a distant relative. In his cold, steady, monotonous voice, Paujol read it, then folded, and handed it respectfully to his superior officer and master. Di Venturini, his yellow face still sickly, greenish white, waited for more.

"The girl—she is still there ?" he asked.

"She is still there, M. le Prince. She is to be sent away in two days. She and madame have had a quarrel."

"Ah ! a quarrel ! What about ?"

"About M'sieu Dennison. M. Dennison came yesterday, came the day before, and both times asked to see the young lady he had picked up on the streets. Madame put him off with a falsehood. Mam'selle was ailing and had declined to see him. This Pauline repeated to mam'selle, who, it would appear, is most anxious to meet again with the gentleman who rescued her. Mam'selle flew into a violent passion, sought out madame and taxed her with duplicity. Madame is not accustomed to being arraigned for her actions, and possesses, as monseigneur doubtless is aware, a fine, high temper of her own. Before five minutes madame was boxing mam'selle's ears. Mam'selle became perfectly beside herself with fury, and tried to rush out of the house, but was captured and brought back by Pauline, who was, as usual, on the watch. Madame then informed Pauline that mam'-selle was mad, quite mad, that her madness consisted in fancying her her mother, that she had run away from her friends under that delusion, and that now she was under the necessity of locking her up, for a day or two, until she could send her safely back to those friends. The passion of mam'selle was frightful to behold, so Pauline says, but she was brought back and safely locked up, and so continues locked up at this present moment. She refuses to speak or eat, and lies like a stone. Madame has made arrangements to have her removed the day after to-morrow—where, Pauline has not as yet discovered."

Paujol pauses. Di Venturini, his face still green, his lips still set, his eyes still gleaming, looks up.

" And the conversation between madame and M. Gordon Caryll—did Pauline also overhear that?"

" Pauline overheard every word, monseigneur, and, as before, repeated it to me. As before, I took it down in writing upon the spot, and have it here. Shall I read it aloud, M. le Prince?"

By a gesture Di Venturini gives assent. Immovably Paujol stands and reads this second report ; immovably his master sits and listens. It leaves no room for doubt—Felicia has deceived him, as thoroughly and utterly as ever woman deceived man. A husband—a daughter—a lover ! and *he* the laughingstock of Paris ! His face for an instant is distorted with passionate fury, as Paujol places this second paper before him.

" This is all?" he hoarsely asks.

" This is all, M. le Prince."

" The girl is still locked up, you say, in madame's rooms, and madame will not return from the opera ball until one o'clock? Wait, Paujol, wait !"

He leans his forehead on his hand and thinks for an instant intently. Then he looks up.

" I will go with you, Paujol, first to see this girl, then to the Gymnase. I have no words with which to commend the admirable manner you and Pauline have done your duty. Go and call a fiacre at once."

Paujol bows low and obeys. Di Venturini sits alone. He does not for one second doubt the truth of all this he has heard. His two emissaries are fidelity itself—their loyalty has been long ago proven. He has long doubted the woman he has asked to marry him. To-night has but made conviction doubly sure; and Cæsare Di Venturini is not a man to let man or woman, friend or foe, betray him with impunity. His face looks leaden in the lamplight, his black eyes gleam with a fury that is simply murderous.

"A husband who divorced her—a child whom she has hidden—a lover for whom I am betrayed!" he repeats through his set teeth, "and all Paris laughing at me. To-night at the bal d'opera, to-morrow at Asnières, and M. le Prince safely absent for another week. Diavolo! it is like the plot of her own plays."

He laughs, a laugh not pleasant to hear, rises and makes ready for his drive. The fiacre is already at the door, he enters and is rapidly driven away to the lodgings of madame.

CHAPTER XII.

HATE her! I wish she were dead! Oh, why, why, why did I ever leave Scotland and come to this horrible place—to her? I will starve myself and die if I cannot get my freedom in any other way! Oh, I wish I had died before I ever came here!"

It was the burden of the moan "Mademoiselle Donny" had been making to herself for the last two days. To Pauline, who brought her her meals, she scorned to speak at all. She lay like a stone, asking no questions, answering none, scarcely touching the food. Then again at times the fierce passions inherited honestly enough from those who had given her life would assert themselves, and her piercing cries would ring through the rooms. She would beat on the locked door and barred window until her hands bled and she sank exhausted and breathless upon the floor. It was known to all madame's household that the poor child, raving so madly in that bolted and barred upper room, was hopelessly insane, and in another day or two would be safely shut up in a *maison de sante.*

She lies now prostrate on the floor, her head resting against the side of the bed. All day long at intervals, her wild cries have rung out, the little dark childish hands have beaten against the unyielding door. Madame's nerves have not been disturbed thereby. Madame has spent the long sunny day amid the wooded slopes and sunlit glades of St. Cloud with her *cavalier servante,* Lord Viscount Dynely, and the pallid curate's widow. Now it is past eleven at night, and she grovels prone here, spent, white, exhausted, her dusk eyes gleaming weirdly in her pallid child's face,

17*

her elfish black hair all tossed and dishevelled over her
shoulders.

" If *he* were here," she thinks with a great sobbing sigh,
" he would save me. Oh, if I had only stayed with him
that night, and never come here ! He was good, he was
kind ; I would have been happy with him."

The face of Terry Dennison rises before her—the honest
eyes, the frank smile, the man's strength and woman's gentle-
ness, and her heart cries out for him now in her trouble, as
though he had been the friend of her whole life.

" He asked for me," she thinks, with another long shuddering sob. " Twice he asked for me, and each time she
told him a lie—told him I was sick and did not want to see
him. And she struck me in the face. Oh, I hate her ! I
hate her ! "

Her folded arms rest on the bed—her face drops on them,
and so poor ill-used, ill-tempered, passionate Donny lies
still. She falls into a sort of lethargy that is not sleep, but
the natural result of so much fierce excitement, and in that
half-doze dreams—dreams Terry Dennison is coming to her
rescue once more, the kindly smile she remembers so well,
and trusts so entirely, on his face—that his foot is ascending the stairs, that he is turning the key in the door, that he
is in the room. Then a light flashes through the darkness,
and she looks up with dazed dreaming eyes to see a man in
the room, shading a light and looking at her—a man who is
not Terry Dennison.

" Hush-h-h !" this man says, putting his finger on his lip,
and noiselessly closing the door. " Not a word, not a sound,
mademoiselle ! I am a friend. I have come to save you.
But all depends on your being perfectly still."

She does not rise. She lies and looks at him, her wide-
open, black eyes full of silent wonder and suspicion.

" Who are you ? " she asks.

He is a little yellow man, in a richly-furred coat, and
with an air of distinction, but Mam'selle Donny does not
like his look.

" I am a friend, as I told you. I have been sent to save

yc.u. I have been sent by him—the gentleman who brought you here—Monsieur Dennison."

She springs to her feet now, the sound of that name electrifying her.

"Take me to him," she cries, breathlessly. "Oh, sir! take me to him. He is strong, and brave, and kind. Oh, take me from this dreadful house, from that dreadful woman to him!"

"Hush-h!" he says again; "softly, mademoiselle—some one may hear. I have come to take you to him presently, but first—madame is your mother, is she not?"

"Why do you ask that?" she impatiently demands; "what has that to do with it? Oh! let me go away at once."

"It has everything to do with it, mam'selle. Monsieur Dennison told me to ascertain. He would have come himself, but you know madame distrusts him and will not let him see you, lest you should tell him the truth."

"I know! I know!" she impatiently interrupts. "She lied to him! She told him I was ill, when he asked for me, and I was dying to see him. She slapped my face, and locked me up here, and I hate her!" Her eyes flashed fire, her hands clenched. "What is it you want to know?" she cried excitedly. "I'll tell you anything — everything so that you take me from here, to him."

"Tell me your story—who you are. She is your mother, is she not? I see the likeness in your face. Who is your father, and where is he?"

"I don't know; I wish I did. I would make Mr. Dennison take me to him. She is my mother—oh, yes! and I was born in Quebec, more than sixteen years ago. My father would not live with her, I don't know why, and there was a divorce. So Joan told me. Joan was there when I was born, and my mother left me with her and went away. Joan brought me up; now she is dead, and so I came here. I wish I never had—oh! I wish I never had. Her name is not Madame Felicia—her name is Rosamond. She called herself Mrs. Gordon when I was born, and my father's name was Gordon Caryll. I don't know whether he is living or dead. Joan did not know. That is all. And now I have told you, I want you to take me away."

But her visitor arose and put her gently back.   One look into her face had settled the question of her maternity.

"Not to-night, petite.   It is late for you to be abroad. But you shall be taken away, and that speedily—you may trust my word when I say so."

Then, before the bewildered child can quite realize it, the little man with the yellow face and furred coat is gone, the key turned in the lock, and she is alone in her prison once more.

*   *   *   *   *   *   *   *   *

The bal d'opera was at its height.   The vast building was one sheet of white gaslight ; perfumes, pastilles, and the rich odor of flowers made the atmosphere almost overpowering. The orchestra, playing the sweet Strauss waltzes, filled the air with quivering melody.   And above the rich strains of the music arose the shrill laughter, the shrill clatter of ceaseless gay voices, as dominoes, white and black, flower-girls, *debardeurs*, gypsies, *paysannes, coryphées, princes au théâtre*, and men in plain evening dress, with masks off or on, as the whim took them, flashed and flitted ceaselessly and noisily to and fro.   A gorgeous picture of one phase of Paris gaslit life—a glimpse of the Arabian Nights—brilliant, intoxicating, wicked.

Among the maskers there came, quite alone and moving slowly, a short, slight man, in a furred and frogged great-coat, which, despite the warmth, he still retained, his mask conceal-ing all but the glitter of two restless black eyes.   He made his way to the centre of the assemblage, and leaning negligently against a statue of the Apollo, watched the brilliant phantas-magoria as it flitted before him.   Suddenly he started slightly and drew in his breath with a sharp, sibilant sound. What he looked for he saw.

There flew swiftly past him, in the dizzy whirl of the half-mad waltzers, a black domino, with a knot of yellow ribbon on her left shoulder.   The tall partner who clasped her so closely, was a gentleman in plain evening dress, a yellow rose in his buttonhole, primrose kids on his hands.   The wild laughter of the lady reached him as she whirled by like a bacchante, laughter he knew well, and had heard often.

The hawk had sprung upon its quarry—from that moment he lost sight of them no more.

The waltz ended. The domino *noir* moved away on her companion's arm to a distant corner, where the glare of gas-light was less blinding, where tall tropic plants cast shade, where but few people were, and where seats for the weary were placed. Quietly, stealthily, the gentleman in the mask and furred-coat followed, unobserved. The lady threw herself into one of the seats, and fluttered open her fan.

"Mon Dieu! but it is hot! Eric, mon enfant, have the common humanity to go and fetch me a water ice. That last waltz was charming, and how well you have my step. We must dance the Krolsbalklange valse together, and then —home. Eric, go for the ice if you would not see me expire."

She removed her mask and showed the flushed, laughing, lovely face of Felicia. Her companion rose to obey, whispering something that caused madame's shrill laughter once more to peal out as she struck him with her fan. "*Fi donc*, Eric, I know what your tender speeches are worth. It is too warm, and I am too fatigued for love-making. Go for my ice."

He departed. Five minutes after, as he was slowly making his way through the revolving throng with madame's water-ice in his hand, a man in a furred overcoat ran rudely against him, knocking it out of his hand and over his immaculate evening suit.

"Mille pardons, monsieur," this personage cried, with a low bow, but a mocking laugh. "But if monsieur *will* be clumsy! I regret exceedingly having spoiled monsieur's best coat; but—"

A chorus of laughter from the bystanders, who were in the mood to laugh at any mishap to their neighbors, however slight, cut him short. The next instant the little man was flat on his back, sent thither by a well-directed blow straight from the shoulder. As if by enchantment a crowd gathered. There is magic in a "row" that speaks to the heart of men of all nations. The insolent gentleman in the frogged coat leaped to his feet with a shrill cry of fury, but

before he fairly reached them he was sprawling on his back
once more.

"Come on," Lord Dynely said, with perfect coolness;
"as my best coat *is* spoiled, I don't mind spoiling it a little
more.   Get up and I'll show you how to walk through a
ball-room without running against your neighbors."

"Mon Dieu, Eric!" cried the voice of Felicia, who had
replaced her mask, and now rushed to the scene; "what is
the matter?   Who is this?"

"I have not the honor of monsieur's acquaintance at
present; but all the same it affords me pleasure to teach
him—"

He paused, for madame had clutched his arm with a
cry of terror and recognition.   With eyes literally flashing
flame, Di Venturini had sprung to his feet like a tiger, torn
off his mask, and confronted them.

"Yes, madame—it is I.   You recognize me, I see.   Tell
your lover who I am.   You know me, if he does not.   We
shall be better acquainted before long.   I have the honor,
have I not, of speaking to Lord Dynely?"

He hissed out his words in English that the crowd might
not understand.   Eric, confounded himself by this sudden
rencontre, bowed also.

"A friend of mine shall wait upon you, my lord, to-
morrow morning," Di Venturini said in a rapid whisper.
"You have heard of me—I am the Prince Di Venturini.
For you, madame," with a low bow, "I shall see you later."

Before either could speak he turned, made his way through
the throng, and quitted the bal masque.   For this purpose
he had come—his end was accomplished.

The crowd dispersed, rather disappointed at having, after
all, been cheated out of a free fight.   Felicia and Lord
Dynely looked at each other blankly for a moment.   Then
madame broke into one of her shrill laughs.

"*Ma foi!* Eric, my friend, but this is droll!   It is like
one of our vaudevilles at the Varieties, where madame
amuses herself in monsieur's absence, and monsieur, furious
and jealous, unexpectedly appears.   What a scene that will
be to-morrow!—he is all that there is of the most jealous—

that poor little M. Di Venturini, and I *did* promise him, before he left, never to coquet more. There is one waltz, mon cher—shall we dance it, or—"

"We will dance it, of course," Lord Dynely answers, " a waltz with you is too rare a treat to be lightly given up."

The soft, sweet strains of the Krolsbalklange float out, and they whirl away with it, in perfect time. Felicia is a perfect dancer, her feet do not seem to touch the floor. Dynely means what he says when he avers that a waltz with her is a rare treat. Then it ends, and he wraps her in her opera cloak, and leads her to her carriage. She leans forward, her witching face in the full glow of the gaslight, a smile on the red lips, in the lustrous, topaz eyes.

"And Asnières, *mon enfant*," she says, "do we go to-morrow down the Seine as agreed, or do we—"

"We go !" he answered, his blue eyes flashing ; "not for all the jealous Italians in Christendom would I throw over to-morrow's excursion."

He stoops and kisses the jewelled, ungloved hand she extends. Once again she laughs, that sweet, derisive laugh he knows so well. Then the carriage rolls away. Circe has gone, and her victim stands alone in the cool February night.

CHAPTER XIII

E stands alone under the cold, white stars, and as the chill wind sweeps about him, as the chill dawn breaks, his senses slowly return. One way or other this intoxicating flirtation of his has ended at least. To-morrow's excursion down the Seine to Asnières is probably its closing act. For M. le Prince Di Venturini, the affianced of Felicia, has been insulted, and M. le Prince is a man to wipe out such insults thoroughly and well. He is a noted duelist—three times has he killed his man ; lighting his cigar coolly and walking away while his adversary lay dying hard among the sweet summer grasses. He is a skilled swordsman, a dead shot. More than once, since the beginning of his flirtation with the fair Felicia, has Lord Dynely been told that. And he—of fencing he knows next to nothing—a pistol he has not fired three times in his life. And " a friend will wait upon him to-morrow," and the morning after, at the farthest, he will meet Di Venturini somewhere amid the wooded slopes of Versailles.

Physically, Lord Dynely was the farthest possible remove from a coward. Life may be tolerably pleasant, and still a man may face the possibility of leaving it with good grace, if his conscience lie dormant. To fear death, one must fear what comes after death. Of that, like most men of his stamp, wholly given up to the pursuit of pleasure, Lord Dynely never thought. After all, taken with all its dissipations, even at its best and brightest, here in Paris, life was a good deal of a bore—not so desirable a thing to keep, by any manner of means, that one should make much of a howling at resigning it. And that the day after to-morrow, when he stood face to face with Di Venturini, under the leafless trees of Versailles, or the Bois de Vincennes, he must resign it, he was as certain as that he lit his cigar now, and strolled slowly homeward under the white, shining stars. Yes, life was a bore ; a man tired of all things. A pretty face with two blue eyes bewitches him, he marries it, and is wearied to death or satiety in a fortnight. One grew tired of women, of wine, of horses, the rattle of the dice, the croak of the croupier, the shuffle of the cards, the whirl of the ball-room, the glare of the gas-light, of all things in this wearisome, lower world. Even swarth-skinned, topaz-eyed actresses pall after a few weeks, after a few thousand pounds spent upon them in presents, for which "becks and nods, and wreathèd smiles" are but a flat return. *Vanitas Vanitatem !* The song Solomon sung so many thousand years ago is wearily echoed by his sons—the *jeunesse dorée* of to-day. And one other day must end it all. There would be the trip down the Seine to-morrow, sunshine above them, music around them, a golden blue river below them, and two yellow, black, lustrous eyes smiling languidly upon him. The morning after, in the gray, cold dawn, there would be that silent woodland meeting, the sharp report of two pistol shots, a yellow, Neapolitan prince flying in haste out of the imperial dominions of Napoleon the Third, and a man lying stark on the blood-stained grass, his dead face upturned to the sky. As in a vivid picture before him he saw it all. And then there would be a wedding in Italy a few weeks later, and the topaz eyes would smile for life on the Neapolitan prince. For the dead man—well, for him, in the creed of the man himself, the best of all things —annihilation !

He walked home very slowly, smoking and half dreamily, thinking all this. He must keep the matter from his womankind, and he must find a friend. There was Boville —yes, Boville would do—he would see him the first thing to-morrow, and refer Di Venturini's second to him. Under ordinary circumstances, Terry Dennison would have been his man, but under present circumstances Dennison was not to be thought of. For a second quarrel had taken place between the two men—a quarrel bitter and deep ;

and for the same cause—Dynely's neglect of his wife. It had occurred three days after the sudden and somewhat surprising departure of Gordon Caryll. Eric still held fast, body and soul, by Felicia, Crystal still drooping with that pathetic, heart-broken face. By command of Lady Dynely, *mère*, Terry had taken Crystal for a drive in the Bois, and there, face to face, in the yellow afternoon sunshine, they had come upon the glittering little equipage of Felicia the dancer. Lying back in her silks and sables and seal skins, her "flower face" smiling behind a little lace veil, her English cavalier, Lord Dynely, beside her, so Lord Dynely's wife had come upon them full. For a second, four pairs of eyes met—then the bright carriage of the danseuse flashed past, and Felicia's derisive laugh came back to them on the breeze.

"Mon Dieu! Eric, a pleasant rencontre for you?" she cried, unaffectedly amused by the situation. "What is the matter with Mr. Dennison? He gave me a look absolutely murderous as we passed."

Crystal had fallen back with a gasping cry as though a brutal hand had struck her.

"Oh, Terry! take me home," she had sobbed, as once before, and Terry, in silence, with flashing eyes and lowering brows and compressed lips, had obeyed.

Four hours later and there was a "scene" in the salon of the Dynelys. Crystal, sick heart and soul, was alone in her room; Eric, waiting for dinner, was reading the evening paper, when Dennison strode in and confronted him.

"Dynely!" he passionately demanded, "how is this to end?"

Lord Dynely looked up, the conscious blood reddening his transparent, girl-like face.

"How is what to end? May I request you to take a somewhat less aggressive tone in addressing me, Mr. Dennison?"

"Your neglect—your shameful neglect of your wife. It is brutal, it is murderous—you are killing her by inches, before our eyes!"

The flush faded from the blonde face of Viscount Dynely.

The livid whiteness of deadly anger took its place. He laid down his paper and spoke with ominous calm.

"May I inquire if my wife has sent you here to tell me this?"

"Your wife knows nothing of my coming—that you know as well as I. But I swear, Eric, this must end! You are breaking, brutally breaking your wife's heart. All Paris is talking, is laughing over your besotted infatuation for that old woman—Felicia the dancer! You spend your time, you lavish your gifts on that painted Jezebel, while Crystal dies day by day before your eyes. And only seven weeks since you married her!"

Eric rose to his feet—the light of deadly rage filling his eyes, but before he could speak Dennison interposed:

"Stay!" he cried, lifting his hand, "hear me out! I pledged myself once never to quarrel with you, do what you might, say what you would. That promise I mean to keep. It is the farthest possible from my wish—the thought of quarrelling with you. But, Eric, I say again this must end."

"Indeed! You speak of my very pleasant platonic friendship with the most charming woman in Paris, I presume. May I ask *how* you propose to end it?"

"For Heaven's sake, Eric, don't sneer! I speak to you as a friend, as a brother. You cannot be quite heartless —you cannot have quite outlived your love for Crystal. Don't you see you are killing her—poor, little soul, don't you see she worships the ground you walk on, the least thing your hand has touched. She would die for you, Eric; and you—you neglect her more shamefully than ever bride was neglected before ; you insult her by your devotion to this worthless woman. If you had seen her after you had passed to-day——" he stops suddenly and walks away to a window. "Don't let us row, Eric," he says hoarsely; I have no wish to interfere with or dictate to you, but in some way I stand pledged to Crystal since her happiness is at stake. Our friendship of the past has given me the right to be her protector at least."

"The right of a jilted lover!" Eric returns, that bitter sneer still on lips and eyes. "Let us understand each other,

Dennison. This is the second time you have interfered in this matter. I warn you now, let it be the last. I have listened to your insolence, because I wish to drag my wife's name into no public scandal, or quarrel with you. It is the last time I will be so forbearing. Be kind enough to quit these rooms at once, and enter them no more! Be kind enough, also, to discontinue your acquaintance with Lady Dynely. If I were inclined to take umbrage easily, I might with reason object to you, her jilted lover, as I said before, playing the rôle of attendant cavalier, but I let that pass— this once. I shall order my wife to receive your visits no longer, and I think she will hardly venture to disobey. After to-day, Mr. Dennison, you will understand our acquaintance is at an end."

And then, before Terry could speak, his lordship had quitted the salon, and nothing was left but to obey. And the only result of his interference was frigid coldness on the part of Lord Dynely to his wife, and increased devotion, if that were possible, to Felicia. They had met more than once since, and Dynely had cut him dead. So matters between those two, who had grown up as brothers, stood to-night. Verily, a woman is at the bottom of all the ruptured masculine friendships of this lower world!

The early dawn was breaking before Lord Dynely reached his hotel. Crystal, pale as a shadow, wasted and wan, lay asleep. A pang of something like actual remorse shot through him as he looked at her, so changed in those few brief weeks.

"Poor little soul!" he thought, "if—if the worst does happen to-morrow, it will be hard lines on her."

Of no use going to bed, he thought; he could not sleep. He threw himself on a sofa in the dressing-room adjoining, still in his evening suit, and in ten minutes was fast as a church.

The breakfast hour was past when he awoke, and Crystal was seated beside him, watching him with eyes of unutterable pathetic yearning. She started up confusedly, as he opened his eyes, coloring, as though caught in some guilty act.

"Waiting for me, Crystal?" he said, rising on his elbow,

with a yawn. "You were asleep when I came home, and I would not disturb you. What is the hour? Ten, by Jove! Is breakfast ready? I have an engagement this morning, and must get off at once."

Breakfast dispatched hurriedly, his dress changed, a note sent in hot haste to Boville, Lord Dynely was waited upon by a tall, fiercely-mustached, soldierly Frenchman. The interview was brief, and strictly private. Boville sauntering lazily in, encountered monsieur swaggering out.

"Who's your military friend, Dynely?" he inquired, "and what the deuce do you want of a man in such a hurry as this?"

"My military friend is Monsieur Raoul De Concressault, Captain of Zouaves; his business here, to bring me a challenge from Prince Di Venturini; and I have sent for you in such a hurry to be my second in the affair. Take a seat, Boville, and a cigar."

"By Jove!" cried Boville, taking the seat, but not the cigar. "I thought it would come to this. Of course Felicia is at the bottom of it?"

"Of course—is not her charming sex at the bottom of all the mischief and murder on earth? Also, of course everything is strictly *sub rosa*—it won't do to let it get wind."

"Certainly not," Boville answered gravely. "Tell us about it, Dynely. I thought M. le Prince was safely away for another week."

"So did I—so did Felicia," Dynely said, with a slight laugh. "He turned up in most dramatic fashion at the *bal masque* at the Gymnase last night, however."

And thereupon his lordship briefly, and not without humor, sketched the rencontre at the *bal d'opera*.

"And the result is to be a duel?" said Boville, still very gravely. "Dynely, are you aware Di Venturini is the best swordsman, the deadest shot, in Europe?"

"To be sure, *mon ami*. All that is a matter of history. Light up, old fellow; I can recommend these Manillas."

"And you?" Boville inquired, obeying.

"I? Oh! well, I know next to nothing of fencing, and never fired a pistol half a dozen times in my life."

"But—good Heaven! Dynely, you have no chance at all then, if the prince means mischief! And he mostly *does*, I can tell you, when he fights. Don't you know he has killed three men already?"

Lord Dynely shrugged his shoulders.

"I can't show the white feather on that account. I've got into this scrape, and I must take the consequences. I've referred De Concressault to you. You'll act for me, old fellow, I know?"

"I shall be helping to murder you," Boville answered, with a groan. "Is there no way, Dynely, by which——"

"There is no way by which this matter can be settled, except by a meeting," Dynely answered, impatiently. Di Venturini came to the ball for no other purpose than to insult me. He did it, and I knocked him down twice. You must perceive there can be but one ending to such a thing as that."

"Devil take Felicia!" growled his friend. "I wish you had never seen the sorceress. She is fatal to all men. She reminds one of those fabled What's-their-names, mermaids —sirens—Lurline—who lure poor devils with their smiles and songs, and then eat them up, and crunch their bones. It's a deuce of an affair, and I never served a friend so unwillingly before in my life. By the way, was the prince masked? How did you know him?"

"He tore off his mask in a fine frenzy after the second knock down. *I* never saw him before in my life. And now I come to think of it, he didn't see *me* at all. I kept my mask on through the whole fracas—never thought of it once. By Jove!" Eric cried, laughing, "the idea of going out with a man he never saw!"

"It's no laughing matter, let me tell you," Boville growled again; "it's an infernal business, and I wish you had chosen any one else to act for you in the matter. However, if you insist that it is inevitable——"

"It is most decidedly and emphatically inevitable; so be off and arrange for to-morrow morning, there's a good fellow. I've an engagement that I would not be late for for worlds."

"And pistols or swords——"

" Are equal to me. Of the two I prefer pistols, as quickest and most decisive. You understand. I have no doubt the result would be the same with either weapon, for I think his excellency means mischief, as you say, only pistols conclude things with dispatch."

The two men shook hands and separated. Boville, reluctantly, to settle preliminaries with De Concressault, and Lord Dynely to keep his last appointment with Madame Felicia down the Seine, to Asnières.

CHAPTER XIV.

CHEZ MADAME.

ALF AN HOUR later Madame Felicia and Lord Dynely had fairly started upon their excursion— their last, they both knew, and the knowledge gave the forbidden fruit fresh zest, even to their jaded palates. You *must* feel an interest in a handsome and devoted young cavalier, lying in the sunshine at your feet, who, this time to-morrow, for your sake, may be lying with a bullet through his heart. As well as Lord Dynely himself, Felicia knew what would inevitably take place in the light of to-morrow's dawn, and, though his youthful and impassioned lordship was beginning seriously to bore her, she had never before been one-half so sweet, so witching, as to-day.

Half an hour after their departure, there rattled up to madame's door a fiacre, from which alighted M. le Prince. That she would be awaiting his coming, with more or less of impatience and anxiety, he did not doubt. He absolutely stood dumb, when the tall chasseur, indorsed by Mam'selle Pauline, announced madame's departure, and with whom.

"Gone for the day to Asnières, and with Lord Dynely!" he repeated, staring at them blankly. The extent of the defiant audacity absolutely took his breath away.

"But, yes, M. le Prince," Pauline answered, with a shrug, "not to return until barely time to dress for the theatre."

"And she left no note, no message of any kind for me?"

"None, M. le Prince."

"How did they seem, Pauline? in good spirits, or——"

"In the very highest spirits, M. le Prince. She dressed with much more than usual care, and so, evidently, had milor. I heard her tell him, as they went away, laughing together, that he was looking handsome as an archangel and elegant as a secretary of legation, and that she looked forward to the pleasantest day of her life."

He set his teeth with a snap, his eyes aflame.

" And he—what said monsieur ? "

" That all days must be the pleasantest of *his* life spent in her company. Then they drove off side by side."

The yellow complexion of the prince had turned dirty white, with jealous rage. If one chance of life had remained to his rival, he lost it in that moment ; if one chance of setting herself right had remained to the woman who slighted him, she lost it in that hour.

" And, mademoiselle ? " he asked, " the little captive— what of her ? "

" Is still captive, monseigneur. She is to be removed tonight, after midnight, safely out of Paris, for the present. Madame holds a little reception after the play to-night. When it is over, Paujol and Mam'selle Donny quietly leave Paris ? "

" Ah ! Madame holds a reception, does she ? " the Prince said, grimly. " Very well, Pauline, I will trouble you no further. I will do myself the honor of being present at madame's little reception after the play. Who knows when she may hold another ? "

He laughed inwardly—a laugh that might have warned madame had she heard it. But, drifting down the sunny Seine to the music of the band of the National Guard, madame heard nothing except the full-blown flatteries of her English knight.

It was a charming day—all that there was of the most delightful. With the abandon of a child, madame threw herself into the pleasure of the moment, and lived, while she lived, each hour to the utmost. " Eat, drink, and be merry, for to-morrow you die," was the key-note of her life. There was nothing new, and nothing true, but the sun shone with summer warmth, and the band played sweetest music, the champagne and truffles were of the best, and her companion was the handsomest man in Paris. To-morrow the Prince Di Venturini would shoot him or run him through—it was

18

well ; there were other adorers left ; but the knowledge added spice to the wine of life to-day.

"Thou art absent, Eric, mon ami!" she murmured, tenderly. " Of what art thou thinking, then ? Tired already of our *fête* day—which I am enjoying like a child, since I am with thee ? "

He awoke with a start.

In very truth, as they wandered here arm in arm, his thoughts, marvellous to relate, had strayed backward to—his wife ! How madame would have laughed had she known it. Poor little soul—poor little Crystal ! When the end came to-morrow, would not the shot that finished him kill her also ? One creature at least of all the women who had smiled upon him for his azure eyes, and golden hair, and Greek face, had loved him. Well, in this world, where there is so much of empty glitter, so little real gold, even that was something.

The brief, bright February day wore on, grew gray and overcast. Madame shivered in her wraps, and turned fretful and cold. They hurried back to the steamer and re-embarked for Paris.

"We will have a storm to-morrow—dost thou not think so, Eric ? " madame asked, wrapping her rose-lined seal-skins closer about her, and looking up at the gray, fast-drifting sky.

He followed her glance, dreamily. To-morrow ! Where, this time to-morrow, would he be ? In this world or the next ?—if there be a next—he thought.

"Still dreaming, mon cher ? " Felicia said, with an impatient shrug. " I begin to think you have not enjoyed our excursion after all."

He answered her, as he knew she expected to be answered, in words of empty compliment, but still with that absent, dreaming face. His wife haunted him like a ghost, to-day. Poor little Crystal !

Yes, Dennison was right—he had been a brute to her. Only seven weeks a bride, and to-morrow a widow ! Ah, yes ; it was hard on her !

"Shall we see you at my rooms to-night ? " Felicia asked again.

"Yes—that is, no, I think not. I have an engagement for to-night that will prevent my having that pleasure."

She shrugged her shoulders. They stood together in the chilly twilight at madame's door.

"Then this is really good-night?"

"This is really good-night."

She gave him her hand, in its perfectly fitting gray glove, and looked at him in silence for a moment. There was a half smile on her lips—so, without a word, black eyes and blue met, in one long, farewell glance.

"*Ma foi!* It is a thousand pities to kill anything half so handsome!" madame was thinking. "Well—he has helped to amuse me for four weeks. What more can one ask?"

"Does she know?" Eric was musing, "but of course she does. Also, of course," rather bitterly this, "she does not care. It is only one more lover, growing wearisome, and safely out of the way."

"Good-night, then, mon ami," madame said, softly, "and au revoir!"

"Good-night, Felicia," he answered, "until we meet again!"

And then he was gone, a smile on his blonde face, and those two had looked at each other for the last time on earth.

Four hours later, and the glittering rooms of Madame Felicia were filled with a very brilliant throng. The best men in Paris, the handsomest and wittiest women met there. And there, when the reception was at its highest, the conversation at its gayest, the music and laughter at their liveliest, came M. le Prince Di Venturini.

Not unexpected. "Who has been here, Pauline?" madame had demanded, when under the hands of her maid, at the dressing-room of the Varieties; and the answer had been prompt, "M. le Prince, madame."

"Ah! and you told him—"

"That you had gone to Asnières for the day, with milor, madame."

Madame laughed.

"How truthful you grow, petite. And M. le Prince—what said he?'

"Nothing, madame ; but that he would see you later at the reception."

So madame knew he was coming, and was prepared for all chances. War or peace—she was equal to either fate, only a trifle curious. Others were curious, too ; that little con-tretemps at the bal d'opera, quiet as it had been kept, was known, and people shrewdly suspected that Di Venturini, noted duelist and fire-eater, would not let the matter drop there. How would he meet madame ?

He made his way slowly through the rooms, and met her with suave and polished courtesy, told her of his journey, of his health, hoped she had amused herself well in his absence, lingered half an hour among the guests, and then, with an elaborate apology for his early departure, went away.

By one o'clock the rooms were empty, the lights out. Madame valued her good looks and lustrous eyes too highly to keep very late hours. Paujol had quitted his post, Pauline had disrobed her mistress of silks and laces, and substituted a dressing-gown. In her room Felicia sat, smoking two or three nerve-soothing cigarettes before going to bed. In the boudoir without Pauline sat, waiting, half-asleep, with her mistress' night draught of spiced wine and eggs on the table before her. Madame often sat dozing and dreaming over her cigarettes for an hour at a time, while the girl waited. So to-night she lay luxuriously back in her chair, her eyes closed, the rose-scented smoke curling upward, when a man made his way noiselessly into the boudoir from the street. He glanced at the sleeping Pauline, at the waiting night draught, and passed on into the dressing-room, into the bed-room, and so came, still noiselessly, upon madame.

He stood for a moment looking down upon her. She had not heard him, but some baleful, mesmeric influence warned her he was there. She sat up suddenly, opened her eyes, and looked full into the yellow face of Prince Di Ventu-rini.

For a second there was silence. She was a plucky little woman, without a nerve about her, and uttered no word or sound. She looked at him straight, silent, then : "Monsieur the prince."

" At your service, madame. I trust I have not too greatly disturbed you ? "

A mocking smile was on his lips. She looked at him disdainfully.

" You have not disturbed me at all. For a moment, I confess, I took you for a burglar, but my nerves are good. What was Paujol about that you entered unannounced ? "

" Paujol was asleep in his loge."

" And, Pauline ? "

" Pauline is asleep also in your boudoir. It is past two, madame."

" And a very late hour for M. Di Venturini's visit. Could it not have been deferred until to-morrow, I wonder ? "

" It could not, madame. By to-morrow I shall be across the frontier, and very far from Paris."

" Ah, I understand ! " she looked at him unflinchingly. " You mean to kill Lord Dynely ? "

" I mean to kill Lord Dynely. Such an insult as he offered me can only be wiped out in blood. I regret that madame must lose her lover, but—"

" Pray, no apologies, M. le Prince ! " madame answered, with perfect sang-froid ; " he was beginning to bore me. Grand passions are always in bad form, and poor boy, he was ludicrously in earnest. Well, monsieur, as you depart to-morrow, I suppose I must give you an audience, even at this improper hour, and in this apartment, or—shall we adjourn to the boudoir ? "

He laughed derisively.

" It shocks madame's delicacy then, that I have intruded here. A thousand pardons, *ma belle*. Where, may I ask, when he paid his last visit, did you receive the painter, M. Gordon Caryll ? "

She never flinched. He knew that then.

" He was your husband, was he not ? And one does not stand on ceremony with one's husband. You see, madame, I know all ! "

She smiled—a smile that fanned his jealous anger into fury.

" And madame's daughter, that she keeps caged up like a

wild animal—what of her ?   You see I know that also.   And
all the lies madame has been telling me from the first—what
of them ? "

" Nothing of them.   And lies is an ugly word to use to a
lady."

" Diable ! do you sit there and mock at me !   Do you sit
there and deny this ? "

" I deny nothing, monsieur.   I affirm nothing.   M. le
Prince will believe precisely what he pleases."

"And do you think—do you for a moment think, I will
marry you after all this ?   You, the cast-off wife of this man
Caryll.   You, the mother of this girl—"

" Stay ! M. le Prince," Felicia said, with one flash of her
yellow black eyes.   "You have said quite enough !   No, I
do .not think you will marry me.   I would not marry you,
with your diabolical temper and jealousy, if you were king of
Italy, much less owner of a beggarly principality.   I don't
really think I ever meant to marry you at all—you are
much too old, and, if you will pardon me, too ugly.   I adore
handsome men—Gordon Caryll and Lord Dynely are that, at
least.   And De Vocqsal—you remember the Austrian marquis, I think, prince?   Yes—well, De Vocqsal is coming to
Paris next week, and is more urgent than ever that I shall
become Madame la Marquise.   He is young, he is handsome,
he has fourteen quarterings, and a rent-roll that is fabulous.
He never calls me ugly names, and is much too gallant a gentleman to intrude into a lady's chamber at two in the morning on purpose to insult her.   Here is your ring, prince ; it
never fitted from the first, and I am glad to be rid of it.   It
is the only present you ever gave me, so I have, happily,
nothing to return.   Now let me say good-night and *bon voyage*, for I am really very sleepy."

She yawned aloud, as she removed the heavy diamond
from her finger and held it out to him.

" Good-night, prince ; and a pleasant trip to you both—he,
pauvre enfant, to the next world, and you—to Italy, is it ?
Take your ring, monsieur, and go."

He took it, and stood looking at her, his face cadaverous,

his eyes like coals. "You tell me this? You mean to marry De Vocqsal?"

"I am growing tired of the stage. Even *that* palls. Yes; I shall marry De Vocqsal, prince, and become a fine lady."

"'This is the end, then?"

"Oh, mon Dieu! yes, if you ever mean to go. How can there be an end while you loiter here? Go! go! I insist."

He laughed.

"I go, madame; pray do not say it again. Thanks for your good wishes. Accept my congratulations beforehand. It is a brilliant destiny to be Madame la Marquise de Vocqsal. Good-night, and adieu."

He bowed low, and was gone—through the dressing-room, and into the sitting-room beyond. Here, Pauline, still guarding the wine, and fast asleep now, sat in the dim light. He went to the table, something between his fingers, a shining globule, and dropped it into the glass. The bell rang sharply at the moment. Pauline started up, with a cry, and Di Venturini vanished through the outer door.

"Madame never misses her night draught, so Pauline tells me," he said to himself, with a sardonic smile, as he leaped into his waiting cab; "she will not miss it to-night; and once drank, there is a longer journey before her than a bridal trip to the imperial court of Francis Joseph. So good-night to *you*, madame, and bon voyage!"

ROM the window of her room, Crystal, Lady Dynely, watched the twilight of that overcast February day close down. She lay on a broad, low sofa, half buried in cushions, her small face gleaming out like marble against their rose tints, the large blue eyes, so brilliant with happy love-light a few brief weeks ago, dim with watching and much weeping now.

Outside the wind was rising. The trees rocked in the gale, the darkness deepened, the first heavy rain-drops began pattering against the glass. Inside the gloom deepened also, until the little, pale face was barely visible. All day long she had been alone, sick in body, sick in soul, crushed of heart. Now she was straining her ears, for the first sound of that familiar step on the stairs, for the first note of that gay whistle, with which he was wont to herald his coming. To her this twilight hour was *the* hour of the twenty-four, for it almost invariably brought Eric, to dress or dine.

Her maid entered to light the lamps, but the soft little voice sent her away. "Not yet," she said, gently. "I like the dusk. Has—has my lord come home?"

"No, my lord has not come home," the Frenchwoman answered, with a compassionate glance at the drooping figure. Alas! was not my lord's defection as well known in the servants' hall as in salon or chamber?

Where was he to-day?—the child wondered. Where was he now? Was he with *her?*—that wicked, beautiful, brown woman? Oh! to be able to win him back, her very own, her husband, and hold him from them all! Was God punishing her for loving too greatly, for worshipping the creature instead of the Creator? She did not know—it might be wicked—this unreasoning worship of hers ; but wicked or worthy, it would last until her life's end. She could see her face now as she lay—the room was lined with mirrors. What a pitiful, pale face it was ! And he liked rosy bloom, peachy, plentiful flesh and blood. The dancing woman had these—*she* had nothing left but the moonlight shadow of her pearl face, and her true and tender heart. Good and pleasant things, but not likely long to hold a sensuous, changeful, beauty-worshipping, thoroughly selfish man. Dimly she knew this, and with a half sob, buried that poor, wasted face in her hands. He had fancied her from the first, only for her pretty, flower-like looks ; let her lose these charms, as she was losing fast, and her last hold on her husband's heart was gone.

She lay thinking this—thinking so intently, that she did not hear the door pushed gently open, and a tall figure come in. It came softly over, and knelt on one knee beside her, and so, in the dusk of the room, looked down upon the colorless, wasted face, the locked hands, from which the wedding ring hung loose. Suddenly her eyes opened.

" It is I, Crissy," he said.

The bewildered look changed to one of electric surprise and joy. She flung her arms around his neck, and held him as though she would never let him go.

" Poor little soul ! " he said, more moved than he cared to show. " You have been alone all day, and have got the horrors. Were there none of them here—my mother—France—all day ? "

" Yes, both. Your mother stayed an hour, and then went to make some calls with Terry. France stayed and read to me all the morning. She is so good—my own dear France. They are all good, but—but," the clinging arms close together, he can feel her passionate heart beat : " Oh, my love ! I only want you.

" Poor little Chris ! "

It is all he can say. He lays his face beside hers for a moment, and is still. He is thinking of this time to-morrow —he knows as surely as that he rests here, that the bullet that kills him will end her life. And it is for that dark

18*

daughter of Herodias, he has forsaken her. All at once a loathing of Felicia, of himself, comes upon him. What a black and brutal wretch he is! how utterly unworthy of this spotless wife, whose heart he is breaking. If the past could but come over again! if what is done could be undone, how differently he would act, how happy he would make her. But it is too late for all that—the end has come.

"Crystal," he says gently, "I've not been a very good sort of husband, I'm afraid—I never was a very good sort of fellow at any time. I've done enough to forfeit all right to your love, but—you care for me still?"

"Care for you!" she whispered. And then the clinging grasp tightens, and she can say no more.

"Yes, I know you do," he says, with a stifled sigh; "it's awfully good of you, Chris, for I *have* been a brute, that's the truth. And look here, I don't mean this really, you know, but if anything happened; if"—with a slight laugh—"I chanced to die, for instance—"

But she interrupts him with a shrill cry, like a child that has been struck.

"Eric!"

"Foolish child! Do I look like dying? It is only a suppositious case—let me put it. If I chanced to die, say to-morrow, you would forgive me all my wrongdoing, my neglect? You would not have one hard thought of me, would you?"

She half raises herself, and tries to look at him. But, still laughing, he holds her so that she cannot see his face. "Answer, sweetheart—would you?"

"I never had one hard thought of you in all my life, Eric, never, so I could have nothing to forgive. If you died"—she catches her breath with a sort of gasp as she says it—"do you think I could live? Oh, love, that is all past. I can never have any life now apart from you!'

"You think so," he says, uneasily; "but you are young, and—you only think so."

"I know so," she answers, under her breath; and instinctively he knows it too.

"Well," he says, at length, after a long pause, "regrets

are useless, but I wish with all my soul the past three weeks could come over again. I ought to have made you happy, little wife, and I have not. If—if the time is given me, I swear I will. Now, let me go; I have letters to write, and much to do this evening."

"You"—she pauses, and looks at him with oh, such wistful, longing eyes—"you are going out, as usual, Eric?"

"No," he says, smiling down upon her. "I am going to remain in, as *un*-usual, Crystal. Lie here until dinner is announced; I will write my letters in your boudoir. You know I must always be alone when my epistolatory attacks come on."

He unlooses the clasping arms and goes. And Crystal nestles down among her pillows, and shuts her eyes to keep back the joyful tears that come to women alike in bliss and in pain. Just now her bliss is so great, that it is almost pain; she cannot, cannot realize it.

He passes through the dressing-room, into the pretty, mirror-lined, satin-hung nest beyond, that is Crystal's sitting-room, leaving both doors ajar. He lights the lamps himself, draws pens, ink, and paper before him, and sits down to write. He must leave a few parting lines with Boville for his mother and Crystal in case of the worst. He wishes he had made a will to-day instead of going to Asnières, but it is too late for that. The title and estate go to a distant cousin of his father's, unless—yes, there is one unless. It is something Crystal has never spoken of—he thinks himself it is unlikely.

"By Jove!" he says, under his breath. "I hope so, for her sake, poor little soul. It will console her; and dead or alive, a fellow likes to perpetuate the title."

He begins his mother's letter first. It will be the easier. He writes, "Hotel du Louvre, February 26, 18—. My dear mother," and there he stops, and gnaws the gold handle of his pen, and pulls his amber mustache, and stares at the blank sheet with troubled blue eyes. What *shall* he say? It will almost go as hard with her as with Crystal. Abso-·utely these preliminaries are worse than the thing itself.

The minutes tick off—still he sits and stares at the white

paper. What shall he say—how shall he word it? Some fellows have a knack of writing things—he has none—never had. Beauty and brains don't, as a rule, travel in company. Eric, Lord Dynely, never felt the want of the latter—that refuge of the destitute, before. By Jove! What shall he say to her? Then, as he plunges the pen in desperation down in the ink, determined to say *something* or perish, the door is burst suddenly open, and Terry Dennison comes impetuously in. Terry Dennison, flushed of face, excited of eye, and strides up to him at once.

"Eric, what is this? Is it true?"

Eric lays down his pen, and flushes also with haughty amaze and anger.

"Dennison! again! and after what passed between us the other day."

"Do you think I would let that stop me now?" Dennison bursts forth, excitedly. "Do you think I would heed anything you may have said at such a time as this? Is it true?"

"Is what true?" still in haughty anger.

"Your duel with Di Venturini. I met De Concressault out yonder, and he dropped a hint, but would not speak plainly. I know that Di Venturini is back, I heard of your rencontre at the bal masque, and I feared something of this. But I did not think you would be so mad—yes, so mad, Dynely, as to accept his challenge. Tell me, is it true?"

"It is quite true. May I inquire in what way it concerns Mr. Dennison?"

"In what way! Great Heaven! he can talk to me like this. In what way—his murder—for it is nothing less. Eric, I say, this must not go on."

"Indeed!"—with a sneer. "How do you propose to prevent it?"

"I will give information to the police. I will—I swear! If I can stop it in no other way, the gens-d'armes shall be on the ground before you. Eric, you shall not fight Di Venturini!"

Eric arose to his feet, that lurid light of anger the other knew so well, in his eyes.

"You dare to stand there and tell me this! Meddler! Fool! If you are a coward yourself, do you think to make me one? Begone! and interfere, tell the police, at your peril. By George, if you do, when the prince and I have met elsewhere, whichever of us survives shall shoot *you!*"

There was a moment's silence—Eric livid with passion, Terry's eyes aflame, his breath coming quick and hard—then:

"You mean to tell me, Dynely, that if I prevent your meeting to-morrow you will meet Di Venturini elsewhere?"

"So surely as we both live I shall meet Di Venturini when and where he pleases."

"But, Heavens and earth, Eric, don't you know he means to kill you? Don't you know he is a dead shot, and that you don't stand a chance. No, by Jove! not the shadow of a chance. A duel! why this will not be a duel, it will be a cold-blooded murder."

"Call it by what name you please, only be kind enough to go."

"Eric, you shall not—you *shall* not meet the prince. He means to take your life; you haven't a shadow of a chance, I repeat. Oh! dear old fellow, stop and think. I don't mind what you say to me—I don't mean to be meddlesome—I don't mean to quarrel with you. Dear old boy, stop and think. It is not you alone Di Venturini will kill—it is your mother—it is your wife."

"This is all nonsense!" Eric cried, angrily and impatiently—"a waste of time. I have letters to write, and I want to get to bed early to-night. If you talked until the crack of doom you couldn't alter things one iota. Let it kill whom it may, I can't and won't show the white feather. Di Venturini has challenged me, and I am to meet him at day-dawn to-morrow—that is as fixed as fate. He means to shoot me, I haven't the slightest doubt; but that has nothing to do with it. The Dynelys have never been noted for rigid virtue of any sort, or an overstock of brains; but at least none that I ever heard of were cowards. I won't be the first to disgrace the name. Have we palavered enough over this, or has more to be said? I warn you, I won't listen. If you will not leave me, then I shall leave you."

He gathered up his papers angrily to go. Dennison advanced and laid his hand on his shoulder.

"Eric! if you have no mercy on yourself, have mercy on your wife and mother. It will kill them—that you know as well as I. Let me meet this Italian cutthroat in your place. I'm a better shot than you, and he'll never know the—"

"You're a fool, Terry!" Eric cried, throwing off the hand. "You talk like a puling baby. Let *you* meet Di Venturini in my place, and I sneak at home like a whipped school-boy, behind the petticoats of my wife and mother! For Heaven's sake get out, and stop talking such infernal rot!"

Terry drew back, and folded his arms.

"It is inevitable then, Dynely? You mean to meet the prince?"

"It is inevitable, Dennison. If your head had not been made of wood, you might have known that from the first. I shall meet Di Venturini as surely as the sun will shine in the sky to-morrow."

A sort of smile crossed Dennison's face at the simile. The rain was pelting against the windows hard.

"The sun will *not* shine in the sky to-morrow," he said, under his breath. Then aloud: "And you are quite sure, old boy, that you know the prince means to kill you?"

"I am quite sure he means to try," Eric answered, coolly; "I am not at all so sure that he will succeed. Now, then, Terry, I'll forgive you everything—everything on my word, if you'll only take yourself off at once, and stop being a confounded bore! When a man expects to be shot at break of day, he naturally has no end to do the night be—"

He never finished the sentence. With a face of white horror, Dennison was pointing to the door of the dressing-room. Eric whirled round, and a cry broke from his lips. There, in her wrapper, her face likes now, her eyes all wild and wide, her lips apart, his wife stood. She had heard every word.

"Great Heaven! Crystal!" Eric cried.

He sprang toward her. She was swaying like a reed in the wind, but at the sound of his voice the blind, bewildered eyes turn toward him, the arms instinctively outstretched. It was the doing of a second—before he could reach her, she had fallen heavily forward on her face, a stream of bright red blood flowing from her lips.

The two men stood petrified, horror-stricken. It was all so sudden that for an instant it stunned them. Then Eric awoke. With a horrible oath he sprang forward, seized Dennison by the throat, and struck him with all his might across the face.

" It is all your doing, you fool ! You meddlesome, thick-witted fool ! If you have killed her, by —— I'll have your life ! "

He flung him from him like a madman. By laying hold of the wall Dennison alone saved himself from falling. The onslaught had been so swift, so unexpected, that he had had no chance to defend himself at all.

Now he was forced to stand for an instant to regain his breath. The flush had faded from his face, leaving it ghastly, only where the red, cruel mark of the brutal blow lay. Then he plunged blindly after his assailant, but in that instant Eric had stooped, raised his wife in his arms, and passed with her into the inner room.

Dennison drew back, laid his arm against the wall, and his face upon it. So he stood for a moment—a moment that was an age of agony. Then he turned, and silently and swiftly went out into the melancholy, rain-beaten night.

STRAIGHT to the Faubourg St. Honore, straight to the rooms of Lady Dynely, Terry went. Crystal might be dying—was, no doubt, and he would be before any of Eric's messengers to break the news to Eric's mother. His teeth were set, his fists unconsciously clenched, his blue eyes aflame. The blow, that for a mo ment had blinded him, burned on his face still, like a brand of fire—the savage that is latent in all men, in far better and deeper-cultured men than this big dragoon, was uppermost now. Eric had struck him, basely and dastardly struck him. If by lifting his finger, he could have saved Eric's life, in this first blind fury he would not have lifted it.

He strode into her private sitting-room, and inquired for Lady Dynely. Yes, my lady was at home, had but just come, was on the verge of again going out, but was at home. She would be with Mr. Dennison directly.

She was with him as the servant said it. She came rustling in, her pale, flowing silks sweeping behind her, a cloak of velvet and fur falling off her shoulders. Her dainty Parisian bonnet was on her head, a flurried, wild look on her ever pale face, an excited sparkle in her light blue eyes. As she entered, Dennison thought, with a thrill of recollection, of the very first time he had seen her as she entered the Irish cabin in the wet twilight, to change all his life for evermore. Had she changed it for the better? If she had left him to grow up ignorant, and poor, and unlettered, among his mother's people, there in the wild Claddagh of Galway, might he not have been a happier man to-night?

"Terry," she cried, coming excitedly forward, both hands outstretched, "what is this I hear? I was just starting for the Louvre as you were announced. Half an hour ago I was at Lady Clarendon's reception, and there the rumor reached me of this horrible affair. Oh, Terry! speak and tell me, it is *only* a rumor, that he will not be so mad, so wicked, so utterly reckless, as to risk his life."

So! that was told! He drew in his breath hard. All must come out now.

" Of what do you speak, Lady Dynely ? "

" Do you not know ? Oh, then it must be false. If it were true you would be the very first Eric would tell. Wretched boy! he is always worrying me to death of late—yes, ever since his return last August. And now his neglect of his wife, poor little creature, and his running after this horrible dancer. Oh ! what a trouble sons are to mothers. Terry, I heard a shocking story whispered about at Lady Clarendon's. Captain de Concressault dropped in there for ten minutes, and it seems he set the ball going. But, it cannot be true."

" Captain de Concressault is a good one to keep a secret," thought Terry, grimly.

" What was it De Concressault said ? " inquired he, aloud.

" Oh ! a most scandalous thing. It would break my heart if I thought it true. That Eric went to a masked ball, at one of those places here, with that woman, Felicia ; that there he met Prince Di Venturini, who had followed to watch them, that a dreadful quarrel ensued, and that Eric knocked the prince down again and again. Every one was horrified —naturally. And I left immediately and came here, to change my dress and go direct to the Louvre. Terry, you are silent ; you look—oh ! good Heaven ! Terry, don't tell me it is true ! "

But Dennison stood silent, his head bent down, his eyes averted, his hat, which he had not yet removed, shading his bruised and discolored face.

' Terry, I command you ! Speak and tell me—is this story true ? "

" Lady Dynely—I am afraid it is."

She laid her hand over her heart, turning ghastly pale.

" And Eric went there with that woman, his wife ailing at

home—went to that wicked dancing-place, and insulted Prince Di Venturini ?"

"My lady—yes."

He spoke reluctantly, each admission dragged from him. Falsehoods came never readily to Dennison, and then, of what use were falsehoods here ?   She *must* know.

" He insulted Di Venturini, a man who fights duels upon the smallest provocation—who will take no insults from any one.   Terry, tell me—tell me the truth, I command !   Has Di Venturini challenged Eric ? "

"Lady Dynely, I am sorry, sorry to have to say once more—yes."

Her blue eyes dilated, the last trace of color faded from her face.

"And Eric ?" she said, in a sort of whisper.   "Eric has——"

"Accepted.   There was no alternative.   I am very sorry," Dennison said again.

She sat down suddenly on a sofa near, so ghastly that he drew close in alarm.

"Lady Dynely, good Heaven ! you are going to faint. Shall I——"

She motioned him to be still, the sick, giddy faintness that was like death, holding her speechless.

"Wait," she said, with a gasp.   "I—I won't faint.   Oh, Terry !   What is this ?   Oh, my Eric ! my son, my son."

She buried her face in her hands and was still, whether crying or praying Terry could not tell.   He stood uneasily looking at her, feeling horribly uncomfortable, not knowing in the least what to do or say.

She looked up after a moment.   Her eyes were red and inflamed, but she was not crying.

"When do they meet ?   The truth, I insist."

" To-morrow morning at daybreak," he answered, almost under his breath.

"And they fight with pistols?" she shuddered, convulsively, from head to foot, as she said it.

"With pistols."

"And Di Venturini will kill him !" she cried out, rising

up. " Oh, I see it all ! I see it all ! They will meet there in some lonely place at day-dawn, and my boy, my darling, my Eric, will be foully murdered. Oh, Heaven, have mercy on me and on him ! "

She flung herself once more upon the sofa, her whole body convulsively quivering.

" He will kill him ! he will kill him. This time to-morrow my darling will be dead ! Oh, I cannot bear it ! I *will* not bear it ! " She started up madly. " This is murder ! " she cried shrilly ; " foul, cold-blooded murder. It must be stopped."

He stood silent, thrilled to the soul by her agony. But again—what could he say, what could he do ?

" Terry ! " she cried, seizing him by the arm and shaking him in her passion, " why don't you say something ? Why don't you do something ? Why don't you tell me what to do ? Oh, you don't care ! No one cares. You stand there like a stone and tell me that to-morrow at daybreak my boy is to be murdered. I asked you to take care of him, to keep him from danger, and you promised, and this is how you keep your word. You stand here safe and well, and to-morrow—oh, my heart ! to-morrow Eric is to be shot ! Go ! " She flung him from her with passionate strength. " You are a coward and a traitor ! You swore to me, and you have broken your oath. You might have prevented this, and you have not. Terry Dennison, I hate you ! "

He put out his hand blindly, as though to ward off a blow.

" For God's sake, mother ! " he said, hoarsely.

" Don't call me mother ! " she cried, in her insane frenzy. " I wish I had never seen you. I wish I had left you there, in Galway, to live and die. Oh ! you might have saved him—you might—you might—and you would not. You come here and tell me that to-morrow you will stand by and see him shot. But you shall not ! " she shrieked. " I will go myself—now—this instant, to Eric, to Di Venturini, and on my knees I will beg for my darling's life. I know the prince—he will listen to me—to me, a most wretched

mother." Her horror, her fear, had driven her for the
moment absolutely distraught. She would have rushed from
the room but that Dennison caught her.
"Lady Dynely, you must not go. For pity's sake stay
a moment longer. Eric will never forgive you if you do this."
"He will not be alive to-morrow morning if I do not do
it ! Let me go, Terry Dennison ! You will not lift a finger
to save him—your own brother—so I must. Let me go."
But he held her fast.
"Wait a moment," he said ; and something in his tone,
in his face, even through all her madness, made her stop.
She looked at him with eyes all wild and wide with terror,
and for the first time saw the bruised and swollen disfigura-
tion of his face. She snatched off his hat and looked at
him full.
"Terry !" she exclaimed, "what is this?"
He turned crimson—a burning, shameful crimson, from
brow to chin. In those supreme moments of life, the per-
ceptive faculties are preternaturally sharpened—like a flash
the truth burst upon her.
"Terry !" she cried out in new horror, "Eric has done
this !"
He did not speak—he could not. Like inspiration, something of the real truth came to her.
"You and he have quarrelled, and he has struck you !
Terry !—you—you have not struck him back ? "
"No," he said, hoarsely and breathlessly, "I did not strike
him back. Mother, be silent ! the devil has been in me
strongly enough once to-night. Let me forget this blow if I
can."
She flung her arms around his neck, and kissed the brutal
mark of her darling's handiwork.
"Forgive him, Terry !" she said. "He is your brother—
your only brother, and he does not know what he does.
Forgive him, have pity on me. In some way you can, you
must, prevent this duel. He is all I have. I have loved
him so fondly—oh ! with more than mother's love—I have
been so proud of him, of his beauty, of his grace, of his talents. Everywhere he has gone people have loved and

admired him. He is all I have--all I ever had. My heart
is wrapped up in him. He worries me—he troubles me,
but I could not live if I lost him. Terry! Terry! pity me
—pity him. He is so young—life is so bright for him. Pity
his wife, whom you love—and in some way—oh, in *any*
way! save his life."

Her arms held him close—her pale passionate face, over
which the tears poured, was upheld to his. So in the supreme selfishness of mother love, she pleaded. In some
way she instinctively felt that her only earthly hope was in
Terry Dennison.

He stood still—a horrible struggle going on within him.
He had gone to Eric in all good faith and fellowship, ready
to take his place to-morrow before Di Venturini's pistol.
And Eric's answer had been a blow. No man had ever struck
him before—no man ever was likely to again. It burned
like a brand at this moment. And he was called upon to
forgive this—this and the hundred other insults Eric Dynely
had offered him, and at all risks save his life.

"Terry," Lady Dynely said, still holding him close, "do
you remember that afternoon last August? We were alone
together at Dynely, and I told you your story. I need never
have told you—who was there to make me? You knelt at
my feet, and I put my arms around you, and kissed you for
the first time. I loved you then—I have loved you since, but
not—oh, no! not as I loved *him*. Do you remember what I
said to you that day? Do you remember what you promised
me?"

He does not answer. She does not know what she is asking him to do. She does not know of the struggle that is
going on in the heart, beating in such hard throbs against her
own.

"I recall it all, as though it were this moment," she softly
went on. "I said to you, 'Be a friend, a brother to my
boy. He is not like you—he is reckless and extravagant,
easily led, self-willed, and wild. He will go wrong, and you
must be his protector. Let nothing he ever says, nothing
he ever does, tempt you to anger, tempt you to desert him.
Promise me that.'"

Still silent—still with that strange, rigid look on his face, that half frightens her in the midst of her supremely selfish pleadings, and which she does not understand.

"You knelt down, "she went on, "you kissed my hand; and kneeling there, alone with God and me, *this* is what you said:

"'Nothing Eric can ever say, can ever do, will tempt me to anger—that I swear. For his sake and for yours, I will do all mortal man can do. You have been the good angel of my life—I would be less than man if I ever forgot it.' You promised that, Terry—the time has come now for you to keep your word."

Still silence. Oh! if he would but speak, if that dark, strange, rigid look would but leave his face.

"My Terry! my Terry!" she whispered, "you have been brave and noble in the past. For sake of him and me, you gave up name, fortune, love—for sake of him and me, I call upon you now in *some way* to save his life."

He drew a long, hard breath, and looked down upon her. Did she know what she asked? No, he saw she did not. All the same though, so that he saved Eric, it didn't much matter.

"Terry, speak to me," she pleaded, "don't stand and look at me like this. Oh! if you ever loved me, if you ever loved Crystal, save him who is the life of our lives. Terry, I call upon you—save Eric!"

He stooped and kissed her.

"Say no more, mother. If mortal man can do it, I will save Eric."

She gave a great sob of unutterable joy and relief, laid her face on his shoulder and was still.

"You need have no fear," he went on; "Eric shall not fight Di Venturini. And now, too much time has been spent here already. You must go to the Hotel du Louvre at once. Crystal is ill."

"Ill?"

Rapidly and concisely he narrated his visit to Eric, only suppressing Eric's own insulting language—how Crystal had overheard, and the result. At any other time Lady Dynely would have been unspeakably horrified—now the greater horror had swallowed up all lesser.

"Yes, yes, I will go to her at once. Oh, poor child! Terry, will you tell me—*how* do you mean to save Eric?"

He smiled.

"You will learn later. At present do not in any way let Eric suspect that you know anything. And—that my plan to save him may succeed—you must give him an opiate to-night."

"An opiate?"

"He must be made to sleep beyond the hour of meeting, else, not even Crystal's death could keep him away. To steady his nerves for to-morrow some sleep will be necessary —he will, therefore, probably retire early. In fact, you must see that he does, and induce him to take a glass of wine, or beer, and administer an opiate in the drink that will hold him for eight hours at least. All depends upon that."

"Oh, I can do that. I have done it often before."

"Very well; that is all you are to do. Now go quickly to the Louvre, and perform your part. In about two hours I will call to see how Crystal is. I have other business of importance meantime. For the present good-by."

* * * * * * * * * *

The last act of " La Sorcière d'Or " is over, the ballet has begun, and a group of gentlemen are loitering about the vestibule of the theatre, not quite sure whether they will re- turn to their stalls for the great display of legs and lime- light, or go virtuously home to bed. Mr. Boville is among them, and Mr. Boville is debating within himself the advisa- bility of a little game of lansquenet, as a soothing preparation for slumber, when a man strides hurriedly up and lays his hand heavily on his shoulder.

"Boville! I thought I would find you here. Will you leave the theatre and come with me?"

Boville swings round and faces his interrogator.

"You, Dennison! Certainly, my dear fellow. But what the deuce is the matter? On my word you look like your own ghost."

"Come with me," Dennison replies, hurriedly, and Boville links his arm through the dragoon's and goes.

Without a word, Terry leads him away from the glare and gas-light glitter of the thronged boulevards to some distant, dimly-lighted, deserted street.

Without a word Boville follows. This is something serious, he feels. Has the duel got wind? Dennison and Dynely are relatives, Boville hazily recollects—relatives of some sort; he is not quite clear about it. No doubt Dennison has come to speak of the duel; but why with *that* face?

"Boville," Terry abruptly begins, "Lord Dynely and Prince Di Venturini fight to-morrow, do they not, and you are Dynely's second?"

"Weluctantly—yes. It's a bad business, old boy. Dynely hasn't a ghost of a chance, and so I've told him. But a wilful man—you know the proverb. Besides, weally, you know," Mr. Boville has a rooted objection to the letter R, "I don't see how he is going to get out of it. The Prince—confound him! would bwand him as a coward far and wide, and Eric's not that. My dear Terry," they are passing under a street lamp at the moment, and the light falls full upon his companion's face, "what *have* you been doing to yourself? There is a bwuised swelling the size of an egg between your eyes."

Dennison's face turns crimson, a deep, burning, tingling crimson once more. He pulls his hat far over his eyes, and tries to laugh.

"An accident, Boville. Never mind my face—I've no beauty to spoil. I've come to talk to you about this duel. At what hour do they meet?"

"At first peep of day, between half-past six and seven. It won't do to be later. But who told you? De Concressault or Dynely himself?"

"Both. Boville, this meeting must never take place!"

"Delighted, I'm shaw, to hear it," drawled Mr. Boville, opening two very small, very sleepy blue eyes to their widest; "never was accessory to a murder in my life—don't want to begin now. But, at the same time, how do you pwopwose to pwevent it?"

"You can refuse to act for Eric."

Boville shrugged his shoulders and inserted his glass in his eye.

"And have my bwains blown out for my pains. Haven't got many bwains, thank Heaven—never was in our family —still, the few I've got I pwopose to keep. That dodge won't work, Terry, twy something else."

"It will be downright slaughter, Boville—nothing less."

"Know it, dear boy—told Dynely so ; but what's the use of telling? He's got into this infernal little scwape, and must take the consequences. He's had his three weeks' flirtation with Felicia—now he's got to pay the penalty. *Apwopos des bottes*, she was in capital fawm to-night—at her loveliest. If it were she that was to be shot to-morrow, I'd assist at the cewemonial with the gweatest pleasure."

There is a moment's silence, and the two men walk on in the rain. Then Dennison speaks in an altered voice.

"There is one way, Boville—only one."

"Vewy pleased to hear it, dear boy. Give it a name."

"I must go out in Dynely's place."

It is the proud boast of Herbert Boville's life that since he was in pinafores he has never felt surprise or any other earthly emotion. But now—he actually stops in the rain, and stares at his companion, aghast. ✦

"Go out in——My dear Dennison, I *don't* think I can have heard you awight. Will you kindly wepeat your last wemark?"

"Oh nonsense, Boville—your hearing's all right. I must go out in Dynely's place ; such has been my intention from the first, and I call upon you to aid and second me."

Boville fixed his glass in his eye, and tried in the darkness to see his friend.

"I always thought," he said in a helpless tone, "that I had less bwains myself than any other fellow of my acquaintance. Now I know I was mistaken. Pway, Terry, *when* did you take leave of your senses?"

Terry muttered something forcible and strong.

"Look here, Boville," he cried impatiently ; "don't let us waste time chaffing. As surely as we both stand here, I mean this. Dynely hasn't a ghost of a chance, as we

19

both know; for him to meet Di Venturini would be sheer murder. Now with me it is different. I may not be the same dead shot the prince is, and I haven't had his experience with living targets, but my pistol hand is tolerably sure for all that. And I mean to meet Di Venturini to-morrow."

He said it with a dogged determination that convinced Boville at last.

"By Jove!" he said, "this is a rum go! Do you mean to tell me, Terry, that Eric will stand by and allow this?"

Eric knows nothing about it—will not until all is over. He is the last man on earth who *would* allow it. The devil himself is not more obstinate or more plucky than Dynely."

"You must be awfully fond of him, Terry, old boy! Gad! I never heard of such a thing in all my life. Knocks Damon and the other fellow into a cocked-hat. By Jove! it does. At the same time you stand no more chance before the prince than Dynely."

"I don't think so," Dennison responded, coolly; "as I tell you, I'm a very fair shot and can hold my own with most men."

"With most men, perhaps—not with the prince. And, then, it's impossible—oh, utterly impossible! You don't suppose, now, Dennison, you *don't* suppose Di Venturini will fight you instead of Dynely?"

"I don't suppose he would, if he knew. It is not my intention to let him know."

"Ah, how will you help it?"

"Simply enough. Di Venturini never saw Eric in his life."

"But he *has* seen you, dear boy, and De Concwessault knows Eric like a book. How do you propose to baffle two pair of eyes?"

"Boville," said Terry, earnestly, "this thing has to be done, that is the whole amount of it. Even if I were sure—which I am not at all—that Di Venturini would shoot me, I would still meet him. It will be the early dawn of a dark and rainy morning. I shall wear this slouch hat, which, to a great degree, will hide my face. And in figure and general air Dynely and I are alike—have often been accosted for each other.   They will never suspect—how should they ?   They will take it for granted that I am Lord Dynely, and the duel will be fought, and there will be an end of the matter."

"An end of the matter !   Ah ! very likely.   And where, all this time, will be Dynely ? "

Terry reddened.

"Dynely will be asleep—drugged.   I have taken care of that."

Again Boville paused—in genuine, unfeigned amazement.

"Dennison ! drugged !   By Jove !   And who will drug him ? "

"His mother.   At my request."

"By Jove ! " exclaimed Boville again, and laughed softly. " if this isn't the wummest go.   By Jove, Terry, *how* fond you must be of Eric ! "

Once more Terry reddened violently in the dark.

"Look here, Boville," he said again, "it isn't that.   It isn't altogether for Eric's sake.   I—I don't mind telling you, it's for the sake of his mother and wife.   Their very lives are bound up in him—if he is killed it will kill them.   And I owe his mother everything—everything, I give you my word, Boville.   I stand pledged to her, solemnly pledged to save her son.   And I mean to keep that pledge.   There, you have it."

"And you expect me to aid and abet you in this Quixotic —yes, Dennison—Quixotic scheme?   By Jove !   I'll see you shot first !"

"You will probably see me shot *at*, at least," Terry answered with a slight laugh.   "Come now, Boville, I rely upon you in this.   It's for the best all round.   Di Venturini will shoot Eric as dead as Queen Anne—now I don't mean to let him shoot me.   I flatter myself my chances are as good as his.   I will not break my word to Lady Dynely. If you refuse to aid me, I will go to Argyll—*he* will not, I know."

"Has Lady Dynely asked you to meet the prince in her son's place ? "

"Of course not—she would be the last to permit such a thing.   All the same ; I have promised to save him, and

there is no other way.   As I tell you, she has been my benefactress all my life.   If Dynely were killed, his mother and
wife would break their hearts.   And," Terry drew his breath
in hard, "there is no one to care for me."

Boville looked at him suddenly.   In the dim light the tall
figure was curiously like Eric's—he noticed it for the first
time.   Was his relationship to handsome Eric nearer than
the world knew ?

They had come close upon the Hotel Louvre—the brilliant boulevards almost deserted this wet night.   Dennison
stopped, and grasped his companion's hand.

"You will do this for me, Boville ?   I can depend upon
you ? "

"Not with my will, I swear, Dennison !   But if you insist—? "

" I do insist.   What is the hour ?"

"Before seven.   But your scheme won't wash.   I warn
you, Di Venturini and De Concressault will know."

"They will *not* know.   Until six to-morrow, then, Boville,
old fellow, good-night, and sound sleep."

*   *   *   *   *   *   *   *

In Crystal's room the light burned dim.   Pale, motionless, she lay, Lady Dynely watching by her side.   It was
close upon midnight, when a servant came in and softly
announced Mr. Dennison.

"Terry ! "   She started up and went to meet him in the
outer room.   " *Well ?* " she whispered, breathlessly.

" It is all right," he answered, in the same tone ; "and
Crystal ? "

"Crystal is asleep and—safe.   It was but a small artery
ruptured, and she will be about in a few weeks, so the doc-
tors say."

"Thank Heaven ! " she heard him murmur.   Then
" where is Eric ? "

" Eric is asleep, too.   I have done as you bade, Terry.
He has had the glass of port, and the opiate in it.   He took
it as quietly as a child."

Her lip quivered.   He took her in his arms for a moment,
and kissed her.

"Keep up heart, mother. I will keep my word. All will be well with Eric. And now," with strange shyness, "before I go—may I go in for a moment and look at Crystal?"

She motioned him to enter, remaining outside herself. He went softly in, and knelt reverently down by the little white bed. Like a lily she lay, so cold, so white, so pure.

" My little Crystal," he said, under his breath, " my little love, if by the sacrifice of my own life I can bring happiness to you, then I resign it willingly. - My own little one ! good-by, and God bless and keep you always."

Lady Dynely had quitted the dressing-room for a moment to glance at her slumbering son. He lay deeply asleep, his head pillowed on his arm, his fair Greek profile turned to the faint light. Then she hurried back to say one last word to Terry, but Terry was gone.

CHAPTER XVII.

HOW THE MORNING BROKE.

THE rain fell softly and ceaselessly all night—it was falling softly and ceaselessly still when morning dawned. The gray, ragged light was struggling wanly through the leaden sky when a fiacre drove rapidly toward the Bois de Boulogne, and three men got out. They were Dennison, Boville, and an English surgeon, resident of Paris.

"You will wait here," Boville said to the cabman; and the three men hurried rapidly along to a secluded and distant spot, where, under the waving trees, scores of "meetings of honor" had taken place before.

They were a very silent party. Boville looked perplexed and gloomy, and gnawed his mustache uneasily.

"I feel as though I were helping to slaughter you, Dennison," he had groaned as they first started. The band of comradeship between him and Terry was one of many years' standing, and the settled conviction was upon him this dreary morning that Terry was going to his death. The miserable weather, perhaps, had something to do with his forebodings, also the unearthly hour at which he had been obliged to get up, but most of all Di Venturini's reputation as a dead shot.

"Wish to Heaven I had never got mixed up in the infewnal business," he growled, inwardly "Eric was bad enough, but this is worse. Nevew heard of such an awangement before—nevew. If Dennison's shot, as he's sure to be, I shall feel like a murdewer all my life."

They strode silently on together now, beneath the dripping trees.

"We're wather ahead of time, I think," Boville remarked

drearily, once, as they passed swiftly over the short, wet grass.

"It's always well to err on the right side," Dennison answered cheerfully. "Di Venturini isn't the sort to keep any one waiting when this kind of thing is on hand."

He was looking pale and rather jaded. He had slept little or none all night. He had written a brief note to Lady Dynely and another to Eric, and intrusted them to Boville, to be delivered in case of the worst. And the worst would happen, that he felt as surely as Boville himself. The quarrel between Di Venturini and Dynely was of that deadly sort that admitted of no half measures. As surely as he walked here he knew that the prince meant to kill him—if he could.

He had altered himself greatly during the preceding night. All his profuse, flame-colored beard had been shaven off, his great, ruddy, trooper mustache trimmed down, and waxed at the points, to resemble Eric's dandy, golden, facial adornment. It deepened the faint likeness between them incredibly—even Boville was genuinely surprised. That impurpled swelling between the eyes had been reduced by judicious applications; the slouched, felt hat, pulled far down, hid it altogether. His coat-collar was turned up, naturally, to exclude the rain, and with the vague, general air of resemblance in their figure and walk, it would really have required a suspicion of the truth to make either Di Venturini or his second suspect the exchange.

They reached the spot chosen. It was deserted. Boville looked at his watch.

"A quarter of seven. They ought to be here. It won't do to loiter about after—"

"Hark!" Dennison interrupted, lifting his finger. Footsteps and voices were approaching rapidly. "I thought his excellency would not keep us waiting long. Here they are."

They came in view at the moment. Terry pulled his hat a little farther over his brow, and busied himself in lighting a cigar. Di Venturini bowed to him profoundly, with all the debonnaire grace for which his highness was justly famed. Dennison, like a true-born Briton, returned it stiffly and distantly. De Concressault approached Boville with profuse gesture and apologies for the brief delay.

"A million pardons. He was disgusted at having neces-sitated their waiting in the rain. It was all the fault of their most infamous pig of a driver. Would they proceed to busi-ness at once? There was no time to lose."

Terry was turned, his face averted, still absorbed by his cigar and refractory Vesuvians, which, dampened by the mist, refused to light. Di Venturini, buttoned up to the throat in a tight black coat, no speck of white anywhere visible, stood leaning against a tree some forty rods distant, a half-smile of devilish malignity and triumph on his face.

The preliminaries of the duel were soon arranged; great practice had rendered M. de Concressault an adept in these nice matters of honor. The combatants were to fire simul-taneously, at fourteen paces, at the dropping of a handker-chief and the old "*une, deux, trois.*"

"Stand here, M. le Prince, if you please," Boville said, marking the spot; and the prince, with that smile of demo-niacal malice and triumph still in his yellow face, bowed and obeyed.

"You'll take your place here, Dennison," Boville con-tinued, in an undertone; "and for Heaven's sake fire the very instant I say three."

Dennison nodded, threw away his cigar, received his pistol, and took his place. His heart beat fast, with absolute ter-ror, lest he should be recognized. But the shaven beard, the hat pulled down, the coat collar turned up, concealed him effectually. A shapely nose and a ruddy mustache were alone visible; for the rest, the general figure and bearing were sufficiently like Eric's to pass muster in that dull light.

There was a moment's pause—Boville held out a white handkerchief.

"Ready, messieurs?" Then a pause, "One—two." Another pause, a quick, warning glance at Dennison. "*Three!*"

The white handkerchief fell, and simultaneously two shots rang sharply out on the still morning air.

Again there was a pause, brief, terrible. The smoke

cleared away—both men stood as they had been placed. The prince's left wrist hung broken. Boville's eyes were fixed on Terry. Was he untouched? *No.* As he looked he saw him sway blindly forward, wheel half-round, and fall like a log on his face.

Boville and the surgeon rushed forward, the latter first, and turned him over and raised his head. The face was ghastly, the eyes closed, and from the breast in the region of the heart a small stream of blood was making its way through his clothes.

" Is he dead? " Boville asked, himself almost as white as the fallen man.

" No—fainted, but—"

He tore open coat and shirt and examined the wound. A small, livid hole beneath the heart was there on the broad, marble-like bosom, from which that slender red stream yet trickled.

" It doesn't look very bad, it doesn't seem to bleed much," Boville cried, in an agony of impatience. " For Heaven's sake, Jackson, speak out ! What do you think ? "

The doctor looked grimly up from his manipulation.

" I think there is internal bleeding, Mr. Boville. This young man won't live two hours."

Boville rose suddenly, and turned away.

" His highness, the prince, does his work well. It's a pity, too—it's the finest physique I ever saw in the whole course of my life. The torso of a Hercules, by George. In the ordinary course of things this poor fellow would have lived to be ninety."

" Can he be moved ? " Hubert Boville asked, in a stifled voice.

" Oh, yes ! he must, I suppose. It may hasten the end, but won't alter it. Where are you going to take him ? "

" To the Hotel du Louvre. His friends are there."

" Poor lad ! By Jupiter, *what* a bust ! " the doctor cried, lost in professional admiration.

At this moment the prince and the captain of Zouaves sauntered up.

" See if he's dead, De Concressault," they heard Di

19*

Venturini say nonchalantly ; "my right hand must be losing its cunning if he is not.　I certainly meant to kill him."

"Oh !　*il est mort*," De Concressault responded, with equal carelessness ; "he's shot through the heart, and the sooner you are over the frontier the better, M. le Prince. Messieurs, *bonjour !* "　He lifted his hat, bowed profoundly, and without another look at their victim, both hastily quitted the ground.

*　　*　　*　　*　　*　　*　　*　　*　　*

Seven ! by the great booming bell of Notre Dame.　Seven, by all the steeples of Paris.　Seven, by the little Swiss clock in the chamber where Crystal lay, feverishly asleep, and Lady Dynely, senior, sat pale and worn, watching.　In the adjoining dressing-room, on the broad, soft sofa, Eric lay still, in deepest, dreamless sleep.　Safe ! and the fatal hour past.

Where was Terry ?　What was he doing ?　In what way had he stopped the duel ?　Lady Dynely's heart was beating anxiously and fast—some dim, prophetic prescience of the truth was trying to force its way upon her, but she would not listen.　No, no !　Terry would never be so insane as that.　He was not reckless and foolish like Eric—he would never think of keeping his word in *that* way.　Only—as she had never longed for any one's coming in her life, she longed for Terry's now.

Half-past seven.　She arose from her place by Crystal's bed and went into Eric's room.　Still asleep—soundly, sweetly—like a little child, his blonde, handsome head still pillowed on his arm, a placid expression of profound rest on his face.　She stooped low and kissed him—a prayer for him in her heart.　He was the idol of her life—he always had been.　And but for Terry he might be lying dead out there in the rain somewhere, even now—yes, even now.　How good he was, how generous, poor Terry !—few would have resigned life's best gifts as he had to his younger brother, for her sake.　She would show him in the future how grateful she was, how noble she thought him.

Eric stirred in his sleep—he murmured a word.　She bent

low to catch it—was it hers, was it his wife's name? He turned and spoke again, more loudly.

"Felicia," he said, "Felicia, *ma belle,* I will meet you to-morrow."

She recoiled with a sudden revulsion of feeling. Even in his sleep it was of that wicked sorceress his thoughts were—that fatal woman, who had so nearly compassed his death. She turned without another look, and hurried from the room.

Eight o'clock. Still Terry did not come. Oh, what detained him? Surely he must know how anxious she was.

A quarter past. She arose impatiently to quit the room, and on the landing, ascending the stairs, she came face to face with Hubert Boville.

At the first glance, before he opened his lips, before a word had passed, she knew something had happened. His clothes were wet with rain, his high boots splashed with mud, his face pale, his eyes excited. He took off his hat as he saw her, and she instinctively recoiled.

"Mr. Boville!" she gasped. "Oh, what is it?"

"I was coming in search of you, Lady Dynely," he said. There was an instinctive coldness in his courteous tone—had not *she* in some way sent Dennison to his doom? "I am the bearer of very sad and shocking news. Poor Terry Dennison—"

He stopped. With a cry he never forgot—a cry whose exceeding bitterness made him pity her even in that hour—she staggered back against the wall, and put out her hand to ward off the blow that must come.

"I see you suspect the truth," he said, more gently. "I am very sorry—sorrier than I can ever say—that I, in any way, have had a hand in this. But the duel has been fought ; he met him in Lord Dynely's place ; and—we have brought him here. He is below in the cab. Will you have a room prepared at once, Lady Dynely—there is no time to lose."

She stood literally gasping for breath. Her hand over her heart. Oh! what was this?—what was this?

"There is no time to lose," Boville repeated again. He had little sympathy for the hysterics of the woman who, to

444 HOW THE MORNING BROKE.

shield her own son, had, he knew, urged Dennison to save him at any cost. "I must beg of you, Lady Dynely—"

She came a step forward, and grasped his arm.

"Is he dead?" she asked, in a voice no one would have recognized as her own.

"No, my lady ; not yet."

The answer seemed to inspire her with galvanic life. "While there is life there is hope." He was not dead. Oh! Heaven be praised!—he might not die after all.

"Bring him up," she cried, starting forward, "at once—at once, to this room."

She pointed to it, and hastened forward to prepare it with her own hands. Boville departed. She summoned her maid, and together, with feverish haste, they made ready the bed.

They carried him up between them—a stark, rigid form—and laid him on the bed.

As she looked upon the bloodless, awfully corpse-like face, the closed eyes, the blue rigid lips, a sudden stillness came over her. Was that Terry—Terry Dennison?—whom only eight hours ago she had seen in all the strength and vigor of youth and powerful manhood? That Terry?—Terry, who never, in all the twenty years she had known him, had had one sick day? That Terry, lying there cold and motionless —so awfully white, so awfully still?

"My dear Lady Dynely," said Boville, with real compassion, touched by the ghastly horror of her face, "come away."

She turned to him.

"You told me," she whispered. "You told me he was not dead."

"Neither he is—only insensible. Come with me—you *must* come for the present. The doctor is going to try to find the ball. The moment the operation is over you shall return."

He led her from the room, her face still fixed in that look of white horror.

"Where is Lord Dynely?" he asked.

"Asleep," she whispered; "*he* told me, and I—for my

son's sake, I made Terry do this—for my son's sake I sent him to his death. It is I—I—who have killed him. Oh, Heaven ! this is how he meant to keep his word."

She fell down upon a fauteuil, her face hidden in her hands. He could say nothing—do nothing—she only spoke the truth. He had a man's natural dislike to scenes, and so left her.

He returned to the chamber he had quitted. The surgeon rose at his entrance from his work.

"Well ?" Boville asked.

"I cannot extract the bullet, and he is dying. You may as well tell them so. He will be a dead man in an hour."

"Poor fellow !" Hubert Boville stood with folded arms, an expression of bitter regret on his face, looking down upon his friend and comrade. "Yes, death is imprinted here. And when the last great muster roll is called," he said, with unconscious pathos, "no truer friend, no braver soldier, will ever answer than Terry Dennison."

CHAPTER XVIII.

"WHILE IT WAS YET DAY."

ALF AN HOUR had passed. Lady Dynely knew that Terry Dennison was about to die.

The truth was broken to her by France Forrester. Miss Forrester, coming early and hastily to relieve her ladyship's watch by the sick bed of Eric's wife, had heard the first version of the truth from the whispering servants of the hotel. Pale with wonder and terror she had asked for Mr. Boville, and Mr. Boville had come forward and told the whole truth. So ! he had crowned all the sacrifices of the past for Lady Dynely and her son by yielding up his life. Surely he had paid his debt.

"Is he conscious?" she asked, with strange, mournful calm. Her own great sorrow had left its traces on her worn, pale face, but still more in the unnatural quiet and gravity of her manner.

"Yes, he has been conscious for the last five minutes."

"May I go in?" she pleaded. "I will not disturb him. I will be very quiet."

"Certainly," Boville said, "and Lady Dynely must be told, too. I—I wish *you* would tell her, Miss Forrester. I hate breaking things to people."

"I will tell her. How long will he live?"

"Half an hour perhaps. Certainly not more."

"Have you sent for a clergyman? No. Then do so at once."

She passed into the room. The blinds were up, the full light of the gray, rainy morning streamed in. She bent over the bed. The face was still and colorless as marble, the eyes closed. Her own filled

" Does he suffer ? " she whispered to the doctor across the bed.

"Very little, if any. The hemorrhage is internal. There is faintness, but no pain."

The low whisper reached him. He opened his eyes, and a smile of recognition came over his face.

" France ! " he said, faintly.

"Yes, Terry." Then all at once a great choking seized her and she could say no more.

" Don't cry," he said, still faintly, smiling, "it will—be— all right."

" Yes, dear old fellow, I think it will." She stooped down with infinite pity and tenderness and kissed him. "You— you are going, Terry—do you know it ? "

" Yes. It's all right, France. Don't cry so. It's awfully good of you to come."

His strength seemed to rally for a moment. He looked anxiously around.

" Where am I ? This isn't my room."

"Don't make him talk too much," the doctor said. " Here, sir, drink this."

He swallowed the spoonful of liquid and still watched France with anxious eyes.

" You are in one of Eric's rooms."

" Eric," his eyes lighted, " where is Eric ? "

" Asleep. Would you like to see him ? "

The light faded from his face. All at once he recalled the livid bruise between his eyes, and averted it even in that hour.

" He—might not—care to come," he said with difficulty. " How is—Crystal ? "

" Crystal is recovering. Oh ! don't think of her, of him, of any one, dear old Terry, but yourself. We have sent for a clergyman. He will be here in a moment. You will see him ? "

He nodded assent.

" Where is the madre ? " he asked.

" In the next room—broken-hearted. Shall I go for her ? "

"Poor mother ! Yes."

She turned at once to go. As she did so the door opened and the clergyman came hastily in.

"I will leave you with him for ten minutes," France whispered, "then we will all return."

She hurried from the room and into the presence of Lady Dynely. As she had fallen down half an hour ago, Lady Dynely still lay in a sort of stupor of dull, infinite misery. France lifted her head.

"Rouse yourself, Lady Dynely," she said : "he has asked for you, poor boy. You must go to him."

To her dying day France never forgot the utter wretchedness of the face uplifted at her command.

"He is dying, France, and I—I have killed him. I made him swear to save Eric, no matter how, no matter how, and he has given his life for my son. And, last night, Eric struck him, struck him full in the face. No, I cannot go to him— I can never look upon him again."

"This is folly, Lady Dynely !" exclaimed the girl, her eyes kindling. "Are you altogether heartless ? He has asked for you—your absence will embitter his last hour. You *must* go to him, Eric must go. Oh !" France cried, "have you not made him suffer enough, you and Eric, that you are so ready to make him suffer still at the last ?"

Lady Dynely arose wildly to her feet.

"I will go to him ! I will do anything ! I will go to him at once."

"Not quite at once. A clergyman is with him. Leave them alone for a little. But rouse up Eric ; fetch him with you ; tell him all."

"Tell him all !" Lady Dynely repeated. She stood, a strange, excited expression crossing her face. "Yes," she said, under her breath, "I will tell him all—ALL. It is time."

She ran from the room, and into Eric's. He was moving and muttering restlessly now, the opiate beginning to lose its effect. She seized him by the arm and shook him roughly.

"Awake, Eric !" she cried; "awake at once."

He opened his eyes immediately and stared up at her in a dazed way.

"What's the matter, mother? Have you gone mad? Crystal——"

He half rose on his elbow with a look of alarm.

"Never mind Crystal—wake up!"

"I *have* woke up. What's the matter with you? What's the hour?" Then, like lightning, memory rushed upon him; his face flushed, turned pale. He pulled out his watch and looked at the time. A quarter of nine. "Great Heaven!" he exclaimed, and fell back among the pillows.

"Ay!" his mother cried, bitterly, "look at the hour. The time for the duel is past, is it not? And the duel has been fought, and your honor saved. Oh, my heart! such honor. You are safe here, and he lies dying there—for you. Your own brother, Eric—your elder brother!"

He sat and stared at her, thinking she had gone mad, quite speechless.

"No," she said, "I have not lost my senses, though you look as if you thought it. The duel has been fought; Terry took your place, and he lies dying in yonder room now, for you, and for me, and for Crystal—the friend whom you struck last night—the brother whose birthright you have usurped all your life!"

Still he sat speechless—still he was staring at her, not comprehending a word.

"Oh, you don't understand—you won't understand, and time is flying and every moment is precious. I must go to him. Eric, rouse yourself! try to comprehend what I am saying. Terry met Prince Di Venturini this morning, and fought your duel for *you*. I made him! I nearly went mad when he came to me last night and told me of Crystal's accident first, and of your challenge. I don't know what I said, I don't know what I did, only I made him promise to save you, and he has, he has!"

He was beginning to understand now. His face turned white, his lips set themselves.

"Go on," he said, speaking for the first time.

"I gave you an opiate and you slept while he went out

and met the prince in your place. He is dying in that room, and he has asked for you and for me ; and he is your brother, Eric, your own brother."

"My brother! Mother, are you mad? I have no brother."

But he grew whiter still as he said it. The resemblance between them—the vague, unsatisfactory story of his relationship to them—all flashed upon him ; and then he knew what manner of man his father had been.

"He is your brother—your very own ; your father's son. Oh, not as you think," seeing the expression of his face ; "his mother was Lord Dynely's wife. I have all the proofs, and he was three years old when you were born."

He rose up.

"His mother was Lord Dynely's wife—his *wife !* And Terry is three years older than I am. Mother, what is this ? "

"The truth! And Terry Dennison is your father's elder son and heir ! I knew it since the night of your father's death ; he confessed all, dying, whilst I knelt by his bedside. You never for one moment have had a right to the title you bear. Terry Dennison is Lord Viscount Dynely ! "

He fell heavily back on the seat he had quitted.

"And you concealed this ? " he said, in a hoarse whisper.

"No—I told him. I told him last August. When he wanted to go down to Lincolnshire and ask Crystal Higgins to be his wife, I detained him. I could not let him go in ignorance. I kept him and told him all—all, Eric ! I thought he would have ousted you and claimed his own. That was why I wanted you so much to marry France Forrester and her fortune. But he gave up all, Eric—name, title, wealth—for the love of you and me."

He buried his face in his hands and turned from her—stunned.

"He might have won Crystal—she was his before you came—she was all he had, and you took her from him. He might have taken from *you* title and fortune, and he did not. Last night he came to you in all good faith and brotherly love, and—and," a great gasp, "you struck him, Eric ! I kissed the brutal mark on his poor face last night. This morning he went out in your place and met the prince, and was shot down as *you* would have been. And he lies dying there ; he will be dead before the hour ends."

He put out his hand with a fierce gesture to stop her.

"Cease !" he said, hoarsely. " Oh, God ! I *cannot* bear it ! "

She obeyed—a rain of tears pouring over her face. He lay mute—quivering through all his strong young frame.

" Leave me," he said, in the same hoarse voice, " I want to be alone."

She turned to go, but on the threshold she stopped.

" You will come, Eric," she said, " when we send ? "

" Yes. Go !"

She went. France stood waiting for her at the door.

" He has asked for you again. He is sinking fast. Come."

She led her into that other room. The clergyman's last offices were over. On the face, lying among the pillows, the cold dews of death already stood. She fell down on her knees by the bed and took the dying head in her arms. He opened his heavy eyes and smiled—a smile of great content. " *Mother*," he said, and lay still.

" Oh, my Terry ! my Terry !" she cried out, " forgive me before you go."

" There is—nothing—to forgive," he spoke, slowly and faintly, but clearly. " You were always good to me. I loved you all my life, mother. Don't cry—it's better so. Eric," his eyes looked wistfully toward the door, he sighed wearily, " Eric won't come ? "

" Eric will come." She bent down and kissed him, and in that kiss whispered : " I have told him all."

" All !" He looked up at her quickly, almost in reproof. " That was wrong."

" It was right. I should have told him long ago. Oh, my boy ! my own Terry ! how good you are."

He smiled—Terry's own amused smile. Then he closed his eyes wearily, and lay still again.

Obeying a motion of her hand, France had gone to fetch Eric.

He came in—white as death itself, an agony of remorse, of sorrow, upon his face, changing it beyond all telling. He knelt down on the opposite side of the bed, and laid his face on one of Terry's hands, without a word.

"Eric ! dear old boy !" The old, glad, loving light lit the dying eyes. "I'm glad you've come. You don't mind what I did this morning ? Di Venturini will never know. It's all right, isn't it ?"

He was watching him wistfully.

Was Eric angry ? But Eric only lifted his face for a minute, and laid it down again.

"All right ! Oh, Terry ! you break my heart."

What was it fell on Terry's hand ? Tears, and from the eyes of Eric Dynely ! For a moment Terry himself could not speak.

"It is all right, then," he said, under his breath. "Dear old boy, I'm glad of that."

Then there was stillness. He lay in Lady Dynely's arms, his face pillowed on her breast, his eyes closed, his breathing coming quick and hard. On the other side knelt Eric, never moving or looking up. The dull, melancholy light stole in and fell upon him, stricken down there, in the glory and strength of his manhood. France Forrester watched him mournfully, from her post at the foot of the bed.

"And his sun went down, while it was yet day," she thought. "My own dear Terry ! as clean of heart, as brave of soul, as loyal a knight as any Arthur or Galahad of them all."

Suddenly his eyes opened, and he looked up in Lady Dynely's face.

"I—have—kept my promise," he said, slowly. "I never quarrelled—with Eric."

"Oh, my boy ! my Terry !" she could only answer through her tears.

He moved a little.

"Eric," he whispered, and Eric lifted his pale face and red, tear wet eyes. "Good-by—*brother*," he said, so low that Eric had to lay his ear to his lips to catch the words ; " be good—to—Crystal."

He closed them once more, exhausted, and lay still. There was a sudden, short convulsion of the limbs—it passed, and he was quiet. So he had lain for fully five minutes, his head resting a dull weight in Lady Dynely's arms. A sharp terror seized her—she looked helplessly around.

" Is he asleep ? " she piteously asked.

Hubert Boville came forward and bent over him. He laid his hand on his heart for a moment, and listened for his breathing. Then he stood up.

" Not asleep," he said, very gently ; " dead."

CHAPTER XIX.

IN *Galignani's Messenger* of next day there appeared this paragraph :

"FEARFUL DUEL.—Yesterday morning, at seven o'clock, a meeting took place in the Bois de Boulogne between a certain princely personage, well known in the Italian political world, and an English lieutenant of dragoon guards. His excellency the prince was attended by Captain De C——cr——lt, of the —th Zouaves, and the other combatant by the Hon. H. B——ville, attache of the British Embassy. As usual there was a lady in the case. The duel was fought with pistols, at fourteen paces. The first fire proved fatal—the Englishman being shot through the heart. The police are on the track of the noble fugitive, but up to the present without success."

In the same column another paragraph appeared which created a far wider and deeper sensation.

"SUDDEN AND MYSTERIOUS DEATH.—It is with deepest regret we announce to our readers the awfully sudden and most mysterious death of the charming actress whose beauty and versatility have crowded the Varieties for the past four months—Madame Felicia. Last night she gave one of the delightful receptions for which she has ever been justly famed, and appeared in her usual excellent health and spirits. She retired about midnight, still seemingly perfectly well. In the morning her maid found her dead in her bed. Suspicion of foul play is at work, and a post-mortem will probably discover the cause of this death, which all theatre-going Parisians will deeply regret.

*   *   *   *   *   *   *

It is the close of an exquisite June day. The old, long-deserted gardens of Caryllynne glow in the warm rose light. Down one of the paths an elderly lady, with snow-white hair, is being wheeled in an invalid chair by a dark damsel, with black sombre eyes and a look of prophetic melancholy on her face. The elderly lady glances over her shoulder with tender, kindly eyes.

"Are you not tired, Donny?" she asks, gently. "You must be. You have been wheeling me for fully an hour. Do call Esther, my child."

The black, melancholy eyes light.

"Oh! no, grandmamma—I never grow tired when with you."

"My dear, how mournful you look, though. Do we not make you happy, little one? Tell grandmamma what it is."

"Happy!" she clasps her hands almost with passion. "Oh, so happy!—so happy that I grow afraid. It is like Heaven to be with you, and papa, and mamma France. No one was ever good to me before since Joan died—except that night—*him*."

"Poor Terry!" Mrs. Caryll sighs; "he was good to all things. And so it is excess of happiness that makes you sad? A paradox, surely, but I am glad it is no worse."

She takes her in her arms and kisses her fondly.

"I want you to be happy, my child—I want to make you happy, to atone in some way for all the unhappiness I have given your father. Love him, Donny, for his past life—oh, my own dear Gordon has been dreary and loveless enough."

"I *do* love him," the girl answers, her great eyes shining. "Who could help it? So noble, so handsome, so good he is. And he is happy now—who would *not* be happy with Mamma France? And to think that to-morrow is their wedding day, and that I am to be one of the bride-maids! How strange it seems."

"It is a happiness he has waited for long—poor Gordon," his mother answers.

"And I have been thinking, too, grandmamma, of—of *her*," she drops her voice, and the great eyes dilate; "it was all so sudden, and so dreadful. Oh! I wonder what it was! —what made her die like that? Did they ever find out?"

"Not for certain, Donny, dear. Ah! don't let us talk about it to-night—on this happy bridal eve. Poor soul! it was a terrible fate." She shudders as she says it. She will not tell the daughter she was poisoned. Poisoned—whether by herself, maid, or whom, has never been discovered. There are those who have strong suspicions of the truth, but —in Naples, Prince Di Venturini reigns in the halls of his forefathers, and in this world at least justice does not seem likely to reach him.

On the terrace above, Gordon Caryll walks, France by his side, and both pace to and fro in the roselight of the summer sunset, with hearts too full of bliss for many words. France looks down at the pair below, the pink flush of the sky kindling into brightness Donny's dusk face.

"She will be very handsome," Miss Forrester says; "and —very like her mother."

His face clouds for a second.

"Poor child!—yes. Let us trust the likeness will end there. How fond my mother seems of her. They are never happy apart. France!" he looks at her suddenly, and a smile that is more radiant than the sunset lights his grave face, "this time to-morrow you will be suffering agonies of sea-sickness crossing the channel. You always *are* sea-sick, you know."

"Yes, I know." She smiles back for a moment, then grows grave. "Don't let us visit Paris, Gordon, I never want to see Paris more. I can never—no, never—suffer again in this life as I have suffered there."

"We will go wherever you please, my own France."

There is silence again. The rose light is fading from the sky—its last rays fall on one of the many painted windows of the old manor, the motto of the house, cut in the panes, shines out:

"*Post tenebræ, lux,*" she reads. "Oh, Gordon! the past has been very dark for you—if my love can lighten the future there will never be another dark hour."

*   *   *   *   *   *   *   *   *

In her dower house Lady Dynely, the elder, dwells alone.

She has never quite recovered from the shock of that death bed in Paris—she never will.

"From first to last my own selfish love for my son spoiled his life," she ever says; "*he* did not know what selfishness meant. I and mine blighted his existence—brought him to his death. *He* forgave me—Heaven may—I never will forgive myself."

So she lives on, quietly doing good to all. No one can accuse her of selfishness now. Her son is a better son than he ever was before, but she knows that he, who died that rainy February morning, loved and honored her, as no human being ever did before, ever will again. They brought him home, and the great vault of the Dynelys was opened, and he was laid to sleep with them. People wondered at it a good deal—but then Lady Dynely had always been a little eccentric since her husband's death. They wonder still more as they read the inscription above him. It is a slab of plain gray granite, with gold lettering, and it says this:

SACRED TO THE MEMORY

OF

TERENCE DENNISON,

WHO GAVE HIS LIFE TO SAVE ANOTHER'S,
FEBRUARY 29TH, 18—.
ÆTAT 25 YEARS.

"*Greater love than this no man hath:—That he lay down his life for his friend.*"

*   *   *   *   *   *   *   *   *

In this same rosy sunset, Crystal, Viscountess Dynely, sits alone, fair and sweet, and youthful, as this time last year when she walked about the Lincolnshire lanes and waited for Terry Dennison to come and ask her to be his wife. She is alone, dressed for dinner in the crisp white muslin and blue ribbons that become her childish fairness best, and which her husband best likes to see her wear. And if that husband fancied hodden-gray or sackcloth and ashes, be very sure this exceptional wife would never have donned other array. She is waiting for him now to come to dinner, listening with love's impatience for the first sound of the foot-

20

step, the first note of the gay whistle she knows so well. For she is happy once more, poor Crystal, and Eric is all her own again.

She knows the whole story. Weeks after, when strength had come back to the weak frame, and light to the dim blue eyes, sitting side by side, his arm around her, Eric had told all—all. Nothing had been hidden, and she learned at last how noble was the heart she had refused, the heart stilled forever. The blue eyes dilated, the lips parted and quivered, the tender face grew very pale, and she flung her arms about her husband wildly, and strained him to her.

" Oh, Eric ! " she cried out ; " to think it might have been you ! "

Oh, selfish human heart ! To the depths of her soul she wondered at the brave generosity of him who was gone ; to her inmost heart she bowed down in reverence. She wept for his loss, real and passionate tears—dear, brave, noble Terry ! her playmate and friend,—but her first thought was for her own idol, her first impulse one of unutterable gladness that it had not been he. She caught her breath, with the horror of it, and while her tears fell for Terry, she held the man for whom Terry had died, close to her impassioned little heart, and cried, again and again :

"Oh, my darling ! my darling ! to think it might have been *you !* "

As Eric never had, never would, she knew Terry had loved her. She was grateful to him ; she strewed his coffin with flowers ; she wept her pretty eyes red, again and again, over his grave ; but she loved Eric, and she never thought of that dreadful morning under the dripping trees of the Bois de Boulogne without a prayer of trembling thankfulness that it was *he* who was taken, and not her beloved.

And Eric is very good to her, very gentle and tender with her, very affectionate, after the manner of men and husbands. And she does not ask much ; she gives so greatly that a small return suffices. That small return, let me say, the Right Honorable Lord Viscount Dynely gives willingly and from his heart ; and Crystal is happy—and the curtain falls to universal felicity ? Well, as the leopard cannot change his spots, nor the Ethiop his skin, so men of Lord Dynely's stamp do not change their nature. Kind he will be to her always—Terry Dennison's dead face would rise from the grave to haunt him if he were not—affectionate, too, after his light, for in a sultan-like, off-hand way, lordly Eric is fond of his little wife ; faithful, also, with a fidelity that will include more or less admiration and attention for every pretty woman he meets ; but for Crystal, or France, or one of us all, to be perfectly happy, is not given to any one born of woman. *This*, Crystal knows—that all the happiness that is hers, all that ever will be hers, has come to her across Terry Dennison's grave.

THE END.